Eugene Coleman Savidge

Life of Benjamin Harris Brewster

With Discourses and Addresses

Eugene Coleman Savidge

Life of Benjamin Harris Brewster
With Discourses and Addresses

ISBN/EAN: 9783337120535

Printed in Europe, USA, Canada, Australia, Japan

Cover: Foto ©Raphael Reischuk / pixelio.de

More available books at **www.hansebooks.com**

Benjamin Harris Brewster

——"I have advised where I should—in the quiet of the night, with my own heart and conscience—and with the only and best friend I have, my mother; and from that I have resolved what I now write."—BENJAMIN HARRIS BREWSTER *to* SIMON CAMERON, 1844.

——"And your good mother! How she would have rejoiced, and how your pleasure would have been increased if she were here! I have enjoyed all that at home. Sometimes I think the good old women do enjoy the successes of their boys!"—SIMON CAMERON *to* BENJAMIN HARRIS BREWSTER, 1881, *upon the latter's appointment as Attorney-General of the United States.*

THE AUTHOR, who is himself irrevocably in maternal debt, and likewise enjoys "all that at home," dedicates this work to the memory of the mother of his subject,

MARIA HAMPTON BREWSTER,

the noble, cultured woman who, in the quiet of the home-circle, won for herself a monument in the fame of her son.

EUGENE COLEMAN SAVIDGE.

LIFE

OF

BENJAMIN HARRIS BREWSTER

WITH

DISCOURSES AND ADDRESSES.

BY

EUGENE COLEMAN SAVIDGE, M.D.,

AUTHOR OF "WALLINGFORD," ETC.

" From the beginning he had a conscience in all that he undertook; whatever he was required to do, that he fitted himself for by thorough and conscientious preparation, and did the work, whatever it was, perfectly; and this sense of conscience will explain the history of his whole career."—*Brewster on Thomas A'Becket*

PHILADELPHIA:

J. B. LIPPINCOTT COMPANY.

LONDON: 10 HENRIETTA STREET, COVENT GARDEN.

1891.

PREFACE.

> " And what is writ is writ—
> Would that it were worthier!"
> —Byron.

I owe to my brother, Frank R. Savidge, of the Philadelphia Bar, the privilege of writing this memoir. I am indebted to him, also, for many fruitful suggestions and much keen and valued criticism.

To Miss Anna Hampton Brewster, whom I visited in her Italian home, "across the Roman Campagna," I owe many facts concerning the youth of her brother.

Many well-known friends of Mr. Brewster have loaned me aid and encouragement, which I hereby acknowledge.

The Star Route trials have been given in these pages as fully as may be done during the lifetime of some of the most influential sympathizers. Later it may be interesting and proper to record more in this regard from the vast amount of evidence which was secured and preserved.

Eugene Coleman Savidge.

New York, September 1, 1891.

CONTENTS.

VIII.

IX.

X.

XI.

XII.

XIII.

XIV.

XV.

XVI.

XVII.

XVIII.

XIX.

XX.

XXI.

XXII.

XXIII.

XXIV.

XXV.

XXVI.

XXVII.

XXVIII.

EULOGIES, DISCOURSES, AND ADDRESSES OF BENJAMIN HARRIS BREWSTER.

LIFE

OF

BENJAMIN HARRIS BREWSTER.

I.

. . . "It is well to read carefully and frequently the biographies of eminent lawyers. It is good to rise from the perusal of the studies and labors, the trials and conflicts, the difficulties and triumphs, of such men, in the actual battle of life, with a secret feeling of dissatisfaction with ourselves. Such a sadness in the bosom of a young student is like the tears of Thucydides, when he heard Herodotus read his history at the Olympic Games, and receive the plaudits of assembled Greece. It is the natural prelude to severer self-denial, to more assiduous study, to more self-sustaining confidence."—*Sharswood's Professional Ethics.*

"You will do the greatest service to the State if you shall raise, not the roofs of houses, but the souls of the citizens."—EPICTETUS.

MEMOIRS of an eventful career are not alone a tribute to an honored man. However much the individual may merit a perpetuation of his fame, the nation has larger need of it.

The spirit of nationality is a production and not a growth. No one following the curriculum of foreign universities can fail to note how European governments make patriots while educating mere readers and writers. In America we are likewise awakening to the national obligation to "sow greatness," along with the other measures for the perpetuity of our body politic.

A people can make no firmer provision for future nobilities than a just appreciation of those of the present, and the dawning recognition of this fact promises for the coming generations a spiritual wealth as great as has been the material.

Benjamin Harris Brewster made a distinct contribution to this national wealth of a spiritual order.

His life was full and long, and stands an object-lesson to strivers in all walks of life. From restricted circumstances he rose to receive the highest rewards of his profession. He lived in the fourth age of our national history: Washington, Franklin, and Jefferson representing the first; Hamilton, Jay, and Madison, the second; Webster, Clay, Calhoun, the third; Lincoln, Seward, Cameron, Grant, the fourth. Of all the forces and movements of this culminating age of our greatness his biography is a direct and vital part.

Mr. Brewster was "a man of letters among men of the world; dazzling scholars by his worldly position, politicians by his culture." He was pre-eminently a literary lawyer. The plethora of learning displayed in his discourses is marvellous. He was especially able in his ecclesiasticism. Almost every religious branch has been the line of his research. Even the local themes he touched are bestrewn with literary gems and rounded with philosophical reflection. This is not the assertion of one or two, nor does it proceed from that "love exceeding the love of biographer." It is a national tribute. The coronet unanimously accorded his work by those whose individual judgments make laws, bestow honors, or guide national opinions, must establish beyond cavil excellence in a sphere incapable of official degrees.

It would be more than human if a long life did not compass errors, and, forsooth, grievous faults. "Whatever the beauty of the sweetest flower, there will be some dust on the petals." The very strength that stamps a man great lends itself to each act of his life,—whatever the direction, the driving power is the same. A successful search, therefore, might be made for seasons of impatience engendered by asceticism, or by an almost super-refinement that abhorred poor taste or grossness. There are undoubtedly to be found, as in every career, errors of judgment, mistaken impulses of a warm heart, apparent inconsistencies which are in truth but increased light and more matured reflection, and, perhaps, inconsistencies real and inexplicable. But search here is conceived to be no duty of the biographer, even though he might desire commendation for critical candor.

The biographer must proceed with mingled humility and confidence,—humility, lest his subject suffer from indiscreet zeal, or the lesson of the life entrusted to him to reflect lose its point or power through lack of discernment or inapt presentation; and confidence in his own fidelity of purpose and the thoroughness of the labor he has made to prepare himself for his work.

Mr. Brewster said of Alexander Hamilton:

"In general, he has been little weighed and appraised—and in spots only—never as a whole. His true valuation will be found in the diamond scales of posterity."

II.

Ancestral Associations and Pride—Early Life and its Sad Accident
—The Cultured Mother—Her Influence upon the Son's Career.

BENJAMIN HARRIS BREWSTER sprang from an
ancient and illustrious race. His ancestry did much
to make our nation and to preserve its liberties.
His pedigree can be traced back into English history
before the landing of the Pilgrim Fathers. The line
in America has had a most intimate connection with
the causes and forces that created and tend to preserve, in face of deteriorating immigration, those
sentiments and principles distinguishing our American civilization from the loose moralities of Continental Europe.

Puritanism, planted on our shores by the Pilgrim
Fathers, was the real beginning of America. "There
were straggling settlers in America before: some
material of a body was there, but the soul of it was
this." And to those who made Puritanism and led
it to this country, in that great primary declaration of
independence,—the independence of conscience, after
which political liberty was but the necessary sequence,
—to the rugged Puritan leaders must be ascribed an
equal share in the building of the nation with their
brave trustees of the following centuries, who surrendered life rather than the spirit of their noble heritage.

Brewster and Standish were the leaders of this
sturdy band of 1620. The cellar walls of the houses

belonging to both may still be seen on Duxbury Nook, a slope of land jutting into the sea, near the historic spot. Both men were of gentle blood. To the former are accorded a superior education in the classics, a large political experience, and an extended association with aristocratic and refined classes in Europe. Standish was the fighting-man, and William Brewster—who is also called Elder Brewster, the Elder of Plymouth, and, sometimes, the Father of New England—was the chief counsellor and sage, the veritable head of the flock. This first ancestor of the Brewster family in America has long since passed into story and song. Says Longfellow:

> " Men in the middle of life, austere and grave in deportment,
> Only one of them old, the hill that was nearest to heaven ;
> Covered with snow, but erect, the excellent Elder of Plymouth.
> God had sifted three kingdoms to find wheat for his planting,
> Then had sifted the wheat as the living seed of a nation !
> So say the chronicles old, and such is the faith of the people."

William Brewster's history is now part of the national history. He was born in Nottinghamshire, England, in 1560, and possessed a coat of arms identical with that of the ancient Suffolk branch. He died in 1644, leaving four sons and two daughters.

Francis Enoch Brewster, his grandson, with a sister, the wife of a Connecticut clergyman, settled at Pittgrove, in southern New Jersey. This name was preserved in the family, and, after a distinguished line of professional men, was given to the father of Benjamin Harris Brewster. This Francis Enoch Brewster married Maria Hampton, daughter of Dr. John Thomas Hampton and Mercy Harris, his wife, and thus chose for our subject a maternal line equally as distinguished as his own in the service of the country. Maria Hampton Brewster, the honored mother of Benjamin Harris Brewster, was a descendant of Sir Andrew Hampton, who settled near Elizabethtown, New Jersey, after the battle of Boyne, exhibited great public spirit, and, among other acts, built a church, described by Judge James D. Westcott* as containing a stone inscription set in the chancel, which recorded that " This church was built by Sir Andrew Hampton and Dame Elizabeth, his wife." Maria Hampton Brewster's father, Dr. Hampton, was a friend of Thomas Jefferson, and served with honor in the war for independence. Mercy Harris, her mother, was the daughter of Benjamin Harris, a " fighting Quaker" of the great struggle for independence, who owned a large landed estate at Bound Brook, received from his grandfather. The future Attorney-General took his Christian name from his maternal great-grandfather, and without doubt bore the impress upon his taste in matured manhood of the influence of his maternal grandmother, Mercy Harris. He was eighteen when she died, and, with his sister, loved to listen to the tragic and interesting incidents of the Revolution frequently related by the stately old lady. She has been described by the sister:

" She was a very handsome old gentlewoman,—a rare picture to recall. She wore her thick, snow-white hair dressed high, with an

---

* Secretary of State of New Jersey for seventeen years, and a brother-in-law of Maria Hampton Brewster.

Indian mull turban, and was fond of a brown levantine gown with the train tucked up in the belt, and a neckerchief and turban, and an old-fashioned silver chatelaine that jingled at her side with its round, silver-bound pin-cushion and numberless accessories that hung on silver chains. This last was a great delight to her grandchildren."

These glimpses of ancestral association and pride will give a clue to the source of those unique tastes in our comparatively new American civilization, which Mr. Brewster exhibited. He was, unquestionably, very proud of his pedigree. Once, indeed, as a prelude to the grasping of a negro's hand in political equality, and as a definition of his previous position, he spoke himself of his ancestry with a pride that would appear almost objectionable were not the heat of the political excitement and the connection taken into consideration :

" I came of a race of men who proudly boast a pedigree that has been honored by historical association with every struggle in England for the cause of popular liberty. Ancestors of mine were conspicuous in the uprising of the Lollards, and followed the immortal Wycliffe in his struggle for the rights of private judgment and the liberty of conscience; and when Charles the First expiated his falsehood and treachery upon the block my kinsmen sat in the Parliament of England, descendants from the franklins, vindicating fully the freedom they had inherited as a special property. Years before that, driven by religious persecution and political tyranny across the dark and stormy Atlantic, that band of Pilgrims from whose head and leader I proudly trace my lineage,—that band of sages, heroes, and saints, by their first act bound themselves and theirs to obey the law. True to my blood, I have kept their covenant."

He had, however, an equal pride in that he had started life a poor American boy, and had made unaided way through misfortune and tight circumstances to success. He was ever the first to acknowledge merit in any walk of life, and to avow that " the race is to the best horse in spite of pedigree."

Mr. Brewster was born in Salem, New Jersey, on the thirteenth day of October, 1816. Twelve months after his birth, Francis Enoch Brewster, his father, brought the mother and child to Philadelphia, and began the practice of law. One year later a daughter was born, Anna Hampton Brewster, who has since become eminent in letters. The son was a remarkably beautiful boy, with a precocious intellect. Greater attention to the early education of children was given at that time than at present, and it was then a mother's pride to teach her children in person. Maria Hampton Brewster was a very superior woman. She had a passion for reading and acquiring intellectual stores, which she tried to impart to her children. Thus, before they were three years old, she had taught them to read, and filled their earliest childhood with stories of Homer, of the Æneid, Æsop's Fables, " Paradise Lost," Spenser's " Faerie Queene," many of Shakespeare's plays, and the traditions of Plymouth. Do we not remember anecdotes of young Pascal and his Euclid, Luther and the Latin Bible, Napoleon and the toy cannon, Webster and his Constitution-printed kerchief? There is treasured in Rome to-day, shown to the writer on a visit to Miss Anna Hampton Brewster, a worm-eaten " Paradise Lost" read by the ten-year-old brother to his sister.

While the father was noted for conversational abilities and great urbanity, it was the painstaking

mother who thus stored their young minds with literary information and cultivated the rare taste for
which both were noted in later life. Mrs. Brewster
related her reading with exquisite grace to her children, and we can easily see whence came the first
development of that rare gift of talking for which
Mr. Brewster was especially famed.

At five years the boy was instructed in Latin and
repeated passages from Virgil. It was the sunny age
of his life. As yet there were no traces of the domestic troubles which later narrowed the means of
the mother. Nor had the golden-haired child received the disfigurement which so strongly modified
his character and disposition in after life. This sad
calamity has been variously described by the press
all over the country, but, owing to Mr. Brewster's
extreme sensitiveness, the true history has never
yet appeared. The burning occurred on Sunday,
shortly after his fifth birthday. The father's habit
was to take the boy walking after church, and the
maid had orders to give the children an early lunch
Sunday mornings that Bennie might be ready. For
some reason the girl was tardy and had only gone
to the kitchen when Mr. and Mrs. Brewster returned. When the door-bell rang and young Ben
heard his father's voice he ran down-stairs to beg his
father to wait. But Mr. Brewster left without the
boy, little dreaming what a lifetime of misery would
have been saved by a half-hour of patience!

Mrs. Brewster, bidding the maid return to the nursery with the children, went to lay aside her wraps,
intending to return and console the little fellow for

his disappointment with some amusing story. But the woman, disobeying orders, left Ben and his sister on the stairs and went to the kitchen for dinner. A bright grate-fire was blazing in the dining-room. This novelty, never allowed in the nursery, was a great delight to the little fellow, and, followed by his two-year-old sister, he ran to the dining-room. His apron had been tied on hurriedly with his arms free from the armholes, leaving it loose to be used in fanning the fire. Fascinated with the flames, he ran to and fro, fanning the blaze with his apron in his eager, childish glee. Little tongues of fire came darting out as if chasing the child. He shrieked with delight and cried out again and again, " Look, sister, look !" Little Anna was less interested with the fire than with a doll-house in a side chimney-closet, and she was busily occupied with the dolls she had there put to sleep the evening before, but from time to time she looked at her brother. Suddenly the boy's apron was caught by the draft and sucked up the chimney. He snatched it out, and, blazing as it was, by some fatality, it fell over his head. In an instant the beautiful blonde curls were ablaze, and the shrieking boy vainly tried to drag the flaming apron from his face. His sister ran frantically to and fro, beating on the door and screaming for her mother. Just then the dining-room servant opened the door. She held a large pitcher of water, but, instead of throwing it over the burning boy, dropped it on the floor and in terror ran screaming up-stairs. The child's nurse was following her into the room with a dinner-tray, which likewise was dropped at the sight, and she also ran wildly calling for her mistress. Mrs. Brewster had already gone to the nursery, and, not finding the children, was coming downstairs to seek them. The conscience-stricken nurse at the sight of her mistress fainted on the stairs. Mrs. Brewster stepped over her prostrate body and ran to learn the cause of the cries and the servants' fright. The instant she saw the blazing child she gathered up a large carpet rug and wrapped it about him. The flames before being extinguished burned entirely through the rug, and in this condition it was preserved for many years a sad memento. Messengers were instantly despatched in all directions for medical aid, but at that hour, one o'clock Sunday afternoon, it was impossible to find a physician at home.

One hour later, when Drs. Physick and McClelland arrived, they found the anguish-stricken mother treating her child. She had, by her presence of mind and intelligence, not only saved his life, but, in a slight measure, allayed the torture. Mrs. Brewster had at once ordered a quantity of white potatoes to be boiled and mashed and then had them mixed with pure olive oil, covering the seared face and head with the soothing paste.

There was not a burn on the child's body except a small spot on one of the shoulders, one arm, and the hands. The whole fury of the flames was spent on the face and head. Weeks of intense suffering and anxiety followed. The boy's life was hung as on a ravelled thread. When Dr. Physick used to relate in his lectures to students the sad case he had so well treated, he invariably closed with these words :

"The best medical skill would have been unavailing if it had not been seconded by the wonderful care and attention of the boy's mother. A delicate, frail woman, she seemed endowed with super-human strength."

Describing her long vigil, holding the suffering child on a pillow, he would add, "To that self-sacrificing mother the boy owed a second time his life."

Mrs. Brewster never recovered from the shock and the subsequent anguish and exhaustion. Other severe domestic troubles came upon her shortly after the son's recovery. She was a woman of great purity, affection, and dignity of character, whose girlhood was beloved and caressed by a large circle of kindred and friends. This great calamity ushered later misfortunes. Her husband failed in some business ventures, domestic troubles followed, and the once happy life became one of privation and sorrow, until the love and society of her two children, whose education she accomplished at great denial and personal sacrifice, remained her only object in life. A complication of heart-troubles followed and kept her an invalid for her remaining years, ofttimes giving her seasons of great suffering. She lived, however, until 1853, witnessing the opening of the successful career of her son, and receiving from him all the return that a son can make for such a debt of gratitude.

A close and peculiar affection bound Mr. Brewster to this admirable mother, and it is impossible to judge of his career aside from her character and influence.

There was the closest sympathy between them, and their intercourse was most delightful. There can be no question of doubt that the mother during that long and painful convalescence was making the future man whose character of mind should bring him eminence. No one can estimate the value of this long contact with the best mental gifts of his mother. As the gifted woman bore him company in the darkened room, renewing the bandages and smoothing his pillow, we may be sure she was not mute. Her seed-droppings sank deep into the good soil, and it became a treasure-gathering time of romance, scriptural incident, and golden precept, which graced his flights of oratory long after her lips had resolved into dust.

There is too little companionship between parents and children, and too large a place given nurse and tutor in moulding our coming generations.

More than a quarter of a century after she rested beneath the marble Mr. Brewster, addressing young men, said:

"We must remember how much is due to the fostering care of those who guarded and trained us in our youth, and how much of the prosperity and promotion and happiness of our lives is the result of that which they imparted to us and brought out of us."

And when he came to sum up his life, his will ordered that he should be placed by the side of her whose care and devotion he never ceased to laud and could never hope to repay.

I I I.

The Lad's Mental Brightness—Great Sensitiveness at his Affliction
—School and College Days.

DESPITE the long illness and great sufferings, the
lad's quick, precocious intellect remained as bright
as ever. When his health was restored studies were
resumed. His lessons were never a task; he understood quickly, and, as his mother often said, it seemed
as if he knew many things intuitively.

His boyhood was that of other boys. He was
active, full of vitality, fond of fun and frolic; but
was extremely sensitive regarding his sad misfortune.
He rarely spoke of it, and on those occasions only
to nearest friends and in a manner quite indirect.
This sensitiveness ever remained, and became the
vulnerable spot sought by unfeeling opponents and
enemies. In 1853 we find in one of his letters:

"Your pretensions to public appointment are identified with those
who have defamed my personal friends and wantonly twitted me in
the public prints of my personal deformity."

At one of these public attacks he is said to have
replied with powerful effect by telling how the curly-
headed boy, fanning the flames, had been picked up
with his "face charred as black as the heart" of the
man whose brutality had thus assailed him. Even
when his deformity had become but another mark
of his distinction, and brought him out in sharp *bas
relief* from the world's crowd, was the quick of his

nature cut by unthinking looks of aversion, or whispered comment.

Although ancestral association and influence had formed an early taste for the antique, it is nevertheless well understood that his singular affectations of dress, first assumed at his mother's request, were preserved principally because they mitigated the severity of his disfigurement.

Year by year, in early life, his dress had become more noticeable for its peculiarity until it finally resolved itself into the picturesque pattern so familiar in his later years.

He wore, almost invariably, a light-colored coat, with a vest of velvet, cut low to expose a shirt-front of the finest cambric ruffles; his collars were those of the Washingtonian period, and ruffles replaced cuffs at his wrists. Old-fashioned gaiter-tops of perfect white covered his boots, and a great white silk hat crowned his head. This, in conjunction with his scarred face, his breadth of forehead, and powerful aspect of personality, made him one of the most striking and unique figures of the century. He attracted universal attention and was forever the subject of newspaper pen-pictures. So great were his attainments and dignity of bearing that the most strained sense of propriety found him even pleasing upon second or third glance.

While the consciousness of the deformity at once vanished under the indescribable charm of his conversation, it sometimes required more than adroitly arranged dress or the fame of high station to counterbalance it. The familiar incident of his *vis-à-vis* at dining, a lady at Long Branch during his Attorney-Generalship, well illustrates this. Expressing all sympathy for the unfortunate gentleman opposite she demanded another seat, and remained uninfluenced when his name and position were mentioned. The sequel proves how Mr. Brewster was hurt; for, as if in revenge, he sought her acquaintance, and by his social graces charmed her into that circle of friends who continued until the end to make of him the admired and revered centre.

In young manhood, however, he had neither station nor wealth, nor the dignity of age, the aid from dress, nor the more matured conversational charm, to shield him from the brutality of attention—if not repugnance—which he must often have felt with keenest agony. His father, even, disappointed by the blight on his boy, seemed repelled rather than drawn more closely to him as was the mother, and for long periods he did not speak to his son.

The result of all this was to drive the boy into closer communion with the gifted mother and sister, and into his books. His labors with books, as he has explicitly affirmed, were reinforced by the specific determination to show those who turned from him that he could rise beyond circumstance and disfigurement.

After finishing his course at the preparatory school of Doctor Wylie, of Philadelphia, his father wished to place him at the University of Pennsylvania; but the mother insisted on Princeton, and prevailed. He entered the freshman class of the College of New Jersey at fourteen years of age and was graduated at eighteen. Dr. McLean, the President, a visitor of his uncle, Judge Westcott, at Trenton, New Jersey, often met his mother there, and always congratulated her on her son's fine mental qualities. " He is a remarkable boy," he would say ; " Ben will make his mark in the world, and a shining mark. He will not distinguish himself at college, for he is too fond of fun ; but he is taking in information on all sides, and has a superior mind." The good old doctor was very fond of the lad, and always stood by him when his innocent boyish pranks got him into trouble. Old schoolmates relate that young Brewster was ever their " lawyer" and advocate, and had brought them out of many boyish scrapes by his dexterity and diplomacy. The lad's selective faculties were thus already at work, casting aside the useless for his aims and ends in life, and appropriating to himself the necessary.

He has always retained for his alma mater a warm love, and reflects Princeton in many of his writings and orations.

Little record has been left of the details of his college life. He graduated with honor, and his subsequent career proves how well he must have applied himself. How he loved the memory of his college days is attested by his words as the orator of a college commencement :

" In retreats like these we all acquire habits of life, and of thought, and of feeling, that can be obtained nowhere else. The peculiar characteristics and qualities of a college student are known with no other order of men, and they have prevailed and will prevail all over the world, wherever such institutions exist, modified only by existing circumstances, but still in all their elements and consequences the same. It is a guild of men,—a brotherhood,—a service that has its traits and obligations and duties that are conspicuous and point out and mark them wherever they may go."

In 1834 he returned to Philadelphia with his Princeton degree.

IV.

Selection of a Profession—Opposition from Friends—Early Struggle —The Financial Panic of 1837—Days of Hardship.

WHEN Mr. Brewster returned from Princeton to Philadelphia in 1834, he had to face the most important issue which ever confronts a youth in

> " The vague but manly wish to tread the maze
> Of life to noble ends—whereon intent
> The bravest heart must often pause and gaze—
> The firm resolve to seek the chosen end
> Of manhood's judgment, cautious, mature."

There is no more weighty step in life than the selection of a calling; and there is no struggle so severe as the young man, in his feeble inexperience, must make for the tool, the instrument, which shall serve him in his largest and fullest maturity. Life is too short to atone for the mistake in deciding at this epoch ; and humanity scarce offers deeper pathos than the sadly frequent sight of a splendid ability misdirected,—a whole life bearing dwarfed fruit from simple misapplication,—all the more pathetic from the very measure of success which attends it.

The very possession of real ability makes this period all the more vitally critical. When the bright boy comes to face the vocation which, in his lisping babyhood, seemed pleasant to his friends, skill and hope in a dozen other directions draw thither his thoughts and promise success. It is a great time of rejection to the fiery youth of wild thoughts. His life hinges as much upon what he decides *not* to be as on what he determines to be. There are an infinity of brilliant careers to renounce, a world of limitations to accept, and a realm of ignorance to acknowledge and thenceforward retain. The thoughtful youth at this crisis may often see how many a fire dies for fuel with ample scattered about its borders, —how squandered, undisciplined energies fall short of greatness for want of concentration.

It would be hard to conceive Mr. Brewster out of the profession of law. His vehemence and dramatic fire might suggest the stage; his strangely devout and religious habit of mind, the ministry; his fondness for letters, authorship; or his wonderful erudition, a professorship,—in any of these lines he would have succeeded, but any one of them would have sacrificed many of the composite attributes for which he found scope in his own profession.

He came up to this epoch with a cherished design to enter the profession of the law. From the character of his mind we cannot doubt that he knew what any definite step involved. But he was met by violent opposition from his father and others, for his misfortune seemed to bar him entirely from any pursuit in which persuasion or personal contact with the

public was required for success. The settling of a
design, the making of a determination, is the work
of one sacred momentous instant. And though it
be denied the biographer to point to just the moment when a determination to be great took birth,
yet Mr. Brewster's action in this exigency approaches
quite nearly to such a sublimity. To the surprise of
his friends, and in spite of their opposition, he prepared to enter the law. His father went so far as to
predict that the very street gamin would hoot at him
as a lawyer. Notwithstanding, by the strength of
his own purpose and the love and support of his
mother and sister as his only capital, he began his
studies. His mother placed him under the direction
of Eli K. Price, where he studied so well that he
was ready for admission to the bar some months before his twenty-first birthday, and was compelled to
await his majority. January 6, 1838, he was formally
admitted to the Philadelphia bar, and so began his
long and illustrious career.

It may give us an idea of the length of Mr. Brewster's life to trace a brief sketch of Philadelphia and
the country at the time he began the study of his
profession. Andrew Jackson was President of the
United States and William the Fourth occupied the
English throne. A popular dollar subscription was
being taken for Thomas Jefferson, who was in pecuniary difficulties. This, possibly, suggested the idea
of the "vow of poverty," which Mr. Brewster later
declared necessary on entering public life. The era
of telegraphs had not yet dawned, and Michigan,
Arkansas, Wisconsin, Minnesota, had yet to receive

the honors of statehood. Webster and Hayne a
few years before had waged their famous debate in
the Senate ; the great Abolition movement was rising
into flame throughout the North ; and the most
serious financial panic in the history of the country
was about to fall upon the land. In Philadelphia,
Arch Street had been built out to Twelfth Street,
Vine Street was paved as far as Ninth, Race Street
as far as Broad, and Chestnut and Walnut Streets
were paved as far as Twelfth. The enormous growth
since was doubtless as unforeseen or as unappreciated
at that time as is our future growth in an equal span.
To acquire from such a retrospection the equanimity
to look forward into the possibilities still within one
lifetime's span is to engender a forethought and
underlying faith which is itself almost a guarantee
of success in life.

But the financial panic which swept the country
when Mr. Brewster was a law-student seemed to
proffer little promise of the future which followed.
Not to go into history it will be remembered that the
result of President Jackson's specie circular* fell in
Van Buren's administration, causing failures in New
York and New Orleans alone reaching $150,000,000.
The Whig party was formed by reason of this act
against the United States Bank, located at Philadelphia, and Mr. Brewster found at his door not only
the sharpest political agitation, but also the severest
effects of the panic. Large numbers of Philadel-
phians became insolvent, city banks suspended, and

---

* Requiring coin in payment of lands.

the City Treasury was compelled to announce a liberal policy to its debtors. The Board of Trade passed resolutions on the " sudden change which had come over the community, and spread calamity and apprehension throughout great interests which support its prosperity, which could be attributed to no other cause than the attitude of the government toward the United States Bank."

At no time in our history has a more depressing outlook been presented to a young law-student.

Mr. Brewster was at a period of life when it was a query not only what sort of lawyer he should make, but into what stature of moral, intellectual, and spiritual manhood he should develop. Doubtless, in his struggles toward the bar, he looked about him at many with the coveted prize of profession, and yet doing no greater things with it than the sad majority of men do with life. Life is indispensable to heroism, noble ends, and the sublimities, and a profession must be had as a tool before one can go to work on the greater purposes of life. But while the nobilities may dim at the place where professional degrees are bestowed and seem so common, life itself is still more universally bestowed. And that so few rise to the possibilities of the one, or do large things with the other, should not cause the tyro at both to value them less.

Later, when the pride of success had become a simple prerequisite of life, Mr. Brewster saw greater things in the hardships of this period than in his success. He loved to contrast his friendless start with the brilliant success which finally followed, but he loved infinitely more those rugged days aiding gathering convictions, removing erroneous theories, and strengthening the true inspirations of early youth. Nor did he ever, for a single moment, lose sight of the nobility of his chosen calling or hold less sacred his intent to mount to its furthest heights.

V.

Philadelphia Bar—Its Plebeian Origin and Later Aristocracy and Brilliancy—Mr. Brewster at the Bar—Eli K. Price—Living Monuments—"Young Lawyers."

WHEN Mr. Brewster took the oath to "behave himself in the office of attorney according to his best learning and ability, and with all good fidelity as well to the court as the client," we may regard him as already marching toward success. He had taken the steps for himself, and had developed those powers of endurance and of positive, almost fierce, aggression which were—to himself at least—an earnest of the recompense awaiting him.

When he became a member of the Philadelphia bar and fought for recognition, it was composed of those justly-celebrated legal giants * who gave it the lustre for which it has ever been noted—laying, in-

---

* The lustre of the Philadelphia bar was at this time reflected from such names as Binney, Sergeant, Meredith, McMichael, David Paul Brown, G. M. Dallas, Barton, Conrad, Reed—men of international fame then in their full maturity.

c

deed, the foundation for the familiar colloquialism,
" As sharp as a Philadelphia lawyer."

The plebeian conditions under which the Philadelphia bar found birth, and the patrician reaction to an
opposite extreme, placed before young lawyers ideals
lofty enough to incite not only the noblest endeavor
but at the same time to invite comparisons equally
as high. The tradition that the law must be " preserved for the patrician class" had changed the old
bar so that before Mr. Brewster's time the privileged
class of the city were expected to furnish the lawyers. This sentiment, no doubt, had its weight in
giving social Philadelphia—even of to-day—its lean-
ing toward rigidity and exclusiveness.

But of the old bar, we quote from Hon. James T.
Mitchell, of the Supreme Bench of Pennsylvania:

" The founders of our Commonwealth entertained a positive antipa-
thy to lawyers. Recently emerged from the great civil conflict in our
mother-country—that great national crisis in which the military system
of feudalism, having outlived its usefulness, was to be swept away forever by the tide of modern ideas and necessities—the followers of Penn
were in that state of mental exaltation which carries away the judgment
even of the sober-minded, and they yielded themselves without hesitation or doubt to chimerical dreams of universal peace and brotherly
good-will. Hence came a distrust of all those whose occupation
savored of strife. The soldier and the lawyer were classed together as
the instruments, if not the promoters, of contention. . . . From these
and other causes it is certain that from the foundation of the province
it was the well-defined and settled policy of the law of Pennsylvania
to discourage lawyers and prevent litigation. . . . Another manifes-
tation of the same spirit is found in the establishment of the unprofes-
sional but apparently regular tribunal called the Peacemakers. . . .
That lawyers should for a time be scarce under these adverse circumstances is not to be wondered at, and we find in 1708 that one John
Henry Sprogel . . . ' doth intervene for a Writ of Error, and hath

retained the *four known Lawyers of the Province.'* . . . It soon came about that the nimble-tongued tradesman found it to his advantage to bring his dilatory customer into court, and by his own eloquence get a verdict; and if, perchance, he failed, his costs were so small that they made little drawback to another venture. The defendant, taken at a disadvantage, found, after a few experiences, that he must bring in some quicker-witted or more plausible friend to his assistance. A few successes in this line turned the friend's attention—perhaps his vanity—to this line of honor or of profit, and the "advocate" was made. Advocates once made, professional training became a matter of course, and so the short round was quickly run. The full-fledged lawyer was prohibited, but the natural advocate was placed where circumstances in a little while made him a lawyer more inevitably than the time-honored course of dinners at an Inn of Court."

Starting with the "nimble-tongued tradesman," the reaction carried it to the other extreme, and for a century the Philadelphia bar was composed of those who with warrant called themselves the best people of the city. But at Mr. Brewster's epoch a greater liberality of sentiment prevailed.

"But with this," writes Francis Enoch Brewster, "there had been a deterioration in the character of the bar. Quacks, public-spoilers, and pettifoggers had crept in among those who, even though they were arrogant and pretentious, were at least gentlemen, and generally learned in the profession."

This second reaction had a twofold effect. Newcomers of the right stamp, incensed at the leaven of charlatanism, and fired with noble ideals of the old bar, were spurred to greater efforts; and a strong professional antagonism toward all *débutants* made a legal career at this period, even for the better classes, far more difficult than formerly.

When Mr. Brewster was admitted to the bar he

retired from Mr. Price's office to establish himself independently.   His relations with this distinguished preceptor were cordial in the extreme.   Mr. Price showed him many kindnesses, and the young student in his love and gratitude learned by experience how much better are monuments builded in human hearts —epitaphs written in a successful -life reaching out a generation beyond that of the hand aiding its start— than neglected marble in a cemetery corner.   Many of Mr. Brewster's students to-day who owe their success and comfort in life to him are, perhaps, reaping the results of this lesson learned by their preceptor in the office of Eli K. Price, their legal grandfather.   Mr. Brewster's love and practical sympathy for young men are his noblest and grandest characteristics.   The biographer cannot too strongly accent them ; he can conceive of no more solacing reflection for a man striking life's balance-sheet than the knowledge that hundreds, 'growing more as he grows less,' shall out in a later day 'arise and call him blessed' to the third and fourth generation.

Of the law student leaving his preceptor's office, Mr. Brewster has said :

" When you leave the office of your preceptor and take your own, you have then but just received permission to study your profession. If before that you have been diligent and industrious, then you can widen the field of your labor; and if you have been negligent and idle, you must straightway trim your lamp and gird. your loins, or woe betide you when the opportunity comes. Do not in the spirit of unrest and anxiety turn your back upon your office and go out into the streets or loiter about the courts, pretending to study while you only idle. Learn ' how to live quietly at home in your own rooms,' as Pascal says—do your duty to your profession ; and when you are reconciled to it your reward will come at last in a contented spirit and in the avoidance of misfortune by your manly self-control and devotion to your post."

Mr. Brewster borrowed a small sum on which to start, and opened a neat office at No. 1 Sansom Street. His early struggles at the bar were severe. Domestic troubles, ascribed by the son rather to mental than moral failings of the father, threw upon the young advocate at this time a large share of the support of his mother and sister.

His life at this period was spent principally in the quiet of his office, the cloister of his library, or the happy and intelligent company of his mother and sister. He was "building his talents on the stillness;" later, he should "build his character in the storms of the world." Shall we not let the pen of the sister picture this happy period of their life? From Rome, half a century later, she wrote:

"How delightful is your description of your walk! . . . Indeed I do remember the lovely walk to Gray's Ferry one heavenly day when you read a book by Sir Humphry Davy to me. What a happy youth we had! So ideal! It does not seem so poor and obscure to me, for I have never had the great wealth and high position since that you have had. As I recall it, it seems very rich in the real things of life. We were well brought up, came of gentle blood, had nice instincts, were passionately fond of books, and enjoyed each other's society thoroughly. I have never in my life met a man so charming and brilliant in conversation as you. You were a wonderful young man. Often now, when I am reading the old poets of England and ancient tomes, enjoying keenly passages and incidents, I see that the first strong outline of my present classical tastes was traced by you in your young manhood. No; we were not poor nor obscure; we were rich and noble, with the best wealth and the best life. I thank heaven that I never had any other life than that of my blessed young womanhood! My old age is a continuation of those days, and therefore is a very happy period to me. And for much that made that youth happy and this old age golden, I have to thank you, my brother! to thank your beautiful mind, and high tastès and noble talk, as well as our dear, dear mother. . . . Take Ben on walks as soon as he is old enough, and give him the good old divine discourses."

It would be difficult to find in all literature a prettier picture. In this school he was preparing for the clients yet to come,—for the responsibilities and honors yet before him. And to this period of his life his retrospection most often took him.

V I.

Early Professional Studies—A Pen Picture of the New Office—Earnings of the Young Advocate—His Escape from the Professional Rut—Chivalric Professional Attitude—Oratorical Capabilities—His own Tribute to Law.

Mr. Brewster once jestingly said, " The lawyer starts life giving five hundred dollars' worth of law for five dollars, and ends it giving five dollars' worth for five hundred dollars." And there is some shadow of truth in the jest.

The first cases of a young practitioner are usually doubtful in nature and contingent, given him by speculative neighbors as cheap ventures which may possibly yield a profit. On those forlorn hopes that even established men would hesitate to lead, often rest his chance of reputation or his permanent undoing. Upon each case, therefore, a wealth of anxiety and research, never given at other periods of life, is expended. A lost cause to the older practitioner can never be the calamity it is to him; for the senior's reputation remains to guarantee the philosophic client that his cause was destined to be lost. But it is doubtful if ever an issue was lost by a tyro that the client did not feel, if not openly say, that "the old foxes would have gotten there."

The scarred face of the new advocate and the predictions of failure did not lessen his anxiety for each of his early cases. His shortcomings would be all the more conspicuous, and eagerly seized as a confirmation, after the manner of prophets. Pride, therefore, joined with ambition and financial need to weight each issue and increase its tremor. Of that interesting period of professional life when the "shingle" has gone up, is furtively viewed from the opposite side of the street, and the novitiate seats himself with mingled hope and fear in the new little office, much has been written and said.* Of every career it is the most interesting period. Can we not picture

---

* Chauncey M. Depew writes of this period in his own career:

"Clients are mostly illogical. They reason from no known commercial basis. In the early days of my career as a lawyer I wrote an opinion for a client and timidly asked five dollars therefor. He grumbled a great deal before paying it. Then he took the opinion to a famous New York advocate to find out whether it was all right. The advocate glanced over it, wrote across the first page the word 'correct,' and asked five hundred dollars for his work. My client paid this sum gladly, and is yet talking about the kindness of the great advocate.

"For the first legal paper I ever drew I charged one dollar and fifty cents. A farmer was my client, and he beat me down to one dollar. Twenty years afterward I wrote a precisely similar paper and received for it five hundred dollars with thanks."

the long mornings uninterrupted by clients, and the pessimism of the drowsy afternoons? Mr. Brewster carefully preserved mementos of this period of wait-ing. We see a glimpse in them of that sentimen-tality which was always a marked characteristic. Though some who wield our literary sceptre to-day decry all approach to sentiment as weak, it was, nevertheless, part of Mr. Brewster's force. It was this strong potentiality, this outgoing from self, that invested objects unattained with a glamour making worth their acquirement, and hallowed and sweetened the rewards earned. Mere sordidness or egoistic love of power are far less inspiring as incentives.

In a well-thumbed account-book preserved by him for half a century are pictures of these first profes-sional steps. His handwriting had hardly formed when the book was opened, and still showed some ambitious flourishes of youth. It might be indelicate to open it did we not appreciate the sacredness of each item, each a step by which an earnest man climbed to success and usefulness. The book records:

Money spent by me in furnishing office, January 7 and 8, 1838.

For Troubat & Haly and Purdon's Digest	$16.00
Coal, $6.50; table, $5.50; 2 bls. coal, .70	12.70
Cards, $2.00; carpeting, $7.50; cashpad, .12½	9.62½
Scuttle, poker, and shovel	1.50
Wages to Rodney	.37½
Signs paid for to Icevil	2.75
Mat, $1.00; moving, .25; portfolio, $1.50	2.75
Paper, $1.00; John, $1.00; putting in coal, .31¼	2.31¼
Miscellaneous expenses	1.94¾
	$50.00
Debtor to Money borrowed	$50.00

This was the opening transaction of a long career. We can almost see " John" or " Rodney" hanging out the signs and the young man making his first entry on the wrong side of the " cashpad." These were poor matters enough, but they were pointing to rich ends.

From early January until the last day of March not a single client promised a contradiction to the prophets.   Then the account begins:

March 30.	To Cash, C. Bulte	$	5.00
" 30.	To Cash from a man for costs		4.00
April 6.	To Cash from Lewis on account . . .		3.00
" 7.	To Cash from Berry for P. of Att'y . .		3.00
" 9.	To Cash of Fearing for lease		5.00
" 13.	To Cash of Warwick for assignment .		5.00
" 14.	To Cash, Capt. Amos, suit in C. Court		20.00
" 20.	Cash, Moss *vs.* Moss		5.00
" 22.	To Cash of Hannah Mitchell on account		2.00
May 10.	To Cash of Rosanna McCarthy . . .		4.00
" 21.	To Cash of Douglasson		1.00
" 21.	To Cash of R. McCarthy balance of fee		1.00

Little dreamed Mr. C. Bulte or the " man for costs" of their important relation to the future Attorney-General of the United States !   The young attorney earned during his first year at the bar slightly over five hundred dollars.   He was then twenty-three years of age.   His second year brought him about nine hundred dollars, and the third slightly less.   In the fourth year of his practice, and the twenty-sixth of his age, however, his earnings were upwards of fifteen hundred dollars.   His balance-sheet reads :

" This year I have made $1500.   There are errors in the account, but this is a fair average.   I have a small sum in bank which remains but to pay old debts, and not that; but, God willing, I will go on and do better—do better by myself and by others, and I *must* prosper!

"January 1, 1842.

"BENJAMIN HARRIS BREWSTER."

Such is a pen-portrait of himself at twenty-six,—success dawning, and he financially in arrears, but with intense earnestness breathing out in secret places a determination to "do better."

The smallest expense items, scrupulously kept, tell of his daily life, his gratuities, pastimes, and aid at home; the surroundings of an intense life of realizing hope at a time when much of our national history was forming.

His office-rent was twenty dollars per quarter. Not thirty days after his first fee there is an item of three dollars for busts of Cicero and Demosthenes. This is not only the first record of that rare love of the fine arts that later distinguished him, but—can we not say it?—it showed the emulous design to become an orator himself. Items, "Mother's bread-bill," "Mother's pew-rent," "Mother's house-rent," in the account, tell how necessary were the fees, while "Cash spent for sister—for mother—for seeing picture with sister—for concert with mother," attest how truly indeed, as the sister has written, they were "rich in the real things of life."

The account, too, shows a fondness for the opera and drama, and it is believed that Mr. Brewster's earliest literary effort was a play from his pen that was produced and given a short run at the Walnut Street Theatre, Philadelphia.

His détours into the surrounding fields of literature

at this time are important in their bearing upon his future, for Mr. Brewster early learned the tendency of professional men to drop into ruts, and sought to avoid it in his own case. The three professions suffer equally in this regard. Students have all remarked the development of special vocabularies in exclusive lines of reading. It is the same in the domain of thought. How often does the lawyer modify the man, and the " bad intellectual habits" of premise and conclusion, which

> " sever and divide
> A hair 'twixt north and northwest side,"

impress themselves upon his vocabulary and deportment. The exclusive study of the mere physical man in the sister profession of medicine involves likewise a risk to the mind—the risk of seeing no laws except those of matter, and of regarding matter as " the one supreme essence of the universe." How quickly the laity recognize and ridicule the regulation doctor is exemplified in the professional controversy over Guiteau's insanity, a case in which Mr. Brewster was prominently concerned, as will be seen later. And the clergy—verily, we all know the unprofitable, exegetical priest as thoroughly as that famous grocer whose epitaph ran, " Born a man; died a grocer." Such a clergyman's manifest narrowness of vision robs even his good of its force, for the most illiterate of his flock instinctively interprets his very truths as but special views from his single stand-point. Such unconscious judgment explains the success of the unclerical Beecher, Talmage, Spurgeon, Gough, and Moody.

Precisely so is it in the law. Its fundamental principle is respect for authority. In a proper degree this is a safeguard of civilization. We cannot help drawing the contrast between Abraham Lincoln, the man, who fought slavery with all his force of logic and debate, and Abraham Lincoln, the lawyer, finally able to crush it by presidential proclamation, re-strained by a lawyer's veneration for the oracles of the law, abrogating Fremont's premature proclama-tion, and resisting the pressure of the whole North until military necessity became a higher law. Then the proclamation came, but not before. Law had bridled even moral sentiment. And we shall see a parallel case with reference to slavery in Mr. Brew-ster's career. But we instantly know the conven-tional, musty lawyer.

" His commonplaces are quaint and professional : they occur to him first in Latin. He measures all sciences out of his proper line of study (and with these he is scantily acquainted) by the rules of law. He thinks a steam-engine should be worked with due dili-gence and without laches; a thing likely to happen he considers as a *potentia remotissima,* and what is not yet in existence, or *in esse,* as what he would say is *in nubibus.* He prefers books bound in plain calf. He garners up his papers with a wonderful appearance of care, ties them in bundles with red tape, and usually has great difficulty when he wants to find them."

Just such a lawyer the laity love to twit, and it is such ultra-professionalism that brings an old age of misery, so well pictured by Judge Sharswood.

With this in mind Mr. Brewster directed his legal studies. He did not go so far into exceptions and subtleties as to lose sight of cardinal principles or to get befogged in his landmarks. He discriminated between what must be known and what was better in reference books,—a greater knowledge than attempting a whole library. Into the vast and enticing field of general literature he boldly launched, persuaded that "power, though better applied at one point, is best gathered over a wide surface."

It is an error to suppose that an absence of leisure must necessarily stamp a man eminent. The lawyer with an unremittingly full docket, or the physician always on the wheel, will undoubtedly become grounded in the principles daily met, and will accumulate gains; but such a one will be robbed of perspective and advance his facility only in one direction. Nothing could be more distasteful to Mr. Brewster than the idea of mere routine law. The "machine lawyer," paying cheap wages to young practitioners and turning out law like sugar over a counter, was to him a prostitution of the profession. "They sell bad goods and charge low prices," said he; "they follow a retail business and take all that comes." He would have it remembered that "the prosperous practitioner," with clouds of clients hanging around him, is not always the safe lawyer. Between such a man and the scholar, the thinker, the jurist, equipped for the underlying principles of law below the surface of every-day formalities,—those great international and constitutional questions never crossing the threshold of the "machine" man,— there is a distinction as wide as human destiny.

Mr. Brewster thus prepared himself to go behind

American law into the English law, back of that into the Roman and Grecian law,—to the very era of Pythagoras, Solon, and Socrates. He was, therefore, only giving his own life views when he spoke:

"Force nothing. In the whirl and hurry of a premature practice you may become apt, quick, sharp, but never solid, steady, learned, self-reliant."

His relation toward the bar was characteristic. His skill was never "a cunning logic, a gilded rhetoric, and an ambitious learning wearing the purple robe of the sophists, letting itself out for hire." Instead, law was to him "our only sovereign on earth" in whose royal domain "the whole power of the state could not take the ewe lamb." The pride of his nature perhaps tinged his professional life, for, whether or not he aspired to social aristocracy, he undoubtedly was a professional aristocrat. Mr. Wayne MacVeagh has characterized Mr. Brewster's chivalric attitude toward the profession of law as rather an impediment to the lawyer under our newer order. "The law," said he, "no longer needs those high qualities that we needed in our criminal as well as our civil jurisprudence of the earlier days, for the lawyer of to-day is to serve the business enterprises illustrating the great material prosperity of the age in which we live."

This seems sad. Mr. Brewster said:

"Any good business man will make a good practical lawyer; but in the higher walks of the profession, when intricate and complicated questions occur,—in those untrodden paths where it is necessary to modify old principles and dogmas, or to reconcile them with the new and various relations created by the ever-shifting wants and demands of society,—then the quick practitioner, the ready business man, is at fault, and the scholar, the thinker, the jurist, and the man skilled in men's affairs must be united in the lawyer to unravel these mysteries and establish the rule of action."

" In the practice of law as an occupation there are many other things needed than mere readiness and dexterity in the application of your knowledge in debate. . . ."

" My experience has been that professional word-mongers and forensic prize-fighters do not prosper as well as the more peaceful, tranquil, steady men. The brawlers of the law receive as their reward the noisy applause of men as empty as themselves; but the calm, dispassionate lawyer, the cool, quiet thinker, the modest and reluctant speaker, commands attention and receives the approving reliance of the public and the profession. . . ."

" The most important part of a man's professional life is made up of a multitude of almost insignificant and obscure points of duty that he dare not omit, and in the faithful performance of which alone he will merit and secure the fame of a good lawyer. . . ."

" Pascal, that marvel of reason and religion, has written, ' *I have often said that all of the misfortunes of men spring from their not knowing how to live quietly at home in their own rooms.*' . . . Apply this thought to your professional habits."

" Of all the dirty speculating a man can make himself a party to, that of jobber in lawsuits is the meanest. Such fellows convert a lawyer's office into a lottery office, a lawsuit into a lottery ticket, and a court-room into a gambler's shop. It is a desecration, as it demoralizes the administration of justice by degrading its officers and its principles into the means of extortion and pillage."

" Oftentimes you will be called on to institute actions to recover damage for defamation. Such suits are not to be encouraged. Never take one of them, however well it may be grounded, upon speculation or on any contingency whatever. Never let your desire to punish a calumniator tempt you to look to the verdict as your means of compensation. Give your service away, if you will, in the cause of one who has been wronged and persecuted and slandered, but touch not one penny of the spoil; it will taint the purity of your hands and corrupt the dignity of your character. I do not mean to say that they should all be discouraged. I know how base a thing is calumny. . . . But with all this our duty as advisers is to soothe and not to irritate and inflame. . . . An action at law is at best but a slow remedy, and sometimes it only helps to propagate a story which would have died out, as lies always do, if you have patience and a firm faith in God's justice. . . ."

"It would be well to imitate Saint Basil, for I have read somewhere, that when attacked by enemies from all quarters, and though so disheartened by their attacks that he was sometimes ready to call the truth and sincerity of all men in question, he nevertheless prescribed silence to himself for three years, lest he should utter anything rashly."

"As Chief Justice Gibson has said in Rush *vs.* Cavenaugh, 2 Barr, p. 187, 'It is a popular but gross mistake to suppose that a lawyer owes no fidelity to any one except his client, and that the latter is the keeper of his professional conscience.'

"Read that case. It will be of service to you."

"In a recent dissertation upon the French bar, you will read that Charlemagne in his 'Capitularies' makes first mention of the profession of the advocates in France, and then directs 'that no one should be admitted therein but men, mild, pacific, fearing God, and loving justice.'

"If I were to wander through a wilderness of words I could not explain to you more correctly the requirements of your profession than they are here expressed in these. Pause over them as I have, and feel their force and be touched with their simple beauty."

"In our bustling times men are all eager to rush into business and gather up practice. Some go abroad and seek it, and they get it; indeed some stoop so low as to make it. If such men have substantial merits they do themselves great wrong. The ranks of the profession are full of such men. They rise rapidly, are conspicuous and prosperous, but are never sound or famous, and when they pass away others succeed them by the same arts and to the same practical ends; and then they are straightway forgotten, and forever forgotten. Not so with the true lawyer. He dies, and another takes his place,— but not his fame,—for that will last untouched by rivalry, and only be conquered by Time himself.

"There are various ways in which such men solicit business, all of which are distasteful and repulsive to true lawyers. They advertise themselves by the multitude of their actions, and secure clients by their mean charges. . . ."

"I have seen a score of such men in my time, and I have seen them deserted, and contemned, and found out. Others not only solicit business, but, worse than that, they make it. They hunt up dead claims; they find out technical errors committed by honest people, who for want of caution have stepped aside from the straight line of legal exactitude, or have been permitted by good counsel to take a step open to doubt, but in a matter wherein they must act. They pick holes in men's title-papers, and they stimulate parties to sue on all such pretexts. There was a time when there was 'a statute for such men.' They are the curse of the profession and a pest to society.

"You must behave yourself in your office of attorney within the Court. Remember upon all occasions to conduct yourself with decorum and respect toward the Court, because it represents the law in its majesty and Justice in her purity. The contempt and slight shown on the day when you are unsuccessful will recoil on you at another time, when, against odds and public clamor, you shall see the Court stand forth to protect a client and prevent a wrong. How then will your commendation sound? How then will the bar be prepared to respect your cause, or to confide in a tribunal it has but recently heard you censure with noise and heated complaints of unjust judgments and partial feeling?"

"Respect the Court. It is wise, and, above all, it is your sworn duty. If you bring the Court into disrespect by your reflecting upon the judges, and by your public and offensive contentions with it, you not only prejudice your cause, but you demoralize the administration of justice, and detract from the dignity and honor of your profession. It is true that judges oftentimes forget themselves, and with arrogant and presumptuous tone shock the feelings of the practitioner. For this there is no excuse, and for this they are soon made to feel the quiet reprehension of the profession and the public, and they suffer in that a reproof that no heat or haste of the lawyer will ever inflict. In all such trying emergencies—when pressed by the necessities of your cause, taunted and provoked by your gratified adversary, anxious for your case and for your own standing, and stung by the unjust and unmannerly conduct of the judge—command yourself, hesitate before you act, think before you speak, and, with a calm, unblenched manner, coldly and courteously waive aside the affront, steadily persevere in the performance of your duty, and your triumph will be perfect without one touch of self-reproach or disappointment."

"Again I say, behave yourself in Court. Be faithful to it, and soon you will feel the value of that fidelity. The roughest scold that ever vexed a bar will subdue his peevish tone when you approach him. He dreads no trap—he fears no contrivance to mislead him under the cover of some smooth but sinister suggestion. He has no occasion to brush you aside or to daunt you with his fretful frown. He knows, and the profession know, that a fair, honest man is up, and, with fidelity to the Court and in sincerity to the law and its usages, he is about to ask for that which he believes to be his right."

"Try no vain experiments with the practice of the Courts; it is undutiful and unlawyerlike. Lord Eldon has said, 'When judicial practice has been settled, counsel do not act according to a right view of their duty if they seek to disturb the settled course of practice.'"

"In the time of Saint Louis we are told that this, among other regulations, was then adopted, that 'all arguments against an adverse party should be spoken with courtesy, without saying anything vile or harsh either as to fact or law.' Who can read this without approving it? Let us all strive to conform to it."

"You must be faithful to your client—yes, loyal as ever true knight was to his bounden duty or his plighted vows. You are not to be the servile, immoral partisan, but the manly, candid protector to your client and his cause; and your constancy will be shown more in the truthful exposure of the defects of his case, and in earnest efforts to persuade him to adopt the right course and do justice, than in all the fierce displays that were ever made to uphold a wrong and shield men from the just consequences of iniquity."

"I could go on in this desultory, rambling fashion for a long way, and, like a musing horseman, wander off with slackened rein till I was enveloped in the thick shade of my own thoughts, and be roused to consciousness by the darkness that gathered round me. So I must now stop, and thus end my journey. I have spoken right on, knowing that you would accept my labor with kindness as I have been faithful to my word, and it has been my effort to deal with you in all sincerity and truthfulness."

Mr. Brewster's whole life was one of design. Every paper he left tells of frequent and prolonged seasons of self-study. He was autobiographical when he once said :

"Before you start out, sit down like true men—like penitential men—and take an account of your mental and moral property."

Mr. Brewster designed to be the order of lawyer he conceived to be the noblest. He became more than the scholar he aspired to be.

As an advocate and orator he was ardent and almost tempestuous, with a passion which could stir and fashion the minds of men. His zeal in every cause was limited only by this intensity. His memory was a marvel. In his famous library—now in the possession of the University of Pennsylvania —he could instantly reach the volume and page desired in all the thousands of volumes piled two deep, and woe betide an intended misquotation by an adversary of some old law conceived to be buried under the dust of the past.

In literature as well as law his resources were marvellous. Admiral Porter has related to the writer that, at one of the state dinners at the White House, Mr. Brewster quoted from memory pages of Cicero, which when compared with an edition at hand were found to be absolutely without omission or mistake of quantity.

He had the rare faculty of weighing testimony and rushing to a logical conclusion from incoherent facts thrust unexpectedly forward in the conduct of a case. He was unexcelled at general repartee. He was of such warmth of sympathy and sentiment that doubt has been expressed as to his ability to have made a good judge. The records he has left of his legal life show a wonderful faculty for downright detail work and a patience therein that it is almost difficult to reconcile with the ardor of his temperament. His style, usually clear and crisp, was occasionally characterized by references resembling, "As ——— said to ——— in his great case before ———." While these glimpses into ordinarily untrodden fields sometimes brought him an imputation of pedantry, they suggested a vast reserve force which enhanced his power. But even in the application of the unembellished there is the same difference between lawyers as between men and men. Mr. Brewster once said:

"We have been sitting down, each in his study, reading the same books, and having the same thoughts, but to a different end. The authorities that we know they know; the authorities that they know we know."

Just as the same order of food produces and nourishes men of different feature, so the same books and thoughts are turned to different account with different men.

Given though Mr. Brewster was to citing authorities, he had no slavish subserviency to text-books, and on occasions he would not hesitate to challenge the book itself.

"Does he fortify it," he once said of a statement made by Wharton, "by reference to statute or clause of the Constitution, legislative or judicial authority, or an adjudication? No; it is only his interpretation. Let him study through the several thousand volumes of adjudicated cases now in the United States, and I deny that he can find one word of judicial utterance or declaration that warrants what he says. Mr. Wharton writes law books; I know him well. He studied law with his father, an eminent jurist himself," etc.

Nothing seemed to escape his vigilance. His vast resource enabled him to extemporize a new line of policy at any unexpected turn of a case. His addresses were always a literary treat. Judge and jury would bend forward to hear him, until it would sometimes seem that the "scales of justice were unfitly swayed" by his eloquence. With choicest applications from literature of all tongues he could graciously compliment an adverse witness or pour down almost boiling invective upon a froward opponent. He was, nevertheless, ever characterized by fairness, concession, and magnanimity, and this is particularly noteworthy with young lawyers.

Professor Loomis, the great New York diagnostician, when thanked by a pneumonic for saving his life, replied, " You owe your life to the young physician who watched your heart overnight, and not to me." Such was ever Mr. Brewster's attitude toward a junior counsel. If, when retained as eminent adviser, he could write a common client that the brief of the junior counsel was right to the letter, therein he found his greatest pleasure. Once when associated in a doubtful case with several lawyers, one quite young, the senior remarked, " Too many lawyers spoil a bad case," and looked significantly at the junior. Mr. Brewster caught the glance, and refused positively to serve in the case unless the young man remained.

Such were his ideas of the lawyer; such was he as a lawyer. Of the profession he has said:

"In Protestant countries, where the discipline of the confessional is unknown, lawyers often supply the place of spiritual directors to those who, were they accustomed to such advisers, would apply to their clergy. Think how dignified and solemn the duty thus cast upon you. How sacred the confidence given to you! The secret griefs and calamities of whole families are revealed to you as one familiar with the mysteries of the human heart and the control of the human reason. The morbid anatomy of perverted moral nature lies spread before you. Fathers, mothers, husbands, wives, sons, and daughters all come to you and tell their griefs and disclose their wrongs committed beneath the cover of domestic privacy, to publish which would make the wrong an infamy. To you masters and their servants expose their unhappy conflicts. These, indeed, are perilous duties and full of trouble. In such matters, remember first and last and always that it is then you most owe your fidelity to your client. You must weigh each thought and guard each word so as not to mislead. You must sift with severe scrutiny the narrative submitted to you, and, on the peril of your soul, strive to heal dissension, to obliterate the recollection of injury, and to establish peace. Treat your client as if he were an adversary, and with a strong compelling hand force him away from the doors of the court-house and bid him sit down with you in the solitude of your office, and there bravely forget his wrongs, and bravely repair his errors. . . .

"In law we should know not only how to control ourselves and our own knowledge and act with honesty and fairness, but we must command others and their knowledge, and force them to be honest and just."

VII.

Mr. Brewster no Success as a Politician—Early Political Associations with James Buchanan and Simon Cameron — The Dominant Democracy.

In an active career of half a century Mr. Brewster was in office five years. Although early ambitious for public life, and possessing abilities of rare usefulness to any party, his political career, from a political stand-point, was not a success. Morally and professionally, however, it was strikingly brilliant and characteristic.

But one paltry appointment was retained by him as a reward for the continued use of his fine powers for his party. Another, highly coveted, was indignantly repudiated because it involved concessions inconsistent with manhood and honor. The third and crowning honor of his career, as we shall see, came to him absolutely aside from political considerations, because the entire national press and sentiment demanded his integrity and legal power in a high post at a critical time. This fact was his particular pride.

When the temptation for public life first assailed him as a young man, we can read his misgivings in his own language:

"... I look around my harvest-field, and, instead of a plentiful crop of good things, I find I have been casting seed of tares and other vile things that flaunt in luxuriance, choking up the good. I do not say this as being in a surly mood, but in a calm, reflective spirit, saying to you a trite but solemn truth. I've been questioning whether I am right in my political pursuits, and whether I am not thus filling my Time's seed-field with tares. And yet I like it. It is a grand pursuit. How it stirs up the noble impulses of a man! How he who with a philosophic spirit contends in this avenue is aroused to all the manhood that nature has given him! What bright prospects of a glorious future are constantly dawning upon him! How, with good in one's purpose and ambition, we dash on in the wild chariot race!

> " Metaque fervidis evitata rotis,
> Palmaque nobilis Terrarum dominos evehit ad deos!

"... You will see, my dear Jones, that I have my harness on. Politics hereafter shall be to me no more a mere pastime, but a glorious contest for principle and the highway for my ambition. I will serve as a foot-soldier, if need be, that I may be an officer. I am ready for work that I may be ready for promotion, and, when promoted, I know my duty.

"To JOHN P. JONES, ESQUIRE, Reading, Pa., November 9, 1843."

Perhaps the country needs the example of a man who, as we shall see, deliberately "advises in the silence of the night" and concludes frankly to avow himself a politician, and work for the success of the organization he deemed best able to guide the Union. Especially so, since the very epithet of " politician" has become an ill-omened description of unworthiness, and the veriest wardsman tries to pose as a statesman to whom the offices come and beg to be taken.

Mr. Brewster made a profession of politics as Webster did; but he never relinquished the law. His career is a significant picture of a vigorous party service, a frank demand for office, and a persistent refusal because of his mental and moral independence.

As early as 1838 he had formed a friendship for Simon Cameron, which led them together on a carriage trip through Pennsylvania. Mr. Cameron, eighteen years the senior, with a promise of future power, was in a position to exert a most intense political influence over the young man, as they drove together through the great State discussing, as they must have done, the future, with its hopes and plans. A few years later, we find in one of Mr. Brewster's letters this estimate of Mr. Cameron :

" No man knows better than Simon Cameron that he is unpopular; but he is a true man, and I, who met him with strong prejudices, have found him faithful, skilful, and bold in our cause. If you have a friend, I believe Simon Cameron to be a true one. Nor do I think he will obtrude himself on the foreground so as to demand of you any unpleasant exercise of that good feeling which you might think you were called upon to show in his behalf."*

---

* Letter to Henry A. Muhlenburg, June 29, 1844.

But more powerful than Mr. Cameron's influence must have been that of James Buchanan. Mr. Brewster's friendship for him, amounting almost to worship, was broken later in life. Mr. Buchanan had entered the Pennsylvania Legislature two years before Mr. Brewster was born, and as United States Senator was now the leading power in State and National politics. Mr. Brewster's words give a pretty picture of Buchanan and his circle of young friends at Philadelphia.

"Allow me to congratulate you upon your happy marriage. . . . And although I cannot look forward to the time when I shall shake off bachelorhood and become a Benedict, I rejoice and applaud those of my friends who manfully assume the duties and responsibilities of a married life. For this has always been to me a subject of serious reflection. Mr. Buchanan and I have often conversed upon it, and whenever it has been the topic, it has filled me with a melancholy regret that one I honor and respect so much should find in the want of domestic ties the only sadness of his life. And we young men whom he so kindly honors with his counsel, his friendship, and pleasant company, should strive to learn by his example to secure those joys and comforts which cluster around the domestic hearth.

"Mr. Buchanan is now with us in the city, and it has been really delightful to see how eagerly all men have hurried to pay their attentions to this great man. . . . Why, there is no man in the country whose pleasant, affable, manly deportment can vie with his. No one once knowing Mr. Buchanan could for a moment wonder at the devoted fealty and allegiance that has always been paid him by the entire people of his State. I speak in seriousness when I say that I honestly think that he will be President of the United States, and that the Democratic party will find in Buchanan their policy and their glory.

"To COLONEL R. FRAZER, Lancaster, Pa., October 31, 1843."

We catch in this some of the enthusiasm of youth, and a prediction part of which was fulfilled when

Buchanan became President.   One of the earliest letters from Buchanan to Mr. Brewster concludes:

"Although not imaginative, my fancy has seized upon your little
snuggery, and, although I have never been there but once in my life,
I feel myself at home among its agreeable and happy inmates."

And we find Mr. Brewster writing:

"Mr. Buchanan has been here and I have had many interviews
with him.   I feel the warmest sympathy with this great and equable
man.   He so identifies himself with all my youthful enthusiasm that
I feel as if he were a dear and respected kinsman who had watched
over me for years, and understood me fully, repressing my folly and
kindly encouraging me to brighter hopes and loftier views.   God
bless him !"*

These relations between the United States Senator
and the young attorney, and those between him and
Simon Cameron, the future Secretary of War, undoubtedly influenced the young man's career.   He
therefore began life as a Democrat, in hearty accord
with the dominant political doctrine of his State, his
family, his two political friends, and, indeed, the
country, for those great changes which have made
our national history were just beginning.

His life began not far from the start of all parties
in this country, as only the fifth occupant sat upon
the Presidential chair when he was born.   Jefferson
had founded the Democratic party,† and its sway

---

* November 9, 1843.

† The first political division in the United States occurred, it will
be remembered, with the framing of the Constitution, when copies
of it were sent to the State legislatures for ratification.   Federalists
supported the Constitution; Anti-Federalists opposed centralization
of power in the general government,—these eventually formed the
Democratic party.

had been almost unbroken until the entrance of Mr. Brewster into politics. The changes which brought Mr. Cameron to declare for protection, induced Mr. Brewster to renounce Democracy, and led to the formation and dominance of the Republican party are the principal part of American history of those turbulent times.

Strengthened by companionship with the two controlling factors in the Keystone State,—who, consequently, spoke authoritatively in national councils,—Mr. Brewster found renewed cause for devotion to the party into which he was born, and which furnished him all his associations and political hopes.

VIII.

Buchanan, Muhlenburg, Shunk, Dallas, and Brewster—Mr. Brewster's First Political Success and Disappointment.

MR. BREWSTER first appeared in political life at the age of twenty-seven as the successful senatorial delegate, over George M. Dallas, afterwards Vice-President of the United States. This first success laid up for him future political embarrassments.

In the Democracy of Pennsylvania at that time there was a violent party schism, and a fierce strife

----

Washington and Adams were Federalists. Jefferson, Madison, Monroe, Jackson, and Van Buren belonged to the party dominant in nation and State when Mr. Brewster took political counsel with his mentors, Buchanan and Cameron, its leaders.

prevailed. The contest for the Democratic candidacy for the governorship was bitterly waged between the friends and followers of General Francis R. Shunk and those of Henry Augustus Muhlenburg, of Lancaster, who presents to history the singular anomaly of clergyman and politician. Mr. Buchanan wrote Mr. Brewster regarding this convention:

"Between Muhlenburg and Shunk I have taken no part. Both my principles and my feelings have kept me neutral, and I shall be in position to render some service to either of them who may be nominated. What I desire to impress upon you, and what I have endeavored to impress upon several of the friends of Mr. Shunk, is *the unexampled importance of your proceedings. . . . The eyes of the Democracy of the Union are intently fixed upon you,* and any serious divisions upon this question may prove fatal to our cause. . . . I have never considered the proceedings of any Pennsylvania convention so big with consequences. Mr. Van Buren will beyond a doubt be the candidate of the party; and I sincerely believe his fate, at least in Pennsylvania, depends upon your prudence and discretion."

It had long been a popular superstition that as Pennsylvania went so the national election would go. Pennsylvania, the Keystone State, was so called by reason of its important position. In the original thirteen States there were six free States on the north and six slave States to the south.

In the light of this great responsibility before the country, Mr. Brewster made Mr. Muhlenburg his choice, and entered the work with his wonted ardor. His documents prove that his labor was unremitting; events show their importance, for Mr. Muhlenburg was nominated. To the uniting of the party factions Mr. Brewster's efforts were next directed successfully, and Democratic victory was assured. So important was his work that he was promised the Attorney-

Washington 1 March 1844.

My dear Sir!

Amidst the gloom & despondency which prevails here I take up my pen to address you a few lines on the subject of the 4th March Convention. What I desire to impress upon you, and what I have endeavored to impress upon several of the friends of Mr. Shunk is the unspeakable importance of your proceedings.

The eyes of the Democracy of the Union are intently fixed upon you; & any serious division upon this question may prove fatal to our cause. I have never considered the proceedings of any Pennsa. Convention so big with consequences. Mr. Van Buren will beyond a doubt be the Candidate of the party; and I sincerely believe that his fate, at least in Pennsylvania, depends upon your prudence & discretion.

Benjamin. H. Brewster Esq

From your friend
very respectfully
James Buchanan

Generalship of the State. He was but twenty-seven, and this high post was practically within his grasp. It was a fairly-won reward worthy of his ambition, and with his ardent temperament it would be strange if he did not exult at the prospect. It was ordered differently, however. Mr. Muhlenburg died shortly before the election, and the candidacy was given to General Shunk. Though Mr. Brewster relaxed none of his effort in securing the success of the ticket, "a Pharaoh had arisen in the land who knew not Joseph," and a subordinate post was offered him with unmanly conditions attached. It drew from him a letter that is typical of his whole political career:

"I now take my position. I want the Attorney-Generalship. If I am to be refused, let it be so; then that is the end of it, and it is over. I stand upon an elevated position as a gentleman, and cannot stoop to make petty bargains with any man. I want to have, or to be refused, the Attorney-Generalship by Mr. Shunk. This is my firm and final conclusion. I want my friends to take this matter in hand, and at the proper time place my claims before Mr. Shunk, and have them considered—but considered even if to be rejected. It would be descending to consent to accept the deputyship when offered— what would it be to run after it, and higgle for it after the fashion that is proposed? That will never do. I turn my back on it when it approaches in that way. I say this early and without feeling. I know no feeling in it except as a manly one of independence. *I have advised where I should—in the quiet of the night with my own heart and conscience—and with the only and best friend I have, my mother; and from that I have resolved what I now write.*

"To Simon Cameron, October 30, 1844."

The Attorney-Generalship was refused him, and how keenly the young man was disappointed we can read between his own lines:

"But this has passed! The same energy which put me forward

with Mr. Muhlenburg shall hold me up where I am, and advance me in the future."

Years afterwards he spoke of this disappointment as seeming to blight his entire future, and loved to contrast the sharpness of such set-backs, apparently closing out the future, with their real significance as seen in their perspective of the past. One needs to be disappointed in the lesser things of life in order to appreciate the greater. The " glories of the Possible" still were his.

IX.

Mr. Brewster in the 1844 Convention—Annexation of Texas—Division of the Democracy on Slavery—Election of Polk—Mr. Brewster's Instrumentality.

MR. BREWSTER was a prominent factor in the National Democratic Convention of 1844. This convention was one of the most important political meetings in our history.

Mr. Brewster became at this convention the direct instrumentality to divide the Democracy on the slavery question, defeat Martin Van Buren, nominate Polk, bring Texas into the Union, and by making Mr. Dallas Vice-President of the United States, change Pennsylvaina from a Democratic into a Republican State. The hostilities and breaches engendered by Van Buren's defeat brought Democratic disaster, indirectly developed anti-slavery strength, and led eventually to Sumter and Appomattox.

It will be remembered that the Whig party had

been formed in opposition to President Jackson's financial policy, already mentioned. The old Federalists, their descendants, and the various factions caused by the personal rivalry of Webster and Clay, united under the new Whig banner, and elected President Harrison. His death, one month after the inauguration, reversed the political decision of the country by placing the administration into the hands of Vice-President Tyler, a life-long Democrat. The storm of indignation that swept the country promised an overwhelming Whig victory at the next contest. As the 1844 Convention approached, even the Democratic leaders conceded a victory for the other side. ·Wrote Mr. Buchanan to Mr. Brewster :

" Amid the gloom and despondency which prevails here (Washington, March 1, 1844), I take up my pen to address you a few lines on the subject of the fourth of March convention."

Henry Clay was nominated by the Whigs, and Van Buren, the conceded candidate of the Democrats, was " caught in the toils of Mr. Clay's diplomacy," and published a letter on the annexation of Texas. Said Mr. Buchanan to Mr. Brewster :

" The letters of Clay and Van Buren against immediate annexation have raised the very devil here among the politicians. The Southern Democratic members are all put aback by Mr. Van Buren's letter. I trust the storm which is now raging may pass away without serious injury, but I fear the result. " [April 29, 1844.]

By the 13th of May the " gloom and despondency" had become almost despair, and Mr. Buchanan wrote Mr. Brewster :

" It cannot be denied that the Democratic party are at present in a sad condition.   Our National Convention will meet at Baltimore this day two weeks, and the majority of the delegates have been instructed or pledged to vote for Mr. Van Buren, while many, and perhaps most of the delegates believe that, if nominated, he will be defeated.   The Whigs have held their Convention at Baltimore, and consider Mr. Clay as good as elected.   If Mr. Van Buren withdraw his name, and the Democratic party unite on any other man (and I think they could), we might yet elect our candidate.   I fear, however, that he will not pursue this course; and should any other be nominated in opposition to him, this will only make confusion worse confounded; for such a nomination would involve the violation of instructions—a doctrine always odious to the Democracy. . . . Should little Van be nominated, he shall receive my active support."

This letter, intimating a contingency which might fulfil Mr. Brewster's early predictions of a Presidential chair for Mr. Buchanan, drew from the former a request for permission to use the name of the latter. He wrote:

". . . The shallow pretensions and flimsy claims of Mr. Van Buren are not again, and for a third time, to be thus thrust upon Pennsylvania.   We who can make the President are not to be always thus forced in the forlorn hope of the contest.   He has twice had his chance, and with a splendid political patrimony inherited from General Jackson.   He left the Presidential chair with a whole phalanx of retainers unknown to the people, beaten, and covered with disgrace.   With thirty-odd Democratic State administrations to support him, with the patronage of the general government, with the devoted allegiance of a noble party, he was routed and our party covered with confusion.   Any other man—I care not who—could have been elected in triumph. . . . If we wanted any better evidence of Mr. Van Buren's ineffectiveness as a candidate, could we find any more convincing than that while he was President his own State was rent asunder, and the Whig party drove his adherents out of the State government?   That New York whipping gave the law to the whole United States, and by nominating Harrison and vigorously supporting him, their friends in the other States swept him into the Presidential chair."

Mr. Buchanan replied, declining to be a candidate against Mr. Van Buren, but expressed a willingness to be the candidate if Van Buren were tried and found unable to secure the nomination.

This was warrant enough for the young man whose heart was for his chieftain and whose convictions were against Van Buren.

It must be remembered that a new issue had been injected into the campaign after the delegates had been instructed. The question of the annexation of Texas had arisen. Van Buren and the whole Northern element, including Webster, Choate, Clay and his whole Whig and Abolition following, opposed the acquirement of this territory. Polk, a Southern man, with the mass of the Democracy, favored it. Mr. Brewster, while opposed to Van Buren personally and desiring Buchanan, was, as the latter, " Texas to the backbone," as the slogan ran, and, hence, he had reason to oppose Van Buren on policy. Therefore, to obey instructions, prevent factions, and at the same time secure Buchanan and Texas, required boldness as well as diplomacy and ability. The limelight of the nation was upon the convention, and especially upon the delegation from the Keystone State, led by the young man of twenty-seven.*

---

* Pennsylvania delegates to this convention were: Benjamin Harris Brewster, H. B. Wright, W. H. Harbeson, Joseph Snyder, Jas. Greer, Benj. Moore, David Lyon, S. L. Roberts, John Hinchman, Jr., Reah Frazier, Charles Kessler, Asa Packer, Luther Kidder, Col. S. Salisbury, Ellis Lewis, E. B. Hubley, Dr. Alexander Small, J. H. McLanahan, Gen. A. Wilson, J. L. Dawson, Gen. H. D. Foster, John R. Shannon, Wm. Kerr, Wm. Gill, Jr., Wm. Beatty,

The convention met at Baltimore, May 27, 1844, in a state of great excitement. It was a notable gathering. Benjamin F. Butler led the Van Buren element, while Benjamin H. Brewster was zealous for Buchanan.

In 1832, Van Buren had been elected on a rule which required that two-thirds of the delegates were necessary to nominate the candidate. This two-thirds rule was now brought forward to defeat him. By its passage instructions might be obeyed, and yet an acceptable man to lead the ticket might be secured.

Mr. Brewster, with Robert J. Walker, of Mississippi,—the great treasury secretary, who afterwards became his father-in-law,—worked with intense earnestness for its passage. It was not until it had been seven times balloted for that success at last crowned their efforts by a vote of 146 to 118. Then came the second step:

"Mr. Brewster arose and said that the delegation from Pennsylvania had been instructed to vote for Martin Van Buren, that the first choice of the State had been Mr. Buchanan, but, he having withdrawn from the contest, they should continue to vote for Mr. Van Buren until New York deserted him; they would not budge an inch until New York, Ohio, and New England had bolted the course."—*New York Herald.*

Hon. J. Bredin. The Whig Convention met at Baltimore earlier in May. Reverdy Johnson called the meeting to order. Tremendous enthusiasm followed Clay's nomination. Pennsylvania delegates were: Wm. B. Reed, J. Strohn, Augustus Baton, John Swift, B. Badger, M. Day, J. Roger, J. W. Hombeck, David Townsend, Thos. E. Franklin, John S. Richards, Henry Maxwell, W. C. Henley, M. C. Moncur, Wm. L. Harris, J. H. Campbell, Edgar Cowen, Thos. M. T. McKennon, Thos. M. Jolly, Sam'l A. Purviance.

The defection which followed induced Benjamin
F. Butler, amid wild excitement, to present a letter
of withdrawal from Van Buren, prepared to meet
such a contingency.* But, while routed themselves,
the Van Buren men prevented Buchanan's nomination, and, to the surprise of all, James K. Polk received the nomination, and Texas and its attachment
of slavery became the issue. The temerity of this
two-thirds party, writes Rufus Choate, was—

". . . strong enough to go into a national convention and there
trample instructions under foot; strong enough to force upon the
body an audacious, not very Democratic, rule of proceedings which
put it out of the power of the majority to nominate the choice of the
majority; strong enough not merely to divide Mr. Butler's last crust
with him, but to snatch the whole of it; strong enough to ejaculate
Mr. Van Buren out of the window."

The electric telegraph flashed from Baltimore the
news of this first convention ever reported by wire,
and on arrival of the train at Philadelphia indignation meetings were held everywhere, denouncing the
action of the delegates who voted the two-thirds
rule. Mr. Brewster was severely censured, and we
shall see how later disciplining was reserved for him.
"No contest for the Presidency, either before or
since, has been conducted with such intense energy
and such deep feeling."†

---

* "I have seen a letter of General Jackson's to Ex-Attorney-
General B. F. Butler, Mr. Van Buren's friend and spokesman in the
campaign of 1844, ascribing the nomination of Polk, after Van
Buren's defeat became certain, to Mr. Van Buren's friends."—*Gen.
Duncan S. Walker to B. H. Brewster*, July 10, 1887.

† James G. Blaine, "Twenty Years of Congress."

The New York *Herald* said, "Of the nomination of Polk we

The peculiarity of this contest was that "while it involved all the mere questions of policy which are ever suspended on the choice of a President, it involved—the first presidential election that has done so—the further more startling questions, *What shall the nation be? Who shall the nation be? Where shall the nation be?*" *

Another peculiarity of the contest was a somewhat ludicrous "moral" issue similar to the prohibition defeat of James G. Blaine and an apparent paradox. Mr. Clay opposed the annexation of Texas because it would involve war with Mexico.† His following among the Abolitionists opposed it because it would extend slavery. The difference in reasons for the same end had great weight in leading the

---

hardly know how to speak seriously. A more ridiculous, forlorn candidate was never put forth by any party. . . . The singular result of these laughable doings of the Democracy at Baltimore will be the election of Henry Clay. . . . Clay will only have to walk over the course. . . . We already see Daniel Webster in the field for the Whig mantle in 1848, and John C. Calhoun for the Democratic."

* Rufus Choate.

† Clay's Raleigh letter said, " Assuming that the annexation of Texas is war with Mexico, is it competent to the treaty-making power to plunge this country into war? . . . I do not think Texas ought to be received into the Union. . . . I think it far more wise and important to compose and harmonize the present confederacy as it now exists than to introduce a new element of discord and distraction into it."

Mr. Webster likewise defined the position of the more conservative North : " While we ought to feel as we do about annexing Texas, we ought to keep in view the true grounds,—the want of constitutional power and the danger of too great extent of territory."—*Webster Letters*, March 11, 1845.

Abolitionists to place in the field a third ticket headed by James C. Birney. Birney drew 60,000 votes; Clay was defeated; Texas was annexed, and the Abolitionists had, with the best intentions, opened slavery into a wider area. This instant defeat was changed by the genius of history into eventual triumph, for the great issues stirred up in this campaign in which Mr. Brewster took so prominent a part led to the point where Lincoln could issue his proclamation and make it possible for our history to relate the death of bondage in America.

X.

Political Sores in Pennsylvania—Feuds of Buchanan, Polk, Dallas, Cameron, Brewster—Robert J. Walker—John W. Forney—An Appointment at Last—Mr. Brewster's Reflections on a Political Life.

MR. BREWSTER's work in the Baltimore Convention made Mr. Polk President and Mr. George M. Dallas, his unsuccessful opponent in his first campaign, Vice-President of the United States. That this was not the intention does not change the result.

To the success of the ticket Mr. Brewster brought all his vehemence. Remembering that President Polk was quoting the very words of the Baltimore Convention when he pronounced our title to the Oregon territory " clear and unmistakable," and recalling the bold " Fifty-four-forty-or-fight" shibboleth that became a later campaign cry when England claimed more than we thought right of our boundary, we are reminded of Rufus Choate's later tribute to the party whose men at that time were of Mr. Brewster's ardent stamp:

"I neither join the Democratic party nor retract any opinion of the details of its policy. . . . I have always admitted that the Democratic party had burned ever with the great masterful passion that this hour demands,—a youthful, vehement, exultant, and progressive nationality. Through some errors, into some perils, it has been led by it; it may be so again; we may require to temper and restrain it; but to-day we need it all! the hopes, the boasts, the pride, the universal tolerance, the gay and festive defiance of foreign dictation, the flag, the music, all the emotions, all the traits, all the energies, that have won their victories of war and their miracles of national advancement,—the country needs them all now to win the miracle of peace."*

In this vigorous strain the Polk fight was made, and in Mr. Choate's language we can almost conceive a picture of the fiery young Philadelphia politician and orator.

Against the protest of Mr. Dallas, Mr. Buchanan was strongly urged and accepted as Secretary of State. President Polk accepted him only upon his written agreement that he would not become a Presidential candidate at the next election. Mr. Robert J. Walker, the Secretary of the Treasury, though requested by Mr. Dallas, declined to make active opposition to Mr. Buchanan's entrance into the cabinet; but seems to have maintained a hostility to Buchanan and his friends that was shown on later occasions. On the other hand, "Mr. Buchanan was never entirely frank, and when failing to secure

---

* Rufus Choate, Lowell address.

appointments because mildly asked, or because the President had no confidence in his promises as to the succession, he would blame it on Walker, Marcy, Johnson, or Bancroft."*　At any rate, Mr. Brewster's friends learned that Mr. Walker was opposing him. Mr. Cameron thereupon wrote:

"I am pained to hear that you have said you would oppose the appointment of my friend Brewster as District Attorney for this State. I am too unwell to leave home to-day, but will be in Washington on Tuesday night to speak with you on this subject. If Mr. Dallas is unwise enough to begin a fight now, I pray God that you will not become a party to it. Brewster is your friend. He has talents, energy, zeal, honesty, and faithfulness. You saw him by your side in the convention which gave you your present position. I am sure you are deceived by some one in regard to him, and I will try to convince you of your error of opposing him. Weak men and small politicians would begin a war in Pennsylvania, but wise men should see its folly.　SIMON CAMERON.

"To ROBERT J. WALKER, April 11, 1845."

Mr. Cameron himself had already been estranged from Mr. Buchanan, for when the latter was debating about entering Polk's cabinet, he consulted Mr. Cameron as to who would be likely to take his place in the Senate. "I think Simon Cameron will," replied Mr. Cameron. Mr. Buchanan turned on his heel and walked away without a word. After this his bearing towards his former lieutenant was always constrained. General Cameron has stated that Mr. Buchanan had another candidate for the place; and so it would appear, for at the following contest Mr. Buchanan warmly seconded the great journalist, John W. Forney, against Cameron, and

---

* Papers, Robert J. Walker.

in the conflict sores were opened which death only could heal.

Mr. Brewster had defeated George M. Dallas as senatorial delegate to the Baltimore Convention, incidentally making the latter Vice-President in the unexpected turn of events. Mr. Dallas, as Vice-President, by his deciding vote in a tied Senate destroyed the protective tariff of 1842 and gave the free trade of 1846. This led Simon Cameron to declare for protection, and brought a reaction which led to the present protective and unequivocal Republican majority in Pennsylvania. It is interesting to speculate upon what " might have been" the political history of Pennsylvania, and indeed the country, if Mr. Brewster had been defeated as a delegate, Mr. Dallas had gone to Baltimore in his stead, the two-thirds measure had been omitted, Van Buren elected, with a protectionist as Vice-President to cast this momentous deciding vote in the place of Mr. Dallas. It is also curious to note from what comparatively small instrumentalities and manœuvres great issues grow, and how important a place the genius of circumstance can give a single individual in the affairs of a great nation.

Mr. Dallas had been fighting Mr. Buchanan for years for the Presidency. Therefore every appointment that the latter urged became to Mr. Dallas a personal obstacle to his own ambition. In Mr. Brewster's particular case he had a personal account,—the memory of a defeat which, strangely enough, had made him such a decisive figure in our political economy. Mr. Brewster, too, was urged by Simon

Cameron, and Dallas hated Cameron with an intense hatred. Mr. Walker's opposition to Mr. Brewster's appointment as District Attorney—magnified by Buchanan—may, perhaps, have been natural in view of the feuds between Cameron and Buchanan, Buchanan and Dallas, Dallas and Brewster, added to President Polk's distrust of the designs of his Secretary of State as to the succession. Mr. Walker's brother-in-law wrote him:

"It is understood in Philadelphia that Mr. Dallas is taking a very active part in opposing Mr. B. H. Brewster's appointment as District Attorney, and that *you* are enlisted in the cause with Mr. Dallas, and that *your* opposition will probably defeat him. You may know the condition of parties both in Philadelphia and Pennsylvania better than I do, yet at the same time I must give my convictions on the subject. You are perfectly aware that those people are the same that opposed Mr. Brewster on his return from the Baltimore Convention, and endeavored to put him down, but did not succeed. These old Van Buren men will never forgive anybody when they have an opportunity of destroying them. I believe myself that Mr. Brewster has more friends in the city than any one of them, but when you get into the country these opponents of Mr. Brewster have not a corporal's guard. *Brewster is an energetic, bold, skillful man in arousing the interests and passions of the people, and exceedingly popular among them, swaying at will their feelings. His stormy eloquence and ugliness please the masses. He is a sort of minor American Mirabeau.* He entered life under the most appalling disadvantages,—deserted by his father, scathed by fire, with an appearance almost frightful, without a single friend to aid him in his almost hopeless career, and a mother and sister dependent upon his youthful exertions. By the force of unaided energies he has gone steadily upward in both his political and professional career. As a proof of this fact I would merely allude to the fact that he was elected as the senatorial delegate to the Baltimore Convention by a large majority over Mr. Dallas. With such an opponent as Mr. Dallas this speaks volumes.

"I hope the interest I feel that you should escape embroilment in Pennsylvania politics and avoid identifying yourself with a mere city clique, and so retain influence in your native State in case of an approaching contest, will prove my excuse for intruding upon you my advice."

WM. COOK to R. J. WALKER, April 15, 1845.

Upon this letter Mr. Walker endorsed:

" Private.   C. Albert.—Tell him I have informed Mr. Dallas that I would most positively decline to take part in his personal quarrels. Mr. B. deserves well for his part at Baltimore as well as for his talents.   I have so informed Mr. Polk."

Even the offices of the Secretary of the Treasury were ineffectual.   Mr. Brewster at this time wrote Secretary Buchanan a most characteristic letter:

" I cannot but believe that I have been designedly misrepresented. . . . But, put all this aside.   I stand upon grounds far above any secret accusations and efforts to overthrow me.   I ask to be District Attorney.   I ask it upon the grounds of my personal, professional, and political standing.   I ask you to bear witness to that.   If I am not worthy of the place, or if a gentleman can be obtained whose services outweigh mine, let him have the place ; but do not let me be set aside from the personal pique of any one.   Let some better reason than this be given.   I know very well that there are many men who have taken umbrage at my course at Baltimore who have been striving to make ill blood between Mr. Dallas and myself even before that time.   Yes ; ever since I was elected senatorial delegate. I did not know they had succeeded so well.   If I was elected over Mr. Dallas I was not conscious of harming him personally, particularly as it made him Vice-President.

" It is doing enough to ask for an office.   I cannot descend to make personal importunities for any place.   If Mr. Dallas and his friends mean to defeat me, let it be so.   I cannot crave favor."

These details are given to show how earnestly Mr. Brewster's friends worked for him and his appointment, and how strictly party discipline was enforced. He did not secure the appointment.   This second

political disappointment has been described by him
in a letter:

"I was refused the place of District Attorney because Mr. Dallas
made a personal request that I should not receive the place. I have
been so informed by a member of the cabinet. I had a letter from
a member of the cabinet that unless the President would assume a
quarrel with Mr. Dallas and deny him the only request he made, by
imposing upon him at his own bar a person he had declared was
personally offensive to him, he could not but refuse me the place.
A few words will explain the cause of Mr. Dallas's hostility to
me. Dismissing all minor considerations, it will be enough to say
that I was the open, acknowledged, and recognized friend of Mr.
Buchanan in this city; that Mr. Dallas was my competitor for the
senatorial delegation for the Baltimore Convention, and was defeated
by a vote of 70 out of 100. I incurred his resentment thereby. Had
Mr. Muhlenburg lived I would have stood unharmed notwithstanding
all assaults. He saw what I would do at Baltimore, and advised it,
and would have upheld me through all trials, for he never forsook
a friend.

"Mr. Dallas has assumed to construe political opposition (indeed,
not that,—personal friendship for another) into personal hostility for
himself. By this he must suffer,—suffer now in the condemnation
of all just men, who will reprove the ill temper that would prompt
him to thwart a young man in his professional hopes,—suffer hereafter in the condemnation of those political friends whose regards
made me his competitor, and whose adhering confidence elected me
so triumphantly.

"I thus speak out as befits a man, that he may know he has a foe
who will meet him openly, and not play the assassin and stab him in
the dark.*

"To Colonel W. W. Smythe, Jackson, Miss., July 15, 1845."

In the second year of Polk's administration a position opened requiring legal ability. Mr. Brewster was

---

* The relations between Mr. Brewster and Mr. Dallas became
amicable a decade and a half after this episode, as witnessed by the
following letter from Mr. Dallas, referring to one from Governor

commissioned to form a court to pass on the serious questions of property which had arisen, following the removal of the Cherokee Indians from Georgia to Indian Territory. Gravest questions of constitutional law, constructions of treaties, and the apportionment of millions of dollars, were before this tribunal. Upon the authority of the Hon. L. C. Cassiday, who at that time was Mr. Brewster's legal associate in Philadelphia, "ninety per cent. of the opinions of the tribunal were carefully thought out and written by Mr. Brewster, and a large proportion of them were acquiesced in by all parties interested."

Mr. Brewster retired from this office at thirty-

Letcher, of Virginia, which showed Mr. Brewster's efforts to push Mr. Dallas for the Presidency.

"Infandum, *amice*, jubes renovare dolorem!

" I am not surprised that your long sickness remained unknown to me : for, in order to forget as much as possible of the past and present, I have immersed myself in the labors of authorship. I ought to thank Governor Letcher for what he was kind enough to feel and write two years ago : doubtless, however, his mind has seceded from his old notions ; and I reserve all my gratitude for steadier and truer friends like yourself.

" My actual trouble springs from an inability to find a publisher for three or four volumes. They lie before me in complete manuscript ; and there they will have to lie, alone in their glory (at least so all the great printing-houses say), until the political convulsion is over. In the meanwhile, the musty proverb, ' while the grass grows,' etc.

" I return with thanks the enclosed letter, and sincerely hope to find you, on an early call, perfectly restored.

" Always faithfully yours,

" G. M. DALLAS."

To B. H. BREWSTER, February 24, 1862.

three, and resumed an undivided attention to his law practice, which had never been entirely relinquished. After six years of private practice and reflection upon the disappointments of political life he said, in an address :

" Be worthy of your country and its fame, but remember that you go far astray from the true path if you are allured from your social and personal duties into the angry contentions of place-hunters and politicians. The time was, in the early history of this country, when great men were wanted in public places to establish our institutions; good men are now needed in the walks of quiet life to strengthen them. All the world over, the trade of a politician is the occupation of a gamester; it is the business of a man whose time is spent in envy and strife. Public stations can confer no rank and bring no distinction to men who run after them. All great public occasions command men best fitted for the necessities of the time. The emergencies that excite great men to action having passed by, tranquillity having been restored, order having been established, new men—inferior men, men of doubtful parts—succeed to their masters, and manage with ease, if not with skill, the vast machine which wisdom created and industry set in motion.

" Let me warn you against the temptations which will beset you to embark in this business of politics. A life well spent in the pursuit of almost any calling will yield you a better income, will give you an independence of position and a manly dignity of character that no office can secure for you. Before you step out of the privacy of your own calling to take office, be sure that you are not unworthy of the place, or impelled by selfish motives, for to the most worthy and upright these stations bring with them trials and griefs that torture men to death. The shores of political life in every country are strewn with wrecks, and some of them were rich argosies. . . . The highest public distinction in this country can have no attractions for right-minded men unless they are the unsought reward of personal worth, dignity of character, mental ability, and a blameless life,—obtained in any other way, they disgrace those who hold them."

7*

XI.

Mr. Brewster's Political Faith—The Native American Party and
the Anti-Catholic Outrages—Riotous Philadelphia—The Native
American Banquet—Mr. Brewster's Letter defining his Position.

A SNEERING enemy by Mr. Brewster's open grave
charged him with "a flighty streak which made him
a political waverer." Other personal or political
opponents have sought at times to connect him
dishonorably with the Know-Nothing party and its
anti-Catholic riots.

About 1855 he did manifest an attitude of dissatisfaction toward the old Democratic party. Not
only were there to influence him the party duplicity,
neglect, and personal disciplining he had received,
but broader grounds of political sentiment and public
policy which were moulding the new political faith
of the whole country. There is nothing inconsistent or illogical in his political attitude at this
time.

The foreign element in American politics has been
a burning question from the start. It involves more
than policy. It cuts to the quick the matter of birth-
right, religion, nationality. So bitter are the prejudices and changes in the quicksand of votes wrought
by its discussion that no man to-day dare suggest it
who hopes for future position or influence in the
councils of his own nation.

Before the beginning of this century the Federalists were an anti-alien party. The founders of the
present Democratic party favored war with England

instead of France, and attracted to its banner the banished enemies of Great Britain from England and Ireland. The alien attachment to the Democratic party has been since maintained. From the start until our civil war, when both sides needed men regardless of nationality, the issue has been raised sporadically.

In 1844 the Gordon riots of England were re-enacted at Philadelphia. The utmost fanaticism prevailed. The worst elements of society made the occasion one of pillage, incendiarism, and murder. Catholic churches and property all over the city were destroyed, and their bishops and clergy were obliged to flee the city for their lives.*

Notwithstanding the denunciation of the outrages

---

* Bishop Patrick, of Pennsylvania, fled disguised as a nun to a Baltimore convent, from which he issued the following :

" BELOVED CHILDREN,—In the critical circumstances in which you are placed, I feel it my duty to suspend the exercises of public worship in the Catholic churches which still remain, until it may be resumed with safety and we can enjoy our constitutional rights to worship God according to the dictates of our conscience. I earnestly conjure you to practise unalterable patience under the trials to which it has pleased the Divine Providence to submit, and remember that afflictions will serve to purify us and render us acceptable to God through Jesus Christ, who patiently suffered on the cross.—FRANCIS PATRICK, Bishop of Philadelphia."

During these disgraceful scenes a journal was issued, of which the following is a prospectus: " THE NATIVE AMERICAN PRESS. *The Yellow Flower and Native Blossom. We'll make all Rome howl.* Vol. I. No. 1. Philadelphia, August 10, 1844. Price one cent.

" PROSPECTUS,—For the publication of a new semi-weekly paper, devoted to the cause of the Native Americans, and sternly opposed to the blighting and withering interference of the Pope of Rome with the Bible and American institutions."

by the Native American party leaders, the order was disgraced and died a natural death. Nearly a decade later, however, a new native movement was started. Its object was veiled from its leaders until they had taken the higher degrees, and their constant replies of " Don't know," finally gave name to the Know-Nothing party. "Americans must rule America" was their platform; their countersign, Washington's famous order, " *Put none but Americans on guard to-night!*"

Avoiding the religious element, the new order rapidly disorganized the old parties. The Whigs did not oppose slavery strongly enough to enter the new Republican party, just forming, and saw neither compatibility with Democratic principles nor a future for their own tottering party. They came almost as a body to the new order. A large number of American Democrats were also drawn to its ranks, especially at the South. Immediate success in State matters emboldened the new party, in 1856, to prepare for a national campaign. But, by an unparalleled piece of stupidity, the anti-Catholic element was introduced at this point, and thus its death-warrant was signed by its own hand.

Before this religious intolerance was avowed— though it was feared and suspected by the Catholics —and while the order was still flushed with State successes, Mr. Brewster was invited to a convention of the American party " to consult calmly in respect to the present political condition of the country, and to declare authoritatively the principles of the American party."

This meeting, the invitation to which remains among Mr. Brewster's papers, was the National Convention of the American party held in Philadelphia in 1855, that broke up in disorder because the Northern and Southern delegates could not harmonize differences on the slavery question. During the convention, however, at a time when it seemed that, at last, the mistakes of all the old organizations would be rectified in the new platform, a dinner was given by the delegates. Mr. Brewster presided at this dinner, much to the surprise of all Philadelphia. The following correspondence ensued:

" PHILADELPHIA, June 9, 1855.

"To BENJAMIN HARRIS BREWSTER, ESQUIRE,—Having been for many years your political friends, we were surprised to see your name published as presiding at the recent dinner of the American Order, and that we may know your views and position there, we take the liberty of asking you if you are to be understood as an advocate of religious intolerance.

" Yours very truly,

"ANDREW STEIF, JOSEPH WATERMAN, DAVID BOYD, LEWIS C. CASSIDAY."

" PHILADELPHIA, June 9, 1855.

"GENTLEMEN,—In reply to your note I must say that I was more surprised at the question it proposes than you were at seeing my name published as presiding at the banquet given to the strangers who were here upon the subject of the organization of the American party.

"I was not there as an advocate of religious intolerance, but because I desired to encourage a spirit of nationality, and to urge the proper administration and revision of the naturalization laws, so as to put an end to the evils we have suffered under, and forever stop the offensive appeals hitherto made by all parties to the prejudices of the large unnaturalized vote of the country.

"No political organization shall receive my support that will subject citizens to a religious test; I will not consent to do anything

f

that can be construed into acquiescence in opinions—political opinions—that would invade the right of private judgment and the liberty
of conscience; and because I am a Protestant I hold it to be my
duty to give my testimony in favor of religious liberty and against
intolerance. In my judgment it is the right of all men—as men—
to think and speak as they please upon the subject of their religion,
being responsible to God alone for their thoughts or words, and any
attempt to deprive them of their civil rights because of those opinions would be an act of injustice and a great public crime.

"BENJAMIN HARRIS BREWSTER."

Mr. Brewster at this time received many letters, giving a good idea of the spirit of the times, notably one from Mr. Seward.

Mr. Brewster has ever been strong in his Americanism, as his addresses will show, but he found the new party principles were not for him, and announced his withdrawal. One year later, in 1856, the anti-Catholic plank was introduced and the party died.

Mr. Brewster cast one more Democratic ballot; then the changes began that involved the country in war and ushered in the Republican régime.

X I I.

Mr. Brewster and Lucretia Mott—The Great Slavery Fight—" The
Underground Railroad"—The Dangerfield Case—An Excited
City—Mr. Brewster Wrapped in the Flag before a Mob—His
Opponent's Grave.

WE could wish a different record on the slavery question for our subject. His convictions as to the legality of slavery were those of the whole bar of the country. The union of the States was only made possible by the concessions to slavery found in the Constitution: without them its existence would have been impossible. From this as a starting-point, Mr. Brewster's course was professional, fearless, and thoroughly characteristic of the man. Reviewing his life near its close, he gives us a manly acknowledgment of just wherein he was mistaken; but he would be the last to apologize for that element of right which dominated him in an unpopular cause. Slavery was wrong, and therein lay his error; but slavery was legal, and in maintaining "the legal principles involved" he was right, and with that content to let the record stand.

The bitterness of the slavery debates has never been paralleled in the history of any nation since the beginning. The Fugitive Slave Act of 1850 had practically turned the whole force of the United States into slave-catchers. The United States bonded marshals, being responsible for the full value of slaves escaping from custody, were empowered to compel by-standers to aid in executing writs, and the Abolitionists at the North faced the dire possibility of being legally compelled to join in the hunt.

The Abolitionists, fired with the rabid fervor of the propagandist, fought the entrenched wealth of the South with the invisible but powerful bludgeon of moral sentiment. "Underground Railways" were established to aid escaping slaves; counsel was retained to protect them; public indignation was stirred to rescue them from the hands of the authorities when recaptured, and all who obeyed the laws in assisting to capture them were placed in personal menace and danger; in short, everything was done to annoy slave-holders and make slavery detestable.* Their power can only be appreciated by viewing the magnitude of the enemy they eventually routed. The two hundred thousand slave-holders of the South were "banded together by one uncompromising tie of common interest,—slavery, its preservation and extension." They put into Congress their ablest men, schooled in native and foreign universities in all the subtleties of statecraft, with one sole political principle,—"The more territory the more slaves; the more slaves the greater wealth."

---

* As a reminiscence of these stirring times, do we not still meet occasionally the lingering vocabulary of "Copperheads, Union Savers, Doughfaces, Southern Sympathizers, Abolitionists, Fanatics, Melanomaniacs, Negro-Stealers, Mudsills," and so on to the exhaustion of ingenuity?

Do we not recall how Webster, Clay, Choate, Cass, Foote, Dickinson, Calhoun, Lincoln, all counselled moderation?

"While the people sleep, politician and philanthropist, the stump, the press, will talk and write us out of our Union!"

"A public opinion is diffused in whose hot and poisoned breath our Union may melt as frost-work in the sun."

"Russia does not hate England more than our North and South hate each other."

"May not duty to the republic be a little too large and delicate and difficult to be comprehended in the single emotion of compassion for one class of persons, or in carrying out the single principle of abstract and violent justice to one class?"

"A whole people,—a reading, excitable people,—hearing nothing, reading nothing, talking of nothing, thinking of nothing, sleeping and waking on nothing for years but an incessant and vehement appeal to the strongest of their passions,—one half aimed to persuade you you were cruel, ambitious, insolent, and therefore hateful; the other half that you were desperately and hypercritically fanatical and aggressive, and therefore hateful. . . ."

The utmost corporate influence possible to conceive in the future will never parallel in power such a compact unit with similar unison of political aim. Others might be divided with personal or political differences, but with them slavery was their wealth, their politics, and their religion.*

At Philadelphia these fires burned most fiercely. It was the home of Lucretia Mott† and the head-quarters of the " Underground Railroad."   The hall used by the Abolitionists was burned by slavery sympathizers, and Mr. George William Curtis, later, announced to lecture in favor of the movement, was stopped by the mayor for fear of bloody work by the mob.‡

Chief-Justice Taney's famous " Dred Scott" decision of 1857 shook all Christendom, and the renewed

---

* Alexander Johnson.

† Lucretia Mott, the Quaker philanthropist and reformer, was a woman of great simplicity and purity of character, whose sympathies made her almost a lioness in promoting the " Underground Railroad" for escaping slaves and in preventing their return to the South.   She was a delegate to the Anti-Slavery Convention in London in 1840, and was not allowed to sit therein on account of her sex.   She was ever ready with her voice, purse, or pen to aid the cause, and was invariably present at all the great slavery trials.   She died in 1880.

‡ Said Mr. Brewster (Cooper Union address), " In Philadelphia, where the Declaration of Independence was signed, they burned that stately edifice—Northern Democrats instigated by Southern men— upon our sacred soil of Philadelphia!   Even within a few months prior to the Rebellion, Mr. Curtis came to Philadelphia to address an audience of ladies and gentlemen as I have come here to-night, and they assembled as you have assembled.   A riotous mob collected around the building, and he was obliged to do—what?   He was turned out of the room, the house was closed, the people separated by back doors and by-ways to prevent bloodshed !"

search for fugitives in the North gave rise to some of the most thrilling scenes in our history, and some as brutal as ever gladiatorial contest afforded.

Believing in slavery as " a social, commercial, and political necessity," both legally and morally right, it was to Mr. Brewster a legal crime to aid in the escape of property which had been purchased by a citizen under the protection promised in the Constitution.   With these views, in April, 1858, he was brought into conflict with Lucretia Mott and her followers in the great Dangerfield slave case.   " Lest affection press upon judgment," and even at the risk of prejudice to Mr. Brewster, the report of the abolition sympathizers is given below.   The case was lost by Mr. Brewster through the intimidation of the Commission by the immense throng of negroes and Abolitionists who surrounded the building; but this account concedes the identity of the slave in exulting over the victory.

EXTRACT FROM A PAMPHLET PREPARED BY J. MILLER McKIM, SECRETARY OF THE PENNSYLVANIA ANTI-SLAVERY SOCIETY.

" On the second instant we were telegraphed from Harrisburg that an alleged fugitive slave had been arrested, concluding with the words, ' do what you can for him.'   We said, ' We must fight it to the last; we must spare no pains; we must dispute every inch of the ground ; we must do all that we can for the poor fellow.'   In less than an hour Wm. S. Pierce, Geo. H. Earle, Chas. Gilpin, and Edward Hopper were engaged to meet the exigencies of the case. . . . .

" The prisoner was produced before the Commissioner, accompanied by his claimants and their counsel, B. H. Brewster.   The Commissioner granted an adjournment until Monday.   Mr. Brewster took occasion to state, before the adjournment, in order that he might not be misunderstood, especially by the gentleman who appeared as next friend to the prisoner, whose feelings and positions he appreciated and respected, how he came to be employed as counsel in this case. It had been kicked about from one to another and refused on various pretexts till it had come to him. He had taken it as a matter of professional duty. He would shrink from no case because of the odium that might attach to it, and he would levy no 'blackmail.' He would charge a fair fee, proportioning it to the amount of his services.

"This adjournment was the man's salvation. Delay gave us a chance to look for testimony *and take our appeal to the people.* By Monday the city was in a hopeful state of excitement. Still we had no hope; the most that we expected to do was to make a good fight, protract the issue, turn the case to general account, and build up public opinion against the recurrence of a similar exigency. . . . Monday morning the Commissioner's office was densely packed with respectable people of both sexes, and the street was crowded with those who were unable to get in. . . . Attempts were made by force to clear the passage and drive back the crowd. Marshal Yost called on his deputies and the city police to aid in clearing the passage. A · remonstrance was borne to the mayor against the interference of the star police, some of whom were rude. The mayor disclaimed any purpose to interfere, and his police were withdrawn. 'Let the trial be removed to where there is room. We demand admittance,' cried the crowd. Still the passage was not cleared. When Mr. Brewster presented himself for admittance he found he could not get in without more effort than he chose to make. He declared he would not attempt to enter until the vestibule was cleared. . . . At last, however, the case was ready to go on. Mrs. Lucretia Mott had taken her seat by the prisoner. Mr. Brewster was about presenting his papers when Mr. Earle rose to denounce the cowardly and despotic policy of choosing an apartment for the trial where the people could not be admitted. . . . *The forenoon was thus consumed.* In the afternoon the same scenes of confusion and excitement took place at the door. The hearing had been removed to the United States District Court, a larger and more commodious apartment, but there was still no space for a hundredth part of the people desiring admission. Mrs. Mott resumed her seat beside the prisoner, and the trial proceeded. At four o'clock the case was adjourned until next day.

"On Tuesday, at the appointed hour, a dense crowd again filled the streets, and the doors of the court-room were besieged by an eager throng, clamorous for admission. The same scenes were repeated that had been enacted the day before. The fact, however, that an applicant for entrance was a medical student from the South seemed to be an 'open sesame.' The proceedings were opened by Mr. Hopper withdrawing from the case, as facts had been developed which must inevitably produce an impression prejudicial to the character of the court for impartiality. Mr. Earle followed in the same strain; he could admire, but could not imitate the consistency of Mr. Hopper; he must stick to his client, let the case take what shape it might.

" Brewster, taken aback by this unexpected move, became much excited. Forgetting his propriety, he allowed himself to become vituperative. He denounced the conduct of the counsel for the respondent as 'indecent and immoral.' They had ' ceased to coax and had resorted to bullying.' ' The conduct of these persons,' said he, ' is beyond all precedent insolent, evasive, and arrogant; and never was the dignity of the profession so draggled through the mire as in the contemptible concoction of the opposing counsel. It is the product of last night's labor, and its intention is to strike justice in the face and set precedent at defiance. I speak advisedly, Mr. Commissioner, when I say in the presence of one Commissioner besides yourself that you have done nothing more than your duty. . . . What you have done is done every day by magistrates everywhere. I do not come here like the opposing counsel, to blurt out sentimental nonsense, but to fulfil the mandate of the law.'

" The case went on. It was half-past twelve at night when the testimony was concluded. The ladies all kept their seats, watching the proceedings with unfaltering interest. Mr. Brewster commenced summing up, which he did with his characteristic ability. Bad as his cause was, it is but just to say that his speech in point of force and clearness was not unworthy of his professional reputation. He was followed by Mr. Earle, who took the floor at half-past two in the morning, and later by Mr. Pierce, who entered the lists at four o'clock in the morning. *It was after five o'clock, and day had begun to dawn,* when Mr. Brewster made his concluding speech. It might—if it were not a paradox—be called an eloquent plea for slavery. He made the most of a bad cause; he managed it with a zeal and ability worthy of a better one. His blood was up; he was irritated; his professional reputation was at stake. To the appeals of his opponents for justice he had nothing to answer but the ' demands of the law,' and on this he rang his changes :

<blockquote>
" ' I crave the law—
The penalty and forfeit of my bond.'
</blockquote>

" He forgot his vaunted gentlemanly bearing and boasted moderation. At the opening of the trial he had complimented the 'next friend of the slave' * for his dignity as a witness, and at the end he sneered at what he called that witness's ' officious testimony.' Then he felt called upon to make an exculpatory statement as to his connection with the case; now he wound up his peroration with language of a very different character,—' I said on Saturday that this was the first case of the kind I have ever undertaken; I say now, *so help me God*, it shall not be the last, if another should ever be offered me.'

" With Mr. Brewster's speech terminated the trial. *It was now ten minutes of six in the morning*. We had been in session since four the preceding day. The sun had set and risen on our proceedings. The friends of the prisoner had kept their seats without signs of uneasiness. The marshal dozed, the Commissioner's eyes grew heavy, the witnesses slept, the prisoner could keep awake no longer, the officers rested their heads on the ends of their maces, and the door-keepers slept at their posts. But Mrs. Mott, Mary Grew, and the twenty or thirty other women who were in the room sat erect, their interest unflagging, and their watchfulness enduring to the end. . . . The prisoner upon his release was almost killed with embraces and congratulations. He was placed in a carriage that stood near; the horses were taken out, and as many as could find places took hold of the tongue and hauled him through the streets amid deafening cheers. The whole city was in a blaze of joyous excitement. Many causes are assigned for the result; there is but one that can rationally account for it. That is, *the twenty-five years' steady presentation to this community of anti-slavery truth*. . . . It was the informing power of the anti-slavery enterprise which has been at work systematically for the last quarter of a century that achieved the triumph. *This was the best slave case that I have ever seen tried*, and I have seen all that have occurred in this city in the last twenty years." †

---

* Doubtless J. Miller McKim.

† The pamphlet ends with the foot-note, " The man on trial as Daniel Dangerfield, or Daniel Webster, *was probably the slave claimed*. It was very imprudent not to change his first name, by which slaves were generally known."

8*

In the great demonstration of the Abolitionists that followed the decision, Mr. Brewster barely escaped with his life. A mob of excited negroes and Abolitionist enthusiasts surrounded his house and howled for his appearance, breathing out the direst threats. The scene has been described by an eye-witness, who affirms that Mr. Brewster appeared to the crowd with the American flag thrown about him, and, with one of his passionate bursts of oratory, dared any one to fire at him for upholding the laws of the United States as plainly and unmistakably written in the Constitution.

There was no middle ground in those days. However much we may to-day sympathize with the cause of the freedman, there is no warrant for all the bitter aspersions that have been cast on Mr. Brewster because he dared face a howling, threatening mob, ready to shed his own blood in seeking what even his opponents conceded was legally right.

The irony of fate brought Mr. Brewster into the same court-room to speak over the remains of Hon. W. S. Pierce, the professional brother who had represented the other side. Under these solemn circumstances he said,—

"I shall never forget how in this very court-room he and I conducted—I opposed to his views, and he opposed to mine—the great Dangerfield case. A case that was almost insurgent and revolutionary in its character and in its methods of administration; the officer of the law, who sat where you now sit, administering justice; the crowded court-room, crowded to excess through two long days and one long night; the building itself surrounded with guards to protect it, and a mob of angry, excited people on the outside,—and there sat Judge Pierce as one of the counsel, calmly conducting that case, anxious, earnest, but unruffled through the excitement, almost terrors, of that case as it was conducted.

"He maintained his equanimity through all his anxiety. I honored him then as I honor him now. That case passed by, and then came the great crisis that threw this country into a condition of intestinal war. . . . Judge Pierce was right in his anti-slavery views. The public judgment was with him in the end. I now look back and see where he was right, representing a high moral principle that it was our duty to have enforced. He possessed advantages of personal experience that very few of us had of the practical workings of slavery. He was born in a slave State, and he knew it in all its wickedness. He knew it in its worst features, not only where it existed, but where families were broken up and children were scattered throughout the country, making them objects of traffic like beasts of the field. He knew it, felt it, saw it in his early experience, and testified to it. I represented the legal principles involved in the case as I had been trained and educated. He represented a high principle, a moral and righteous principle, which was right."

XIII.

The First Republican Convention—Relations with Buchanan—The Rebellion.

In June, 1856, the first Republican Convention was held at Philadelphia, and history was again being made at Mr. Brewster's very door. John C. Fremont, the "Pathfinder," was the Republican candidate. James Buchanan was the candidate of the Democrats, and Millard Filmore led the Native Americans.

Mr. Brewster was not yet reconciled to the new Republican party. Their slavery attitude repelled him. His former relations with the President, too, had been somewhat restored. Mr. Buchanan wrote him, October 15, 1859,—

" You must well know that at an earlier period in your life I was your friend, faithful and true, and I heartily rejoiced when the ancient relations were restored previous to the late presidential election."

Mr. Brewster's reply was,—

" You say you were my friend, faithful and true, at an earlier period of my life. Suffer me to say that at that time I served you with an intense zeal and in a population hostile to you. At that time I brought to your service a power acquired by my own unaided efforts, and for exerting which to this very day I have the hostility of the very men who used your federal office-holders here to injure me."

The injury to which Mr. Brewster here refers was opposition to his *second* effort for the post of District Attorney. He wrote to the President regarding it,—

" You say correctly when you say that the nomination ' was not of the least consequence to me.' Indeed, if my friends, the heads of the profession here,—Mr. Meredith, Mr. Mallery, and others,—are good counsel, it would have been an injury to me. They deprecated, one and all, the idea of my accepting the nomination, because they believed I would be elected, and in that way would 'injure my civil business for life.' *But because it was of no consequence to me, I am not to submit quietly to the hostile action of a set of men whose first duty was modest obedience to the will of the people.*"

But graver matters were exciting the people. The following month, October, 1859,—six months before Lincoln was nominated,—John Brown made his famous Harper's Ferry raid. The country flamed with excitement. Mr. Brewster spoke at a meeting at Jayne's Hall, Philadelphia,* earnestly counselling

---

* Addresses were also made at this meeting by Richard Vaux, Wm. B. Reed, Charles Ingersol, Robert Tyler, James Page, Isaac Hazlehurst, Henry T. King, and John C. Bullitt.

moderation and allegiance to the law. "Within the forms of law we are safe; beyond them we are in ruin."

In May following Mr. Lincoln was nominated, in November he was elected, and in December, 1860, South Carolina withdrew from the Union. Buchanan's cabinet was in sympathy with the South. He himself "wrote a political essay to teach the North its duty," and then virtually abdicated. President-elect Lincoln, at that time in Philadelphia, was hurried to Washington by a circuitous route.* Philadelphia— the metropolis of the Keystone State, which then controlled the Union; the centre of the panic that organized the Whigs; the riotous scene of the Native American party's conventions, outrages, and disruption; the head-quarters of the "Underground Railroad" and hot-bed of Abolitionists; the seat of the first Republican Convention; the home of the vacillating occupant of the White House † and the

---

* The lamented S. M. Felton, shortly before his death, gave the writer a vivid account of this secret night journey of Mr. Lincoln, planned by him. As president of the railroad connecting Washington with the North, Mr. Felton sought aid from the government to protect his line. Failing to secure it, he garrisoned the line with his own detectives, and in this manner became apprised of the bold plot to capture Washington, assassinate Lincoln, and seize the government. Mr. Lincoln was hurried to Washington, on a special train, by way of Harrisburg, in charge of General Superintendent H. F. Kenney, and action was taken which thwarted the grave conspiracy.

† "Buchanan's Presidency was for the first time a distinct and avowed marshalling of a solid South against a solid North on the slavery question. . . . His influence precipitated civil war where it might have averted it by firm measures. . . . In November and

embarking point of the President-elect on his adventurous night journey—became at this time the raging battle-field of warring passions.

Simon Cameron, then United States Senator, was serenaded about this time, and, in responding to the compliment, declared himself "willing to make any reasonable concession not involving principle to save the country from anarchy and bloodshed."

A few weeks later, we find a proclamation from Mayor Henry, protesting that " treason against the State of Pennsylvania or the United States would not be suffered within the city."

In this caldron of seething political activity, Mr. Brewster came out vigorously for the Union, waived his views on slavery, and declared vehemently that there was no principle of government that he would not " deliver over to instant death if it were the cause of such foul treason as this principle of involuntary servitude had been."

In 1863 the National Union Club was formed at Musical Fund Hall, Philadelphia, and a call was given to the " unconditional friends of the Union, and to all engaged in sustaining the general government in suppressing the present unholy rebellion."   Mr. Brewster delivered an address on this occasion, breathing in fiery eloquence the spirit of the times.

December he was angered at the verdict of the country ; in January and February, frightened and harassed by the conduct of his trusted Southern advisers. . . . He lacked will, fortitude, courage, self-assertion,—desire to shoulder responsibility. . . . He closed his term not only emancipated from Southern thraldom, but, in some degree, embittered against Southern men."—*Nicholay and Hay's Lincoln.*

When Mr. Lincoln became a candidate for re-election, Mr. Brewster warmly espoused his cause.   In the Grant campaign four years later, he spoke at the Cooper Union.

A great political change had swept the country. A new party had been born out of the dismemberment of the old parties.   Said Mr. Brewster,—

" The Republican party in Pennsylvania has a peculiar history. All the strongholds of the Republican party of this day were once the only strongholds of the old Democratic party in its proudest days. The whole of the Eastern tier of counties, and the whole of the Northern tier of counties, were once the citadels of the Democratic party, and in those counties began . . . the teaching of those doctrines . . . which revolutionized the State and carried it over forever to the cause of Republican liberty in this country.   The Whig party in Philadelphia was broken up by the destruction of the old city proper. . . . Then we had the Know-Nothing party, the Native American party, the People's party, the divided Democratic party, the Abolition party,—and out of this grew up gradually a party called the Republican party."

XIV.

Simon Cameron—Important Connection with Mr. Brewster's Career —Burdens at Washington as Secretary of War—Renouncing Political Life in Russia—The Senatorship.

MR. BREWSTER's political career is so closely associated with that of General Simon Cameron that they can scarcely be treated apart.   They were intimate from the start, and, though occasionally clashing in ambition, remained constant until the old War Secretary was called from Donegal to bear the remains of his junior to the grave.

The author was robbed by death of valued assistance promised him upon the present work by General Cameron,—as also by Ex-Governor Pollock and Samuel Savidge, his grandfather, all three of whom were intimately associated early in life, and passed away since the present task was undertaken.

General Cameron was born in 1799, became powerful in the councils of the Democratic party, and followed Mr. Buchanan's heels rather too closely for the comfort of the latter when succeeding him, in 1845, as United States Senator from Pennsylvania. General Cameron declared for protection at the time of Mr. Dallas's decisive vote, and forever afterwards commanded Pennsylvania politics. Like Mr. Brewster, he came into the Republican party when the whole nation was overhauling and reconstructing its political faiths. In 1862 he wrote Mr. Brewster from Russia :

" Is it not strange that of all who started out in 1844 to reform the Democratic party, you and I are the only ones who have not wandered off with the ' strange gods ?' "

Mr. Cameron became President Lincoln's Secretary of War. The circumstances that attended his appointment, and his independent views about arming the negroes, are well known. The trials of his position at this critical time, and how he felt them, we can judge from his letter to Mr. Brewster :

" No one in Pennsylvania seems to be content with anything I can do, and none but you make allowances for my annoyances, and after having tried to serve every one, I shall probably go home as much cursed as poor miserable Buchanan, who neglected every one,—such is patronage."

Mr. Cameron served ten months as Secretary of War, at a time when the War Department was something more than a mere social appendage to the administration. His effective measures for subduing the Rebellion were opposed by Secretaries Chase and Seward, and he resigned to accept the Russian mission at St. Petersburg. From here he wrote to Mr. Brewster a pathetic commentary on the pleasures of office :

" It was no pleasure for me to be in Philadelphia when no one understood me and when I could speak to no one."

At St. Petersburg his shrewdness and diplomacy prevented the Russian Government from joining England and France in active support of the Southern States, and turned Russia from a spectator into a warm and active friend of the North. This accomplished, he conceived his duty to be at home, and wrote Mr. Brewster :

" It is my determination to reject in future all ambitious associations and ambitious schemes which will entangle me with office or place. I shall go home and sit quietly there, trying to do some good to my country or to those who are serving it in this unholy war. In truth, I am distressed with apprehension for the fate of our country, and this apprehension is wearing out my nervous system. I think that now is the time for every one to be at home, and that there, as a private gentleman, I can do more than here or anywhere else in public station. I do not fear for the ultimate success of our arms, but I dread the effect of this long delay upon our institutions and upon the character of our people. Long wars are always followed by great calamities. We must conquer the rebels, and do it soon."

Three days later, in a longer letter to Mr. Brewster, we see more of these perturbations,—also the necessity to pour out his soul to his friend, and a stimulation to the ambition of the junior:

"I am inclined to think that you and I are both fools, and yet I would not allow anybody but myself to say that of you, and I would not say it of myself to any one but you. Why, you will ask? Because we are always looking for sympathy! For friendship! For kindness! It is so with me, and your letter convinces me that it is so with you. At this moment I am ready to abuse you for this weakness, and yet perhaps before night I shall need some one to tell *me* that it is foolish and silly and extremely weak! You have accomplished *more than any man that has lived* under the circumstances. You have ability, education, knowledge, and have won, under difficulties such as no other man has ever battled with and conquered, a professional reputation that is equal to any man in our land, so full of wonderful successes. And I, too, with scarcely a merit, have had all the distinctions and honors conferred only on the great and good of the world. Still, you grumble, and so do I. Why is this? The secret is in the human heart. We are never content. I would give all the world for your genius, your learning, your knowledge, and your power over the human mind by your high qualities. And you would give all these for my petty distinctions? Such is human nature! We are never content with what we have. Divines tell us that this discontent is evidence of the future world. God grant that it may be so! I believe in the goodness of God and His overruling providence! I am going home to renounce all wish to enter again into public life, and to devote all my energies and all the influence I have to the service of my country. One advantage of my coming here is that I have seen another phase of the world in the entire folly of looking for worldly distinction. *I have now seen it all!* Every sphere in which man can enter I have seen, and I shall feel prouder when I go home than ever I have been to sit on the porch of my farm-house, and as a private citizen do all that man can do to make those around me happy, and do what I can to aid my country by my example in this its hour of need. If you wish to run the rounds that I have run, you shall have my help. For me, my course is run."

This promised Mr. Brewster what he had always regarded as a distinguished honor,—the Senatorship. When Mr. Cameron returned Mr. Brewster wrote him :

"I am happy to hear of your safe return. Ever since my return many persons have been urging me to be a candidate for the Senate. I have said to all that I should consult you. Now I take this early occasion to advise you of this purpose. I cannot ever conflict with you. Is it your wish to return there? From your letters to me from Europe I believe you have surrendered all idea of future political life. In those letters you offered to advance my wishes for political promotion. Are you to be a candidate for the Senate? If you are not can I ask you to aid me and help the friends who have prompted me to this ambition?"

In Mr. Cameron's proffer of the Russian Mission and Mr. Brewster's reply we have between the lines the only clashing of interests that ever occurred :

" As to your proposal to have me replace you in Russia, although, as you stated in St. Petersburg, it would show your power, and although I then felt elated at the idea, yet on reflection I would rather stay at home, and, if I enter at all into the line of political promotion, use your influence you so kindly offer to lend me to get me into the Senate."

General Cameron had reason to reconsider his renunciation of political life, for in 1867 he returned himself to the Senate, Mr. Brewster deferring to his senior from feelings of loyalty and friendship.*

---

* The peculiar circumstances under which the 1867 Legislature met will doubtless explain why it became necessary for General Cameron to reconsider this decision. Governor Curtin, Thaddeus

Mr. Brewster, however, closed the year with the following significant entry in his book, dated December 31 :

" So ends the year as I began it,—at work in my office."

X V.

Belligerent Politics—Attorney-General of Pennsylvania—John W. Geary.

WE have seen how every political preferment frankly sought by Mr. Brewster eluded him. Death robbed him of the post of Attorney-General of Pennsylvania at twenty-seven; the opposition of Mr. Dallas prevented his appointment as District Attorney; the hostility of the Pennsylvania leaders in Mr. Buchanan's administration made this same office—confessedly of " no importance" to him, as the President wrote him—impossible of attainment; and Mr. Cameron's personal pre-emption of the field kept him from the Senate. Other posts were possible

---

Stevens, John W. Forney, and General Moorehead were all striving for the Senatorship. In this fight Colonel A. K. McClure, who was then managing Governor Curtin's interests, selected no less a personage as lieutenant than Colonel Matthew S. Quay, just entering political life. General Cameron went to the Senate, Governor Curtin to Russia, Colonel McClure quit the Republican party and politics, and Colonel Quay started upon his own independent career. It will be remembered that Colonel Forney had been pushed by Buchanan against Cameron years before, and much feeling at that time had been engendered.

to him,—as, for example, the Russian Mission, at a most critical time; but, declining these, he characteristically "took his position," and fought with stubborn pertinacity for what he deemed his right. Such belligerence was his pride and principle. No matter what personal cost or hostility was incurred in combating a disingenuous opposition, or of how little moment the end might be to him, he was right, and therefore would fight regardless of consequences. The one life-long exception to this grew from his loyal friendship to General Cameron, and the latter's just claim to priority.

This spirit was not politic. It involved continual political strife; but there was nothing of the time-server about it. The key-note of his political career is fierce opposition to political meanness. It lost him every appointment he sought, and made him spurn with contempt a high post that came unsought; but it was his pride until the day of his death.

In 1866 the following letter from Governor Geary made possible to Mr. Brewster the office promised him twenty-two years before:

"New Cumberland, Pa., December 25, 1866.

"Hon. B. H. Brewster, Philadelphia, Pa. :

"My dear Sir,—Having the fullest confidence in your ability as a lawyer and your integrity as a man, I have the honor to tender you the appointment of Attorney-General of the Commonwealth of Pennsylvania. Earnestly soliciting your acceptance,

"I am truly yours, John W. Geary."

Mr. Brewster accepted. The duties of the office were discharged by him with distinguished success.

Among his more notable official achievements were the strangling of the Gettysburg lottery scheme, which he regarded as a project for making money under the pretext of helping orphans of soldiers, and breaking up the practice of judges who were remitting sentence and discharging prisoners before their sentences had expired.*

Mr. Brewster served two years as Attorney-General of the State, and suddenly resigned in a manner in keeping with his whole career, but reflecting seriously upon the Governor. During the Star Route trials in Washington, when the ring were moving the whole country in their efforts to remove Mr. Brewster from the cabinet, a preposterous story of a pistol encounter between Governor Geary and Mr. Brewster was telegraphed over the country. Mr. Brewster said,—

"Neither Governor Geary nor any other man ever shut me in a room and pointed a pistol at me. That cannot well happen and turn out as it is described, I hope. It is absurd, for the Governor had the power to remove me, as he did, without exacting a resigna-

---

* This practice prevailed in the city and county of Philadelphia. Both the Governor and Attorney-General held that such procedure was illegal. Judge Allison, of the Philadelphia bar, however, took issue with them upon the ground that after sentence it was his practice to enter a rule to remit the sentence, which rule remained over from term to term, until the court should see fit to act. Judge Allison also stated that this practice had prevailed in Philadelphia courts for many years, that it had its sanction in the common law, and that it was required by necessity, to avoid unjust and hasty action by the courts. Mr. Brewster in his test of the matter secured the opinion and practice of every judge in the Commonwealth. No judge outside of Philadelphia County claimed the privilege except Judge W. J. Woodward, of Reading, Pa.

tion with a pistol. The facts are these: during Geary's campaign, when I found that there was disaffection and dissatisfaction about me among some of the politicians who were not satisfied with my severity, of course, with regard to them, I went to him personally and asked to resign. He refused my resignation. I sent a friend to him afterwards, finding that that hostility increased, and I told him that I would like to go away to Europe to see my sister. He begged me to remain, though, and said it would injure his prospects. Again hearing he was in difficulty, I went to him in person, and he positively refused to accept my resignation, and told me he would never listen to it. After he was elected, and before he was finally declared elected, he sent me a letter in Philadelphia requesting my resignation. That letter was delivered by Alfred C. Harmer. I refused, and told Mr. Harmer I would give the Governor a reply. I wrote him a sharp, severe reprimand for the unfair and unmanly way in which he had treated me. I knew that this had been brought about by the men who threatened to count him out unless he removed me. I reminded him of what had passed between us, and how he had refused to accept my resignation, mentioning the names of gentlemen who had called upon him at my instance offering my resignation, went over the whole ground, and published the letter, and it created a great sensation throughout the State."

The following are both letters in full:

" EXECUTIVE CHAMBER, HARRISBURG, October 21, 1869.

" HON. BENJAMIN HARRIS BREWSTER, ATTORNEY-GENERAL:

" DEAR SIR,—You have on several occasions told me that whenever I deemed it to my interest, or to the welfare of the Commonwealth, you would at once relinquish the office of Attorney-General into my hands. That time has now arrived, and I, therefore, respectfully and earnestly request that you immediately tender to me your resignation, to take effect without delay. Your compliance will oblige

" Yours, etc., JOHN W. GEARY."

"OFFICE OF THE ATTORNEY-GENERAL, PHILADELPHIA, October 23, 1869.

" TO GENERAL JOHN W. GEARY, GOVERNOR OF PENNSYLVANIA:

" SIR,—Yesterday Mr. Harmer handed me your letter of the 21st of October. It requires my resignation 'immediately and without delay,' and assigns no cause for the request. It is a peremptory demand, most unusual among gentlemen, and uncalled for in this particular case.

"After my receipt, in July last, of the letter of Mr. Covode, made public in the columns of the daily press, in which he requested my resignation, and assumed to do so by your authority, you sent a special message to me by Mr. Lewis Waln Smith, deputy attorney-general, desiring me not to regard his letter and assuring me that it was unauthorized and its publication was unauthorized. Notwithstanding I felt a sense of wrong in your silence and neglect to make public disclaimer of the letter, yet I submitted quietly for the sake of the party and its cause, knowing that any agitation of the subject on my part would involve you and imperil your election. This you applauded at Corry a fortnight ago, when, of your own accord, you came to see me, and when we last saw each other, and then you expressly said to me and Mr. Lowry, and I believe to General Kane, that our relations were unchanged; to me you said that all of the action of Mr. Covode in the letter before mentioned and in the telegram sent by him to me, and which I exhibited to you, was unauthorized, and you then in severe terms condemned his conduct as brutal and meriting punishment.

"You wished me to wait until after the election, when I might deal with these men who had put an affront on me. You then thanked me for the services I had rendered, and repeated your personal and official confidence in me, and then left me, making arrangements with me for an important official duty to be performed with you. To Mr. Cummings, who went to you specially deputed by me to confer with you on the subject three weeks ago, you expressly iterated and reiterated your confidence in me, saying that you had no cause of complaint and no wish to remove me or have me resign. The offer of my resignation referred to in your letter was frequently made by me and others for me, and was always refused by you as hurtful to your prospects. It was made from motives of personal convenience and to help your renomination and to silence the calumnies of men who were your enemies. As an instance of your feeling towards whom I would recall your course in reference to Mr. Kemble, whom you told me you suspected of being a defaulter, and by your express direction had me send you twice an accountant from the city to verify your supposed discovery of his delinquencies, and against whom you said I should proceed as soon as you were re-elected.

"Now you write to me demanding my resignation, and assign no cause, but leave me open to imputations to which I will not submit. *I will not permit you, at the instance of a class you denounced to me as corrupt factionists, and one of whom you instructed me to prosecute, and after you have answered your own convenience and received my help, thus to evict me from a place I never sought and which you solicited me to accept and which I have held with due respect to my public duty and my own honor.*

"After this course of duplicity, or vacillation, to me it is indifferent which, serve with you I cannot and will not, and you may have my office vacant and fill it with whomsoever will be base and mean enough to run the risk of like treatment, or receive it as the price of some dishonorable bargain.   I am, sir, etc.,

"BENJAMIN HARRIS BREWSTER."

XVI.

Mr. Brewster at Fifty—Emory Storr's Contrast with W. M. Evarts—
Mr. Brewster as a Lecturer and Orator.

MR. BREWSTER had passed his fiftieth year upon his retirement from the attorney-generalship of Pennsylvania.   The impetuous fires of his youth were being modified into the proud and dignified repose of manner which characterized the two last decades of his life.

During all the tempestuous times outlined in the last few sections he had, despite his political activity, ever paid the most careful regard to his profession, and he was now one of the famous advocates of the country.

In 1869 an effort was made by his friends to secure as a crowning recognition of his abilities the appointment of Attorney-General in President Grant's cabinet. Among others advocating his cause was Emory Storrs, of Chicago, who described him as "the greatest lawyer in the country,—greater even than William M. Evarts," whom Mr. Brewster was being urged to succeed, and who was thus quite naturally brought in contrast with the Philadelphia lawyer.

Robert J. Walker wrote President Grant urging the appointment:

" . . . Mr. Brewster stands in the foremost ranks at the bar of this city and is Attorney-General of the State. As a lawyer I have known him long and well. I possess some familiarity with the duties of Attorney-General of the United States. With many of the points connected with that office Mr. Brewster's practice has made him very familiar, *and I think his intrepidity on such questions, and especially the suppression and detection of fraud*, would greatly assist the officers of the Treasury, who seem to be doing their full duty on this subject. Making due allowance for my great friendship and regard for Mr. Brewster, I am influenced in making this recommendation exclusively by a desire to promote the public welfare."

The office was, however, bestowed elsewhere. It was to come later to Mr. Brewster, at a time when even greater intrepidity was needed.

Following this came a period of great legal and literary activity. His law practice was large but select. In 1872 he made an address before the Fairmount Park Art Association, and delivered the lectures on Frederick the Great. His discourses on Thomas à Becket and Gregory the Great followed some time later, as also a number of anniversary and college addresses.

In 1874 the corner-stone of the great Public Buildings in Philadelphia was laid. Historic Independence Hall, where the Declaration of Independence had been signed, and the first Continental Congress' held, had long since become too small to accommodate the affairs of the growing municipality. The magnificent edifice designed to supersede the old structure, and every ceremony connected with it, were sought to be clothed with every possible significance,—suggesting, as it does, not only the municipal but the national growth and prosperity since the time when Liberty Bell rang from the old belfry. For this occasion of national significance, Mr. Brewster was selected as orator. His name was thus indissolubly linked with one of the most momentous contrasts in our history, and his discourse was full of patriotic commentary and meaning.

At midnight, as the dial pointed to the birth of 1876, the Centennial year of National life, at the request of the Select and Common Councils of Philadelphia, Mr. Brewster stood before the Hall of Independence and made the first of his memorable Centennial addresses. The mystic midnight hour, the sacredness of the place, and the profound significance of the occasion, drew from the orator a matchless discourse,—a model of patriotism, brevity, and purity of diction.

Mr. Brewster's superb oratory and fame had made him the unanimous selection of the Commonwealth for all great and imposing occasions. Six months later, on the first of July, 1876, he stood in the same historic place, and, at the request of the Historical Society of Pennsylvania, delivered a second Centennial address.

Not only on local affairs, but upon almost every striking event or great movement of our national history does his name seem to be impressed. The Nation was born at Philadelphia; the Union was controlled by the Keystone State from its metropolis; and the principal events of American history had been enacted in Philadelphia, or by men sent out from Philadelphia. Now, all this century of history making was to be symbolized at the Centennial Exhibition, opened by President Grant May 10, 1876.

The Pennsylvania Day, therefore, embodied almost the entire import of the Centennial. It fell upon September 28, 1876,—the centennial anniversary of the adoption of the First Constitution of Pennsylvania. Again the choice of Pennsylvania fell upon Mr. Brewster. Governor Hartranft wrote, when requesting him to be the orator,—

"I know of no one of Pennsylvania's sons who is better fitted for the task."

The occasion was momentous, the assemblage august, and this third Centennial address—by which Pennsylvania made Mr. Brewster the exclusive spokesman of the Commonwealth during this great national jubilee—was in keeping with the occasion and the reputation of the orator. Such discourses are histories by history-makers, and voice directly the sentiment of the great living people held and swayed by the man they had sought from among them, and placed upon the rostrum to stand for their holiest thought.

XVII.

Richard Henry Dana on Mr. Brewster as United States Senator—Senators J. Donald Cameron and M. S. Quay—Mr. Brewster and Mr. Cadwalader working for the Dramatic Copyright—George H. Boker on the Subject.

In 1877, Mr. Brewster's name was before the Republican Convention of Philadelphia as candidate for the nomination to the post of District Attorney. The Democratic party had held this important post for two terms, and the Republicans felt sure that Mr. Brewster's high reputation, if he received the nomination, would bring success to their ticket. This was the same post which President Buchanan's leaders, years before, had denied Mr. Brewster when the President consoled him with the suggestion that it was of "no consequence" to him. The people again were by the convention denied the opportunity of voting for Mr. Brewster, and the result was a Republican defeat. The people of Philadelphia, however, unwilling to accept the prohibition of the convention, made Mr. Brewster the candidate of the so-called "United Labor" party, and, although he uncompromisingly refused the nomination, over five thousand votes were cast for him,—enough to defeat the Republican ticket.

In 1881, Mr. Brewster's name was again before the Legislature during the five weeks' struggle over the United States Senatorship. Among the celebrated men whose ideas of the fitness of things induced them to advance the name of Mr. Brewster was Richard Henry Dana. He wrote to Miss Brewster:

"It will be a great satisfaction to the American bar if Pennsylvania will honor herself by sending to the Senate (the first time for many years) a person who has not sought the post which 'stands candidate for him.'"

Mr. Brewster had a high conception of the senatorial function, and if he had been sent to Washington in that capacity, his name would have gone upon the list of American parliamentary nobles. In this instance, and a later one, the efforts of his friends were futile. The offices on both occasions were preempted, and Messrs. J. Donald Cameron and M. S. Quay were chosen instead.

This may be said to end Mr. Brewster's political career. It is idle to pretend that any public man is coy about public office. Chauncey M. Depew, when asked if he would accept the Presidential nomination, frankly responded, "Yes; who would not?" And it is not the biographer's purpose to affect that his subject was annoyed by the clamor of offices for his occupancy. But it is worthy of note that Mr. Brewster received no position for which he or his friends sought.

Before passing to his greatest honor and work, his labor in behalf of the dramatic copyright should be noted. This is well set forth in the following letters of Mr. George Henry Boker:

"MY DEAR MR. BREWSTER,—I shall only set down a few heads for your observation, leaving it to the suggestion of your brain to find logical reasons in support of them:

"*First.*—The United States is the only civilized country that does not secure to dramatic writers the right of representation.

" *Second.*—The chief value of a play is in the right to represent it. The right of representation, as compared with the ordinary copyright, is, so far as value is concerned, immeasurably in favor of the former.

" *Third.*—Of all literary property, a successful acting play is the most valuable; but this value arises, not from the right to print, but the right to represent it on the stage. Bulwer, from his two popular plays, derives a revenue from the British theatres of two to three hundred thousand pounds. Knowles's ' Hunchback' is acted, on an average, three hundred times a year in Great Britain alone. Dr. Bird's ' Gladiator' has been acted over a thousand nights. I might multiply examples on this point, many from my own experience, but they all go to prove the fact stated with sufficient clearness in the first sentence of this paragraph.

" *Fourth.*—Under the laws of the United States a successful dramatist is unable to print his plays. He must keep them in manuscript in order to secure the right of representation to himself. Even this security is imperfect, for a stenographer may take the plays down as they fall from the actors' lips, and produce them at rival theatres without leaving the unfortunate author any remedy at law. Instances of this kind have frequently occurred in the United States.

" *Fifth.*—The mere copyright in a play is of small value, the popular taste of the reading public not inclining toward such productions. Therefore, this noblest form of poetry has fallen into disuse in America, nor will it revive until the right of representation is secured to dramatic authors.

" *Sixth.*—The want of such a law in Shakespeare's time is the reason that his plays have come down to us so full of errors. He was obliged to secure his property by keeping it in manuscript; nor was any authorized edition of his works printed until long after his death. What a treasure to the world would have been an edition of Shakespeare's works edited by himself!

" *Seventh.*—As I have before said, it is the universal custom of the few successful dramatic authors of America to secure their plays by keeping them in manuscript. All of Dr. Bird's plays are unprinted; Stone's plays are in like condition; Conrad's remained so until within a short time; Cornelius Mathews's plays are in manuscript; I have six unpublished plays in my portfolio; and there are scores, by authors of greater or less note, in the same seclusion. What justice can a critic do an author under such circumstances?

Not having the text of his works before the critics, he is abused for the misinterpretations of the actors. I once listened to a tragedy of my own in which no one of the actors spoke any ten consecutive words of my text, and yet I was obliged to shoulder the odium belonging of right to their vulgarity and ignorance. All my works have suffered more or less in this miserable way. The right of representation would remedy all this. I should print my works before they were acted.   GEORGE HENRY BOKER.

"MY DEAR MR. BREWSTER,—The deed is done. You may have noticed that our bill passed the House of Representatives on Saturday last, and, according to the information contained in Mr. Cadwalader's letters, was signed by the President on Monday last; so that it is now the law of the land. . . .

"I suppose, my dear sir, that you begin to grow weary of my wordy gratitude to you, and ask yourself why I dwell upon this particular instance of your kindness to me, when your general conduct has been nothing but kindness. I have many reasons for singling out this act from among so many others. You suggested my present successful efforts; you employed your private friendship with Mr. Seward in my behalf; you spoke nobly of a man whom you do not like, and obtained for me the invaluable aid of Mr. Cadwalader; and I will be sworn that there is no man living who more heartily rejoices over our joint success than yourself. *From the first to the last you have been the mainspring of this whole movement;* and through you alone a darling object of my desires has been reached. Therefore I thank you again and again; nor shall I ever grow weary of thus expressing my gratitude.   GEORGE HENRY BOKER.

"August 9, 1856."

XVIII.

The Star Route Trials—Their Wide Range of Interests—Public Misconceptions—The Buried Truth and Published Scandals.

THE famous Star Route trials are without parallel in American history. The impeachment of Warren Hastings, of England, hardly equals them.

Not only did they involve grave legal questions, the recovery of fabulous sums of money, and the punishment of an army of evil-doers, but they struck deeply and relentlessly into the strongest influences surrounding our body politic.

Never were participants in any legal contest so widely dispersed in distance, or so greatly varied in intelligence and position. From the peculiar conglomeration of Washington life the influences of these trials reached outward to the cactus plains of Arizona, along the sandy shores of the Pacific, and on snow-shoes into the frozen Northwest. They entwined in their subtle meshes the long-haired stage-driver under his sombrero in the far West, and the kid-gloved Senator fleeing to his Canadian exile. At focal, brilliant Washington, where the ablest meet and the meanest follow to gather the crumbs,—where peculiar crimes develop special talents, and where the man with baseness to sell ever finds a ready market,—from the lowest dregs of the foul cesspool of political life, amid jury-fixers, suborners, harlots, professional jurymen, and detectives, the intricacies of these great trials led up to the very Presidential chair itself. They involved the political control of the United States Senate, the financial policy of a great government, the peace of two Presidents, one Presidential candidate, and two distinguished Cabinets. They drew tears and the wringing of hands from the very Senate Chamber, charged with heaviness an atmosphere to resound to the sharp crack of the assassin's pistol, and injected a Democratic interregnum into the long rule of the Republican party.

They display the quaintest medley of influences and motives,—vanity, ambition, revenge, avarice, fear, —and yield an indescribable aroma of the underlying strata of Washington life. From the professional juryman with unsavory record, anxious to defeat the government whose challenge "took bread from his mouth,"—or the court official rewarding a tradesman for placing his portrait on a brand of cigars,— or a committee chairman caught in the toils of a queenly Delilah sent out in the interest of the ring, and threatened with exposure,—up to the efforts of the President-maker himself to sit in judgment on his own misdeeds,—there is symbolized a range of motives as wide as destiny itself.

For an almost interminable time the reports of these proceedings were spread before the country in the morning journals. The conflict was fought in the newspapers as well as in court. Journals were subsidized and editors hired to defend the ring and prejudice the government officials. The most ingenious misstatements were sent broadcast over the land, and the real issues and real triumph of the trials were carefully masked under pre-arranged scandals against the Department of Justice. The court records went into their dusty oblivion, the dreary thousands of pages bury the truth in their tiresome embrace, while many persons remain ignorant of the gigantic abuses discovered, the heroic efforts made to correct them, and the signal success which crowned these efforts.

Behind this great contest, opening with the crack of Guiteau's pistol, and waged under the continual menace of murder, through a Niagara of misapprehension and designed vilification, stood one man, Benjamin Harris Brewster, with steadfast purpose and inflexible will. His whole career had pointed to this work and fitted him for it. A man less strong would have yielded to personal comfort or expediency; one less able would have been crushed. Aided by a mere handful of fearless, upright men,* in disregard of his own political future and at the sacrifice of personal comfort and health,—day after day, month after month, with entreaties of friends, threats of enemies, and great weariness of flesh,—he persistently and untiringly maintained the high ideal of public duty he had set up for himself, and pursued these robbers of the government to the extremest limit.

The Star Route ring did not go behind the bars because in both trials members of the jury were shamelessly bribed. The proofs of corruption were so clear that the purchased verdict was tantamount to a conviction. Said Mr. Brewster,—

"The public men who were involved as defendants in these cases were not on their trials before these juries alone: they were on their trial before the people of the United States, and they were convicted by the common judgment of the whole country. They were not punished by imprisonment, but they had better be in prison than now at large, objects of scorn and aversion. The effect of these trials has been to deter all of the adventurers who throng about the departments of Washington. The wholesome terror of these trials has ex-

---

* The men who aided Mr. Brewster, and whose names merit union with his own in the lasting history of these trials, were P. H. Woodward, Henry D. Lyman, R. J. Merrick, W. W. Ker, and Brewster Cameron.

pelled these dishonest jobbers. The thoroughness of these investigations has made it plain that there is no place so high that it could become a sanctuary for a thief and public robber."

Greater than the punishment of individuals was this victory for the government. It is a monument of achievement to those who started upon this almost hopeless contest against the cohesiveness of public plunder.

XIX.

Mr. Tilden's Campaign Ammunition—Charles A. Dana's "Turn the Rascals Out!"—Star Route Antecedents and Complications—President Garfield's Moral Marathon—The Trials begun—Tragedy in the Atmosphere—"The Gentlemen in Washington."

. . . "President Garfield expressed regret that he had exposed me to such attacks by connecting me with a matter not necessarily part of my duty; but I told him that I regarded it as an honor to be abused in his company. I added the general proposition that in these days the abuse of thieves is the only decoration in our public life worth the winning or the wearing, and it is the surest possible passport to the good opinion of honest men.

"WAYNE MACVEAGH."

. . . "This terrible prosecution has attracted on me, as a focal point, the open, avowed, aggressive hostility of the worst men in the United States of America, scattered over its surface from Maine to the remotest territory; and their hatred and hostility is my public compliment. . . . I will follow, expose, and punish them, despising them and their vulgar threats. . . . When I cannot do that without molestation, I will leave my place. I took it up with honor, and I will lay it down with honor as clean as I took it up.

"BENJAMIN HARRIS BREWSTER."

RUTHERFORD B. HAYES, in 1876, was declared President of the United States upon the report of the Louisiana Commission. Mr. Tilden's adherents claimed the election for their chieftain, as the first returns seemed to show. In the work of the Louisiana Commission, William Pitt Kellogg, United States Senator from Louisiana, figured prominently.

The bitterness between the two parties at the inauguration of President Hayes, the intensely energetic efforts made by Mr. Tilden and his friends to prepare for the next election, and the relation of Senator Kellogg to the Republican party, are important antecedents of the great Star Route trials.

As the 1880 election approached, an effort was made by the friends of General Grant to secure a third term for the hero of Appomattox.* Senators Conkling, Cameron, and Logan, representing New York, Pennsylvania, and Illinois, expected to carry the Convention with a burst of hero-worshipping eloquence. Chester A. Arthur was a distinguished delegate from New York; James A. Garfield, from Ohio; Benjamin Harris Brewster, from Pennsylvania. Conkling headed the Grant movement, while Garfield was accorded by the mind of the Convention the lead of the other faction. Simon Cameron was chairman of the National Committee.

Intense excitement attended the balloting. For a time the success of Grant seemed almost assured.

---

* Senator Conkling began his eloquent nominating address with—

"When asked what State he hails from,
Our sole reply shall be,
He comes from Appomattox
And its famous apple-tree !"

In unwavering and dogged loyalty his famous " 306" phalanx stood firmly for their hero until all hope of his nomination departed, when James A. Garfield was borne forward on an unexpected wave of enthusiasm, and received the nomination. Chester A. Arthur, as the most prominent advocate of General Grant, and the representative of the opposing camp, received the second place, and thus for a time the conflicting Republican factions were welded on one ticket. The contest, however, was only deferred.

A few days later the Democratic Convention convened at Cincinnati. It was expected that Samuel J. Tilden would be nominated. The work done by Mr. Tilden for campaign purposes directly concerns our subject, and indicates his own expectation. Hancock and English, however, received the nomination, and the campaign opened favorably for the Democratic ticket. Democratic gains in Maine foreshadowed a national success, and stirred the Republicans to unwonted activity. Indiana was the critical State. Ex-Senator Stephen W. Dorsey, secretary of the Republican National Committee, made this section his special battle-ground. General Grant and Senator Conkling went west and made a series of campaign addresses to aid him, and under his direction the State was carried, and Garfield and Arthur were elected. The jubilant Republicans gave their national secretary a dinner at Delmonico's the following February. Vice-President-Elect Arthur presided, and made an address congratulating and commending Stephen W. Dorsey, the guest of the evening. Prominent among those around the board was Mr. George Bliss.

To our direct purpose, then, are the factions in the Republican party, the campaign work of Mr. Tilden, the party services of Ex-Senator Dorsey, the complimentary dinner, the address of General Arthur, and the presence of Mr. Bliss.

Following the inauguration of President Garfield came the selection of the Cabinet. The secretary of the National Committee, the successful manager of the Indiana campaign to whom the President almost directly owed his election, and with whom he was on terms of personal intimacy, had, as might be expected, a candidate for a Cabinet portfolio. Mr. Bliss, by a coincidence, was one of the supporters of this candidate. Other considerations prevailed with the President, however, and he soon had occasion to be thankful for his "escape from a snare to entrap him."

As early as 1872, Mr. A. M. Gibson, of the New York *Sun*, and Messrs. Carson and Root, of the New York *Times*, had learned of certain mail frauds. The former, from time to time, supplied Mr. Charles A. Dana, editor of the New York *Sun*, with the material upon which to base his famous appeal, "Turn the rascals out!" which closed each of his editorials. When Mr. Tilden began his quiet preparations for the 1880 campaign, he went deeply enough into the matter to furnish the money for the investigation, and to send Mr. Charles F. McLean, an associate, to Washington to learn if the frauds really existed. Mr. McLean reported that the frauds existed, and that their evidence was being properly prepared. Mr. Tilden, failing to secure the nomination himself, refused to allow the material to be used in Hancock's behalf,—either from lack of interest in Hancock's success, or from a desire to retain his ammunition in the event of a future nomination for himself.

Mr. McLean had a law partner, Mr. Henry E. Knox, who had been a college chum of President Garfield. Mr. Knox, having learned of these frauds and knowing that Senator Dorsey stood in relations of confidence and influence with the President-elect, late in February received permission to place before the President-elect evidence that Dorsey was implicated. This explains why Mr. Dorsey's influence with the President-elect failed to move him in regard to Cabinet appointments.

More than ordinary importance, therefore, attached to the selection of a Postmaster-General. Messrs. Whitelaw Reid and Charles Emory Smith, with Mr. Thomas L. James, met the President by appointment, and the interview resulted in Mr. James's acceptance of the post. The President said, as soon as Mr. James's appointment was agreed upon, that, "from what he kept hearing, he feared something was very wrong in the Post-Office Department. If so, the Postmaster-General must find it out, and then put the plough into the beam, and after that sub-soil it."

The inauguration of Garfield, therefore, was the inauguration of the Star Route investigations. On the 9th of March, Mr. James received renewed instructions from the President, suggested and had approved the appointment of Mr. P. H. Woodward, and employed and assigned him to the special duty of investigating the suspected frauds. The Postmaster-General then visited New York, and through Mr. John Swinton, one· of the editors of the New York *Sun*, met Mr. Gibson and obtained what information he possessed. Mr. Woodward was assigned a room in the Post-Office Department, took possession of the papers, began tabulating them, and kept them in a safe in the room. The developments were startling.

The " Star Route service" was a vast and important service, stretching for thousands of miles in a region of country infested by hostile Indians, cowboys, and desperadoes. The lines ran by stages along mountain-sides, into sunless canyons, through almost virgin forests, and across the waterless alkali plains in the great Southwest. In many cases the territory was accessible only by " buckboard" or on horseback. It was found that this extraordinary service was relegated to the supervision of one man, occupying a desk in the office of the Second Assistant Postmaster-General. There was method in this.

Mr. P. H. Woodward has prepared the following statement of details of the frauds :

" The work of unearthing the truth was systematically begun. While one inspector exhumed and explained the facts buried in voluminous piles of departmental papers, eight or ten other inspectors,*

---

* In this connection, as deserving of special praise, let me mention the names of Messrs. A. G. Sharp, George L. Seybolt, J. E. Stuart, John B. Furay, G. W. Porter, J. D. King, S. P. Child, R. B. McGaughey, and Edward E. Boyd.

selected for superior fitness, were despatched to the frontier to go over a part of the manipulated routes.

" In the early days of the republic our inland mail transportation was graded by stage, two-horse coach, and horseback service. After various modifications of the system the law of 1845 wiped out the distinctions and provided that the lowest bidders engaging to carry the mails with ' certainty, celerity, and security' should be accepted. These words were indicated by the departmental clerks on their registers by three stars (* * *), and hence came to be called ' star bids,' and the routes ' star routes.' Since 1845 all the inland mail service of the country, except railway, steamboat, and messenger, has been technically known as ' star service.'

" After due advertisement the above service is let for four years to the lowest bidder on each route tendering sufficient guarantees for its faithful performance. For convenience in supervising the work the country is separated into four divisions, the service in one of which is let each year.

" The contract term for California, Oregon, and some other States west of the Mississippi, as well as for the Territories, began July 1, 1878, and terminated June 30, 1882. The manipulations practised in this division during this term constituted the chief subjects of investigation.

" The law of the land aims to secure the utmost fairness and economy in letting the service. Section 3941 of the Revised Statutes provides :

" ' Before making any contract for carrying the mail . . . the Postmaster-General shall give public notice by advertising . . .; and such notice shall describe the route, the time at which the mail is to be made up, the time at which it is to be delivered, and the frequency of the service.'

" Section 3949 provides that all contracts shall be awarded to the lowest bidder tendering sufficient guarantees.

" ' Section 3965. The Postmaster-General shall provide for carrying the mail on all post-roads established by law, as often as he, having due regard to *productiveness* and other circumstances, may think proper.'

" Thus the law peremptorily requires that before contracts for carrying the mail are made, the service shall be fully advertised, the route described, the schedule time and frequency of the service set forth, and finally, that the award *shall* be made to the lowest bidder tendering sufficient guarantees. It is the right and privilege of every citizen who can furnish the required security at every letting on any route to compete for the service on fair and equal terms. Any device which gives one an undue advantage over another inflicts a wrong and injustice, and hence is prohibited. On the other hand, it is the right of the public to obtain the service at the lowest responsible bid. The policy of the law, as repeatedly enunciated, aims to secure impartial competition. Any statute intended to meet exceptional emergencies must be construed in subordination to this fundamental principle.

"In a rapidly growing country such emergencies are liable to arise. In a few months a small mining settlement may develop into a populous community. When the service was advertised, perhaps one or two mails a week fully supplied the needs of the hamlet. In the course of a year or two its growth may properly require perhaps that the number of weekly trips shall be increased to three, or six, or seven. Hence, to avoid the delays of a re-advertisement, section 3960 of the Revised Statutes provides for additional trips, stipulating that the compensation therefor 'shall not be in excess of the exact proportion which the original compensation bears to the original service.'

"During the contract term cases may also arise when the rate of speed, sufficient at the beginning, may have become too slow. Two railways approaching each other may demand that the connecting stage-line shall be run on a faster schedule than the public interests required at the time of the lettings. Section 3961, intended for cases like the one supposed, enacts:

"'That no extra allowance shall be made for any increase of expedition in carrying the mail, unless thereby the employment of additional stock and carriers is made necessary, and in such case the additional compensation shall bear no greater proportion to the additional stock and carriers necessarily employed than the compensation in the original contract bears to the stock and carriers necessarily employed in its execution.'

"The orders of Mr. Brady giving extraordinary allowances to certain contractors, and which were charged by the prosecution to be fraudulent and corrupt, were made under cover of sections 3960-1, quoted in part above.

"Mr. Brady became Second Assistant Postmaster-General in July, 1876. Service on the routes embraced in the indictments for conspiracy went into operation July 1, 1878, two years later. He had been sixteen months in office before the advertisement for the same was issued. During the last six months of 1878 and the first six of 1879,

Mr. Brady made orders for additional trips, and for expedition of time, which increased the cost of mail transportation above the original contract price about two millions of dollars a year in the western division alone.   Did the public necessities so change during the brief period between the appearance of the advertisement and the subsequent inflation of contracts as to justify even a small fraction of these colossal expenditures, ordered in defiance of the spirit of the fundamental law, and under the screen of two statutes enacted with the view of meeting promptly rare and exceptional emergencies?

"On looking over the advertisement of November 1, 1877, for the service to begin the following July, the persons charged with the investigation discovered that on most of the routes it called for infrequent trips and slow time.   In the light of subsequent events, they inferred that this arrangement was intended to be the initial step in a far-reaching scheme for enriching certain combinations at the expense of the public treasury.   They also discovered that most of the beneficiaries, under Mr. Brady's system of administration, obtained the routes on very low bids—bids, in fact, often below the actual cost of doing the work.   As the favorites were men whose wits had been sharpened by wide and varied experience, a prophetic spirit seemed to assure them that the ordinary rules of business might here be safely disregarded.

"A glance will show that, under the system developed by Mr. Brady, the *bona fide* bidder had no chance whatever.   If he based his figures on the cost of the work, he was certain to be underbid, and thus excluded.   If he dropped below the initiated, he was held to a strict performance of the contract, and taught by depletion to keep out of the way thereafter.

"The government prepared cases against several groups of contractors, but owing to the length of time consumed, and the magnitude of the labor, only one was brought to trial.   There were a few preliminary hearings against minor offenders before United States commissioners, but these soon sunk out of sight in the presence and under the pressure of more important work.   The combination actually proceeded against on the charge of conspiracy to defraud the government consisted of John W. Dorsey, John R. Miner, John M. Peck, Stephen W. Dorsey, Harvey M. Vaile, Montfort C. Rerdell, Thomas J. Brady, and Wm. H. Turner.   Of these, Mr. Brady had been Second Assistant Postmaster-General, and as such had charge of all contracts for transporting the mails; Mr. Turner was a clerk in his office; S. W. Dorsey had been United States Senator from Arkansas; John W. Dorsey was his brother, and Peck his brother-in-law; Rerdell for several years had been the confidential clerk of Senator Dorsey; Vaile was a professional contractor.

"Counsel for the government consisted of Attorney-General Brewster, R. T. Merrick, Esq., of Washington, George Bliss, Esq., of New York City, and Wm. W. Ker, Esq., of Philadelphia. The accused were openly defended by ten lawyers, several of whom enjoy a national reputation. . . .

"A few facts, selected as samples, will give the reader a knowledge of the character of the frauds. Having secured the award of certain routes at low figures, favored contractors, with a confidence in destiny amply justified by subsequent events, despatched agents to the frontiers to work up petitions among the settlers, asking for more frequent trips and for expedition of time. Senators and Congressmen were specially solicited to indorse the petitions of their constituents. Anxious to oblige, and ignorant of the scheme, many of them lent the weight of their names quite promiscuously. According to the text of these papers, each particular route supplied a region which was just entering upon a career of unprecedented prosperity. Immigrants were hurrying in, populous villages were springing up where the latest maps indicated no break in the wilderness, smelters, schools, and even churches were bodily translated from the ardent imaginations of the writers to the plateaus and valleys of the Rocky Mountains. All that was needed to complete the felicity of the settlers and to insure the stability of their town was more mails. Their letters must come often and come quick. As a partial compensation for giving up the comforts and advantages enjoyed in the older States for the purpose of extending the boundaries of civilization, and adding to the wealth of our common country, could not the Postmaster-General yield them this small boon?

"When a sufficient quantity of this class of literature had been accumulated to serve as a pretext for compliance, it was taken to Mr. Brady. What followed can best be illustrated by a few examples.

"Route No. 38,135, from St. Charles to Green Horn, Colorado, thirty-five miles, service twice a week, was awarded to John R. Miner at his bid of $548 per annum. It was afterwards quite properly extended twelve miles to Pueblo, with a *pro rata* addition of $328.40 to the annual pay. It was now forty-seven miles long; the schedule time was sixteen hours; and the yearly pay for two trips a week, $876.80. June 26, 1879, Mr. Brady ordered an additional trip, allowing therefor $438.40. The three trips now cost $1315.20, and so far one can discover nothing worthy of harsh criticism.

" But at the same time Mr. Brady ordered an expedition from sixteen to seven hours, with an additional allowance of $2630.40.

" The annual cost of the service was now—

" Three weekly trips	$1315.20
Expedition	2630.40
Total	$3945.60

" It will be seen that the Department paid just twice as much for the expedition as for the trips. How were the figures reached ? Right here will be found the key which opened the vaults of the treasury to the alleged conspirators.

" Referring back to section 3941 of the Revised Statutes, it will be remembered that no allowance is to be made for increase of expedition in carrying the mails, unless thereby the employment of additional stock and carriers is made necessary, and that the ratio of increase shall in no case exceed the ratio of the new equipment required to that in use before. The pecuniary gains of the contractor are promoted by making the difference between the two as great as he can, and in the absence of the restraints of conscience, he can accomplish the desired results either by understating the number of men and animals used on the long schedule, or by overstating the number needed for the short one. By either device, the desired ratio can be reached.

" Till the time of Mr. Brady the computations were quite complicated, ' stock' being understood to cover vehicles, harness, stations; in short, the entire outfit. He simplified the matter by construing ' stock' to mean animals, and by accepting the unsupported affidavit of the contractor respecting the numbers required under both schedules.

" The key used in this case reads thus :

"' Hon. Thos. J. Brady, *Second Assistant Postmaster-General:*

"' The number of men and animals necessary to carry the mails on route No. 38,135, three times a week, on the present schedule, is one man and one animal. The number necessary to carry the mails three times a week on a reduced schedule of seven hours, is two men and four animals.

"' John R. Miner.

"' Sworn to April 17, 1879, before W. F. Kellogg, Notary Public.'

"In the estimates a man is treated as the equivalent of a horse or 'animal.' Hence the problem is reduced to the simple proportion 2 : 6 : : $1315.20 (pay for 16 hours) : $3945.60 (pay for 7 hours). Of the total, two-thirds, or $2630.40, is for expedition.

"Neither Mr. Miner nor either of the other defendants ever performed the service on any one of these routes themselves. It was their uniform custom to relet the work to persons living in the vicinity who are technically known as 'sub-contractors.' All fines and deductions imposed by the Department for imperfect performance were thrown upon the latter.

"Wm. B. Farish, Wm. H. Higgason, and J. H. McDaniel, successive sub-contractors on this route, testified at the trial that on the schedule of seven hours they all performed the service with one man and two horses, and that on a schedule of sixteen hours it could be performed with no less. Hence the change in time did not in the slightest degree necessitate the employment of additional stock and carriers, and the donation of $2630.40 per annum was ordered not only without authority, but in direct violation of law. The sub-contractors also testified that they received $840 per annum for doing the work, leaving to the contractor an annual profit of $3105.60, without the investment of a dollar.

"The annual net revenues of the offices supplied by this route for three years prior to June 30, 1881, were $60.42, $172.23, and $175.43 respectively.

"Let us now pass on to route No. 41,119, Toquerville to Adairville, Utah. Its length is 132 miles, and it was advertised for one trip a week on a schedule of sixty hours. In due time the contract was awarded to John M. Peck at $1168.00 per annum. November 1, 1878, the trips were increased to three a week and the pay to $3504.

"*April* 12, 1879, M. C. Rerdell wrote to Nephi Johnson, of Johnson, Utah:

"'I enclose herewith a petition for increase of service on route 41,119, which please have numerously signed. Also, write other petitions somewhat after this form, for other points along the route, and have them signed. In writing other petitions do not use the exact language of the enclosed petition, and give as many reasons as you can for the increase. . . . Also have the county officers, members of the legislature, postmasters, etc., write letters to the P. M. General and to your delegates in Congress, earnestly requesting the increase.'

"June 25th, the identical petition sent by Rerdell to Johnson, having been vitalized by numerous signatures and favorably indorsed by the Utah Congressional delegate, was filed in the Department. It asked for daily service 'on a less schedule than now carried, that is to say, in about forty-eight hours.' Along with it was also filed a companion piece, asking for seven trips a week, 'the running time to be forty-eight hours.' Note that these petitions were placed in the Department *June 25th*, and that they call for a schedule of *forty-eight hours*.

"The oath of John M. Peck, intended to measure the cost of expedition, ran thus :

"'The number of men and animals which are necessary to carry the mail on route 41,119, seven times a week on the present schedule, is three (3) men and six (6) animals. The number necessary to carry the mail on said route on a schedule of thirty-three hours, seven times a week, is five (5) men and eighteen (18) animals.'

"This document purported to be sworn to in Colfax County, New Mexico, before J. S. Taylor, N. P., *January* 22, 1879. Its unessential framework is in the handwriting of John R. Miner. The vital figures and words '41,119,' 'seven,' 'three,' 'six,' 'thirty-three,' 'seven,' 'five,' and 'eighteen' were interpolated by the pen of M. C. Rerdell. It was filed at the same time with the petitions, June 25th. The prosecution inferred that Miner, having prepared the skeleton, sent it to Peck, by whom it was sworn to in blank, and returned to the managers in Washington, who, as the occasion arose, could use it for any route awarded to Peck. It was evident that Mr. Brady was unwilling to make a satisfactory allowance for a reduction of running time from sixty to forty-eight hours, as asked in the only petitions presented, and insisted on thirty-three hours as giving the transaction a more presentable appearance. In conformity with his demand thirty-three hours were inserted in the affidavit, and it must have been done after the petitions had been circulated. Otherwise on this point they would have agreed.

"The above inferences were afterwards corroborated by Rerdell when he exposed the secrets of the ring, and at the second trial appeared as a witness for the government. He testified that a stock of blank affidavits from both Peck and J. W. Dorsey, a resident of Vermont, were kept on hand and filled in as the different routes awarded to them were expedited.

"July 8, 1879, Mr. Brady ordered four additional trips with an annual allowance of $4672, and a reduction of time from sixty to thirty-three hours with an annual allowance of $12,718.22 'being *pro rata.*'

" Seven trips a week cost yearly	$8,176.00
Expedition	12,718.22
Total	$20,894.22

9 : 23 : : $8176 : $20,894.22

" On analysis, the affidavit, the joint product of Miner, Peck, and Rerdell, leads up to some curious, not to say impossible, results. According to its statement, daily service on a schedule of sixty hours required three men and six animals. The route was 120 miles long, twelve less than as advertised. Daily trips necessitated 1680 miles of travel each week, or 240 each day. Hence, each of the six animals must be driven so as to make on the average forty miles a day. As the oath called for but three men, each of these had to travel eighty miles a day, and as the schedule was two miles an hour, *in some way they must manage to do duty forty hours in every twenty-four!* The expedition was grounded on two petitions emanating from the contractors, and its cost—$12,718.22 per annum—was measured solely by this false and absurd affidavit.

" Rerdell testified that by direction of Stephen W. Dorsey, to whom this route had fallen when the combination divided their interests, he filled up one of the blank forms sworn to by Peck, without trying to obtain information on the subject, and merely following the instructions of his employer to make the proportion yield an increase of from 150 to 250 per cent. Scores of sub-contractors testified that they were never questioned by the affidavit-makers with reference to the men and animals required on either schedule. During the investigation we never found a truthful oath, or one not grossly false. The perjuries by which the treasury was robbed tower defiantly skyward like the mountains whose gloomy wastes they proposed to enliven by the frequent and furious trips of the mail-driver.

" Nephi Johnson, sub-contractor, received after the expedition $8444 a year for doing the work, leaving for Mr. Dorsey an annual profit of $12,450.22. The roads were rough, the mails small, and the time impracticable. Very soon both the postmasters along the line and the people sent petitions to Washington asking a restoration of the sixty hours' schedule. The petitioners say, ' We consider the present increased speed entirely unnecessary to the wants of the people and an uncalled-for expense to the government.' But papers

i

intended to stop waste from the treasury seemed to have little influence upon the mind of Mr. Brady. The remonstrances slept in the files till unearthed by the investigation, and the expenditure went on till lopped off by Postmaster-General James.

"Route No. 44,160, Canyon City to Camp McDermitt, Oregon, length 243 miles, advertised for one trip a week on a schedule of 130 hours, was awarded to John M. Peck at $2888 per annum. Early in the season there were Indian troubles along the line, but they were practically over by midsummer. Service, however, instead of starting July 1st, did not begin on the upper end till November and on the lower end till December.

"Vigorous efforts to secure the much-coveted increases began long before the first mail under the contract was taken from the post-office. The affidavit of Peck bears date September 18, 1878. The petitions, mostly in the disguised handwriting of John R. Miner, are importunate and loaded with signatures. In tapping the treasury the contractors were more expeditious than in putting on the service, for December 23, 1878, Mr. Brady ordered two additional trips, and an expedition to ninety-six hours, allowing therefor the lump sum of $18,612 per annum. July 16, 1880, he ordered four additional trips with an allowance of $28,666.66. The annual pay had now become swollen to $50,166.66, of which $20,216 were for trips and $29,950.66 for expedition. Sub-contractors performed the work for $20,000 a year, leaving a net profit of over $30,000 to the 'gentlemen in Washington.'

"In July, 1881, the inspector selected to go over the route reported that 'except within twenty miles of Canyon City there is not a residence, cabin or otherwise, along the entire line to McDermitt, except the stations built for the accommodation of the contractors.' The country is either mountainous or given up to sage brush and practically not cultivable. It has no mines. For most of the distance the road was but a trail. There was but one intermediate post-office and no through mails. The weight of letters and newspapers averaged about three pounds a trip. For the fiscal years ended June 30, 1880 and 1881, the net revenues of the offices supplied were $473.69 and $108.58 respectively. Annual outgo over $50,000; net revenues $108; net profits of the contractors over $30,000; the country supplied, a barren waste; the daily mail, literally a handful!

"While the writer was going over the petitions for increase with three or four witnesses summoned from the route, he found many names of persons whom none of them knew. Among these was the signature of Nephi Johnson. It so happened that Mr. Johnson was sitting in the next room at the time. He was called in, and recognized the handwriting of two of his sons and many of his acquaintances living on route No. 41,119, *a thousand miles distant from Canyon City!* The list had been cut off from some other petition and pasted on to this.

"The goose continued to lay her golden eggs till killed by Mr. James.

"Route No. 40,104, Mineral Park, Arizona, to Pioche, Nevada, length two hundred and thirty-two miles, advertised for one trip a week on a schedule of eighty-four hours, was awarded to John W. Dorsey at $2982 per annum. In due time letters were obtained from three or four public men, none of whom lived near the route, and presumably knew nothing about it, recommending increase of service. The letters were reinforced by a single petition, which seems to have been accepted as voicing sufficiently the views of the settlers. Its appearance was suspicious. It ran thus:

"'We, the undersigned citizens, furnished mail on route No. 40,104, from Pioche, Nevada, to Mineral Park, Arizona, wish to have more frequent mails, and would respectfully request that the service on this route be increased to three trips on a schedule of sixty hours instead of eighty-four hours.'

"The paper bore forty-one names, eleven written by one hand, and five by another. The words and figures 'Three trips on a schedule of sixty hours instead of eighty-four hours,' 'Pioche, Nevada,' and the last '4' in 40,104, were written by Rerdell over erasures. He testified that he did this mechanically at the request of Miner. Not a person signing it lived on the line. In short, it was gotten up for route No. 40,105, Ehrenberg to Mineral Park, and was afterwards altered and adapted to No. 40,104. However, notwithstanding its foreign birth and unnaturalized aspect, it subserved the purpose of the contractors to their complete satisfaction. By July, 1879, at two jumps, the pay had gone up from $2982 to $52,033.33 per annum. Of the aggregate, $20,874 were allotted to trips and $31,159.33 to expedition.

"In the fall of 1879 'mail bills' were placed in the through pouches on expedited lines for the purpose of securing an accurate account of the time actually made. Through a misconception of instructions, the postmaster at Mineral Park wrote on the thirty-nine which left his office for thirty-nine successive days, beginning November 16, 1879, an inventory of the contents of the pouch. On nineteen trips there was not a single letter, and for the period they averaged less than one a day. *In this case over $30,000 a year was paid for 'expediting' an empty mail-bag.*

"Only two intermediate offices were supplied, and these were so small that they yielded to the government a yearly revenue of less than ten dollars. Pioche was supplied by four other routes, and made little use of this one.

"Isaac Jennings, of St. Thomas, Nevada, took a sub-contract to perform the service at $28,000 a year, subject to fines and deductions, leaving a net profit of over $24,000 to be divided in Washington. Through some misunderstanding, he did not hurry the empty pouch through on the fast time, so that the penalties imposed upon him for the fourth quarter of 1879 amounted to $7789.83, or $789.83 more than his entire proportion of the pay.

"With financial ruin staring him in the face, Jennings, after some fruitless correspondence, proceeded to Washington in search of redress. He was still there when the accession of the Garfield administration brought new methods to the Post-Office Department. His principals, however, would do nothing for his relief, and the government could not. A prosperous farmer in 1878, he was reduced to beggary by his connection with the ring. He remained at the capital many months after hope had died out of his heart, and finally started for home on a ticket purchased by the charity of those who pitied his sorrows.

"The above routes are samples, by no means the worst, of over one hundred similarly manipulated.

"So far as Mr. Dorsey and his associates were concerned with the business, the sub-contractors furnished all the capital, did the work, and took the risks at starvation prices. They were kept in ignorance of the large sums paid by the government. The reader has caught glimpses of the enormous profits made by the principals, who did not on the frontier own a horse or wagon, a blanket or bucket,— whose sole cash investment consisted of ink, stationery, and office-furniture in Washington.

"If space permitted, the story might be told of route No. 40,116, Phœnix to Prescott, Arizona, W. M. Griffith, contractor, which was twice expedited, and the pay, without re-advertisement or competition, advanced from $680 to $32,640.32; or of route No. 32,024,

Vinita to Las Vegas, New Mexico, V. W. Parker, contractor, where the annual pay was run up from $6330 to $150,592.03. To describe adequately, however, the tortuous devices by which, in this case, the treasury was made to pay much and get little, and the manner in which one by one the essential features of the job were laid bare, would require a volume instead of a page. Enough has been here told to explain the general character of the transactions. In the execution of details, each combination had a system of its own, but in all, petitions with indorsements from public officials were used to persuade the mind of Mr. Brady, and affidavits respecting men and animals were produced at the right juncture as the jimmy to crack the safe."

This enormous work was unearthed by Mr. Woodward and abstracted with his own hand.* The routes

---

* Mr. Woodward's important relation to these trials has been stated by Mr. Brewster, who said,—

"When I first went into the case I did not know Mr. Woodward. He was a stranger to me. After the case went on he was necessarily detailed and handed over to the Department of Justice. He was at the elbow of Mr. Bliss all the while, and at Mr. Merrick's elbow whenever he was needed. I do not think there was a fact in the case they did not acquire from him. When I prepared the short argument I made in the first case, I consulted a great deal with Mr. Woodward. I had learned his value. I think without Mr. Woodward these cases could never have been instituted. I think he was, to use one word, invaluable. He is a man of remarkable intelligence; he is a man of great purity of character; he is an educated gentleman. In all my life, in an experience of over forty-six years of legal practice, I never have met with a man who could assist a lawyer better than Mr. Woodward. He understood his subject thoroughly. He understood all the bearings and relations of each point he submitted, and he would instruct himself in the law bearing upon it by conference with counsel. He was the most valuable assistant I ever had, and I believe to him mainly is owing the fine preparation that was made in these cases,—the complete and thorough preparation. The government, I think, is in debt to Mr. Woodward for his intelligence, industry, and integrity. I have learned to admire and respect him very much."

thus expedited were held by seven powerful and influential combinations. The whole service was honey-combed. These combinations were growing rich at railroad speed, and post-office inspectors, who might have unearthed the frauds at small cost and the most superficial inquiry, were found to be forbidden to trench on " star route" domains by a power whose unspoken word was obeyed as law.

Swiftly came evidence that intense hostility to the new order of things existed. No sooner had work begun than bitter and malignant attacks appeared in Star Route organs on the President, the Attorney-General, the Postmaster-General, and others. Swarms of contractors, their attorneys and beneficiaries, raised a deafening clamor, and made common cause against the administration. From all points of the compass the plunderers arose to aid their brethren in distress. The battalion was formidable, and the rumble of its muttered thunder was borne on to Washington and filled the air.

These were stirring political times. The Democrats, claiming the victory for Tilden and working confidently to repeat it all during the Hayes administration, now looked hungrily on at the clouds lowering over the fortunes of the Republican party. The union of the two factions at Chicago had only deferred until now the storm that was at hand. The chief clash occurred in the Empire State. The " Stalwarts," headed by Mr. Conkling, supported by Vice-President Arthur, claimed the right to dispense the appointive offices of the government in the State of New York, after the manner that had prevailed in the preceding administrations. The "Half-Breeds" followed the leadership of the President himself, who insisted on making appointments according to his own judgment and discretion. The appointment of the collector of customs for the port of New York is considered the best office in the appointing power of the government. The President named for this post Judge William Robertson. The New York Senators, Messrs. Roscoe Conkling and Thomas C. Platt, supported by the entire Stalwart faction of the party, including the Vice-President, the Postmaster-General, and Governor A. B. Cornell, of New York, resisted the appointment in an open letter to the President, and in the Senate and lobby. The conflict waged in the public press perhaps more fiercely than between the principals. Caricatures in the illustrated press represented the President and the New York Senator in gladiatorial garb, wrestling together, and the editorial columns, according to their point of view, praised presidential "backbone," or berated presidential ingratitude. Senators Conkling and Platt, failing to prevent the confirmation in the Senate, resigned, returned to New York, and put the issue before the people in a campaign arranged at the New York home of Vice-President Arthur. The struggle which followed was characterized with the bitterest hostilities, and both gentlemen failed of re-election.

The condition of the party was deplorable. Even its most able and honorable men were in a state of intense excitement,—chafing at opposition, smarting under defeat, exulting at victory, or foreboding as to the future. The baser elements, with baser passions, went to the extreme of partisan rage, while the thieves, sycophants, and parasites fattening on public plunder, threatened, brazenly defied, and trembled. Astute politicians, skilled at taking the public pulse, shook their heads at the mutterings and looked askance at the indications of what could not be defined, located, or described. There was a tragedy at hand: there was murder in the atmosphere!

Meanwhile the secret work went steadily on in the room assigned Mr. Woodward in the Post-Office Department. One Saturday afternoon in early April, the Postmaster-General was asked to examine the work already accomplished. Amazed at the revelations, he hurried to the White House with Mr. Woodward, and placed the matter before President Garfield. The President at first doubted the genuineness of the figures; then, with great impressiveness of manner, averred that he had been providentially saved from a snare to entrap him,—the meaning of which was now first revealed. The next day, Sunday, a lengthy consultation ensued between the President, the Postmaster-General, Mr. Woodward, and Attorney-General Wayne MacVeagh. Grave political complications were presented. Mr. MacVeagh modestly understates the decisive part he took in inaugurating these trials when he said,—

"One of the gentlemen accused had been a United States Senator, and had been an active agent of the Republican party in the then recent canvass which had resulted in the election of the President. Another gentleman whose name was connected by common rumor with this matter I believe was then a United States Senator, and a

Republican Senator, and at that time, according to my recollection, the Senate was Republican by one majority. In addition to that, there was a perfectly well-marked and universally known division of opinion in the Republican party. . . . I remember explaining very fully to President Garfield, in the presence of the Postmaster-General, the very great gravity of the initial step of these investigations. I explained that at the first appearance the figures were so startling, and the uniformity of evidence of mismanagement so absolute wherever we touched the matter, that it seemed to me that the President, as chief executive, ought to consider well before taking any step from which retreat would be impossible, and what the consequences of that step would be; that, if I were joined in those cases and started upon them, there was no way to stop them short of an exhaustive examination through the judicial machinery of the country before grand juries and petit juries, except, of course, the resource he always had of dispensing with my services, but that also might become embarrassing; and that therefore it was of grave consequence to everybody that this matter should be well considered before we started. I was induced perhaps, partly, to state this view more fully than I otherwise would have done because of allusions appearing in the public prints to certain relations that had existed between these gentlemen and General Garfield, certain letters said to be in their possession, to which allusions had been made, and various such things about which I knew nothing, but which caused me to feel it my duty, as a confidential adviser of the President, to lay this matter before the President in the way I did lay it before him.''

The Postmaster-General suggested that it would be wiser to institute civil suits for the recovery of the money obtained through fraudulent contracts, rather than proceed criminally against the parties implicated.

The President arose from his seat, and walked to and fro across the room in deep thought. There can be no doubt he felt the profound weight of his decision. It was the climacteric moment of his life. At the very threshold of his administration it meant for him that martyrdom which seems already to have foreshadowed itself upon his mind.*   It was a great moral conflict of a few seconds within the counsels of a single individual: a conflict whose results should reach out beyond the span of his own life and administration into the future history of his party.   He turned abruptly in his pacing and said,—

" No, gentlemen.   I have sworn to execute the laws.   I shall do my full duty.   Go ahead, regardless of whom or where you hit.   I direct you not only to probe this ulcer to the bottom, but to cut it out— no matter whom it hurts!"

This conference, so impressive and weighty in results,—disclosing a moral victory as striking as any in history,—ended after some detailed discussion of plans.

The Attorney-General assumed charge of the criminal prosecution.   His first move was to secure the facts already in intelligible form, and then despatch a number of the oldest and most experienced inspectors to the frontier.   The next step was the removal of Thomas J. Brady, Second Assistant Postmaster-General.   His chief clerk was also removed, and Mr. Henry D. Lyman was appointed chief clerk of contract office, and at once became acting Second Assistant Postmaster-General, pending the confirmation of General R. A. Elmer as successor to Brady. Mr. Lyman came at once with great skill and intre-

---

* The fatalism of President Garfield was curious, and has often been remarked by his friends.   It was shared and perhaps augmented by his mother, whose last words were, as he bade her farewell at the train not long before the tragedy, " James, I wish you would take care of yourself.   I am afraid somebody will shoot you."

pidity to the support of the government. The Contract Bureau was thoroughly reconstructed by him. Nearly all of the fraudulent contracts had still sixteen months to run from the time of his appointment. No time was lost in collecting evidence of fraud and cancelling these contracts, or restoring them to their original proportions. So skilfully was this performed that no appeal was ever sustained. Mr. Lyman thus not only saved the government enormous sums of money, but effectively crippled the ring by cutting off their financial supplies. "We don't mind your criminal proceedings," said one; "but this is what hurts."

Meanwhile A. M. Gibson was appointed to assist Mr. Woodward. Mr. Gibson almost immediately urged the employment of Mr. William A. Cook. Attorney-General MacVeagh appointed Mr. Cook assistant district attorney to aid in the preparation of the criminal cases. Messrs. Woodward, Gibson, and Cook went diligently to work, and both Woodward and Gibson, it is important to remark, had the combinations to the two safes containing the criminating papers.

EX-SENATOR DORSEY'S CONNECTION AND INFLUENCE.

The interest of Mr. Dorsey in the pending investigations soon became apparent. This was disclosed not only by the evidence unearthed in the Department, but also by Mr. Dorsey's efforts to disturb the relations between the President and his Cabinet, clog the investigations, and convince the country that "persecution" by Messrs. MacVeagh and James was the primary motive of the administration.

Messrs. MacVeagh and James, knowing the difficulty of acquiring the secrets of a rich, powerful, and well-organized ring, quietly announced that the administration would protect from harm the minor tools of the principals who would give valuable information to the government. It became Mr. Woodward's duty to receive these confidences, and he thus acquired the secrets of the ring, which he reduced to writing. Many of these, seen by the writer, are startling in the number of eminent men they implicate. Mr. Woodward's position was unique, yet perilous. The criminals learned to trust him implicitly; he never broke faith with one of them. They understood that their disclosures should guide the government in preparing the cases, but should not harm themselves, or be used in court, unless they were to be accepted as State's evidence and given immunity.* It was the policy of the govern-

---

* In the case of McDevitt, who was sent to the penitentiary upon his own confession, the government broke its pledge made through Mr. Woodward. This nearly lost them Mr. Woodward's further services, and did frighten many who would otherwise have given valued information. Mr. Woodward strove earnestly to save McDevitt. He wrote,—

" At the indirect solicitation of a Cabinet officer, upon conditional promises of immunity, Thomas A. McDevitt came to Washington at his own expense, and under oath made statements which, provisionally at least, were accepted as satisfactory. He did nothing subsequently to forfeit his claims.

" The innocent part borne by me in this and in one or two other transactions, which somewhat similarly have gone amiss, has caused me intolerable pain and humiliation, and has seriously embarrassed me in the performance of my official labors.

" While not primarily responsible for the pledges referred to, I

ment to mention no man's name in connection with the matter unless he was to be taken into court and prosecuted.

Mr. James was shortly thereafter informed that Montfort C. Rerdell desired to make a " clean breast" of his relations to Senator Dorsey and the Star Route contracts. Messrs. James, Powell Clayton, and Woodward thereupon met Rerdell by appointment at the Arlington Hotel, where Rerdell went further in his disclosures than he intended, and produced papers that would have substantiated his statements before a jury. He confessed that he had kept the books of the combination, and that the share of Brady, the Second Assistant Postmaster-General,—entered under the name of "Smith,"—was thirty-three and a third per cent. of the "expedition" for one year, and one-half of the remission of fines and deductions. This statement was repeated the following day to Attorney-General MacVeagh, and several days later Rerdell, in company with the Postmaster-General, went to New York for Dorsey's ledger to verify this statement as to Brady's share. Postmaster Pearson and Inspector Newcomb met the train at Jersey City, the latter " shadowing" Rerdell until he rejoined the Postmaster-General later the same day and returned with him to Washington, carrying a package wrapped in a newspaper, which he said was the ledger. Rerdell claimed to have met Dorsey, who charged him with treachery, and said

---

cannot shirk my duties to the men who have been asked through me to trust the government of the United States."

they had parted after a stormy scene. On the train he was handed by the conductor several telegrams from Dorsey, and passed them over to Mr. James. The first requested him to leave the train and return to New York ; the second was a piteous appeal that he should not ruin Dorsey's wife and children. Rerdell remained unmoved for the time, and continued to Washington. Here, however, Senator —— and others, friends of Dorsey, and finally Dorsey himself, succeeded in getting from Rerdell a sworn recantation. Thus was lost to the government his evidence, and all the papers he had exhibited remained in the possession of the combination. Said Mr. Woodward, " I shall never forgive myself that undue deference to official station deterred me from seizing the papers in a friendly way, and from cleaving to Rerdell night and day until the last scrap of evidence had been wrested from him." Rerdell subsequently made affidavit covering the influences which induced his recantation.

Ex-Senator George E. Spencer, about this time, reported to the Postmaster-General that the previous Sunday, while conversing in his room at the Everett House, New York, with Hon. S. B. Elkins, Dorsey entered unannounced, and

"appeared terribly demoralized, smoking incessantly, drank deeply, and said that Rerdell, his clerk, had 'squealed' and betrayed him, and had shown his papers to the Postmaster-General and the Attorney-General. Dorsey begged both of them to help him, making at the same time the most abject apologies for the harsh things said in the past. Dorsey called at the Everett House again June 16, but was then in a state of exhilaration, asserting that everything was all right, after all. Subsequently he exhibited Rerdell's recantation."

When this testimony, which would have proved a confession of guilt from Dorsey, was desired in court, Mr. Spencer, who was thought favorable to the government, sped beyond the reach of the government inspectors, in disregard of his subpœna, and remained an exile in Canada, and later in Europe. When the cables told that the trials were at an end, he sailed for home.* Thus his testimony was lost by the government.

President Garfield and his Postmaster-General returned together from Elberon the last Monday in June. In the car, between Baltimore and Washington, the President called Mr. James's attention to a bitter personal attack upon himself in the *National Republican*, then owned by General Brady,† and asked why Messrs. Cook and Gibson had been so slow. He requested Mr. James to meet him at the White House that evening with Mr. MacVeagh. Mr. MacVeagh was absent, but Wednesday afternoon, June 29,—three days before the memorable

---

* Mr. Spencer on his return was arrested and brought before Judge Wylie for contempt of court. Said he, in defence: " I called on Senator Conkling and showed him my subpœna. Mr. Conkling turned to the Revised Statutes, and said, ' This is not a legal subpœna. . . . The courts would so hold and decide. If I were you, I would go off and attend to my business.' I regarded his legal advice as very good advice, and I followed it."

Mr. Bliss drew the subpœna. The court dismissed Mr. Spencer, on the ground that his papers were illegal. The difficulty of obtaining witnesses against Senator Dorsey is the point.

† In addition to the *National Republican*, General Brady had also purchased the Sunday *Capital* and the *Critic*, of Washington, and was using all three journals most vigorously in his own defence.

2d of July,—Messrs. James, Woodward, and Cook went to the White House. At the moment of their entrance Senator Dorsey and Colonel Robert G. Ingersoll were in earnest consultation with the President. Rerdell was waiting in an anteroom, expecting to be called in to confirm his recantation in person, while the assassin Guiteau at the very moment was skulking around with revolver in pocket looking hungrily for the chance to open his murderous fire.

The President left Messrs. Dorsey and Ingersoll and came to the red room. Here Mr. Cook was for the first time presented to him. He explained what had been done by Gibson and himself, and then pleaded earnestly that Senator Dorsey might be saved on the ground of his great services to the Republican party. Mr. Woodward argued, in reply, that partisan services should not be allowed to condone crime. The President patiently heard Cook's plea for Dorsey, but made no reply. Mr. Cook further stated that an agent of Thomas J. Brady had already attempted to corrupt him, and that, as a mere measure of self-protection, he had secreted a detective under the sofa in his office to be a witness to the conversation. A most unpleasant sensation was left on the minds of those present, but the remarkable avowal found no response upon the impassive features of the President. Mr. Woodward had mildly recommended Cook, at the earnest and repeated requests of Gibson. He had already been called to account by the President for Cook's connection with the case, and was now filled with the gravest misgivings. The close of this remarkable twilight meeting—but a few hours before the assassination—is described by the Postmaster-General:

"The President suggested that they were too slow, that they should be more earnest in their work, and should have the guilty parties indicted and tried. Mr. Cook promised that no time should be lost. On rising to leave the room, he said, 'Mr. President, you know I am a criminal lawyer, and that my associations are not always with angels. I hear a good deal of what is going on, and I feel it is my duty to say, from knowledge which has come into my possession, that something dreadful is about to happen. I do not know what it is, but I think I can learn during the coming week.'"

A slight, spasmodic start and a nervous change of position were the only signs of feeling given by the President; then he responded that he apprehended no danger.

Be this a coincidence, merely a love of the mysterious,—a striving for effect in the desire to shield Dorsey,—or the true deductions of a man acquainted with Washington criminal classes, it was nevertheless strangely prophetic. The twilight faded into the gloom of night, and the sun thrice arose. Then Guiteau's pistol-flash laid the President at the feet of his Secretary of State, and the passions of the nation rose to a critical point!

Senator Dorsey continued his efforts to secure immunity, or, at least, a separate and "whitewashing" inquiry. These efforts culminated in a meeting between Messrs. MacVeagh, Dorsey, and Ingersoll in the Post-Office Department. Mr. Dorsey here stated that a separate investigation was deemed feasible by the President. Said Mr. MacVeagh,—

"My impression is that at that meeting Mr. Dorsey asked me if I proposed to disregard 'the orders of the President,' or the 'wishes of the President,' and that I answered that I had no knowledge of any wishes or orders of the President which I was contravening. . . . Of course it would not be telling the whole truth to be silent upon the fact that these prosecutions were a source of very great anxiety, and I might almost say, at certain stages of them, distress, to President Garfield. It would be strange if it had been otherwise ; and I have no doubt that at times gentlemen may have felt that there were other methods of correcting these wrongs than the methods which General James and I were pursuing, though I have no knowledge of that ; I was never present when such a thing was said."

Mr. Dorsey was informed that it would be useless to attempt any other settlement than by a judicial investigation ; that any other kind would be of no value to any accused person ; that behind Mr. Mac-Veagh was the President, and behind the President was an aroused public opinion and the press of the country, and no value could be given any investigation conducted otherwise than through the ordinary channels, where every innocent person would have every possible chance to be vindicated.

Failing in this, attempts were made to remove Messrs. MacVeagh and James from the Cabinet. Upon his return from a vacation, Mr. MacVeagh was told that evidence had been laid before the President of very base conduct on the part of General James and himself in suborning witnesses and being engaged in a plot to steal papers. Said Mr. Mac-Veagh,—

"I was interested only in one phase of that matter, and that was to know whether the President had seen fit to receive charges of that character about me in my absence ; and, upon my asking him about it, he said that he had declined to receive any such paper whatever, and had answered that, if it was left with him, the only action he would take upon it would be to have the man who had made it immediately arrested for perjury."

Other influences, however, were at work. Evidence that the defendants had warm sympathizers in the government employ became distinctly apparent. Rerdell had warned the Postmaster-General at the Arlington interview that Cook was in secret communication with Dorsey since entering the government employ, and that Dorsey had manifested complacence at his relations with him. Daily, in unexpected quarters, the work of sympathizers was developed.

It was only in September that a systematic attempt was made to prepare the cases for the grand jury, for work in the Departments had been practically stopped by the assassination of the President. Then, to the surprise of those interested, the grand jury was suddenly dismissed by the District Attorney, and the statute of limitations threatened to allow the accused to escape before it could be again convened. The District Attorney, George R. Corkhill, was known to be on intimate social terms with the accused. Said Mr. MacVeagh,—

"According to my recollection, Colonel Corkhill asked me when I thought these Star Routes would be ready for the grand jury; and I said that, in my anxiety for the President, I had not lately been concerning myself about the details, but of course his own special assistant (Mr. Cook), appointed for that purpose, could give him any information he wished. Mr. Corkhill's recollection of that conversation is that I said that when the grand jury was needed for the Star Route cases he would be informed."

Mr. Cook subsequently protested—rather too much—in open court that, as he had been absent from the city when the grand jury was dismissed, the government could not be responsible for it.

MESSRS. BREWSTER AND BLISS JOIN THE CASES. MR. MERRICK AND MR. KER RETAINED.

Mr. Brewster and Mr. George Bliss, of New York, were at this juncture joined to the cases, with Mr. Brewster as senior counsel. Mr. MacVeagh said,—

"I employed Mr. Bliss. When I saw the President, shortly after his wounding, on the floor of the dépôt, I was profoundly impressed that his death was a question of a very little time. I was continuously in Washington from that moment until we took him to Elberon, where I remained with him continuously until his death. In all that time it was a matter of newspaper talk that I was the gloomy member of the Cabinet. It was my misfortune to think each week, and almost each day, that the President was rapidly nearing his grave, and I therefore regarded it as a question of only a little time when the duties of my office would cease technically. To a very great extent they had already been paralyzed by the wounding of the President; and I felt it was undesirable . . . and improper to complicate these cases by any action I could avoid when I was not to be responsible for their final conduct. Whatever was necessary to be done in the interest of public justice I did, but I desired that . . . my successor in office should come to these cases as little embarrassed by any committals of mine as possible. . . . Shortly before the President died, it was felt by the gentlemen having charge of the matter, all of them, that something ought to be done in the way of selecting leading counsel to represent the government. By that time it was known that many eminent counsel had been employed by the defendants, and it was felt that we ought not longer postpone the selection of counsel on our side. I then stated that I proposed to ask Mr. Brewster to come into the cases, and, as Mr. James did not know Mr. Brewster, I would be glad to associate with him any lawyer of competent position Mr. James might select. It was impossible to consult with the President, and we had to act according to the best light we had.

I felt it was my duty to select members of the profession, if I could find them of proper professional standing, who had heretofore maintained cordial personal and political relations with Mr. Arthur. . . . I knew Mr. Brewster had for many years entertained such relations. He had been Attorney-General of my State, and had discharged the duties of that high post with honor to himself and the profession. I knew him to be a man of courage, and, so far as I could judge of the qualities needed, he possessed the other qualifications which I thought extremely desirable. I therefore invited him to come, and he came. Mr. James suggested Mr. Bliss, and I accordingly invited Mr. Bliss on that suggestion. That was a few days before the President died, and at a time when each hour I was expecting his death."

Mr. Bliss immediately took charge of the cases. Mr. Brewster was detained in Pennsylvania, and did not come into them until the day after the "information" proceedings were filed. These "information" proceedings, turning on whether conspiracy was an infamous crime, were left to Mr. Cook, the local lawyer, who assured Mr. Bliss that there was nothing to prevent them in the laws of the District of Columbia. Mr. Brewster argued upon the question, but the proceedings were not sustained.

In the mean time Mr. Brewster became Attorney-General, and, although devoting much time to the cases, was obliged to leave their preparation and detail largely to Colonel Bliss.

At this time Mr. R. T. Merrick, of Washington, was appointed "Special Assistant Attorney-General for the Star Route trials," to represent the Attorney-General. He took a leading and brilliant part. Said Mr. Brewster,—

" Mr. Merrick was selected for the reason that it was considered a proper thing to dissociate the cases from all political feeling, and to select a prominent Democrat to appear in them for the government with the other counsel, so that there could not be any charge of anything being done that was not known to all parties, and so that the prosecutions should be manifestly in the interest of the public, and not of any party."

To draft the indictments for those not yet exempt under the statute of limitations Mr. Brewster employed Mr. W. W. Ker,* of Philadelphia, who had gained a national reputation as a draftsman of indictments. Mr. Ker was known to be a man of unassailable integrity; furthermore, he was a Democrat, an additional reason for his employment, as the Attorney-General was determined that, if the indictments proved defective, there should be no ground to charge intentional error from political relation and sympathy.

DIFFICULTIES OF THE CASES. SPIRITING WITNESSES AWAY. SYMPATHIZERS IN GOVERNMENT EMPLOY.

The ordinary difficulties of the Star Route cases are hard to grasp. The laws in the District of Columbia were defective in the first place. Conspiracy was the only offence with which the defendants could be charged.

Witnesses, furthermore, were with difficulty secured. Around a camp-fire at night, along a distant route in the Far West, there are hot words spoken

---

* Mr. Ker found thousands of papers to examine, names and dates to obtain, and but a short time remaining before the adjournment of the grand jury and the exemption under the statute of limitations. Provided with six stenographers, and working daily until after midnight, he had six indictments under way at once. There were seventeen to be prepared, and the last three were only furnished the day of adjournment.

by cowboys and stage-drivers. They know it costs more to run their routes than is received by their employer, and fear the loss of their wages. Pistols are drawn, threats are made, bloodshed is imminent, —but tranquillity is instantly restored. It is explained that this is only part of a " deal ;" that the chairman of the Post-Office Committee, sitting in the United States Senate Chamber at Washington, will soon expedite that route, and there will be plenty for all. Shreds of this row reach Washington. Inspectors, armed with subpœnas, go from mining-camp to mining-camp to track out the participants in this debate, and bring them—in buckskin moccasins and personal armament—to Washington. In the majority of cases the expenses and fees to witnesses had to be advanced,—as much as $800 in one case, —and then the government counsel were obliged to find boarding-places and guarantee the board-bills of this motley crowd of frontiersmen.

This was by no means the chief difficulty. Not only were ill-gotten gains used to pay eminent counsel, but newspapers were hired to defend the accused and make common assault on the Department of Justice, witnesses were spirited away, and sympathizers were bought among hitherto trusted government employees. The marshal who drew the jury was in their interest, if not employ. The District Attorney,*

---

* It is justice to Colonel Corkhill to say that his relations with the accused did not cause him to disregard his duty to the government. The indictments were promptly signed, without perusal, upon the desk of the Attorney-General before the statute of limitations applied.

whose signature was required to complete the indictments, was suspected of a design to delay a few days on a pretext, and give the accused the benefit of the statute of limitations.

Furthermore, the house was divided against itself. In addition to Messrs. Woodward and Gibson, Mr. Cook had abstracts of government papers at his office. Here his law partner, Mr. Cole, had access to them, and, as was proved, had copies made of them by a St. Louis lady. Mr. Cole at the time was the legal adviser of some of the accused, and was dividing his munificent fees more than equally with Mr. Cook.* John A. Walsh testified,—

" Mr. Cook came to me when I was waiting to be called before the grand jury, and suggested that Mr. Kellogg was disposed to ' do what was right in the matter.' He spoke in a Delphic way, looked mysterious, looked at the ceiling, looked around in every direction, and said to me, ' You see which way your interest is.' "

Mr. Gibson, likewise, was engaged in the arduous task of representing both sides of a question. Contractors have sworn that they paid him large fees to have contracts undisturbed in the Department, and to prevent implicated parties from being indicted. The increase of $680 to $32,640 on a certain route, according to one of his decisions, " while suspicious, implied no *proof* of fraud, and its interference, in his judgment, would be illegal and unwise public policy." To have withdrawn a letter written by Mr. Bliss to the Postmaster-General on this subject, five thousand dollars was offered. Mr. Bliss testified,—

---

* See Appendix, testimony of P. H. Woodward.

"The result was that I went to the Second Assistant Postmaster-General, and told him that if that letter of mine was ever withdrawn, he might conclude that somebody had made five thousand dollars out of the withdrawal."

The government was in abject confusion at this time. President Garfield was dying at Elberon. General Arthur, almost crushed by the attitude of the country, had retired to New York. There was neither policy nor Department head. The Cabinet were with the dying President ; everything was at a stand-still.

The accused, however, were intensely active in making good their escape. Mr. Woodward learned that " Cook and Gibson were selling out the government, that a burglarious seizure of the papers had been discussed, and that when the catastrophe came it would be so contrived as to ruin me [Woodward], if possible."

Soon the government files would be barren of proof. Decisive action was urgently required. Mr. Woodward testified,—

"The presence of Mr. Gibson had become unbearable. . . . Having reflected maturely on the subject and notified Mr. James and Colonel Bliss of my purpose, I suddenly changed the lock-combination on our two iron safes. The following day I caused a full inventory to be made of the contents, and about the same time partially reconstructed the clerical force working under my direction. Mr. Gibson tacitly confessed the justice of the proceeding by never asking of me any explanation, or making any complaint, though he continued for two or three weeks to come to our rooms."

This was the pivotal point in the cases. It practically ended the connection of Cook and Gibson with the government. Both were later in the active interest of the accused, and both most shamefully maligned Mr. Brewster.

SYMPATHY FROM EMINENT REPUBLICANS. MR. BLISS PERFORMING DUTY AGAINST INCLINATION.

In addition to defective laws, the difficulty of gathering witnesses, the disappearance of important papers, the purchase of sympathizers, and the " fixing" of the jury, the trials were impeded at almost every point by the sympathy of some of the most eminent men of the party. Bound to some of the accused by ties of personal and official relation, and careful of the party reputation which must necessarily suffer by these exposures, these gentlemen unquestionably had extenuating circumstances lifting their latent and perhaps unconscious obstruction entirely out of the venal category of those who waged the detailed opposition. This influential sentiment came nearer to Mr. Brewster himself, and more largely concerns his own steadfastness, than the other, which was out of his sight.

Even the principal prosecuting attorney for the government has been charged with inclination to shield friends among the accused, notably Senators Kellogg and Dorsey. Mr. Bliss occupied a delicate position. As an eminent and powerful Republican he was a personal intimate of the President and the majority of his advisers, and with them had shared close relations with the accused. He had helped with General Arthur to honor Dorsey at New York, and had co-operated in the latter's attempt to place an appointment in the Garfield

Cabinet. His supposed desire that Dorsey might not be convicted can therefore hardly be called unnatural. Said Mr. Merrick,—

" That desire may have been the desire of an honest man determined to perform his full duty, yet, whilst he did perform it, still wishing that the result might not be achieved, though he put forth every effort to achieve it."

Mr. Bliss had entire control of the details of the cases after Mr. Brewster entered the Cabinet, and in view of his delicate position repeatedly requested to be relieved. The papers of the Attorney-General record anxious and prolonged consideration on this score. Mr. Brewster wrote him,—

"What could I do at that time? Let you leave the cases, and expose myself to the imputation of damaging the whole prosecution, and leave the Department charged with doing so with the purpose of aiding the accused? I could not help myself."

He also said,—

" Mr. Bliss I confided in above all men in the case. When I came into the cases they had been given him in special trust by the Post-Office Department. I was made to understand that Mr. James had selected Mr. Bliss, and, as those prosecutions were, to a certain extent, instigated by the Post-Office Department, and were urged in the interest of that Department and the postal service, I recognized him as the most important person in the cases, as representing that Department, and I so recognized him all the way through. At that time I did not know Mr. Woodward's position in these investigations."

The Attorney-General did not wish to risk the government's case by relieving Mr. Bliss. Later, however, it became possible to grant Mr. Bliss his request, and he was allowed to withdraw.

A difference in policy,* coupled with the enmity of several witnesses for the government, gave rise to some transient feeling among the government counsel, and led to these reports that Mr. Bliss did not use his full ability to bring several of the accused to justice.

This cannot be urged as a cause for the failure in the Dorsey cases, as the record shows that the juries were purchased to acquit the accused.

Mr. Brewster's relations with Mr. Bliss were those of personal friendship at the opening of the trials. That they were strained at the close was to him a source of pain and regret.

GOVERNOR KELLOGG. HIS IMPORTANCE TO THE PARTY AND CONNECTION WITH THE CASES.

William Pitt Kellogg was Republican Senator from Louisiana. He constituted the one majority by which the Republicans at that time controlled the Senate. He was a most important man politically, and was bound to the party and its leaders in close relationship. He had handled the money used in the

---

* Mr. Merrick took the ground that a high officer of the United States, whether the Second Assistant Postmaster-General, or a member of Congress, or a Senator of the United States, who took bribes under such circumstances, was far more guilty than a contractor who was acting under more or less compulsion, although acting voluntarily. Mr. Bliss, on the other hand, contended that the evidence against Price was strong and conclusive, that he was already indicted, and that the government had no right to give him up to take anybody else; that he was sufficiently guilty to hold him, and that it would be wrong to give him up for the sake of taking Senator Kellogg. That was the ground of difference between them.

Louisiana Electoral Commission, and, furthermore, controlled fifteen delegates to the approaching Chicago Convention which should nominate a successor to President Arthur. The President was, be it remembered, a candidate to succeed himself. Action against Senator Kellogg was therefore hazardous not only to the personal interests of the President and his entire administration, but to the party itself and the principles it was pledged to the nation to maintain. It required unexampled boldness to proceed against such a man. And the proceedings were frankly opposed by a large portion of the party upon mere considerations of party policy.

Senator Kellogg was charged with having received twenty thousand dollars from one Price, for securing "expedition" of a route. Price and John A. Walsh were witnesses against him. Mr. Walsh, as the banker, held drafts bearing Kellogg's signature, and had other corroborative witnesses connecting both Brady and Kellogg with the transactions. Mr. Bliss presented the case twice to the grand jury without securing an indictment. Mr. Ker took it the third time before the grand jury, and the indictment was secured. By this time, however, the statute of limitations had applied, and the charge was dismissed by the court on this ground.

Of the second presentation to the grand jury, Mr. Walsh testified,—

" I never got into an atmosphere so unmistakably hostile. I felt it intuitively and instinctively. The case was so overwhelmingly strong that even Mr. Bliss . . . had to come out and state that if he had been a member of that grand jury he would have had to indict; but he omitted to say that he told the grand jury it was a serious thing to indict a United States Senator. . . . I recognized that the defendants were ably represented there. . . . As the case came out there was one member of the jury, Mr. Semken, a jeweller here, who seemed appalled at the idea of one of the anointed being in danger of being indicted. He would look at me in a dazed sort of way as if inquiring whether the case could possibly be as stated, and I would say, 'Yes; that is so!' Bliss evidently got very angry with me."

After the second failure Mr. Walsh openly charged that the government did not desire to indict Senator Kellogg, and, taking refuge in Canada, refused to testify again until Mr. Bliss was removed.

Said Mr. Brewster,—

" Mr. Walsh wrote a letter to the President, in which he charged . . . that I was party to Mr. Bliss's determination to suppress the case. . . . The letter was intended to leave an impression that I was participating in the attempt to strangle the case. Among other things Mr. Walsh charged that ' a member of the Cabinet had a conference with Mr. Bliss on the subject, the purpose of which conference was to suppress the case.' I wrote to Mr. Bliss about that. . . . He replied in a most emphatic way, denying the charge, and said a great many things in that letter. He intimated, among other things, that Walsh was a witness for the government, and I ought to be very careful not to let his denial, or anything to the prejudice of Walsh, be made known, as Walsh would take advantage of it as an excuse for not appearing. . . .

" In the mean time it seems that Mr. Chandler spoke to the President and said that he wished to take notice of this charge, and wanted me to write him a letter asking him if the charge was true. When I was applied to about it, I said, ' Walsh's letter does not name Mr. Chandler; there is no Cabinet officer named. . .' Still I was given to understand that Mr. Chandler believed it was intended for himself, and wanted me to write him a letter. . . . By and by Mr. Bliss's reply came, and I took it and wrote a letter myself to Mr. Chandler, stating why it was I wrote to him, apologizing for so doing, and saying that it would be a very indecorous thing for me to do if he had not expressed a desire that I should do it. . . . Then I said to him, as an act of civility, that he need not regard Mr. Walsh's statements; from what I could learn of Walsh he was a shameless kind of a person; that I had been waiting for Mr. Bliss's reply, and now sent him a copy of it. I also said to him, 'You will observe that Mr. Bliss gives a caution as to the use that is made of his letter or anything he says about Walsh. . .' I got a reply from Mr. Chandler in which he positively denied the whole matter, and concurred in Mr. Bliss's suggestion as to the caution that should be observed not to let it be known to Mr. Walsh that there were any remarks made about him. . . . There the matter rested. I never showed that letter to any human being; I am sure I did not. It was locked among my private papers, . . . in my special custody, kept by me privately, and not put on the records of the Department."

The Attorney-General had only known Mr. Walsh by the report of Mr. Bliss, and but reflected that gentleman's words regarding him. Curiously enough, Senator Kellogg learned of this letter,* and threatened to place Secretary Chandler on the witness-stand to prove that even the Attorney-General regarded Walsh—the principal witness against him—as a "shameless kind of a person," and thus render his testimony valueless. Mr. Walsh also learned of the letter, and wrote both Secretary Chandler and the Attorney-General demanding a copy, and made it an excuse to remain in Canada until visited by Messrs. Brewster Cameron and W. W. Ker, who were authorized to give the personal word of the President and the Attorney-General that it was not the government's purpose to "morally assassinate

----

* According to Senator Kellogg (unpublished MS.), Secretary Chandler showed him the letter. He told Ex-Governor Warmouth, of Louisiana, Governor Warmouth told Mr. Norton, and Mr. Norton, a firm friend of Mr. Walsh, told the latter.

him," as he had charged, and that the case would go to the grand jury with Mr. Bliss out of the way and Mr. Ker in charge.

Before this, Mr. Kellogg had besieged the Department of Justice in personal endeavors to have the matter suppressed, claiming that Mr. Merrick was persecuting him.   Said Mr. Brewster,—

"I told him I did not believe Mr. Merrick would persecute anybody . . . but that I would see about it, and Mr. Kellogg went away. Soon after I saw Mr. Bliss and asked him about the matter. I told him it was a sad thing to have Mr. Kellogg coming to me and going on as he did, and I felt very bad about it; and I was pleased to hear Mr. Bliss say that ' Mr. Kellogg is all wrong. . . . I am doing it, not Mr. Merrick.'   A day after that I was tired and worn out, having been sitting up the night before working on the Star Route cases then on trial, and I was lying in bed in my room in the afternoon, at Wormley's Hotel, when there was a knock at the door.   I was asleep at the time.   The knock at the door awakened me.   The servant came in and brought Mr. Kellogg with him.   Mr. Kellogg was in a high state of excitement; he cried, wept, clasped his hands and wrung them, and expressed himself in terms of great anxiety and distress.   It was a painful thing for me to witness it, and it wearied and annoyed me very much.   I pacified him and talked with him, and told him he ought not to come and annoy me in that way.   I was lying in bed undressed, and he continued this sort of distressful talk, and complaining about Mr. Merrick persecuting him. I told him that that was not so; that Mr. Bliss had told me the day before that Mr. Merrick had nothing to do with it; and finally I said, ' Why don't you go and see Mr. Bliss?   He will tell you all about it.' . . . He said Mr. Bliss would not receive him.   I said, ' Yes, he will;' and I asked him to hand me a piece of paper, and I took a pencil and wrote him a note on my knees, lying in bed, and gave it to him.   Just as I had finished it and handed it to him, Mr. Brewster Cameron came in to see me, and Mr. Kellogg told him in an undertone to go out, that he wished to be alone with me.   I called Mr. Cameron and said I wanted him there.   I said that because I wanted to be done with the scene.   Mr. Cameron came in, and then Mr.

Kellogg got up—for he was kneeling at my bedside sobbing—and, in a very excited way and with a great deal of feeling, expressed his gratitude, and took me by the hand, and said he would never forget my kindness, and said that he would deliver the note to Mr. Bliss, and went off. After he was gone . . . I said to Mr. Cameron, 'Go and tell Mr. Bliss exactly the circumstances under which I gave that note.' He did go away, and subsequently swore that he told Mr. Bliss. To all of this Mr. Cameron has sworn. That letter was never alluded to until Mr. Bliss brought it out here. I am told he stated here that it embarrassed him. He never displayed to me any of the embarrassment about it. It was months after the date of that note that we met at my house, and he never spoke of it then.

" I will add here that Mr. Kellogg was constantly seeking opportunity to see me and importuning me to dismiss the proceedings. Once he followed me to Newport, in September, 1882, and was so noisy in his excitement and solicitations that my wife, who overheard him, thought it was some one asking pardon for a condemned man. *I persisted in following the Kellogg matter up. . . . And it was all the more necessary that the case should be followed up because there was an outcry made by Mr. Walsh that Mr. Bliss and I and ' a Cabinet officer' were concerned in suppressing it.*"

Senator Kellogg, in his interview with Mr. Bliss above referred to, is said to have made a practical confession. When told later that his indictment had rested as much on this as anything else, another curious phase was divulged, which will show the difficulty of proceeding against men of influence.

" Mr. Kellogg said that after he had presented the Attorney-General's note to Mr. Bliss he called on Secretary Chandler. Secretary Chandler immediately told him he had made a great mistake, and that Bliss would betray and ruin him; he paced the floor a few minutes in an excited manner, then said he would see Mr. Bliss and ask what Kellogg had said. When Mr. Chandler returned he said that he had ' coppered Bliss;' that Mr. Bliss had admitted to him that the conversation was one of ordinary character, that nothing unusual was said, and that Mr. Bliss, among other things, had said that he ' believed Mr. Kellogg to be an innocent man.' Mr. Kellogg then said that if Mr. Bliss would testify against him to the effect that he had admitted his guilt, Mr. Chandler would take the stand and testify that Bliss said immediately after the interview that he did not believe Kellogg to be a guilty man."

Mr. Ker, as already stated, made the third appearance before the grand jury, and secured an indictment against Senator Kellogg. The cases were dismissed by the court because the statute of limitations applied.

THE ATTORNEY-GENERAL'S PERSONAL LABORS IN THE CASES. HIS APPEARANCE IN THE FIRST TRIAL.

The first Star Route trial began June 1, 1882, and continued until September 15, 1882. During these hot summer nights the Attorney-General personally followed the testimony, and prepared himself to appear in court at the close of the cases. Said he,—

" For the purpose of preparing myself, I went over the whole of the testimony that was taken; then I had it cut out and condensed, and here in this mass of papers you see evidence of the preparation I personally made for my argument in the case. I went over it with great care. I sat up at nights—many a night—working at it, because in the daytime I had other duties and I was interrupted. It was very hot weather, but I remained here, at great personal inconvenience, long after Congress had adjourned, in order to conclude that case. There was not a line of testimony or a line that counsel spoke that I did not read and study."

His appearance and address have been thus described:

" The idea of convicting such men as Dorsey and Brady was met with incredulous laughter. People thronged the court-house out of curiosity and because the irresistible Ingersoll was a never-failing source of mirth. In fact, he was not only irrepressible, but for a long while the judge made no effort to repress him, but often joined in the general levity, and gave out strange utterances that led men to believe that the government had no case. Everything seemed to be in harmony with that awful spectacle when packed hundreds greeted with laughter they were ashamed of the idiotic or hellish utterances of the assassin Guiteau. A foul enchantment of irreverent mirth seemed to be the legacy handed down from that trial, so hideously burlesque in its surroundings, and only redeemed by the verdict, which satisfied public opinion if not legal acumen. And so, void of all dignity, of all sense of respect to a court of justice, the first Star Route trial dragged its weary length.

"But one day, the last day of the trial, a change came over the scene and the laughter ceased, and it has not been resumed since. The friends and journals of the defendants scowled at the idea of an Attorney-General of the United States stooping so low as to practise in an ordinary criminal court, and, when it was fully known that he feared not to stoop to that low level, it was proclaimed as an act of persecution without any precedent in this country, or in any other civilized land since the Bloody Assizes.

"The Attorney-General appeared, and made a speech that every one praised,—a speech, as one man said, that was as epochal as Webster's reply to Hayne. And as great as was this praise, it was the least praise it deserved. Showing that his presence in the court was sanctioned by two sources of American precedents, he proceeded to magnify the court, the supreme court of the nation's capital, where the murder of a nation's chief had been avenged. His argument was clear, his manner impressive, his gesticulation perfect, his words wise and at times strangely eloquent. This gives but a faint idea of the speech. Briefly meeting Ingersoll's closing argument, revealing at once to every mind the difference between mental power and brilliant smartness, he went on. It was the impalpable, the intangible, that made his effort so great. His picturesque garb, the personal idiosyncrasies of his speech and personal appearance, all added force to the occasion. He seemed like some grand impersonation of the dignity of justice, calling judge, jury, and spectators to the solemnities of the hour. He was there to disinfect the court-room, to banish unseemly mirth, and to bring home to the jurors the important fact they seemed likely to forget,—that pilfering from the government was a mortal, not a venal, offence.

"It was a remarkable display of personal power, an impressing of his character upon others. He seemed less anxious that his arguments should convince a jury than that judge and jury should feel their responsibilities and be awed into reverence by the dignity of justice. And, as he spoke, men felt that this was a solemn place, which their irreverent mirth of the past months had profaned. And as he continued Ingersoll's features became grave, and the illustrious defendants looked as though they saw prison-cells opening for them. In Brewster's manner there was no assumption of solemnity, no cant, no rebuke in words of past levity; but it was what he seemed to embody in his own personality that so strangely influenced all and so cast dark shadows before men who had believed that former position and usefulness, allied to wealth, would save them from their crimes.

" From that hour levity left the court-room, and, despite the occasional efforts of Ingersoll to be natural, it has not returned. The venerable Philadelphia lawyer had shown how a man could be natural, genial, eloquent, and even witty in his speech, without trenching upon the *rôle* of the comedian or transferring the hall of justice into the chamber of mirth."

It was proved that the combination had sent agents out along the routes to sublet them, and that these agents stated that there would be an increase of pay. Said Mr. George Bliss,—

" We proved their statement that there would be an increase of pay on a given route to a certain sum within a given time, and so much within another given period; these statements being made as inducements to the subcontractors. . . . We proved also that in three successive cases the increases were made precisely according to the predictions made by these agents. We put on the stand the agents who made the statements, the men who said they had made the subcontracts with that understanding; and we proved that the orders of increase were made precisely as those agents had predicted—we proved all this, and yet the jury failed to convict."

Said the New York *Herald* editorially,—

" The evidence against them is overwhelming. For months the prosecution piled proofs upon proofs of their guilt. Against this mass of evidence the defendants made virtually no reply from the witness-stand. For the sake of appearance, their lawyers went through the form of calling a few witnesses to testify on irrelevant matters, but this pretence could not long be kept up, and soon there was an utter collapse of the defence in the matter of evidence."

Eight of the twelve jurymen at the close of this first trial voted to convict all the defendants. The votes of the other four were curiously divided. These men, according to sworn testimony, were bribed, and hence a conviction was a physical impossibility. The panel agreed that the conspiracy existed; and that Rerdell, a mere tool of Senator Dorsey, and J. R. Miner, the humblest and only insignificant member of the ring, were guilty.

The verdict was a legal anomaly. Mr. Merrick characterized it as disgraceful to the records of the court, and moved that it be set aside. This was done, and the government made immediate preparations for a second trial.

JURY CORRUPTION.

The details of the debauching of both Star Route juries, and the efforts to bring scandal upon the Department of Justice and remove Mr. Brewster from the Cabinet, would form an interesting study in criminalogy. They are too long for our purpose here.

Abstracts from sworn testimony, given in these pages, will show how insidiously third and even fourth parties by prearranged and tortuous paths brought jurymen in the direct hire of the chief of the accused; how in some instances the agent of the accused appropriated and " scalped" the bribes placed in his hands for individual jurymen ; how additional money, late in the day, had to be outlaid to cover this treachery; how jurors prearranged signals and used them from the jury-room, so that the accused knew in advance the verdict, and assembled with their friends, retainers, and in some cases wives and children, so that in overwhelming force they might celebrate in the court-room the verdict when announced by the foreman of the jury.

The foreman of the first Star Route jury, an ally of the Dorseys, Brady, and Vaile, alarmed at the strength of the government's case, prearranged an attack on the Department of Justice to screen himself from the odium he knew his course would bring upon him. He failed in his attempt to secure an interview with a trusted agent of the Department of Justice,—with the evident purpose of giving a false report of the affair afterwards,—but notwithstanding prepared a flimsy, sensational paper for use in the jury-room with those whose verdicts had not already been purchased. This paper, which falls to pieces on the slightest analysis, set forth an alleged attempt of a government representative to buy of him a verdict against the accused. It was hoped that it would arouse those emotions with the ignorant jury which would impel the jurors who had not been bought to vote with those who had agreed in advance to acquit.

Through these efforts of the foreman the jury agreed that a conspiracy existed, but voted to acquit the prominent conspirators.

The government agents learned later that the accused were very indignant against foreman Dickson at the verdict, although it involved only the insignificant Rerdell and Miner. When Dickson was arraigned by the courts for this misconduct in the jury-room, and whined about the ingratitude of those he had acquitted, who, though he had fulfilled his contract, refused longer to affiliate with him, they denounced him as an idiot for not comprehending that " in trade the greater always includes the less."

INTRICACIES AND CONFLICTING INFLUENCES. A CABINET MEETING. EVERY HEARTH IN THE LAND A BENEFICIARY OF THE STAR ROUTE TRIALS.

The intricacies of these trials render chronological order in their presentation impossible. The influences which warred in their progress cannot all be sharply catalogued as directly right or directly wrong. Sympathy, malice, party policy, fear, cupidity, doubt,—all formed motives too subtly interwoven to be placed on one side or other of the line. Many of them are curious.

President Garfield owed his election to one of the distinguished defendants. President Arthur's chances of renomination rested partially on the influence of another. The Cabinet and the defendants, the counsel for the defence and the prosecution,—all useful politically, all able,—had for years been accustomed to pay one to the other the deference that rank and station render one another's due.

By a coincidence, Attorney Cook had represented Mr. Kellogg in his legal contest for his seat in the

Senate, while Mr. Merrick had opposed him. Witness John A. Walsh had a large claim against the government and one of about equal amount against Brady. Testimony on either side might jeopardize payment on the other. Dickson, foreman of the first jury, was president of an electric light company largely owned by Brady, one of the defendants. So all through were conflicting interests and associations.

To those who believe in the principles of a great party, and its relation to the whole people, it may not always seem policy to hazard it to punish individuals. A choice of evils may at times be deemed necessary. In this narrow light, which excludes the broad, far-reaching reforms, is explained much of the opposition from eminent men which sought to stay these trials. Even around the Cabinet table this question arose.

Mr. Brewster wrote,—

" I think the disinclination to pursue these suits was because some of the members of the Cabinet not only felt sick of the prosecutions, but had a lingering inclination to hush the matter up from a kind of sympathy with some of the sufferers. But to that I would not consent. That intimation was never very pronounced, but it was an intimation. I very promptly objected to that, and insisted that, no matter what the result would be, the administration had but one duty, and that was to pursue them, and Mr. Gresham backed me in it most strenuously, and after a pretty positive talk around the table it ended in a very positive determination to pursue these people."

He also said,—

" I made up my mind that I would not permit anybody to talk with me upon the political relations of this case or of any other case. I thought it would be a scandalous thing for me to do. I did not come into the office of Attorney-General to dispense the justice of the United States upon political considerations. I would rather never have taken it; I would rather leave it than do that."

The government accumulated an extraordinary amount of evidence regarding the debauching of both juries, which was reported to the Attorney-General. It was his desire to have the corrupted jurymen and those concerned in their crime presented to the grand jury. He wrote Mr. Woodward, to whose hands all these lines of evidence converged,—

"While I am in office (which will now be but a few months), I recognize the importance of completing my Star Route work by using all the information that you propose to obtain in securing the secret history of these detestable cases, and of those wicked men, and putting upon the record evidence of their guilt in securing their unjust acquittal,—in fact, of their guilt in every direction,—as a part history of the whole thing and as a final justification of our joint efforts.

"To P. H. WOODWARD, August 15, 1884."

Again, November 27, 1884, he wrote,—

"It is necessary that you will take in hand as speedily as you can, and have prosecuted and pushed, those cases that relate to the bribing of those Star Route juries.

"That is a subject the public is not fully aware of, and does not fully understand in all its force. The effort here is, upon the part of some responsible people, who not only favor the Star Route men, but would flatter the local sentiment, to allege that all we say upon the subject is not so, and that we are in error. Furthermore, it is the policy of others to avoid allusion to the fact that the verdicts were obtained by bribing, and to intimate that from some unknown cause connected with the method of prosecution the cases were lost, which is not true. We owe it, therefore, to the government and to those who prosecuted the cases, and also to the administration of justice, that this thing should be put in its proper light before the public. I wish you would take it in hand."

Still later, January 2, 1885, he reiterated,—

"It is due to this administration that these proceedings should be had, if it is possible, with any prospect of success, before it closes. And I, therefore, again, in a most emphatic and earnest way, repeat what I wrote you upon the 29th of December, and that which I have said in this letter: 'If these proceedings can be had with a prospect of success, let them be taken up at once.'"

The administration was soon to change, however, and it was extremely doubtful what attitude the new Democratic Cabinet would take in regard to these cases.

Mr. Woodward, careful of his promises to the confiding criminals and reluctant to begin a prosecution with no assurance that it would be pushed, wrote,—

"No one is more anxious than I am to secure all obtainable evidence in reference to the bribing of the Star Route juries. In the teeth of great difficulties, I have obtained possession of many facts.

"I have developed enough facts already to convince any man whom it may be desirable to satisfy. Many facts could not be used in court, and others still would lose their force through the necessary withholding at the time of trial of the correlated facts. If taken into court, the entirety of the case as regards evidence would be lost. *The results were accomplished by many distinct crimes converging to a common end.* If presented, each would have to stand or fall by itself, and thus the stock of evidence separated into the facts belonging to each particular crime, and broken in its connections, would prove insufficient. As the instruments employed are for the most part kept in ignorance of what their associates are doing, it is exceedingly difficult in such investigations to develop a complete chain of legal proof.

"P. H. WOODWARD.

"February 12, 1885."

The new administration was soon ushered in. Oddly enough, Postmaster-General Vilas, of the

Cleveland Cabinet, made not a single official inquiry in regard to the cases up to the time of Mr. Woodward's retirement,* and thus the matter dropped. The Republican party, in purifying its own ranks, had purchased an eventual triumph at the cost of instant defeat. It required a boldness of the hardiest type.

Said Mr. Brewster,—

"One thing I know, that I have never done a thing in this office that I have not done it from a desire to do my public duty in an honorable, upright way, and with an eye single to the interests of the public; with no advantage to myself in any way, political or personal. I have striven to do my duty, and I believe I have done it, and done it correctly. . . .

"I am remarked upon on both sides for my course in this matter,— by ignorant people who don't know what they are talking about, for not doing my duty; and by those who know better, because I did my duty. Urgent efforts were made to dissuade me from these prosecutions, but there was too much to be remembered,—the honor of the Department of Justice, but besides that, the honor of Mr. Brewster. That I pursued the right course I am perfectly satisfied, and the people of the United States will be, too, some day."

That day has come. The party turned out its own rascals. Unscrupulous contractors for years were so strongly intrenched that they fancied their dislodgement impossible. They were sustained by all manner of personal, political, and financial supports. The corridors swarmed with them. In sections paying the largest profits they literally owned the clerks, and the official who incurred their enmity was

---

* It is also worthy of passing remark that an effort was made to get several Star Route representatives into President Cleveland's Cabinet, and that the President received definite and distinct warnings similar to those given President Garfield.

doomed. Even upright men sought safety in silence, and the department head who joined battle with them would have fallen in the fight. Nothing short of criminal proceedings would have accomplished the far-reaching economies.

These proceedings did not send the accused to prison, but they did what was infinitely more important. They are therefore the greatest success of our recent national and political history.

The results came instantly. Two million dollars were saved to the Post-Office Department in 1881 in mail expenses, and more in the succeeding years. The annual deficiency was converted into a surplus, making it possible to reduce the letter-postage from three to two cents. Thus to the writer of every letter to the remotest corner of the land—to the hearth of every home in the nation—came directly and instantly the benefit of these reforms started by the Garfield administration, and faithfully executed by President Arthur and Attorney-General Brewster at such fearful cost.

The conflict in every sense was a moral one. It was not waged upon field of battle, amid the gay dash of color and inspiration of martial music. It lacked all the dramatic concomitants of Wagram, Marengo, or Waterloo. Its field was in the silent precincts of the inner conscience of a few men. The combatants were duty and honor set firmly against every worldly prospect the tempter ever offered man.

In some cases the tempter prevailed; in others honor carried the field, and calumny was accepted and worn as "public compliment."

X X.

President Chester A. Arthur—Resignation of Mr. MacVeagh—Mr. Brewster Attorney-General of the United States.

PRESIDENT ARTHUR began his administration under the most sombre and unpromising auspices. His position while the nation breathlessly watched at the bedside of Garfield was full of the keenest mental agony.

That he had been in open opposition to the dying President made this position almost unendurable. General Arthur's name had been signed to the protest to the President over the New York collectorship; he had been most intimately associated with the "Stalwart" faction of the party; and had held at his own home in New York a meeting with the personal and political enemies of the President in furtherance of their conflict. These facts, with the assassin's maudlin boast of aid from the party his pistol was bringing into power, lashed unthinking men into passionate words and the harshest misjudgments of General Arthur and all who were closely associated with him. Even the friendly journals of the country insisted that—

"An ordinary sense of justice will suggest to fair-minded men of every party and faction to suspend judgment until they have something to judge. The same votes that made Garfield President made Arthur his legitimate successor, and he should be made to feel that he has the same constituency behind him ready to uphold his hands and strengthen his purposes."

How keenly both he and his friends felt their terrible position, we may judge from the following letters to Mr. Brewster:

"New York, August 25, 1881.

"My dear Mr. Brewster,—

". . . Since my return I have been so overwhelmed with other matters that I have not been able before now to make acknowledgment to the friends who thought of me and sent me words of encouragement and sympathy in those dark and dreadful days.

"The expression of your sentiments in the Philadelphia *Press* which you sent to me was extremely gratifying to me, and I thank you cordially. We shall meet again, I trust, one of these days; and in the mean time, I am, my dear sir,

"Very faithfully yours,

"Chester A. Arthur."

"My dear Mr. Brewster,—

". . . The brutality and falsehoods of newspapers have, from long endurance, become so much a thing of course that its present illustration would not have impressed itself upon me but for the indignation which many valued and respected friends besides yourself have been considerate enough to express. For the sake of General Arthur, who, though generous, upright, and brave, is sensitive, I sincerely regret his having been buffeted so.*

"Time, the great altar at which all things must bow, will, however, set it right.

"Roscoe Conkling."

---

* As the recently published memorial of Mr. Conkling elicited, President Arthur found himself later in as strained relations with the New York ex-Senator as was the Garfield administration. The occasion of this estrangement will show the difficulty of General Arthur's position. The breach arose shortly after President Arthur's inaugural. Mr. Conkling first suggested and then insisted that the President remove Judge Robertson, whose appointment to the collectorship of the port of New York had involved Senators Conkling and Platt in their famous controversy with President Garfield.

"President Arthur refused to profit by the tragedy to accomplish what he had failed to do before Garfield's death, and argued, in

" With the knowledge of these hatreds before him, and keenly conscious of the intense and painful sense of public anxiety and expectancy, General Arthur calmly and firmly accepted the murdered President's place, and took up the reins of public authority. From the hour that he felt the obligations of the high duties thus forced upon him, he seemed by a sudden and natural aptitude to be filled with power to execute them. From that moment he made it evident to all that he knew what he ought to do, what he wanted to do, and how to do it."

More important, perhaps, than any one question the President had to meet at the outset was the great Star Route scandal. The clamor for the conviction of the accused had been dropped during the terrible suspense attending Garfield's illness; but, now that Garfield was buried and Arthur was President, the

---

addition, that the country would be shocked if his first act should be so radically hostile to Garfield's friends. Mr. Conkling insisted that the President was not responsible for the tragedy; that it was the Arthur and not the Garfield administration, and that the President's first duty was self-protection. The firmness of the President was a surprise to Mr. Conkling, and they parted, the former in grief and the latter in passion. Their relations were never restored. It is said that a year later the President actually made out the nomination of Marvelle W. Cooper as Judge Robertson's successor, and even telegraphed Mr. Cooper that his name would go to the Senate that day, when a prominent member of the party opposed it so strongly, in a private interview with the President, that an hour later, with face as white as snow, he recalled the nomination from his secretary, and rather passionately destroyed it. This is the first time in his political career that General Arthur ever broke a promise, and it is not known what powerful argument was brought to bear on this occasion."

people recalled the matter and intently watched for an announcement of policy from the new administration. The nation was in no mood to brook trifling. There was an awful solemnity in its silent judgment on the acts of the new executive. Garfield's Cabinet one by one resigned, and the President selected with deliberation advisers to succeed them.

When it became known that Mr. Wayne Mac-Veagh, the Attorney-General, would resign, the Star Route organs hastened to place a motive in his mouth,—namely, that the trials were to be abandoned because the government had no case. Mr. MacVeagh's political faiths and traditions practically closed his connection with the Department of Justice at the death of President Garfield in September, although as late as December his successor was still unnamed.

Mr. Brewster was at this time senior counsel in these great trials. His fame as an advocate was world-wide, and the very qualities that had moved politicians to deny him all nominations throughout his long career commended him to the public at this crisis. Not only was he by attainment pre-eminently worthy to bear the mantle of Crittenden, Black, Stanton, and Evarts, but, as a noted non-conformist, he was famed for fighting in a losing cause, if it involved honor or principle, in preference to ease, expediency, or political preferment on the side of the casuist. The national clamor for the pushing of the trials, therefore, pointed directly to him as Mr. Mac-Veagh's successor. Mr. MacVeagh himself warmly urged the appointment, and the Star Route organs gave distinct evidence of their views at the prospect by opening upon him a tirade of abuse at the first mention of his name for the place. The unsubsidized press of the country, too, was insisting that—

"The right selection of Attorney-General is still needed to leave no doubt anywhere of the determination of the administration to show no mercy to the thieves. For this no better choice could be made than Benjamin Harris Brewster. His abilities would dignify the office."*

Thus, pronounced public sentiment made it evident that his appointment would "signally unite high personal qualities with a peculiar public significance," and it became almost a necessity to the administration, in the logic of circumstances, to invite the famous lawyer into the Cabinet. Mr. Brewster was proud of the manner in which this honor came to him. All through his long life party duplicity had robbed him, for his very frankness and independence, of post after post desired from those he had largely helped to make. Now, however, an aroused public sentiment pointed to him as the man needed for the occasion, and brought him to this his unsought and crowning honor,—the post of Attorney-General of the United States.

His nomination was confirmed by the Senate December 14, 1881, and, when the appointment was announced, public confidence in the sincerity of the administration in respect to the Star Route cases revived at once.

Said the great New York dailies,—

---

* Charles Emory Smith, in the Philadelphia *Press.*

"There is no reason to suppose that he was in any way responsible for the various mishaps that have tended to give these prosecutions the appearance of a needless failure. He is now, however, in a position where he can be fairly held responsible, and upon the results he will be judged. If the Star Route conspiracies, through any delay, or the disappearance of witnesses, or insufficient preparation of evidence, break down, Mr. Brewster's niche in the gallery of Attorney-Generals of the United States will not be an enviable one." *New York Tribune.*

"The best testimony to the fitness of this appointment has been found in the disgust it excites in Star Route circles."—*New York Times.*

"He is an able man, and a ready orator."—*New York Sun.*

"The selection of Mr. Benjamin Harris Brewster is one of the best the President could have made. Mr. Brewster is always of great ability and a gentleman of the highest character. He is not especially identified with either faction of the Republican party; he is liked by the leaders of all shades of political belief and opinion, and he is eminently qualified to discharge the duties of the great office to which he has been called. The country will be satisfied with the appointment. By the vigor with which he prosecutes the Star Route trials, he will be judged."—*New York Herald.*

Among the hundreds of congratulations received by Mr. Brewster, several are peculiarly noteworthy. This warm-hearted letter from General Cameron is prophetic and striking:

"HARRISBURG, December 18, 1881.

"DEAR BREWSTER,—

"I am glad you have obtained the very highest honor of your profession. Any man may become a Cabinet Minister, but very few are fitted to be the highest law officer of a nation of fifty million people. No one can be more proud than I to say you will discharge its high duties with signal ability and entire integrity.

"You will receive many hundreds of congratulations, but great success always creates jealousies with the unsuccessful and spiteful below you. But if you don't heed them, they won't hurt you.

"You will be severely and perhaps cruelly criticised and slandered about the 'Star Route' cases, but you need only to do your duty as you have done with everything trusted to you, and you will leave that office with the highest honors that have been worn in it.

"And your good mother! How she would have rejoiced, and how your pleasure would have been increased if she were here! I have enjoyed all that at home! Sometimes I think the good old women do enjoy the successes of their boys!

"SIMON CAMERON."

"MY DEAR MR. BREWSTER,—I congratulate you on your accession to the high office which confirms your priority in our profession. I am sure your zeal, energy, and talents will be employed in that exalted place to promote your country's welfare, and will establish your fame on a basis far more perfect and enduring than could be insured by the mere possession of official rank.

"CHARLES O'CONOR.

"January 21, 1882."

"HON. BENJAMIN H. BREWSTER, Atty.-Gen.:

"MY DEAR SIR,—I received your very kind letter of a few days since, in which you attribute more to me than I deserve in the matter of the President's selection of his Attorney-General, but I sincerely congratulate the President on his selection, and I was delighted when I saw the nomination sent in. Senator Cameron spoke to me on the subject of your appointment to the place when he was last in the city, now two or three weeks since, and expressed his anxiety in the matter, and I agreed with him in the propriety of the appointment. This much the Senator may have stated to the President. But I am inclined to think the appointment is the President's own, only wanting to feel assured that it would not be disagreeable to his friends. With sincere congratulations and best wishes, U. S. GRANT.

"December 24, 1881."

"MY DEAR ATTORNEY-GENERAL,—

"I congratulated you in person on your appointment; let me now do so on the universal approval that the appointment receives.

"I look forward with much pleasure to our association, and the ladies are much gratified in contemplating Mrs. Brewster's company.

"I hope we may aid our excellent President in having a model administration. Trusting I may soon see you in Washington, I am
"Yours truly,

"FRED'K T. FRELINGHUYSEN.

"NEWARK, N.J., December 26, 1881."

Mr. Brewster took his oath of office January 2, 1882, before Judge Wylie, the jurist who should preside at the great trials that the new appointment guaranteed. Record of the instructions of the President at this juncture has been left. Said Mr. Brewster to the President, November 24, 1882,—

" I have never forgotten my instructions on my first accepting the office, to pursue these cases with the vigor and rigor of the law, so that the innocent should be acquitted if clearly innocent, and that the guilty should be punished if clearly guilty; and that there be no half-hearted sentiment in the purpose of the government and its officers in the prosecution."

January 12, 1882, ten days after taking his official oath, Mr. Brewster was given a complimentary dinner by the bar of Philadelphia. Mr. Brewster was deeply gratified at the honor, and yet the closing words of his remarks show how fully he appreciated the thorns of which General Cameron had warned him.

Mr. Biddle, in introducing him as the guest of the evening, said,—

" Mr. Brewster has won, and fairly won, one of the few political prizes the lawyer cares to possess, and now has his name added to the roll of remarkable men who have held the office of Attorney-General of the United States. Most of these names are surely such as should quicken into the highest activity the best faculties which he possesses. Among them we find the judicious and well-learned Bradford, the profoundly learned and argumentative Pinkney, the elegant and accomplished Wirt, the refined, industrious, and exact Gilpin, the scholarly Legare, the versatile, many-sided Cushing. But none of them surpassed the gentleman whom we have among us as our guest to-night, in a qualification which should be conspicuous in him who is called upon to be the mouthpiece of the legal department of the government,—the ability to express thoughts in clear, pure, nervous, and elegant words. Ofttimes have we been delighted

Philadelphia
Dec. 20. 1881

To the
Hon. Benjamin Harris Brewster
Dear Sir

Desiring to show
our personal regard and express
our gratification at your
appointment to the high office
of attorney General of the
United States as members of
the Philadelphia bar we beg
to request the honor of your
company at a dinner at
such time as may suit your
convenience.

We are, with great respect
your friends
Geo W Biddle
Eli K. Price
Rich T. White —

Wm Henry Rawle

F. Carroll Brewster.

Jos: B. Townsend

Samuel B. Huey

Daniel M. Fox

Rufus E. Shapley

Wm. W. Wiltbank

Wm Henry Lex

Daniel Dougherty

Richard Vaux

Isaac Hazlehurst

Wm Nelson West

John Cadwalader

Wm Rotch Wister

Francis Rawle

P. V. Morris.

Henry St. Hagert

Chas S. Pancoast

J. C. Sinkler

Victor Guillou

S. Sergeant Price.

John K. Valentine

Geo. Northrop

Wm. W. Kerr heh.

Francis Page

E. C. Mitchell

R. Ashhurst

Saml Dickson

Pierce Archer

Lewis Cassidy

Sam C. Perkins

Furman Sheppard

Geo. S. Graham.

David W. Sellers

Rob Grafson

Dallas Sanders

James H. Campbell

W. W. Drayton

H. S. Caven

Leonard Myers.

Henry R. Edmunds

Rudolph M. Schick.

Furman R. Elcock

Amos Briggs

Mayer Sulzberger

James G. Dickinson

James A. Henderson

Thomas J. Dreel

John M. Campbell

Chas. S. Vancanes

Thomas Hartig

John J. Toner

Henry P. Brown

Isaac Norris.

Cornelius Welsh

Pierce Archer.

Enoch Taylor Hopkins

Warren Carleton

Wm. M. Meredith

A. M. Adams

William B. Mann

Wendell P. Bowman.

James H. Heverin

W. E. Littleton

as we have heard or read the polished periods which flowed so smoothly and gracefully from the tongue or pen of our friend—the exact thoughts intended to be conveyed in the most accurate and tersest language. This is a high, a very high, excellence, of a value hardly to be overestimated by those who cherish the preservation of the beauty and vigor of our noble tongue.

" Of Mr. Brewster's legal attainments it is useless to speak here. We have all of us so often seen and felt the force of his abilities in our encounters with him in the halls of justice, as to make even a passing reference to them unnecessary. One part of his professional life, however, I must be allowed to touch upon. Succeeding, as he did, one of the first men of this or any other community as Attorney-General of this Commonwealth, he conducted the business of his office with so much honor, decorum, and courtesy as to excite our warmest commendation, and to make professional contact with him always agreeable. He never used official power for the purpose of personal or official triumph ; he never bore unduly upon the parties he was obliged to contend with while advocating the interests of the State. All was done fairly, openly, and with moderation. In saying this I speak that which I do know, and I testify to that which I have seen.

" But there is still another quality of our distinguished friend to which a brief reference should be made in conclusion ; I mean his attachment to those who have served along with him at the Altar of the Law. *He has ever rejoiced in the success of every one of us ; he has sympathized with our difficulties and our troubles ; he has held out the hand of encouragement to the young, the timid, and the disappointed.* It is this particular quality which has brought us together to-night with so much spontaneousness to tender to him our gratulations, and to drink from our hearts the words of the sentiment which I now offer to you :

" Our guest, Benjamin Harris Brewster : a long life of professional labor, rewarded by the highest professional honors."

Mr. Brewster then rose and said,—

" I appreciate this compliment so much that I cannot express the feeling that overwhelms me. I must be, by your kindness, excused. You must not expect much from me. Yesterday I sat down to prepare a written speech to present to you. I attempted it, but I could not ; my hand trembled, and my mind refused to express the thoughts and feelings with which it was crowded. My eye was filled with tears. I threw the pen aside, determined to depend upon the promptings of the instant and your generous forbearance."

Turning to Mr. Biddle, he said,—

" Sir, we have been friends from school-days. You have said many things in my behalf that remind me not of what I am, but of what I ought to be. For you I feel a personal respect, and from you the good words that have come touch me deeply, for I know that they are the utterances of your personal convictions as well as the performance of the task now put upon you. You have welcomed me with your whole heart as our brethren would have you do. We have read the same books, have studied the same grand thoughts, uttered in the same noble and forcible language, have lived the same life together, professional and personal, and now we here stand in the presence of each other enjoying the result and fruit of our careers, and both thankful for what we have enjoyed. You have undertaken to express, in terms that startled me by their warmth, your judgment of me. Men judge you in a spirit of commendation and confidence. May I cite a passage from Sir John Denham as expressive of that which I would hold to be a calm description of yourself :

> " ' Though deep, yet clear; though gentle, yet not dull;
> Strong without rage ; without o'erflowing, full.'

" When I thus describe you I describe those qualities which I conceive make up the perfect lawyer. What more shall I say ? Indeed, indeed, I cannot say anything. This occasion overpowers me ; your presence, your exhortation overwhelms me and silences me.

" Before me I see my friend Dickson, who, among a multitude of others, wrote to me a letter of congratulation. I answered him as I shall now conclude to you : ' What have I done to merit all these kind words from all you good men ?' So I now say to you as I said to him. When the Lords of Courtenay had fallen from their high estate they adopted a motto which is now suggestive in its application to my position under different circumstances.

" Descended from Pharamond, the father of the French monarchy, enjoying lordships in France and scattered over the face of Europe in their different branches, they became the possessors of great principalities. Time passed on, they ascended the throne of Constantinople and ruled the Eastern Christian world. They became the Earls of Devon in England, and then came their calamities. They were overwhelmed and degraded, and in their sorrow, the night of their calamity, one of their branches adopted the motto, ' *Ubi lapsus quid feci* ' Now they in their grief cried out, What have I done thus to lose all this greatness and all this glory ? So do I now, in the midst of my exaltation and honored as I am, so do I cry out, ' *Quid feci*'—What have I done ? What have I done ? Thus I wrote to our friend Dickson, who now looks at me applaudingly and with gentle tokens of affectionate regard. What have I done that you should thus come together to honor and exalt me ?

" Gentlemen of the bar, forty-four years have I been one of you, and here I am now, surrounded with you, giving me every token of your confidence and respect. Believe me, I never can forget this. I started with you, and I will remain with you. I will be with you to the end. My greatest honor from the first was, and to the last shall be, that I was one of you, and enjoyed your respect and confidence. THE OFFICE THAT I HAVE TAKEN UPON ME, AND WHICH WAS SO GENEROUSLY BESTOWED UPON ME, I HAVE RECEIVED WITH A SENSE OF HUMILITY AND CLEAN HANDS, AND, WITH THE HELP OF GOD, I WILL LEAVE IT AS PURE AS I RECEIVED IT."

The organs of the Star Route sympathizers had now opened upon him their most active warfare. Their detective reporters were sent to Philadelphia and Harrisburg to stir up and manufacture scandal, so that every circumstance of his life was dug up in the search for material to be used against him. And when he went to Washington every species of ingenuity was devised to ensnare and entrap him.

But Mr. Brewster had been trained by a long career of public effort for his great work. He had long fought deception at the hands of politicians and tricksters, and was not now to be involved even by those who made villany a systematic study. His first precaution was that a stenographic report of everything transpiring in the office should be kept. In this way a record,. as complete as that of any court, anticipated all misrepresentations, and saved the Department and himself from a most skilfully planned disgrace.

Heavy as were the burdens upon the whole administration, thus so inauspiciously begun, those upon the Department of Justice were greater than upon any other branch of the government. President Garfield's Cabinet had consisted of James G. Blaine, Secretary of State; William Windom, Secretary of the Treasury; Robert T. Lincoln, Secretary of War; William H. Hunt, Secretary of the Navy; Samuel J. Kirkwood, Secretary of the Interior; Thomas L. James, Postmaster-General; and Wayne MacVeagh, Attorney-General. President Arthur's Cabinet was subjected by death and resignation to many changes. Postmaster-General James, of the Garfield Cabinet, was followed by Timothy O. Howe, who died and was succeeded by Walter Q. Gresham. Upon the death of Mr. Folger, Secretary of the Treasury, Mr. Gresham was given the Treasury portfolio, and Frank Hatton, the Assistant Postmaster-General, became head of the Department. October 23, 1883, Mr. Gresham resigned his portfolio for a place on the bench, and was succeeded by Hugh McCulloch. This made three Secretaries of the Treasury and four Postmaster-Generals having at one time or another a connection with the Star Route trials. The Arthur Cabinet was composed as follows :

Secretary of State . . . . . . Frederick A. Frelinghuysen.
Secretary of the Treasury . . . Charles J. Folger,
                                         Walter Q. Gresham,
                                         Hugh McCulloch.
Secretary of War . . . . . . Robert T. Lincoln.
Secretary of the Navy . . . William E. Chandler.
Secretary of the Interior . . Henry M. Teller.
Postmaster-General . . . . . . Timothy O. Howe,
                                         W. Q. Gresham,
                                       Frank Hatton.
Attorney-General . . . . . . Benjamin Harris Brewster.

XXI.

The Murderer of Garfield—Details of the Assassination—Guiteau's Cunning—Scientific Struggles for his Pardon—An Army of "Cranks" at Large—The Insanity Commission's Report—The Attorney-General's Action—Dr. George M. Beard on the Subject.

"We are not responsible for the thoughts that cross the threshold of our brains. The human brain is forever acted upon by external impressions, and is as automatic as a machine. But we have the power to say to these thoughts, 'You stay,' or, 'You get out!' That power is *the human will*.

"It is not mental gifts, but mental habits; it is whether a man possesses his thoughts or whether he is possessed by his thoughts. Self-possession is the highest gift of God to man.

           "WILLIAM H. THOMSON, M.D., LL.D."

HAD not the gigantic Star Route question overshadowed all else, the trial of Charles Jules Guiteau, the dastardly assassin of President Garfield, would have been the memorable case of the Arthur administration.

Guiteau's revolting sacrilege during the trial is still

fresh in the public mind. When he was deservedly sentenced, after a long trial turning solely upon the question of his sanity, extensive efforts were made by eminent neurologists to save his neck and have him remanded to an asylum.

The details of Guiteau's movements prior and up to the shooting have been summarized by District Attorney George R. Corkhill:

"Guiteau came to Washington March 6, stopping at the Ebbitt House, remaining one day. Then he secured board and room at various places, of which I have record. May 18 he determined to assassinate the President. He had neither money nor pistol at that time, but he went into O'Meara's store, in Washington, and examined some pistols, asking for the largest calibre. He was shown two, the same in calibre, only differing in price. June 8 he purchased the pistol, for which he paid ten dollars, having in the mean time borrowed fifteen dollars of a gentleman in this city, on the plea that he wanted to pay his board-bill. The same evening, at seven P.M., he took the pistol to the foot of Seventeenth Street and practised firing at a board, firing ten shots. He then returned to his boarding-house, wiped his pistol dry, and wrapped it up.

"On Sunday morning, June 12, he was sitting in LaFayette Park, and saw the President leaving for the Christian Church on Vermont Avenue, and at once returned to his room for his pistol, put it in his pocket, following the President to church. He entered the church, but found he could not kill him there without the danger of killing some one else. He noticed that the President sat near a window. After church he examined the window, and found he could reach it without trouble, and that from that point he could shoot the President through the head without killing anybody else. The following Wednesday he went to the church to examine the location and window, and became satisfied that he could accomplish his purpose, and determined therefore to make the attempt at the church the following Sunday.

"He learned by the papers that the President would leave Saturday, June 18, for Long Branch. He therefore determined to meet him at the dépôt. He went to the foot of Seventeenth Street again and fired five shots to practise his aim, and be certain that his pistol was in good order. He then went to the dépôt, and was in the ladies' waiting-room of the dépôt with his pistol ready when the President's party entered. He says Mrs. Garfield looked so weak and frail that he had not the heart to shoot the President in her presence, and as he knew he would have another opportunity he left the dépôt. He had previously engaged a carriage to take him to the jail. On Wednesday, the President, his son, and, I think, Marshal Henry, went out for a drive. The assassin took his pistol and followed them, watching the carriage for some time in the hope that it would stop, but no opportunity was given. On Friday evening, July 1, he was sitting in the park opposite the White House when he saw the President come out alone. He followed him down the Avenue to Fifteenth Street, then kept on the opposite side of the street until the President entered the residence of Secretary Blaine. He watched at the corner of Mr. Morton's late residence (Fifteenth and H Streets) for some time, and then, afraid that he would attract attention, he went into the alley in the rear of Mr. Morton's house and examined his pistol, and waited. The President and Secretary Blaine came out together, and he followed them to the White House, but could get no opportunity to use his weapon.

"On Saturday morning, July 2, he breakfasted at the Riggs House, and then walked into the park and sat for an hour. Then he went to the dépôt, had his shoes blacked, and engaged a hackman, for two dollars, to take him to the jail, went into the water-closet and took his pistol out of his pocket, unwrapped the paper from around it, which he had put there to prevent perspiration from his body dampening the powder, examined the pistol carefully, trying the trigger, and returned and took his seat in the ladies' waiting-room, and, as soon as the President entered, advanced behind him and fired two shots."

As the President fell at the feet of Secretary Blaine, Guiteau was immediately seized and borne to jail. The following letter was found upon him:

"July 2, 1881.

"To the White House:

"The President's tragic death was a sad necessity, but it will unite the Republican party and save the republic. Life is a flimsy dream, and it matters little when one goes. A human life is of small value. During the war thousands of brave boys went down without a tear. I presume the President was a Christian, and that he will be happier in Paradise than here. It will be no worse for Mrs. Garfield, dear soul, to part with her husband in this way than by a natural death. He is liable to go at any time, anyway.

"I had no ill will with the President. His death was a political necessity. I am a lawyer, a theologian, and a politician. I am a Stalwart of the Stalwarts. I was with General Grant and the rest of our men in New York during the canvass. I have some papers for the press which I shall leave with Byron Andrews and his co-journalists at No. 1420 New York Avenue, where the reporters can see them. I am going to jail. CHARLES J. GUITEAU."

At the jail he immediately assumed a heroic pose, and with keen enjoyment entered into the notoriety he had gained. Just as bridge- and balloon-jumpers, who hold life cheap, and risk death for the sake of the notoriety to be had if successful, so Guiteau had calculated an adventure. He had reasoned his escape thus legally:

"I shot the President without any malice or murderous intent. I deny any legal liability in this case. In order to constitute the crime of murder, two elements must coexist: first, actual homicide; second, malice—malice in law or in point of fact. The law presumes malice from the fact of the homicide; the degree of the malice depending upon the condition of the man's mind at the time of the homicide. If two men quarrel and one shoots the other in the heat of passion, the law says that that is manslaughter. The remoteness of the shooting from the moment of its conception the greater the malice—because the law says shooting a man a few hours or a few days after the conception, the mind has a chance to cool, and therefore the act is deliberate. Malice in fact depends upon the circumstances attending the homicide. Malice in law in this case is liquidated by the facts and the circumstances as set forth in these pages, attending the removal of the President.

"I had none but the best of feelings personally towards the Presi-

dent. I always thought of him and spoke of him as General Garfield. . . .

"My conception of the idea of removing the President was this:
Mr. Conkling resigned on Monday, May 10, 1881. On the following Wednesday I was in bed. I think I retired about eight
o'clock. I felt depressed and perplexed on the political situation,
and I had retired much earlier than usual. The idea flashed through
my brain that if the President was out of the way, everything would
go better."

Thus, all the bitterness occasioned by the raging
political strife had found lodgement and concentration in the brain of Guiteau. During the trial he
said,—

"I have a right, as my own counsel, to ask your Honor that General
Grant, Senators Conkling and Platt, and President Arthur, and those
kind of men who were so down on Garfield that they would not
speak to him on the street and would not go to the White House—I
have a right to show my personal relations with these gentlemen,
that I was on friendly terms with them; that I was cordially received,
well dressed, well fed at the Fifth Avenue Hotel by the National
Committee. I want to show my personal relations with these men."

Guiteau's trial took place, beginning November
17, 1881, before Judge Walter S. Cox. Benjamin F.
Butler and Emory Storrs were requested to defend
him, but declined. Mr. R. T. Merrick was willing
to argue the question of jurisdiction. G. M. Sco-
ville, his brother-in-law, of Chicago, took charge of
the cases, and had associated with him Leigh Robin-
son and Charles H. Reed. Messrs. W. S. Davidge,
of Washington, J. K. Porter, of New York, Edwin
B. Smith, and Colonel George B. Corkhill, District
Attorney, had charge of the prosecution.*

---

* Guiteau's jury were Messrs. John P. Hamlin, restaurant-keeper;
Frederick M. Brandenbaugh, cigar-dealer; Henry J. Bright, retired

The defence tried to establish two lines: First, that the prisoner was insane; second, that the wound was not necessarily fatal, and was not the cause of death.

The prisoner, for purposes of diagnosis, was permitted "to interject statements into the proceedings." Later, it became impossible to control his interruptions short of a gag in his mouth. He claimed "divine pressure."

The following distinguished gentlemen gave, as their expert opinion, a statement that the prisoner was insane: Dr. James G. Kiernan,* of Chicago; Dr. Charles H. Nichols, of New York; Dr. Charles F. Folsom, of Boston; Dr. W. W. Godding, of Washington; Dr. James McBride, of Milwaukee; Dr. Walter Channing, of Brookline, Mass.; Dr. Thomas W. Fisher, of Boston; Dr. E. C. Spitzka, of New York.

---

merchant; Thomas H. Langley, grocer; Michael Shehan, grocer; Samuel F. Hobbs, plasterer; Ralph Wormley (colored), laborer; George W. Gates, machinist; W. H. Brawner, commission-merchant; Thomas Heinlein, iron-worker; Charles J. Stewart, merchant; and Joseph Prather, commission-merchant.

* Dr. Kiernan said, "Guiteau is insane, but one out of every five in the community is morally insane." Many students of mental phenomena are disposed to regard the entire tramp class as mentally unsound. Dr. Oliver Wendell Holmes intimates, as the logical deduction from his medical training, that "*a man is no more responsible for a crook in his brain than one in his back. . . . Bad men should be treated precisely as though insane.*" Dr. Kiernan, during the recent Frank Collier insanity trial at Chicago, is reported to have admitted that, "in stating one person in every five insane at the Guiteau trial, he was not correct: he was 'rattled,' in fact."

The following experts pronounced the prisoner morally responsible: Dr. Fordyce Barker,* of New York; Dr. Noble, of Washington, D.C.; Dr. Francis D. Loring, of Washington, D.C.; Dr. Allan McLane Hamilton, of New York; Dr. Samuel Worcester, of Salem, Mass.; Dr. Theodore Damon, of Auburn, N.Y.; Dr. S. M. Talcott, of Middletown, N.Y.; Dr. Henry P. Stearns, of Hartford, Conn.; Dr. James Strong, of Cleveland, Ohio; Dr. Abram M. Shaw, of Middletown, Conn.; Dr. Orpheus Evarts, of College Hill, Ohio; Dr. A. E. Macdonald, of New York; Dr. Randolph Barkesdale, of Richmond, Va.; Dr. John H. Callender, of Nashville, Tenn.; Dr. Walter Kempton, of Winnebago, Wis., and Dr. John P. Gray, of New York.

The trial ran its course. The issue narrowed and turned on the sanity of the prisoner. In the light of the fullest testimony on every phase of this question, the jury gave a verdict, "Guilty as indicted." As the name of the last juryman was called and his response given, Guiteau shrieked, " My blood will be upon the head of that jury; and don't you forget it. God will avenge this outrage." The prisoner was sentenced to be hung on June 30, 1882.

The trial had been reported over the entire world, and when the verdict was announced it was universally discussed, in its political and scientific aspect. It afforded an unprecedented opportunity for morbid individuals, and others eager for notoriety, to get into print on one side or other of the question.

---

* Dr. Barker said, " Moral insanity is nothing but moral weakness."

Many really eminent men were impelled or solicited to enter the discussion.   Those who opposed capital punishment* on principle joined with those who believed Guiteau insane, in the effort to have the assassin reprieved.

Miss A. A. Chevaillier, of Boston, secretary of the Society for the Protection of the Insane, presented a petition from numerous physicians and experts for a reprieve, and the appointment of a commission to examine his mental condition.

A committee waited on the President, and were referred by him to the Attorney-General.   They protested, " Psychology is not pleading for Guiteau, but for the American people."   This brought some amusing counter-protests from " the American people," who felt well able to care for themselves.†

---

* Garofalo, in his recent work on " *Criminalogie*," says,—

" . . . Everywhere where the death penalty has been altogether or almost abolished, murder has increased in an extraordinary degree. In Belgium murder increased in a frightful manner whenever the knowledge of the abolition of the scaffold spread among the masses. From 1865 to 1880 the murders increased from 31 to 120.   In Prussia, where for many years there had been no executions, murder increased from 242 in 1854 to 518 in 1888.   In Switzerland, where capital punishment was abolished in 1874, murders increased in five years to the proportion of 75 per cent."

† " The societies making this demand, in the name of science and humanity, are a queer lot.   Among them the reader will recognize the titles of several concerns that affect an immense amount of erudition and occult knowledge, but whose ' strong hold' is their mystery and abstruseness. . . . The general impression will be that the petitioners regard the assassin as a psychological curiosity upon whom they desire to try a few experiments.

" These pseudo-alienists and neurological persons are nothing if

Dr. Isaac H. Hazleton, of Wellesley Hills, Mass., wrote,—

" All of the specialists of mental diseases who theoretically believe that insanity makes a patient irresponsible were asked to sign the petition. . . . There are a large number of specialists who hold different opinions, and who have had an equally large and practical experience with the insane.

" I have seen Dr. Godding take a patient, who committed an assault on one of the attendants, into the bath-room and there threaten to drown him if he did not promise never to make another attempt. At first the patient refused, but, after being completely submerged several times, begged that his life be spared, and made the promise. Afterwards he was the most quiet patient in the hospital. A patient, therefore, can control his impulse to kill.

" I witnessed a will made by an insane man which was afterwards admitted to probate, because all the attendants testified that he had disposed of his property uninfluenced by his insanity. In other words, an insane man frequently performs a sane act.

" From the time of David until the present. insanity has been successfully feigned.   The reporter of a New York daily, who deceived people at the hotel, his nurses, and the two examining physicians, and finally all the officers of Bloomingdale Asylum, is the best-known modern instance.*   Every hospital has had several, mostly criminals, and it is not infrequent in the army and navy.

---

not empirical. Assuming to speak for the 'profession,' they say there are several circles in the craft holding different views as to Guiteau's responsibility. . . . Says the spokesman, ' Psychology is not pleading for Guiteau, but for the American people.'   The American people are undoubtedly very greatly obliged to these scientific twaddlers for their disinterested labors.   There is no more reason to suppose that the 'profession' represented in this novel and pertinacious petition is any more trustworthy than the profession that diagnosed the case of Garfield.   There never was, and never will be, any considerable number of doctors who will agree on any given point."—*New York Times*, June 23, 1882.

* The journalist referred to was Mr. Julius Chambers, who, by a coincidence, read law in Mr. Brewster's office. Mr. Chambers was formerly managing editor of the New York *Herald*, later established

"I think Guiteau ought to be hung, because I am positive that there are five hundred thousand men to-day in the United States as insane as Guiteau, who will kill as many innocent and worthy members of society, if the highest power in the land shall declare that this man had not had a perfectly fair trial, or that any man who can exhibit as much method in his madness as to await until he had perfected himself in the use of his murderous weapon, and then select a proper time and place and opportunity, and reason that he will be declared insane and so escape punishment, is a fit subject for the insane asylum and not the gallows."

The vast array of expert testimony had the usual result of all such " expert" conflicts. Confused judges, lawyers, and jurymen, knowing little of the scientific distinctions debated in such cases by the eminent gentlemen, each usually with a " hobby," are prone to disregard both sides and accord with the proverbial judicial utterance that " the common sense of twelve men is better than all the expert testimony in the country." In this case, what was established on one side seemed to be equally as ably controverted on the other.

The Attorney-General, when it became known that he was considering the subject, received numerous protests against a reprieve from specialists quite as able as those urging it. Besides, he knew that actions bear fruit. There was evidence enough in his mail * that Guiteau was only one of a numerous

---

the European edition of that journal in Paris, and is now one of the editors of the New York *World*. Mr. Brewster was familiar with this celebrated effort which launched Mr. Chambers into prominence.

* The mails of the President and Attorney-General were loaded with anonymous suggestions, some comic, others startling. Numbers scattered over the country seemed to be eagerly watching every de-

fraternity at large, as mentioned by Dr. Hazleton. Students of mental diseases well know how apt any popular fancy or subject is to take the minds of the unbalanced and show itself in the wards of an insane asylum. An anniversary, a newspaper discussion, or even a new song, of some personage or event, will often reflex itself in the asylums by sending thither its representatives. The "histories" of such cases bear a curious yet startling sub-relation to the questions of the times. These grim and awful undercurrents follow the great surges of human progress and form one of the most interesting yet pathetic phases of disordered intellection. By no means do the asylums contain all who are thus susceptible, nor are they all adjudged mentally unsound by the communities in which they live. Such persons cannot be denied responsibility.

It must be remembered that the Czar of Russia was assassinated in March, only a few months before Guiteau became an imitator of the regicide, and that Guiteau's trial was conducted at a time when

---

tail of this trial, seemingly anxious to save or hang Guiteau. They sent hints, suggestions, threats, appeals, diagrams. An example:

"ATTORNEY-GENERAL BREWSTER: A lady of exceptional character and well known for her practical common sense made to the writer this statement. 'I was alone in my residence with an infant so ill with the scarlet fever that it could not swallow. The Good God told me that I must hold the child's nose. I started to do it, but was afraid I would kill it. I took my seat; the Good God told me I must do it. I arose, went, and held the child's nose.' The lady is arraigned for murder. The President and the Cabinet are the jury. Verdict, Guilty of murder in the first degree. Did you ever hear of such a remedy for scarlet fever?"

the untried and suspected Arthur administration was facing the most turbulent season of political unrest and passion in our recent history. There were multitudes of lawless, excitable, and desperate men ready to remove any figure from public place that a disordered fancy might suggest, and by the mere pressure of a trigger spring into instant notoriety the moment the government showed any vacillating deviation from the equable and dignified course of the law.

Sergeant Mason, who attempted Guiteau's life, September 12, 1881, while guarding him at the jail, was only a feeble imitator of the assassin himself. There can be no doubt that in the dim intellections preceding his act he conceived a public sympathy making of him a species of hero and saving him from punishment.* A month later, November 18, 1881, Mason himself found an imitator in William Jones,† the man who followed the prison van and fired into it at Guiteau. Undoubtedly these examples would have been numerously followed had Guiteau been reprieved.

Besides this wholesome check on the numerous others burning with fanatical zeal to fulfil some

---

* Mason was dismissed from the army and sentenced to eight years imprisonment.

† Jones, indeed, escaped, as he had doubtless expected. District Attorney A. S. Worthington, who represented the government against Jones, writes, " Jones was acquitted. The general impression was that the jury acquitted him not because he did not try to kill Guiteau, but because they did not think anybody ought to be punished for a little thing like that."

public mission, there was some political significance attached to Guiteau's trial. There were not a few in the country who believed Guiteau had accomplices, and was the tool of the Stalwart faction that his pistol had brought into power, especially since he openly and boldly avowed his relation with the men of that faction and claimed their aid. To have granted him a reprieve for the purpose of retrial before those whose verdicts were ready in advance, might have seemed a confirmation of this theory to these few individuals fond of the idea of conspiracy and plot.

But this was the lightest consideration. This very belief abroad did more to reprieve him than the reverse, for it seemed to point to his death as a political necessity forced upon the administration to clear themselves from all taint of sympathy with the instrument of their accession to power. In this light Guiteau—be he lunatic, tool, or simply an egotistic fanatic, calculating on his probable chance of safe notoriety—became in some minds a martyr whom the government was obliged to execute to allay public distrust. A great clamor thereupon went up that the assassin was to be executed as a political measure, whether insane or not, and the mail of the President and Attorney-General was filled with such missives as the following:

"It is reported throughout the United States That YOU insist on the hanging of Guiteau, SANE or INSANE, for *Party* sake. ☞ *Americans like Justice.* Let him have a Commission. Then if sane hang him—But if you hang him and deny that which can do no harm to enquire into—you condemn you and your Party to Historic Infamy. Had he killed any one but a President he would now be in a lunatic asylum."

The President himself was moved by this outcry, calculated in its very sinister nature to make a fair-minded man hesitate and examine well his course. And when the petition borne by eminent men reflected indirectly this same effective taunt, the committee to whom it was referred by the Attorney-General were sufficiently moved by it to recommend a reprieve. They said,—

" We have carefully considered the papers you have referred to us. . . . These papers come from persons connected with the following-named medical societies and others : 1, The Association of American Superintendents of Asylums for the Insane; 2, The American Neurological Society; 3, The New York Neurological Society; and, 4, The New York Medico-Legal Society.

" Eminent physicians, distinguished as students and experts in the matter of insanity, have expressed opinions which are contained in their several printed letters to be found among the papers referred to, to wit : Dr. W. W. Godding, superintendent of the District of Columbia Asylum for the Insane; Dr. C. A. Walker, of Boston, president of the Association of American Superintendents of Insane Asylums, and for thirty years superintendent of the Boston Lunatic Asylum; Dr. Theodore W. Fisher, superintendent of the Boston Lunatic Hospital; Dr. Walter Channing, a writer of recognized reputation on the subject of mental diseases, officially and professionally connected with what is said to be the only criminal lunatic asylum in the country, that at Auburn, N.Y.; Dr. George F. Zelby, late superintendent of the MacLean Hospital, Mass., and at present committing physician for the city of Boston; Dr. A. MacFarland, late superintendent of Oak Lawn Retreat, in that State; Dr. W. A. F. Browne, a distinguished writer on psychology, formerly Scotch commissioner in lunacy; Dr. William F. Morton, editor of a New York journal on mental and nervous diseases; Dr. William A. Hammond, formerly Surgeon-General U.S. Army; Dr. George M. Beard, of New York City; and Dr. Spitzka, who was a witness at the trial of the prisoner. These gentlemen express very positive convictions as to the mental condition of the prisoner as it, in their opinions, was at the time of the homicide, at and during his trial, and since. These opinions they profess to have formed from careful study of what transpired, as stated in the public prints at and about the time of the homicide, of the daily record of the trial, of the prisoner's conduct during and since the trial, and of his previous history as developed at the trial. And they submit that, notwithstanding the examination by the government of medical experts before the court, the defence upon the ground of insanity was not fully or fairly presented.

" They ask for a respite, in order that the President may have the opportunity, beyond what is afforded by the history of the trial, to inform himself as to the question they present, to wit: whether there is reasonable ground to believe the prisoner insane ; and that he may employ such agencies and consult such sources of information as may be in his opinion reliable and best fitted to satisfy him on the subject. Should it prove to be the fact that the prisoner is not and was not sane and responsible at the time of the act or now, they suggest the important proposition that the government of the nation shall not be charged with the execution of a man under such conditions.

" In view of what these gentlemen thus present, without reference to anything they have to say in connection therewith respecting the conduct of the prisoner's trial, we cannot but think that their request is entitled to favorable consideration, and that it may well be further examined under the directions of the President, so that every proper caution may be observed, and the life of the prisoner may not be taken unless it shall appear that he was beyond any reasonable doubt responsible for his act, and not irresponsible by reason of his mental condition at and before the time of its commission.

" Respectfully submitted,
" ALEX. T. GRAY,
" WM. A. MAURY,
" A. J. BENTLEY.

" WASHINGTON, June 23, 1882."

The question thus rested with the Attorney-General. The eyes of the civilized world were upon his decision. The case was destined to become as historic as the murder of Cæsar, the Guy Fawkes fiasco, the stabbing of Marat, the beheading of Charles the First, or the assassination of Lincoln, and his decision for all time would be discussed wherever the political history of our great nation is read. There was no middle ground of expediency. To have reprieved Guiteau would have been a cowardly concession to this public clamor. To hang him would seem cowardly from the very logic of events. And yet, the easier course, merely as a matter of expediency, would have been to take the side of seeming magnanimity, and reprieve the assassin. To hang a lunatic for party purposes would have been worse than cowardly, and a man as careful of his personal and official honor as the Attorney-General would be likely to shrink from the faintest appearance of such a thing, and go to the opposite extreme.

The petitioners understood this tendency, and used its strong leverage to the utmost limit. It therefore required both firmness and boldness to take the side of apparent prejudice, override the recommendations of his own committee appointed to report on the subject, and declare to the President that he should establish a dangerous precedent in substituting his own judgment for the judgment of the law and its forums. By deciding against the reprieve, the Attorney-General ordered the hanging of Guiteau.

"DEPARTMENT OF JUSTICE, WASHINGTON, D.C., June 23, 1882.

"TO THE PRESIDENT:

"SIR,—Yesterday were sent to me by your secretary the papers presented by Miss Chevaillier, of Boston, consisting of petitions and letters of physicians and experts in support of an application for the appointment of a commission to consider the mental condition of

Charles J. Guiteau, and also praying for a reprieve pending such an investigation. In addition to the papers transmitted to me by your secretary, I have had presented to me to-day a written argument or statement from Dr. W. W. Godding, and also an argument signed by George M. Beard, M.D., W. W. Godding, M.D., and Miss A. A. Chevaillier.

"The whole question has been carefully and thoughtfully considered, and I have arrived at the conclusion that I cannot recommend a reprieve for the purpose requested. It is doubtful if the President, in a case like this, has the power to appoint such a commission to reverse the sentence of the law. The case of this man has been thoroughly and fairly tried in a prolonged, public, judicial investigation, in a court of competent jurisdiction, before an able, upright judge and a jury of impartial men. Abundance of testimony was offered upon the question of his sanity or insanity; in fact, that was the main and only issue and the only point contested. The wilful, deliberate, and premeditated killing of President Garfield by the defendant, Charles J. Guiteau, was an undisputed fact. It was conceded to have been done by lying in wait for his victim with a deadly weapon, carefully prepared for the purpose; the weapon was used with intent to kill, and the shooting by the defendant caused the death of President Garfield. All these facts were undisputed. The only question mooted was that of the moral, mental, and legal responsibility of the accused. The question of sanity or insanity, I repeat, was the only issue on that trial. He had a painfully protracted trial, during which latitude in every particular, almost to the straining of the law in his behalf, was allowed,—more latitude than was ever known to have been allowed to any defendant in all of the recorded annals of the law. He, himself, was permitted to say at pleasure all that occurred to him, whether in order or out of order. The evidence was overwhelmingly against him upon this very point of insanity. The case was submitted to the jury by a judge of acknowledged learning, a discerning, cautious, upright officer, in a charge that was calm, deliberate, and fair, and within one hour after that charge the jury found the prisoner guilty in manner and form as he stood indicted. In view of this, I again express my decided conviction that the requests submitted in these petitions ought not to be granted.

"The application comes at a late day. It has no legal status, and it is an attempt to secure by an extra-judicial hearing a reversal of a solemn verdict and judgment obtained in the regular and orderly administration of the law. Such attempts must be discouraged. The law must be maintained and confirmed by a strict conformity to its determinations and conclusions obtained in a regular and orderly manner.

"The attempt to assert that the sense of all the best medical talent sustains this application, because it believes the defendant insane, is contradicted by Dr. Godding, who to-day, when heard orally by me, admitted that, outside of those now applying for this reprieve, the preponderance of the medical talent in this country was the other way, and believed him to be sane.

"I will further add that the defendant has exhausted all of the remedies of the law for his relief. Since his trial his cause has been heard with deliberate care before the whole bench of the Supreme Court of the District, and no error in fact or law has been found; but that court dismissed his appeal, and ordered judgment on the verdict. After that, he applied to Mr. Justice Bradley, of the Supreme Court of the United States, for a writ of *habeas corpus*, and again the subject was considered by that learned justice, and the careful conduct of the Supreme Court of the District commented on and applauded, and the writ of *habeas corpus* refused.

"At the last hour, you are asked to reprieve this justly condemned man, to investigate, in an unusual if not irregular way, a fact that has been solemnly determined by the constituted authorities of the law.

"I submit it ought not to be done. It will establish a dangerous precedent. It will shake the public confidence in the certainty and justice of the courts, by substituting your will for the judgment of the law and its forums, at the instigation of a few who assert that he was and is insane, and who press their application, contrary to the 'preponderance of the medical talent of this country, who believe the other way and think him sane,' as is admitted by one of the most conspicuous, earnest, and important of the petitioners.

"I am, sir,

"Very respectfully,

"BENJAMIN HARRIS BREWSTER,

"Attorney-General."

Guiteau was hung on the 30th of June, 1882, at the Washington jail. Dr. D. S. Lamb, of the Medical

Museum, held the autopsy in the presence of a number of distinguished physicians. Some deviations were shown from the typical brain, but, in the language of the official report, "*they have absolutely no significance from the point of view of mental derangement.*" The skeleton was added to the curiosities of the Medical Museum.

Among the sharp comments on the Attorney-General for this decision, Dr. George M. Beard wrote,—

"This is the most important case of the kind of this age, of any age; a case that will never cease to be remembered to the dishonor of our nation until we cease to be a nation."

The case, however, was tried before competent authorities in a thorough manner. In refusing to be taunted or threatened into giving the assassin over to the advocates and witnesses of one side of the question, the Attorney-General stood upon the law and its findings after a fair trial. He took this responsibility, and was willing to go into history with it.

XXII.

Turning out the Rascals—The Great Work of the Arthur Administration—Congressional Investigation—Democratic Success of 1884 due to Mr. Brewster's Efforts to Purify the Republican Ranks.

"It would be straining political necessity pretty far to say that it is not the best thing an administration can do to expose and punish its own delinquent appointees. . . . Better that we should perish and expose them than that our enemies should do so; better that we should get rid of these *fungi* that are a stench in the nostrils of the Republican community in which they live and over whom they exercise official authority."

" The President said to me, as he has said all the way through, ' I want this work to be done as you are doing it ; I want it to be done earnestly and thoroughly. I desire that these people shall be prosecuted with the utmost rigor of the law. I will give you all the help I can. You can come to me whenever you wish to, and I will do all I can to aid you.' And he did so all the way through, without a moment's hesitation,—always stood by me and strengthened me and gave me confidence.

" BENJAMIN HARRIS BREWSTER."

THE masterly manner in which President Arthur met the perils of his delicate position won the admiration of the best men of both parties. When the immediate prejudices faded, restored confidence grew into a distinct appreciation of his fitness for his great office. He became, therefore, as the administration progressed, the recognized candidate to succeed himself.

Early in his administration, however, President Arthur was confronted by his Attorney-General with a decisive test of his character, which involved the loss of the renomination, but stamped him with moral greatness. This moral victory, greater perhaps than Garfield's, is not only interesting as biography, but forms the pivotal point of one of our most important political changes. Upon it directly turned the 1884 election which gave the Republican party their brief interregnum.

Mr. Brewster found, soon after entering upon his duties, that United States marshals and commissioners throughout the country had for years been defrauding the government by rendering false accounts, and were outraging the rights of citizens by arrests on frivolous charges made solely for the sake of fees.

Many of these officials, located principally in the South and west of the Mississippi, were powerful in their communities. Some of them, like Senator Kellogg, whom the Star Route trials were antagonizing, controlled delegations from their respective States, whose votes were anxiously desired by friends of the President at the Chicago Convention. Said Mr. Brewster,—

"The inspectors who went out to pursue these people had been neglectful of their duty. Hundreds of thousands of dollars have been stolen from the public treasury by these marshals, and their corrupt lives and vicious practices have brought discredit to the Republican party. It is the shame of their misconduct, scattered throughout the country, that has created this sense of hostile opposition in the way of independents within our own ranks."

These abuses he determined to abolish. It was a herculean task. The profits accruing from these dishonest practices from long custom had grown to be looked upon as personal perquisites. Nothing short of criminal proceedings could accomplish the results desired. These Mr. Brewster determined to take. Accordingly, in organizing his Department he sought anxiously and carefully for the proper person to place in immediate charge of this responsible and difficult duty. The appointment fell upon Mr. Brewster Cameron,* of Pennsylvania, who was made gen-

---

* Mr. Cameron, as inspector of the Post-Office Department, had, by his industry, ability, and courage in correcting abuses in the postal

eral agent of the Department of Justice, and thus became chief of the executive branch of that Department. Mr. Cameron had supervisory control of the United States attorneys, marshals, clerks, and commissioners throughout the country, and was also chief of the examiners of the Department, and therefore became charged with the responsibility of directing the investigation into the accounts and conduct of all court officers.

Mr. Cameron entered conscientiously into his work, and after careful consideration made a number of arrests. Mr. Brewster, with a conscientiousness as admirable as his intrepidity, gave the most careful

---

service in the West, won the esteem of the Postmaster-General. The fitness of his appointment is a matter of history. He enjoyed the entire confidence of the Attorney-General, and was thereby able to relieve the latter of many anxious cares. Without his faithful and intelligent co-operation the reforms instituted by Mr. Brewster must have failed. Mr. Brewster wrote him on his retirement,—

"Your resignation as tendered is accepted, and with great reluctance. You have been so useful in organizing the branch of this Department which was committed to your charge, that I am unwilling to part with you.

"For some months past your requests to be relieved have been suspended by me, for I could not see how I might supply your place. But General Cameron is right; a man of your energies and experience and prospects in active life should be elsewhere than in a minor official position in this city.

"You have assisted me more than I can tell in a short note in meeting the necessities cast upon this Department by the growing population and extent of the country. Without you in the beginning I would have had great difficulty in executing fully those duties of the Department that belong to the portion of it which was confided to you. Your judicious organization and arrangement will make it easier for some one that I may appoint to take up what you leave than to have begun where you started, yet I had hoped to have you to the end.

"However, go wherever you may, you will be useful; for you are diligent, dutiful, truthful, and must prosper and prevail in whatever you undertake.

"BENJAMIN HARRIS BREWSTER,
"Attorney-General.

"January 10, 1884."

attention to the minutest details of each case,* making it impossible for his subordinates to place the
name of an innocent man on the criminal records of
the country.

A storm of wrath was created by these arrests.
Appeals, based on party welfare, were first made to
Mr. Cameron. Friends of the President then tried
to dissuade him by assuring him that he was ruining
the Attorney-General, coupled with threats of dis-
missal. Failing in this, the Attorney-General was
importuned to remove Mr. Cameron. When it was
found how closely the Attorney-General had followed
each case, and was himself responsible, the President

---

* Said Mr. Cameron : " It is due to the Attorney-General more
than to myself that the practices of marshals rendering fraudulent
accounts was discovered, exposed, and broken up. The only praise
due me is that I have endeavored faithfully, with industry and
fidelity, to carry out his instructions. As his confidential agent, I
was the instrument that met the public eye, but, as I turned to him
for counsel and support on all matters of consequence, the result
would have been the same, practically, no matter who had been the
general agent of the Department, if he had courageously done his
duty. . . .

" There never has been a prosecution against a marshal, deputy-
marshal, or other court officer, that the facts have not been first
submitted to the Attorney-General and carefully examined by him.
This business he usually attends to at night . . . remaining until
eleven or twelve o'clock, and sometimes later. It has been my in-
variable rule to go over the reports with him in detail, and he has
then directed that the case be pursued or abandoned.

" Mr. James R. Young also knows that Mr. Brewster came to the
Department at night to give personal attention to matters which, in
my opinion, an Attorney-General must intrust to subordinates; or, as
Mr. Brewster has done, imperil his health to promote the efficiency
of the service."

was solicited to remove Mr. Brewster from the Cabinet as a political necessity, as his prosecutions of influential Southern Republicans were disrupting the party in those States. The attempts made by Republicans of national repute to thwart the prosecutions show the almost insurmountable difficulties a Cabinet officer meets when undertaking to uproot a system of wrong founded on the precedents of many years.

Republican journals, organs of the men accused, raised a cry of "persecution" all over the country, and were thus led to lend their sympathy with the Star Route organs, against the administration.

Presidential ambition and political expediency have swerved from the path of duty some of the most distinguished men of our nation. This was counted on. President Arthur's closest personal and political friends were given distinctly to understand that a continuance of these arrests would cost the President the delegations from their respective States,—principally in the South, where they threatened to consign to the penitentiary some influential political leaders. The discontinuance of these reforms would banish his Attorney-General from the Cabinet, but would insure him the nomination and a second term. This was Arthur's temptation: he met it manfully, and made the choice of the right rather than the Presidency. It was not an easy decision; it could not have been made without a struggle; it had its penalties, and they were paid. This is to his lasting honor. Said Mr. Brewster, speaking of an individual case,—

" In consequence of the outcry, I detailed Mr. Blair to examine all the papers. I then sent him to Alabama, and he investigated the matter there, and he came back and made a report to me that he was of the opinion that Mr. —— was guilty, and that it was the opinion there that while he was marshal he could not be convicted. I then directed papers sent to Mr. Bentley, of the Department of Justice, not giving him Mr. Blair's report, but asking him to make a report on those papers as to what ought to be done. Mr. Bentley, without knowing Mr. Blair's opinion, gave a written opinion of his own that, in his opinion, Mr. —— was guilty. . . . Then I sent the case to Mr. Maury, solicitor for the Department in the Supreme Court of the United States. He, not knowing what the others had done, gave a similar opinion. Then I gave the case to Mr. Solicitor-General Phillips and Mr. Simons conjointly, and they examined it and came to a like conclusion. . . . The President said that if there was any persecution it ought to be stopped and the matter investigated. . . . He did not like the idea of a man he had just appointed to office being prosecuted, and he wished me to have the matter investigated. I informed him of the reports that had been made, and there it rested. . . . Mr. Bliss wrote me a letter in which he maintained the doctrine that where the President had made an appointment the subsequent prosecution of the person was improper, no matter when the facts were discovered or known; and he did say to Mr. Cameron that the appointment condoned the offence, and he also said it in words to me. I reprehended it and refused to listen to such a proposition. . . . I do not think there is any gentleman in the administration who would have the hardihood to stand up and maintain such a doctrine. If he did, he had better prepare to leave office. I think public sentiment would put him out. *It was reported that if these things were persisted in I would have to leave the Cabinet. They have been persisted in and I have not left the Cabinet.*"

Mr. Brewster's course in this matter is in keeping with his whole career. The moral heroism required to face, not only every species of personal and political antagonism, but estrangement even from his President, is to be equalled only by the fidelity and integrity of President Arthur himself.

President Arthur's character was never subjected to a sharper test. Not only were his personal ambitions being jeopardized, but the very party itself was being disorganized. The Democratic party was making all possible capital out of this discord in Republican ranks and the great public scandals consequent upon it.

Incited by manufactured scandals, the Democratic Congress hoped to break down the administration by an investigation of the Department of Justice. This was done by a special investigation of several months' duration, made by the "Springer Committee," during which Mr. Brewster's acts and motives were subjected to the sharpest criticism from his political enemies; and not only were his sterling honesty and integrity proved, but it was found that he had shown the highest qualities of statesmanship and executive capacity in an atmosphere filled with suspicion and treachery from those in whom he was compelled to trust.

Through all these misrepresentations and jarring influences, President Arthur's character stood the test, and the cordial relations between the President and his Attorney-General ripened into friendship, that continued warm and unbroken until the end. In the quiet and retrospection that came to both after the administration, Mr. Brewster wrote to his chief, "I have always found you true."

When the Chicago Convention met to name the Republican candidate to succeed President Arthur, it became evident that the "rigor and vigor of the law" invoked by his orders on public despoilers had made him too many enemies to succeed before the Convention.

Mr. Blaine received the nomination. General Arthur's disappointment is historic, and was shared by his friends. Mr. Blaine's campaign was brilliant and memorable. By a combination of innumerable fortuitous circumstances, any one of which would have changed the result, Mr. Cleveland was elected.

Certainly it is not unduly magnifying the Star Route trials and the crusade against fraudulent marshals by claiming for them a very important place among these deciding circumstances. Aside from the votes directly influenced by the scandals they unearthed in the Republican party, had not these trials and prosecutions existed to engender their intense antagonisms, General Arthur would have been made the candidate at Chicago, and the success of the Republican ticket would not have hinged upon the personal antipathies of a few enemies of Mr. Blaine in New York State,—notably, Roscoe Conkling,* Henry Ward Beecher, George William Curtis, and Carl Schurz.

---

* The famous personal feud between Secretary Blaine and Senator Conkling is undoubtedly one of the many circumstances to be separately and directly charged with having lost for Mr. Blaine the Presidency. It arose from a sarcastic comment from Mr. Blaine upon the Senator's personal appearance. Senator Conkling's recent biography has adduced, with show of authority, the statement that Mr. Blaine would have cordially welcomed any attempt at reconciliation from the New York Senator, at any time since the unfortunate collision occurred. In explaining the affair to a mutual friend, Mr. Blaine declared this famous allusion to Mr. Conkling's personal appearance

Notwithstanding the peculiar and unparalleled opposition in the Empire State, and the rather lukewarm support of the Stalwarts who still remained in the party, Mr. Blaine's hold on popular enthusiasm was such that even the most astute politicians believed that he would be elected. Mr. Blaine, however, lacked a few hundred votes in New York State, and the Democrats were given their long-desired opportunity to " turn the rascals out." The cleansing of the natural refuse which always collects around a ruling party had been done by the Arthur administration. Then the other party was intercalated for a brief inspection period to attest how well the work had been accomplished.

The work had been thoroughly done. The next administration found none of the rascalities expected. The efforts of the Arthur administration had resulted almost in a revolution in favor of honesty and efficiency, which has lasted to the present day.

Mr. Brewster's appointment and later activities are so linked with Star Route and similar matters that we are apt to think of him unduly in this connection, to the exclusion of the other surroundings and duties of a Cabinet officer. He came to the office almost

entirely unpremeditated on his part. He was in the gallery while Mr. Conkling was speaking, and went back to the floor, intending to speak but for a moment, and in the warmth of debate uttered a sentence which cost him a life-long enmity and the Presidency. Mr. Blaine understood how vitally he had wounded Mr. Conkling, and in his readiness to make advances he is said to have gone " further, he believes, in that direction than any other man controlled by self-respect would have permitted himself to be led."

every night, remaining until after midnight, and appeared in court without cost to the government at a time when they were paying one hundred dollars per day to individual counsel. At the same time he was far more than a simple prosecuting attorney for the government. He was pre-eminently a statesman in all matters coming before the incumbent of his high post. Nor was he lacking in the fulfilment of any of the social duties devolving upon a Cabinet officer. On the contrary, his appearance was a new feature in Washington society. He was described all over the country as " a descendant of those courtly men of whom history says so much and of whom this generation sees so few," and as an " oddly-dressed, comely old grand seigneur and his beautiful wife, a new element in the conglomerate mixture of Washington society."

His marvellous conversational powers found here larger scope. Unlike Macaulay, of whom Greville said, " Conceding his extraordinary power and astonishing knowledge, he was not agreeable," Mr. Brewster had the rare gift of subordinating a powerful personality to his subject. He was not clogged or hampered by his culture. He had not, like the Grecian youth, worn out his shield in polishing it. Nor did he write or speak "above his ability," as men may who practise writing to the exclusion of speech, or the reverse. Thus his graces of conversation joined with his picturesque appearance to make him the central figure of this confessedly most brilliant administration, socially, since the Rebellion. At all public occasions it was " Brewster" the people scanned most closely, and for " Brewster with his famous ruffles" the press of the country constructed the most romances and gossip. Washington correspondents seemed never to tire of describing him and his beautiful wife and idolized boy.

In the Cabinet meetings, in the social gatherings, in the upper diplomatic circles, Mr. Brewster shone with unusual brilliancy. To the other Cabinet officers he ever held, in their own words, " the touchstone, the loadstone, the guiding star to the source of all classical allusion," and in the inner life of the administration we see him appealed to as interpreter of passages from Tennyson, or the authority to whom questions in ethics were submitted.

" GENEVA, N.Y., July 31, 1884.

" MY DEAR ATTORNEY-GENERAL,—

" A friend writes, ' Can you explain a passage in Tennyson's Gareth and Lynette :

> " ' In letters like to those the vexillary
> Hath left, crag-carven o'er the streaming Gelt.'

" In my forlorn ignorance I lift my eyes to my dear Attorney-General, who holds the touchstone, the loadstone, the guiding star to the source of all classical allusion.

" I trust that you are mentally and physically at rest at the top of enjoyment on the sea-beach at Long Branch.

" Yours faithfully,

" CHAS. J. FOLGER."

The relics of that inner court tell of all the graces of refined social and official life. " In your busy life," writes a friend at the receipt of a *morceau*, " you have taken time to give me pleasure." Others, in hosts, paint unsuspected but charming pictures of rare intellectual and social feasts. The biographer cannot touch the letters of those brilliant departed days without the utmost sadness. Most of the writers passed away at the wane of the administration, and left indescribable pathos in the " Lights out !" after the one glorious hour, so vividly pictured in the faded letters,—now " all dead ashes !"

XXIII.

Joys of Official Life—" Happy Days" Abroad—An Episode at Paris —Baron Rothschild—Social Slavery at Washington—Arthur, Conkling, Cameron, Brewster, Folger, Frelinghuysen, and the Wane of the Administration—Ingratitude of Republics.

NOT many days after his release from office, Mr. Brewster prepared for a trip to Europe.

General Cameron at this juncture, as ever all through their long association, had for him a word of almost paternal comment and counsel. The old sage from his life of retirement and retrospection knew by experience the sweets of official life and the joy of being a controlling force in a large body politic. He knew, too, without doubt, how insipid are the first months of the retirement, when life seems to offer no further object, and there is but flatness in mere professional or social endeavor. Against this *ennui* General Cameron was providing when he wrote,—

" You will soon be relieved from the cares of office. For a time, and only a short time, you may be unhappy,—but it will only be a short time. My retirement has been a continual pleasure. I am no longer annoyed by the parasites, nor vexed by the petty envy of jealous rivals, while my friends of all parties make me happy by their presence and their good humor. . . .

" I think you are right in going to Europe before setting to work in the old routine."

Mr. Brewster sailed on the " Gallia" with his wife and son. He had ever a fondness for European travel, and had gone abroad nearly every summer he could escape from professional engagements. Coming thus from the highest professional honors our country could proffer him, and bearing letters from leading diplomats to their potentates and friends, he was given an unbounded welcome by the celebrities and nobility of England and the Continent. They vied with one another to entertain this unique man from across the water.

At Paris one day his singularly distinguished presence, with the undertone of conjecture that it always occasioned, drew from the excitable populace, " *Vive l'Embassadeur Americain !*" Though not exactly comprehending his position, he was instantly recognized as an American celebrity, and was spontaneously honored, much to his amusement and discomfiture.

While upon the Continent, Baron Rothschild entertained him in regal style, and conveyed him from point to point in his private car. Mr. Brewster visited his sister at Rome on this trip. In his calendar he marked, " Happy days !"—as they must have been, after the luridness of the Washington atmosphere from which he had escaped.

On his return to Philadelphia late in the autumn,

however, he was soon to record sad days. Not many months later, March 9, 1886, his wife died, and on the 14th was buried in Washington. This brilliant ornament of so many White House receptions had paid the sad penalty of Washington life. Mr. Brewster wrote of her to his sister,—

"The exciting life she led at Washington, the social slavery she endured to official and social pleasures against my will, brought her home tottering on the edge of the grave."

Mr. Brewster keenly felt this blow. General Arthur, then stricken by his fatal malady, left his death-bed to write him,—

"My poor, dear, desolate friend! I wish I could help you in any way. And poor Ben—what will you two ever do without her? She was such a good friend to me, and you know, I am sure, how devoted I have always been to you both. God bless and help you. I am quite ill and confined to my room. If I were able to go I would be with you now.

"With a heart full of most affectionate regard and sympathy, I am, always, Faithfully yours,

"CHESTER A. ARTHUR."

Mr. Brewster replied,—

"I opened your letter with trembling hands. I did not believe that you could find strength or heart to trouble yourself with my sorrow; but here you are, as you ever have been, faithful in sorrow as in all things. I never have known the hour since we were brought together at Washington that I did not deeply and earnestly revere and honor you; and now I feel and see how advantageously and well placed was that confidence and affection.

"I fairly feel your hand touching mine as I place mine upon the lines you have traced."

K 19

Mr. Conkling also wrote,—

" Two deaths in my own house, and still others in our narrowed circle,—all within a few weeks,—have made up only in part un-wonted perplexities and absences. But ever recurring have been tender thoughts to you in your darkened home, and longings for power to help you upbear your burdens.

" *After all, the whole is so brief—so little—so questionable !* May calmness and blessing enround you, and bring you back from night into day.

" In sincerity, your friend,
" ROSCOE CONKLING."

There is indescribable pathos in these sad words from men who faded from the great arena of public life about the same time.

Wrote Mr. Brewster,—

" I was living in a very dreary and wretched way. Mrs. Brewster was gradually passing away, day by day. The doctor says this has as much to do with my condition as anything, and perhaps more.

" This has been a year of frightful calamities to me. Our dear friend Arthur, too, and then Frelinghuysen before him, and, not long before we parted and separated at Washington, Mr. Folger, for whom I had a deep sense of affection,—all these blows one after another have given me a cause of sore unhappiness."

Listen, also, to Simon Cameron, on the very verge of eternity :

" I have made enemies because I have had opinions and the courage to assert and defend them. I am an old, old man now, who has lived through the most wonderful days of our history, and when I am gone all that I ask is that people may say that I did the best I could, and was never untrue to a friend."

In all this can we not picture the sadness of each on leaving the great Capitol,—gathering up the remaining effects, gazing about on the field of past labors and power, tying the last red ribbon about the final package, then looking around to see if anything had been left!

" How soon men get through their honors, and how soon they wear out! The less than four years of Mr. Arthur's administration made him look fifteen years older. The wear and tear of public life are terrific. All the months following Mr. Arthur's abdication of office were spent in trying to recover from the overstrain. How tired he must have been when, just before his departure, he said, ' Life is not worth living.' Instead of being ambitious for the honors of our public men, better be sympathetic for their restraints and their fatigues. Macaulay, after all his bright career in the English Parliament and imperishable fame, wrote, ' Every friendship which a man may have becomes precarious as soon as he engages in politics.' Daniel Webster, after his wonderful career and in the close of his life, writes, ' If I were to live my life over again with my present experience, I would under no circumstances allow myself to enter public life. The public are ungrateful. The man who serves the public most faithfully receives no adequate reward. In my own history those acts which have been before God the most disinterested and the least stained by selfish considerations have been precisely those for which I have been most freely abused. No, no; have nothing to do with politics. Sell your iron; eat the bread of independence; support your family with the rewards of honest toil: do your duty as a private citizen to your country, but let politics alone. It is a hard life, a thankless life. I have had in the course of my political life, which is not a short one, my full share of ingratitude, but the unkindest cut of all, the shaft that has sunk the deepest in my heart, has been the refusal of this administration to grant my request for an office of small pecuniary consideration for my only son.'

"That is the testimony of a man who ought to know! Daniel Webster died at Marshfield of a broken heart. Under the highest monument in Kentucky lies Henry Clay's broken heart. Henry Wilson sleeps at Natick with a broken heart. Under the sod of Auburn is Wiliam H. Seward's broken heart. In a Cincinnati cemetery is Salmon P. Chase's broken heart. At Albany, in a casket covered with flowers that have not yet faded, is Chester A. Arthur's broken heart!

"From all the graves of Presidents and ex-Presidents there sounds out this solemn charge, ' Be content with such things as ye have. You brought nothing into the world, and you can carry nothing out. Having food and raiment, be therewith content.' " *

---

* Talmage.

XXIV.

Marriage—Mary Walker Brewster—Her Illustrious Father—Benjamin Harris Brewster, Jr.—Anna Hampton Brewster.

MR. BREWSTER was unable to marry until rather late in life. The subject of matrimony, however, had been one of serious consideration to him as early as his first acquaintance with Mr. Buchanan, as was evidenced in his letter regarding the domestic relations of that gentleman.

A letter written to General Cameron some time later discloses a prominent reason for this long delay, and conveys also another idea of the sad influence of his misfortune upon his social as well as his public life. He writes, almost bitterly,—

"I have learned that I best consult my own tranquillity when I keep away from those gatherings in Vanity Fair, where I am exposed to the brutal sneers and affected sighs of the 'tender sex,' who have never lost a chance to remind me of my misfortune, and hold me responsible for it as though it were a crime."

In 1857, however, he became the attorney for the estate of Dr. Shulté, of Paris, and subsequently married the widow, Elizabeth von Myerbach de Reinfeldts. Mr. Brewster, after his marriage, spent many vacations with his wife's parents in Germany, near Cologne. She died in 1868.

In 1870 Mr. Brewster married Mary Walker, the daughter of Robert J. Walker, a lady of rare beauty, who graced his later positions, and afforded the press of the country many fruitful contrasts and descriptions. W. H. Seward, congratulating him on his marriage, wrote,—

> "I congratulate you on your marriage, which, from my knowledge of your wife, I am sure is a happy one. No more intellectual family than that to which she belongs has ever existed in the United States; none more highly cultured and refined. If her father's bold and enlightened statesmanship could have ruled in his time, the republic would now have been the continent of North America. It will be accepted hereafter."

Robert J. Walker, her father, was born in Pennsylvania, represented Mississippi in the United States Senate, and stood with Mr. Brewster for the two-thirds rule in the 1844 Convention. As Secretary of the Treasury in President Polk's Cabinet he made an enviable reputation among American financiers. His policy upon the subject of the annexation of Canada and Cuba is referred to by Mr. Seward,— a policy whose wisdom is becoming daily more apparent.

It was while in Polk's Cabinet that he was joined for a time with Mr. Dallas in opposition to Mr. Brewster.

General Walker opened our trade with China and Japan, and followed Governor Geary as constitutional Governor of Kansas.* Like Geary, he also was

---

* "A convention, called in Kansas against Governor Walker's authority by a fraudulent Legislature, met at Lecompton, and submitted a proslavery constitution to the people. Shameless as this was, Buchanan approved it and abandoned Walker to disgrace. A Southern man as he was, he was honest enough to do right in the matter of Kansas."—*Nicolay and Hay.*

treacherously served by the Buchanan administration, and no more striking career than his can be cited to confirm what Webster said of the ingratitude of the public. By the very irony of fate, after his long and brilliant public career and almost penniless demise, it became the privilege of Benjamin Harris Brewster, the young man he had opposed when a powerful Cabinet officer, to erect and pay for the memorial now marking his resting-place. He died one year before his daughter became Mrs. Brewster. He was an illustrious statesman, and his daughter united with Mr. Brewster's renown and pedigree a lineage direct from Benjamin Franklin.

Mr. Brewster's union gave him one son, Benjamin Harris Brewster, junior, born in 1872. The son bears a great name to shadow him in comparison, but has rare endowment from an illustrious ancestry to meet this disadvantage. In his early manhood he promises to maintain worthily the traditions and dignity of his family line, which in him united the elder of Plymouth with the ruling spirit of our Revolution, the ambassador whose power at Versailles made our nation a possibility.

Anna Hampton Brewster, the distinguished sister of the Attorney-General, was his playmate in childhood and helpmate in his earlier struggles for success. Her beautiful feminine chirography in his yellow, time-stained ledger recalls pretty pictures of the well-born cultured maiden adding her mite to the success of the brother, and tells of the physical as well as moral support the young attorney received in his home.

Miss Brewster, enjoying a mental endowment in no degree inferior to that of her brother, has attained eminence in letters, and has given an exclusive attention to literature, art, and music, while the brother's time was occupied with the technicalities of his profession and his political and legal activities. From her home in Rome, where she established herself some twenty years ago, Miss Brewster has contributed most able treatises on European art, literature, archæology, and music to American and English periodicals. Added to this large miscellaneous work of a scholarly and critical nature, she has also written two novels, " Compensation ; or, Always a Future," and " Saint Martin's Summer," the first published in Philadelphia and the second in Boston. Both are works of exquisite taste and culture, and have indescribable charm, especially for those familiar with the classic scenes and incidents amid which they are laid.

XXV.

Piety of Public Men—Religion for Campaign Purposes—Mr. Brewster on the Subject—Friendship with Catholic Prelates—Proselyting Efforts—The Pope's Benediction.

THE religious element in Mr. Brewster was so marked that his personality cannot be viewed aside from it.

He believed that Christianity and that which it involves are the greatest considerations facing the rational being. Religion was not to him merely the vocabulary of a narrow sect or circle : it was, instead, a realizable force, appealing to the highest elements in human nature. Therefore, he had no shamefaced desire to exclude it from his daily discourse. On the contrary, his whole public and private utterance abounded with " fragments of a real church liturgy and body of homilies strangely disguised from the common eye." Nevertheless, he was a man of the world, mingled in sharp political contests, and sustained high honors. Nor did he conform to the straight and narrow rules by which many Christians are wont to guide their lives.

It is customary to doubt the piety of public men, the more so when political renegades report committee meetings, at campaign head-quarters, to manufacture biographical shreds of sentiment and religion in the candidate to catch the popular heart. Such disclosures are an undesigned tribute to the popular heart, that makes sentiment and religion a necessary part of a campaign, but they dispose us to be incredulous and insincere in our judgments of other public men.

Though a man may sometimes be religious in public for effect, and verily have his reward, quite another interpretation must be placed on that motive which withdraws him to the cloister of his home, to spend the major part of his leisure in Christian reading, research, and meditation. A belated French infidel, housed overnight in a forester's hut, paid Christianity an undesigned but effective tribute. Watching to escape robbery, he discovered his rude host at secret prayer, and at once abandoned his

p

vigil for fearless and undisturbed slumber. So, when we find a man's private library filled with religious books, his public discourses replete with religious thought, and the record of his inner life, placed in his sacred places of repository, one of continual moral stock-taking, we, like the sardonic infidel, may repose free from misgiving and doubt as to his sincerity, whatever may be our own attitude in religious matters.

And yet it is natural that we should doubt the humility of the great. The allurements of ambition, the pride of contest and flush of success, the wild scenes of excitement wherein the sublime stimulus is caught, are not the most efficient aids to Christian lowliness. They are, like life itself, dangerous; yet it is hardly the brave man who would forego life for fear of its danger.

Regarding the piety of an outwardly brilliant life, Mr. Brewster has written,—

"Before À Becket became Archbishop he was supposed to have led a life of elegance and luxury,—almost sinful worldliness in its character . . . It was found that he had been misunderstood, and that amidst the whole of his splendid public career he had been mindful of his spiritual duties, and in secrecy and with humility, by prayer and supplications, had daily sought the Divine help. To the world, the outward sign of splendor that surrounded him was no sign of the inward and spiritual grace that ruled him."

Mr. Brewster was raised and died in the Protestant Episcopal Church. His religious sympathies and associations, however, were spread over the entire breadth of the religious world.

He saw no monopoly of truth in any one division

of the Church Universal. From this narrow, excluding view, which is perhaps necessary at the start to give a framework for conviction, he early cast off. This sad necessity of breaking away from the narrower traditions of old—this " downfall of habitual beliefs which makes the world totter for us in maturer life"—comes but too often to men of wide reading and association. What Anglican, Arminian, Baptist, Calvinist, Methodist, or Romanist can do more than honor in the merest externals his early excluding views if his friendships in books or living souls lead out upon the wide ocean of universality? It is somewhat a fact that narrow men are the best propagandists. Light can be discussed geometrically by single rays in one plane, but no one can grasp its entire effulgence pervading space.

This independence, however, with its indefiniteness and distinct inability for sharp partisanship, is apt to be misunderstood and misjudged by strict denominationalists. Its very breadth has an element of danger; and its unrest may drive one after Cardinal Newman,—with his last, swan-like note, " Lead, kindly light,"—into the extreme of an infallible interpretation and papal guidance.

Mr. Brewster interpreted the Baptist immersion, the Methodist mourners' bench, the Roman and Anglican confessional, as but outward steps towards the spiritual child's estate. In a similar manner did he view the Catholic's submission to church authority. All to him were means to the same great end, modified by temperament, by tradition and circumstance, but of equal potency when received with equal sincerity,—all true, with rays of truth blending as the colors blend in the spectrum. The lawyer believes the State, the King, can do no wrong. The Catholic attributes infallible church authority to the Holy See. The Methodist, at the other extreme, believes that "all things work together for good." Did not Mr. Brewster in his creed compass both extremes when he spoke,—

"To deny the overseeing power of Providence is, to my mind, practical infidelity. This is a disobedience and rebellion that will sooner or later be visited with punishment."

Mr. Brewster was deeply versed in technical theology, and better read in the dogmas of St. Augustine, Calvin, Luther, and the great prelates of the original church than many clergymen. Yet his attitude, in speaking as a Protestant to a Catholic audience, is noteworthy. At controversial points he invariably stopped, and disclaimed right or ability to trench upon the prerogatives of their clergy. The dark ages when the church, as yet undivided by the Reformation, was making the history of Europe, formed his favorite reading ground. Many of his friendships, heightened by this literary taste, were prelates in the Roman Catholic Church. When, under the impulse of that passion that drives man into brilliant climes, he indulged his taste for European travel, he bore with him Latin letters of introduction from clergy high in authority, and thus the doors of the oldest monasteries were opened to him, and the hearts and lore of the monks. In these sequestered spots in Europe, amid the ivy and ves-

Die 14. Martii 1875.

Deus sit tecum, et det tibi gratiam et
virtutem: nam Ipse incepit, et gratiabitur
te confirmet solidetque.

Pius PP. IX.

pers, he drank deeply from fonts of learning, and gathered those rare treasures which make his discourses a storehouse of information even to the most profound scholars of our country.

He thus had friends and correspondents in these institutions of research, reflection, and piety all over Europe and America, and it became the natural desire of the distinguished prelates to bring him into their faith. Many were the efforts to this end in their letters. Wrote Archbishop P. J. Ryan,—

"I feel sure I shall some day meet you and Mrs. Brewster both as devoted children of the dear old church which you have already learned to appreciate in its historic and æsthetic character."

Pope Pius IX. himself, upon the receipt of Mr. Brewster's lecture on Gregory VII., gave him with his own hand the blessing which is given in fac-simile in these pages.

While Mr. Brewster had no sympathy for exclusive or pharisaical denominationalism, he loved all religious effort that had for its object the love of a soul and the lightening of human sorrow, no matter what the theology, the denomination, or the style of presentation. Sects and denominations are as requisite as military divisions, but as inconsequential as nationality itself so far as the ultimate end is concerned. Nevertheless, it is proper that the Castilian, the Frenchman, the Teuton, the Englishman, and the American should each glory in belonging to no other nation.

Mr. Brewster was a potent lay preacher. His discourses were all delivered for a charity, and in them and his college orations are found evidences of his love for all branches of Christian effort. Said he, of a Catholic order,—

"I am not a Catholic, and yet I appear each year to help these holy women, and will continue to do so while life and strength last, because their order is Catholic (that is, universal) in its beneficence. The Catholic and Protestant alike enjoy its blessed protection. The object of these lectures is to obtain your encouraging help:

> "'In faith and hope the world will disagree,
> But all mankind's concern is charity.'"

There was a peculiar appropriateness in the subjects he selected for these discourses, and his own peculiar appearance: stories of Thomas à Becket, Gregory VII., Frederick the Great, St. Patrick, and St. Francis, came from him as the "comely old grand seigneur" almost as from one of the old arch-prelates themselves.

To his own church, the Episcopal, he was especially devoted. His students well remember, in an office talk to them on the beauty of the Episcopal ritual, its conservative associations, and classic utterances, how he once closed by repeating with powerful effect, in deliberate, rolling measure and almost golden-tongued flavor, St. Chrysostom's prayer:

"Almighty God, who hast given us grace at this time with one accord to make our common supplications unto thee, and dost promise that when two or three are gathered together in thy name thou wilt grant their requests; fulfil now, O Lord, the desires and petitions of thy servants, as may be most expedient for them, granting us in this world knowledge of thy truth, and in the world to come life everlasting. Amen."

Methodists and Presbyterians likewise will find, in

his Dickinson College address, his warm admiration for their bodies, and an outline of the important parts these denominations have played in the history of the world,—the Methodists staying anarchy and revolution in England, the Presbyterians giving us a basis for our Constitution.   Said he,—

"Irreligion is a blackguard; no gentleman could entertain such thoughts without waiving his rank and descending to the level of a low-bred man."

"They may fathom the depths of science, and yet may be outstripped by a little child in the knowledge of that which passeth comprehension,—the knowledge of him in whom we live and move and have our being.   The element of piety is the purest instinct of our nature. . . . An abiding faith in him whose service is perfect freedom."

"Believe me, when I say to you that the life you have before you is one of duty.   Let no man start out from this place, decorated with the high commission of his degree, exulting in the false belief that life is a play-game merely.   Morally, mentally, socially, physically, this life is a trial. . . . I say to you again, and earnestly entreat you to take counsel by one who has come here covered with the dust of the world's wayside and sometimes weary with his journey, that the surest road to pain and shame and sorrow is the path of frivolity and pleasure. . . ."

"The lad leaving this school of learning, bent only on using what he has acquired for his own personal gain or promotion, will find before he has gone far that he has left behind some of those equipments that are necessary for success.   The most precious elements of his nature he has neglected, and when he should touch the prize he will find, alas! he is too feeble to grasp it. . . ."

"I do not presume to touch with unhallowed hands the sacred subject of your duty to your bountiful Creator.   Would that I could feel that I was worthy to do so, but I must exhort you, with all the sincerity of my heart, to honor if you will not adore, to believe if you do not profess.   That which was once religious tolerance I sometimes fear has almost degenerated into the recognition of irreligion. . . ."

"Christianity is the common law of this land.   Obliterate it, and the nation would crumble into fragments and perish in a day. Our fathers brought it with them as their most precious treasure, and from it they took all that is pure and true in the institutions they bequeathed to us. . . ."

"From foundations such as these can the thoughtful man only take hope of his country. Let no one mislead himself with the belief that we owe our prosperity and happiness to our political institutions only. That in which modern civilization excels the civilization of the past, whether it be Grecian, Egyptian, or Oriental, is, first, in its higher standard of moral duty, social and individual; second, in the successful application of the revelations of science to the practical purposes of life. Both of these, under God's providence, I believe to be the necessary and immediate result of the faith and doctrine of our holy religion."*

Let us interpret Mr. Brewster autobiographically when he said of Chester A. Arthur,—

"Before I close I must remind you that all those fine qualities of his character were not unconsecrated by religious convictions. If this were wanting we could have found no consolation in our sorrow. His excellence of nature would have been but a shadow. He was not tainted with any philosophical pretensions. He had no affinity with the hostile opinions of unbelievers. He was blasted with no such intellectual conceit. He believed that Christianity was the product of Divine revelation, not the result of human reason; that philosophy did not make it and could not destroy it; that it dwelt in realms of thought and understanding far above the region of the philosophy of schools. He thought that 'to reduce Christianity to philosophy would be to strip it of the future and to strike it dead;' that there is one science which is religious, and another which is not, and that is impious science. By these convictions he lived and died."

---

* Address at the laying of the corner-stone of the Marine Hospital, Erie, Pa., 1868.

XXVI.

The Relation of Mr. Brewster's Literature to his Personality—
Literary Friendships—Memorabilia.

" There is great danger that law reading, pursued to the exclusion
of everything else, will cramp and dwarf the mind, shackle it by the
technicalities with which it has become familiar, disable it from
taking large and comprehensive views."—*Sharswood's Professional
Ethics.*

" The study of letters is the only true consolation in adversity, and
the only embellishment of a prosperous and happy life."

" If you wish to know what public fame is, remember that the
long line of Roman consuls and Grecian magistrates is now forgotten,
while Æsop the slave, Socrates the mechanic, and Horace the son of
a freedman, are immortal."—BENJAMIN HARRIS BREWSTER.

" The thrill of awe is the best thing humanity has."—GOETHE.

MR. BREWSTER'S literature, friendships, and religion were closely related.   He enjoyed a positive
worship in literature that is missed by those who
know it only as an art, rather than " that delicious
self-confessional, the transfusion of thought to
writing."

To make literature but an art would rob it of this
autobiographical character, banish the man behind
the book, and exile our choicest mental comrades.
It is in this nobler literature, whatever may be its
art, that we meet our most thorough sincerities.
Here the fleshly environment—that " thin film of
some emotional non-conductor"—is laid aside, and

the gentler graces, the loves and religions of men, resort, for—

> "—— the ideal, to blow a hair's breath off
> The dust of the actual."

The proud man, guarding his secret tears from public eye, confides their fruit to his manuscript.

> "I knew the mass of men concealed
>   Their thoughts, for fear that if reveal'd
>   They would by other men be met
>   With blank indifference, or with blame reproved:
>   I knew they lived and moved,
>   Trick'd in disguises, alien to the rest
>   Of men, and alien to themselves,—and yet
>   The same heart beats in every human breast."

So it sometimes surprises us to find the theme of all poetry, the burden of all great utterance, resembling closely that natural sincerity of sentiment and belief we have carefully avoided in shamefaced wisdom since the days of childhood. Indeed, this very shamefacedness standing between us and perfect sincerity—even though that sincerity demand confession and tears—is part of the barrier between us and greatness. To apply experience, however harsh, to these early inspirations is greater than to discard them with scoffing self-pity. "Heart speaketh to heart" was Cardinal Newman's motto.

In this light we can interpret aright those cheery assurances of our literature, and see, behind these passages that have helped the world through its despair and revived hope in disheartened souls, the earnest writer striving to reinforce his own melting morality, his own faltering faiths. Such soul-tonics are stronger because coming from the soul most needing them. Thus we have made for us those literary congenialities whose influence upon our destiny is beyond compute, and whose companionship cannot be lost, even at exceptional periods, without emptiness and demoralization. In every life brisk efforts to attain special ends will at times banish these comrades of the mind. And it will be a common experience that life grows insipid and barren when thus for a time narrowed by the rut of engrossing labor. The better nature lies dormant, and there persists a vague protest like an accusing conscience. President Garfield * felt this when, turning in disgust from the details of appointments and places, he sighed for the mental companions of that unseen domain of purposes and ideas—

> " Where loyal hearts and true
> Stand ever in the light."

The real personality awakes when these are restored. We are once more participants at the great centres of thought and purposes, and dwell again among the centuries, instead of in our own brief allotment of time. " Death itself does not divide the wise; thou meetest Plato when thine eyes moisten over the Phædo." Writes Sir John Lubbock, "Poetry has been called the record of ' the best and happiest moments of the happiest and best minds.' Poetry

---

* He said, " Heretofore I have lived in a world of purposes and ideas. Now my days are taken up in deciding whether this man or that man shall have this place or that place."

lengthens life; it creates for us time, *if time be real-ized as the succession of ideas* and not of minutes. It is 'the breath and finer spirit of all knowledge.'" This, then, makes literature a repository of friend-ships. It explains the charm of epistolary passages from friend to friend, and accounts for the fact that letter-writing is pre-eminently a feminine gift, reaching its highest possibility where there is most of soul. It brings from us our best. If we delight in the heroic, is it not "because we have already domesticated the same feeling in our small houses"? The author's text ever needs the key of the reader's sympathy.

It is this very joy of the " fit audience though few" which enables us, through literature, to approach human friends. By finding them fond of what we love in books we ascribe to them the qualities both discern in the medium which so reveals one to the other. It is impossible to picture a loveless, selfish, insincere man dwelling constantly in a literature redolent of the nobilities, keeping a *Memorabilia*, and sending gems to friends,—as though to learn by *that* test if they too love the same rare thoughts and lofty ideals. On the contrary, such an atmosphere implies a wide, broad life,—the only real life. " The hours when the mind is filled with beauty are the only hours when we really live, so that the longer we can stay among these things so much more is snatched away from inevitable time. These are the only hours that are not wasted,—these hours that absorb the soul and fill it with beauty. This is real life, and all else is illusion or mere endurance."

This was the worshipful office of literature that

Mr. Brewster knew. This connected his literature, friendship, and religion. Laying aside all entailed by the incarnation, and entering, within the retirement of his library, into the holy of holies, he "saw the bright countenance of truth in the still air and quiet of delightful study." Said Mr. Wayne Mac-Veagh,—

"I have never been able to forget when I first met Mr. Brewster. In an argument before the court I had indulged with the enthusiasm of youth in a quotation from one of the masters of the English tongue, 'pure and undefiled;' and, as soon as the argument was over, Mr. Brewster came to me with a cordiality of greeting I shall never forget, and insisted upon my going to his house, sitting at his table, and spending the evening in his company; and there in his library he read to me from some of the masterpieces of our prose literature with which he was so familiar,—from Milton, Burke, Lamb. . . . From that day forward we were friends, and our friendship never knew a moment of diminution until the day of his death."

The excellence of Mr. Brewster's work attests that Coleridge spoke well when advising literary men to have another profession. Galileo, Pascal, Goethe, Descartes, Priestley, who laid the foundation of chemistry, Scott, Goldsmith, Charles Lever, Sir Thomas Brown, and our own Franklin, Emerson, Holmes, Longfellow, and Holland,—and hundreds of others whose names will readily occur,—were professional men as well as writers. Of Sir Walter Scott it was said, " His capacity for law he shared with thousands of able men, but his capacity for literature with few or none." The same may be said of Daniel Webster, who lives to-day more distinctly as an American author than as a lawyer. History proves that the highest professional eminence is directly compatible with the noblest order of literary work.

> " Man's genius is a bird that cannot be always on the wing; when the craving for the actual world is felt, it is a hunger that must be appeased. They who command best the ideal enjoy best the real." *

> " It is hardly possible for a man to give out his true inspiration— the real, profound conviction he has won by hard wrestling, or the few-and-far-between pearls of imagination; he must go on writing and talking by rote, or he must starve. Would it not be better to take to tent-making with Paul, or spectacle-making with Spinoza?" †

It is to be regretted that Mr. Brewster wrote so little. He left enough, however, to give the flavor of the soil in which he delved, to disclose the riches he had fallen upon,—and not too much to prevent an easy acquaintance with his work.

Mr. Brewster dared to be sentimental, epigrammatic, heroic, and lofty in his literature. He had no fear of being called a tearful man. He had all the penalties which go with a noble spirit and an impressible nature. The clam's lot has been extolled in popular apothegm as one of considerable beatitude, and to the unfeeling feeling has ever been a crime.

Mr. Brewster's sentimentality was the parent of many of his noblest actions. Cherishing mementos, maintaining a memorabilia, abstracting literary gems, and the " taking of moral stock," all approach this worshipful office of literature. When a downright person rather proudly disclaims such follies, he nearly always gives a clew to his life. and confesses that he has had no self-examinations, no recon-

----

* Bulwer. † George Eliot.

structions of faith and purpose, no transformations by "the renewing of the mind." Without such seasons of purpose-making and self-study, life degenerates into mere designless sleep-walking and sleep-talking,—the theft of our existence—so much of it only automatic reflex with no end in view, so little of it really willed and purposed. It is when a reasonable *because* proceeds each volition that man, self-determinating, has found the way to moral if not temporal greatness.

Lacking congenial friends in the present one may transmit best thoughts to a later self, or when awakened by warmth in books become a self-confessor. We pass this way but once, but one may "ripen the wine of the present in the glooms of the past."

> " Hoc est
> Vivere bis, vita posse priore frui."*

To this worshipful office of his literature, to this calm and intelligent "moral stock-taking," may be attributed the preservation of Mr. Brewster's great dignity of character and ultimate success. They helped him fight self-distrust and morbidness that naturally attend an introspective life, and made him bold to demand that place in the world he knew was his despite disfigurement and contumely.

Literature was not to him a skilful juggling of words and fancies, a faultless art of writing nothing in beautiful chirography, or a fine technique as precise as the mechanical render of an opera. It was

---

* 'Tis twice to live to be able to enjoy the past life once more.

not even the mere genial glow of conversational amenities. It was more. It was an impress upon a personality, a part of his best life, a psychological entity as distinctly a computable force as is the force of electricity,—ay, it was to him one of the eternal verities on which rested his faiths, his loves, and his friendships. Yet he did not allow it to supplant 'that higher office—the surer and stronger panoply of religious principle.' Said he,—

" De Quincey tells us that literature itself will not answer all the desires and ends of the intellect; that the human mind calls for something more with which it *must* be satisfied, or men will waste themselves upon the vulgar excitement of business or pleasure. Selfish, sensuous indulgence of the mind will be visited with stern punishment. Nature resents all excesses. There must be a moral object and end in all you do—a sense of duty and obedience to a nobler purpose than your own enjoyment or your own advancement."

The purity and finish of his style, his gifted fancy, keen wit, singular facility of chaste and copious diction, make his brief literature a model for imitation. Its very brevity commends it, and makes its careful, painstaking study a possibility.

XXVII.

Enmities and Friendships—Associations with Elders and Juniors—
Simon Cameron, James Buchanan, Eli K. Price, W. H. Seward,
and others.

" He has ever rejoiced in the success of every one of us; he has
sympathized with our difficulties and our troubles; he has held out
the hand of encouragement to the young, the timid, and the disappointed."—*The Bar Dinner Tribute to Mr. Brewster by George W.
Biddle.*

MR. BREWSTER's attachments were strong, even
intense. He has been said to be more ready to go
into bankruptcy of pocket than bankruptcy of affection. His enmities, likewise, were strong. No man
of his force of character could pass a long life of
legal and political activity without making enemies.
The numberless causes won by his vehemence made
no friends for him on the opposing side, and his
aggressive and belligerent political course brought
him almost a political ostracism from those who, like
Governor Geary, were made to feel the keen edge
of his invective. As Attorney-General of the United
States he had the "open and avowed hostility of
the worst men in the country," proudly declared to
be his public compliment.

Then, he was an aristocrat, bore himself proudly,
and was outspoken in his pride of ancestry. He had
the broad views and ways of a man whose life has
been made various by learning, whose stand is upon
"the vantage ground of truth." This is always met

with criticism and antagonism. The very consciousness of inferiority makes every low fellow an enemy of the gentleman, and no hatred is more brutal than that of coarseness for refinement.

Mr. Brewster, however, was gentlemanly in his aristocracy,—a condition by no means universally fulfilled—and those near to him knew how warm was his heart, how intense his love for humanity, and how sincere was his respect for honest worth wherever found. One morning he spoke impatiently to a coal-heaver whose baskets blocked his way. "You were born rich and I am poor," said the laborer, and the lawyer bared his head to apologize for the thoughtless words.

His emotional nature made his attachments intense, and drew the warmest devotion from those around him. As a young man, he sought and revered the friendship and counsel of older men. Said he of Eli K. Price, his preceptor,—

"The personal relations between Mr. Price and myself were very close. We were constant to each other. My veneration for him and habit of deferring to his experience from the very beginning gave me a thorough understanding of him; *and it also created an inclination rather to prefer and solicit the friendship of such old and able men. I would encourage all young men to cultivate such associations,* and not to think or feel as Cardinal Reginald Pole did, when he wrote to Henry the Eighth that, 'although a young man, he had long been conversant with old men, and had long judged the eldest man that lived too young for him to learn wisdom from.'"

Mr. Price had written him,—

"Well do I remember the day, though not now the year, when you came to my office, a stripling boy, and the impressive circumstances that preceded; and gratefully do I recall the memory of your uniform respect and kindness, and I may add filial reverence from that day to this; and I am sure these feelings will be with you when I am gone.

"The good I was happy to do you when you were a boy has been many times compensated by your many marks of respect as a man; and you have greatly added to my happiness and pride in that you have made your manhood distinguished in our high profession, by learning, ability, and eloquence. My kindest wish is that you may live to a happy old age, and find as many grateful juniors to cheer your declining years.

"You say forty years ago you left my office for your examination. Forty years ago I was about double your age; I in the maturity of life; you at early manhood, untried in the severe experience of professional life. Time, instead of widening the distance between us, has brought us nearer together. We are now but one-fourth of the years of my life apart; and your experiences are as full as mine, if not as prolonged. Our sympathies run, as they should, nearer together. You confess to a shade of sorrow and look back regretfully to the peaceful days spent in my office. I have had afflictions: they have been blessed to me; by them my faith has been deepened, my immortal hopes made brighter. The peace you love shows your desires to be what they should be. You say *we* are. I more accurately say *I* am 'within the twilight of the setting sun of life.' I sincerely thank God for the force and vitality left me, of which you so kindly speak. I thank you for the repetition of the benediction of the head of the Catholic Church, which you well deserve. The religious element in your character I have always liked. It is immensely preservative and refining to all who are so blessed."

Mr. Brewster's relations with James Buchanan were similarly close at the outset of his career. In a letter already given, we see how thoroughly the culminating President of the Democracy had enlisted the enthusiasm and sympathies of his young manhood. We find Mr. Buchanan writing him, "Pardon me for thus playing Mentor to your Telemachus."

General Simon Cameron was eighteen years his senior. They had met in a political convention in Pennsylvania at which Mr. Brewster had most sharply attacked the rising leader. Cameron remained quiet during the onslaught, only remarking, "*That is a man of convictions,*" and at the close of the convention went to him, discussed with him their differences, and made of him a life-long friend.

Writing from St. Petersburg, while Mr. Brewster was yet in the heyday of his manhood, General Cameron said,—

"I have seen another phase of the world in the entire folly of looking for worldly distinction. *I have now seen it all.* Every sphere in which man can enter I have seen. . . . If you wish to run the round that I have run, you shall have my help. For me, my race is run."

Age, however, brought them nearer together and made them almost contemporaries. In this letter from General Cameron, there are melodies of " Auld Lang Syne :"

" MY DEAR OLD FRIEND,—

"How happy your kind, old-timed congratulations made me. It turned my memory back more than forty years ago when, like boys, we rambled once over ' this broad State of ours,' in the buggy drawn by the black horse, who seemed so glad and proud of his work, while we admired the rich valleys and richer mountains, then only begin-ning to show their long hidden treasures which have since given so much wealth to Pennsylvania.

"Don't you remember Dr. Paliken, of Danville? He was a char-acter, and how glad he was to see us ! and Patterson, of Pottsville,—how full of gentleness and country love he was ! and Mr. Muhlen-burg, of Reading,—what a grand old Roman was he ! so polished, so cultivated, and so hospitable ; and his daughter Rose, so graceful, and so proud of her father! And they are all dead, with hundreds of others who greeted us on that trip through the coal region, between the Susquehanna and the Delaware!

"Why can't we renew that trip next spring? The green sward will still be there, and the bright flowers on the hill-sides and in the meadows, with the grand mountains and the crystal springs flowing from their sides, and babbling over the rocks; and, better than all, the sons and the grandsons of the men who greeted us then will be there still to welcome our coming, in the old-fashioned and hearty manner. Let us try it!

"I want you to come up to my farm, when you have a couple of days to spare, and we will have a nice old time. I have books there, and eggs and milk, and bread and butter, and warm rooms, and no one to make us afraid. A happy New Year to you!

"January 4, 1878."

The tears of Thucydides would never have been drawn by Herodotus had the youth been loitering with boon companions in sylvan dells while the father of history read to the assembled Greeks. So the young advocate at the Philadelphia bar would have lost some of his mightiest aid and inspiration had he not wisely chosen the friendship and counsel of seniors.

When an old man himself, he cherished the friendship of younger men. They were links binding him to life. They were fresh, emulous, appreciative, still holding their youthful sincerities, and unspoiled by worldly contact. Destinies were beckoning them ahead, and perhaps because his own fight had been hard, he loved to help and encourage them, and watch their glowing enthusiasm over what had long since lost its charms to him. This is the great lesson of his life,—that monuments in human hearts and prosperous, happy lives, are better than epitaphs in marble.   His juniors were, too, an actual support to him : they were growing more as he felt himself growing less, and he loved to lean on their strength and sincerity.

"Do you wonder why I ask you for advice on so weighty a subject?" he once asked a young associate; "it is because I know the value of advice from the standpoint of a young man."

"You are now at the bar," he said to another; "I must see that you have practice enough to live comfortably."

Many a young man to-day owes his position in life to Mr. Brewster. "Do I not take care of my boys?" he once said, in affectionate playfulness.

We are never harmed by asking favors for another. The very demand asserts for ourselves a dignity and a position we may not have been accorded before. Besides, all love the attitude of benevolence, and a benefactor is ever afterwards interested in the object which makes this relation possible. Mr. Brewster understood this phase of human nature, and hence never had the small man's fear of asking a benefice for his friends.

Mr. Brewster was therefore worshipped by his young friends with an ardor that no man, however exalted in position, can affect to disdain. Such attachments bring responsibilities that dare not be disregarded. His files teem with letters of gratitude:

"My association with you has been a liberal education, and I shall remember your kindness fondly and gratefully as long as I live.

"BREWSTER CAMERON."

" For kindness at all times, for advice which made me, a lonely boy, a resolute man resolved to make his way in the world,—for the marked attention of your family, but above all to the constant friendship and unvarying kindness of your mother, who I trust watches at the footstool of ' Our Father' over us all, I am indebted for my position and success.

" Lewis C. Cassidy.

" September, 1854."

But so warm and willing were his efforts for the young men with whom he was thrown, that at times preposterous expectations would be aroused. There is a gleam of humor in the motive that preserved evidence of these misconceptions. One young man, just admitted to the bar, modestly desired a judgeship on the Philadelphia bench, which he was sure the influence of his " dear preceptor" could obtain for him. Another, while yet a student, had a difficulty with a government employé over an attempted infraction of the rules of the service, and left him with the threat, *"I'm a student of Benjamin Harris Brewster, and I'll have you bounced!"* The fearful guard sought to protect himself from Mr. Brewster's wrath by appealing to friends, while the great lawyer himself was exceedingly surprised, and both vexed and amused, at requests from influential persons that he reconsider his determination to have this faithful man removed,—upon closer inquiry he would be found blameless of any fault !

Mr. Brewster showed the breadth and range of his sympathies in his very friendships. They spanned all stations in life, from the unknown, untried student in his law office to the prince of statesmen, the kings of finance, the arbiter of social fortune, and the President at the White House;—from the flicker of the garish footlights, the pass and play of journalistic wit, to the nun in the convent, the cowled monk in his cloister, or the prince of the church in pink cassock and cape.

In the hoary monasteries of Europe were spent some of the happiest hours of his life. At the diplomatic board in foreign lands he shone as the brilliant guest of the ambassadors of our own and other nations. At his own home the master and mistress of the histrionic—Joseph Jefferson and Charlotte Cushman—have partaken of his viands, admired his bric-à-brac, and felt the delightful charm of his talk.

William H. Seward was Mr. Brewster's senior by seventeen years. Their friendship was ever constant, and Mr. Seward, like Simon Cameron, had for his junior a word of counsel or commendation at almost every turn or utterance. Mr. Seward was entertained at Mr. Brewster's Philadelphia home when at the height of his popularity. When it was noised about that the great anti-slavery secretary was in the city, admiring friends filled the street in front of Mr. Brewster's home. Their enthusiasm was almost as great as had been the rage of another gathering, similar in slavery sentiment, which, as a coincidence, had filled the same street only a few years before, threatening Mr. Brewster's life for his connection with the Dangerfield case. The contrast between these two gatherings is a striking commentary upon the changing spirit of the times. Mr. Brewster was strongly pressed, and at one time half decided, to accompany Mr. Seward on his trip around the world. It is worthy of comment that when this great leader of New York State passed away and the mantle of his leadership fell upon Roscoe Conkling, Mr. Brewster's relations with this later generation were quite as strong as with the former. By friendships with seniors in his youth and juniors in his age, he thus stretched his political associations over a double generation.

Honorable Jeremiah Black was another celebrity whose friendship Mr. Brewster enjoyed, and whom he often entertained at his home. The toga of Black, in a subsequent generation, fell upon Brewster, and fate willed it so that the junior, whose day had fallen in a later administration, had the sad duty of moving the resolutions before the Supreme Court of the United States at the death of this distinguished Attorney-General of the United States.

General Grant was not only associated with Arthur, Conkling, Cameron, and Brewster in the Stalwart branch of the party, but had a warm personal regard for Mr. Brewster. Just how much he did to favor Mr. Brewster's entrance into the Cabinet is told in his own characteristically frank words.

In the social world Mr. Brewster's connections were equally as marked.

A social leader* has written of him:

"While quietly eating my soup, I saw an apparition. In walked a stately, handsome woman, by her side an old-fashioned, courtly gentleman, in a black velvet sack coat, ruffled shirt, and ruffled wrist-

---

* Ward McAllister, " Society as I have Found it."

bands, accompanied by a small boy, evidently their son. 'There he is,' I said to myself. . . . I stealthily viewed the man on whom my hopes hinged. Remarkable to look at he was.

"A thoroughly well-dressed man, with the unmistakable air of a gentleman and a man of culture. As he spoke he gesticulated, and even with his family he seemingly kept up the liveliest of conversations. No sooner had he reached his coffee than I reached him. In five minutes I was as much at home with him as if I had known him for five years.

"'Well, my dear sir,' he said, 'what made you go first to Frelinghuysen? Why did you not come to me at once? I know all about you; my friends are your friends. I know what you want. The office you wish I will see that you get. Our good President will sanction what I do. The office is yours. Say no more about it.'

"From that hour this glorious old man and myself were sworn friends. . . . He was the brightest and the best conversationalist I have ever met with. His memory was marvellous; every little incident of every-day life would bring forth some poetic illustration from his mental storehouse."

Mr. Brewster was a guest of Mr. McAllister at the latter's Newport villa. Mr. McAllister was one of his warmest friends, and one of those chosen to bear his remains to the grave. Mr. Brewster graced the highest social circles of the metropolis, and his mails were ever filled with remonstrances that his appearances were so infrequent among those who loved to denominate him the prince of their social life.

Notwithstanding all that naturally tended to drive them apart, the relations between General Arthur and Mr. Brewster were of the closest nature. It was because of this close association that, with Hon. Chauncey M. Depew, Mr. Brewster was requested by the New York Legislature to deliver the eulogy upon his departed chieftain at Albany. Mr. Brewster has written of this:

"I had and have a sense of affection for Mr. Arthur which is very lasting; and I have been made to know how fitting it was for me to entertain my regard for him since his death; for, while living, he never failed in giving me his utmost confidence under all circumstances, and since his death his family have told me, to my great content of mind, that all he gave in sentiment was more than felt by him. It was because of that they requested I would deliver the address, saying to me at the time that, from what they knew of his regard and sense of endearment for me, they were assured that it would have been a request that he would have wished."

Among the leaders of his own bar he had many warm friends. In his legal as well as political associations he spanned a double generation,—from David Paul Brown and William M. Meredith, of the older bar, to John K. Valentine, George L. Crawford, Rudolph M. Schick, and Lewis C. Cassidy. Notable among the others was Hon. Furman Sheppard.

Prominent among the literary and journalistic celebrities numbered in Mr. Brewster's immediate friendships were Honorable John Russell Young, who was a constant correspondent, and bore to him the saddest of all relations on the day of his funeral, and his brother James R. Young, who assisted him in administering the affairs of the Department of Justice.

XXVIII.

Last Trip to Europe—Land of the Midnight Sun—Friends Passing
Away—The Brewster Law Library—The End.

MR. BREWSTER made a final trip to Europe after
the death of his wife. Accompanied by his son, he
journeyed into the Land of the Midnight Sun. Here,
July the fourth, 1886, he delivered a patriotic address
as orator of the company of Americans in whose
company he had travelled.

Upon his return to Philadelphia he met many sad
changes. His friends and contemporaries were fast
passing away, and his first public appearance was to
deliver a eulogy upon his old preceptor and friend,
Eli K. Price. The loneliness and change had a most
saddening effect. Standing at the grave of another
dear friend, Hon. William S. Pierce, he said,—

"I have been away from this my home for some years, and now,
when I return and find gone many who were my advisers and early
friends, I feel as if I were not at home. When I returned here to
live with you, and to die with you, when I returned here to be with
you as I have been from the beginning one of you, and every day,
certainly every week, or every month, I find that some one with
whom I was related, with whom I had connections, passes from
sight, I feel as if I were alone. The links that bound me and bind
me to those days when you and I, Mr. Chairman (Hon. Joseph
Allison), were hand in hand, as we were from the beginning, and I
know we will be to the end,—as friends,—are one by one dropping
away, and I am alone.

"These brethren around me, many of whom are personally unknown to me, younger men, can well appreciate and feel as I feel

when they remember that which I now say, how sad and irksome this life is coming to be to me."

It was with this sadness that he set about preparations for the end, and the gathering together of the scattered details of his estate for his son. This involved the disposition of his famed library, reputed to be the finest private law collection in the United States, which is now at the University of Pennsylvania.* Mr. Brewster has expressed himself on the subject:

"I am reconciled to parting with these books because they go together in a place where they ought to be, for a purpose so solemn and, if I may be permitted to say it, so honorable and praiseworthy. . . .

"Before I close, I must say while you were with me, and after you left, I felt and thought that the subject was embarrassing to both of us, but that you with great delicacy smoothed the restless sense that occupied my mind. Neither of us was made to traffic, and least of all on a subject so personal in its character.

"Before I had a boy, my direction by my will was that the public should have my books; but Ben is now here, and I must have a regard for a suitable provision for him. While I have sufficient for myself—and thank God I am not rich!—the price of these books must be added to his patrimony.

"To A. SYDNEY BIDDLE, July 6, 1887."

Mr. Brewster's health had been sadly undermined by his work in the Cabinet. The tranquillity follow-

---

* The Biddle Law Library comprises the noted collection of American, English, Scotch, and Irish Reports, numbering four thousand two hundred volumes, formerly the property of the Hon. Benjamin Harris Brewster, and the gift of George W. Biddle and family, in memory of the late George Biddle.—*Catalogue of the University of Pennsylvania.*

ing his preparations for death, however, left him in better condition. Dr. George R. Morehouse, his physician and friend, at this time made a careful examination of his condition and pronounced him sound in every organ. This cheering assurance impelled him to shake off the gloom of political retirement and broken circle of friendships, and to enter again into active legal business. He was retained as eminent counsel in some great cases, and contemplated adapting himself to the changing order of things. Indeed, he went so far as to negotiate for a branch office at New York, and to outline a law firm of Brewster, Schick, and Savidge.

As the year 1888 opened, however, he became aware of the inroads of disease. He knew the disabling possibilities of uræmic poisoning, and, in fear of impairment of his faculties, he executed the following paper:

"PHILADELPHIA, March 16, 1888.

"Being now about seventy-two years of age, and conscious that certain infirmities and diseases may overcome me, such as paralysis, softening of the brain, and other disabling afflictions, I have considered it prudent to say this:

"I wish that my friend Frank R. Savidge shall be my attorney, guardian, trustee, or committee, if I am in such disabled condition; to manage my estate and be guardian for my son until I die, and if anything prevent him from acting I desire that he shall employ counsel who shall apply to the court to have some competent person perform this duty. I desire Mr. Savidge, if he is called upon to act, to consult with Doctor Morehouse and be guided by his judgment in whatever he may do.

"BENJAMIN HARRIS BREWSTER.

"Witness, JAMES S. NICKERSON."

Mr. Brewster also drew his will at the same time,

witnessed by his friend and associate James S. Nickerson and his two students.

When both papers were drawn, he handed them to Mr. Frank R. Savidge, saying, with some tremor of voice, " Now I am ready for marching orders."

The orders were not long delayed. Several weeks later he was forced by increasing disability to go to bed. Then the end came slowly. His mind was unclouded until the last. From his death-bed he directed Mr. Savidge about the preparation of a case he expected to argue before the Supreme Court at Washington, asking also about some details of his estate. On the morning of April 4, 1888, he passed away, attended by his son and a trained nurse.

Philadelphia and the country at large responded with genuine grief at his loss. The Department of Justice at Washington was draped for thirty days, and the whole national tribute was one of love and esteem.

He was borne to his last resting-place by General Simon Cameron, Ex-Attorney-General Lewis C. Cassidy, Senator Henry M. Teller, Furman Sheppard, Judge Joseph Allison, George L. Crawford, Ward MacAllister, and John Russell Young,—all of whom had been significantly associated with him in his long career.

It was eminently fitting that this comely old apostle of departed days should receive the *Nunc Dimitis* in Christ Church, Philadelphia, hoary with the rime of years,—so ancient that it is classic in American literature. The life had been very, very full. Its activity had been intense. It had reaped the highest honors that can come to a professional man. Its influence, heretofore, had worked with only scattered effect. It had touched other lives only at the visible point of the present. Now, however, as the insubstantial pageant of mortality faded, the completed career became a crystallized lesson, and the most powerful, most beneficent life began. " Now, O Lord, lettest Thou Thy servant depart in peace !"—so went the service. Then the remains were placed by the mother's dust—the life ended, the trophies won, and laid beside the grave.

> " Out of the shadows of the night
> The world rolls into light;
> It is daylight everywhere."

THE BAR MEETING.

THE custom of the Philadelphia Bar to convene at the loss of its worthy members was a tribute greatly beloved by Mr. Brewster. At the Bar Meeting called in honor of Honorable W. S. Pierce, he had said,—

"Meetings of this kind are sometimes the subject of criticism and exception. I know of lawyers who have been heard to say that they wished no Bar Meeting. I hope such meetings will never cease. They are wholesome in every way. They testify to the public that we know what death is; that when it warns us we gather together to mourn for those who are taken, and to express our sense of admonition that the loss conveys. It testifies to the world our affection for each other, and our honor for our profession. . . . Never then let it be wanting to any one of us. Let us gather together filled with a fraternal sense of affection, filled with a sense of sorrow for loss, filled with those high and noble thoughts which, being considered and accepted as an established rule in the profession, prompt all men to live up to purer lives, good deeds, and the conscientious performance of their professional duties."

April 7, 1888, the members of the Bar met to pay to him their last tribute. Justice Gordon, of the Supreme Bench, presided, and Rudolph M. Schick, Dallas Sanders, William Henry Lex, and Frank R. Savidge, Esquires, were named as secretaries.

Resolutions were presented by the Honorable Furman Sheppard, which paid tribute to the rare natural endowments, the legal attainments, the varied scholarship, the forensic powers of the dead jurist; which spoke of the high offices " he had successively held with honor to himself and profit to the public, in which he manifested the same rectitude, fearlessness, ability, and devotion to duty which characterized his entire professional career;" and conveyed the sincere sympathy of the Bar to his family.

Honorable Lewis C. Cassidy moved the adoption of the resolutions, with a biographical sketch and eloquent eulogy. Said he,—

"In his social life, Mr. Brewster was naturally a retiring man He was what some people considered peculiar, but when you knew him it was not a mere oddity. Often that which was thought eccentric or odd about Mr. Brewster was simply the effort to prevent in some degree his appearance from making not only the man himself unhappy, but those who came to see or hear him. But when you crossed his door, got within the influence of his soft, sweet, gentle voice, and elegant manners, all idea of appearance was forgotten, and you were ever afterwards charmed and attached to him. As a conversationalist, I do not exaggerate when I say that he was almost without equal. He attached himself to home and friends with the greatest possible warmth, and I trust that I am not infringing upon the sanctity of Mr. Brewster's home when I say that in the death of his wife he received a stroke from which he never entirely recovered; and when a little while afterwards the President who had called him to a confidential place in his Cabinet, as his Attorney-General and adviser, was stricken to death, I say advisedly that Mr. Brewster was not again the same man. He kept himself to himself, among his books, and saw but few. His life was solitary.

"He was dearly attached to the men that were about him. Forty years ago, and a little more, the speaker, by the kind direction of Providence, sought his office as a student. He not only took pains with me as a student, as he did with all, but he literally took me to his arms, and from almost that day to the day of his death, I felt that I could say to him, 'Wheresoe'er thou goest, I will go. Thy home shall be my home, and thy God shall be my God.' He had attachments, and they were written in brass. He had enmities, but they were written in water."

Honorable George W. Biddle seconded the resolutions, and said,—

". . . Mr. Brewster had another professional trait which it will not be amiss to dwell upon. He was a man whose kindness sprang from the heart, not involved in mere manner, not got up for display; for he was ever willing, ever anxious to assist the rising tyro as well as those whom he had drawn around himself by close relations. His heart and his feelings went out warmly to every one who had proper claims upon him.

"I can recall a single incident, and I suppose it is not out of place to make a passing allusion to it. When he held the highest office that can be held by a professional man, in his effort to oblige a friend he purposely went out of his way to show his personal interest in the matter, and by that display of personal interest he accomplished what was desired. . . .

"He was singularly well read in the noble tongue which is the common inheritance of two mighty nations on both sides of the Atlantic. . . . He had by no means confined himself to the authors of this century, but he was well read in the writings of the earliest masters, and displayed marvellous facility, both with his pen and in oral speech. . . . I know of nothing that can surpass his address on Alexander Hamilton for happiness of expression and comprehensive grasp of character. . . . Again, in 1876, when about to enter upon the Centennial year, he addressed his fellow-citizens in terse and beautiful words, all within the compass of a very few minutes, taking a rapid retrospect of the past, seizing the opportunity to speak of the progress of the country up to the present hour, and speaking of the great Fathers of the Revolutionary period, with marvellous aptitude and beauty, so strikingly, so impressively, so beautifully, that no man could have read it, much less have heard it, without being moved to the depths of his soul. He was a wonderful orator, both with his pen and his mouth, and I know of no man whom I can call his equal."

Honorable Richard Vaux said,—

" . . . Mr. Brewster had two marked characteristics. To those who knew him, and knew him well, and to those who knew him only as an acquaintance, he presented entirely different aspects of character. To those who knew him but slightly, he appeared to be an austere, cold, unsympathetic man, and he was regarded by many as arrogant and aggressive. To those who knew him intimately, who were fortunate enough to become his friends, those impressions proved to be unreal, and they found that he was a man of the strongest possible cordial and kindly feelings. As a friend he was honest, upright, unswerving, unfaltering, and true. In his professional relations he was sometimes aggressive and strongly antagonistic, but it was only in the performance of a mere professional duty with which his inner character had nothing to do. He was a man of vast influence among the people of this city, of this State, of the country. There were those who disagreed with him on many subjects, but like all such men he had warm, devoted friends, and he has left to his friends no other duty than to speak the truth of his character and life. Those who may have differed with him will learn by and by that their impressions of him were mistaken because they did not know him. . . .

" Well, in this case, these associations have at last to be severed. In this case we have at least the character of our departed friend as the highest solace and consolation. His character is pure, his reputation untarnished, and he stands before this Bar, and before the country, as one who deserved high commendation for his integrity and for his sense of honor. While we are thus surrounded by this cloud of sorrow, our faith is encouraged and our hope brightened, because we who remain behind, knowing what we know of him, can see the silver lining around the cloud, and believing, rejoice that he rests in happiness.''

Honorable Wayne MacVeagh said,—

" . . . I am not quite sure that it is a good thing that the profession of the law is so visibly and steadily changing as it is; but I am quite certain that it is wise for both juniors and seniors of the Bar to recognize the magnitude of the change which is occurring. We are not burying to-day the last of the race of great lawyers which have made the Philadelphia Bar famous the world over. Some of them still remain to guide those of us who are left by their side, and every one of them, as well as one of them who is here to-day,—Mr. Biddle,—will echo the wish : ' Serus in cœlum redeas ;' but, after all, the work of the law is changing, and it is not likely that its service will ever again see a class of men such as Mr. Brewster. The law no longer needs those high qualities which were needed in our criminal as well as in our civil jurisprudence of the earlier days. I share thoroughly with Mr. Cassidy the views he entertains as to the inherent importance, usefulness, and dignity of that branch of the profession, though it is no longer as highly esteemed as it once was, nor will the practice of the profession in either branch probably again require the courage which illustrated the character of Mr. Brewster. Every man instinctively felt in his presence that he was a brave man. He did not need to tell it. It did not need to be spoken of while he lived. In his courage and in his sense of duty to his profession he was of a chivalric temperament.

" We are likely to spend the balance of our professional years in different kind of labor. We are, in greater or less degree, destined to serve the great business enterprises which illustrate the great material prosperity of the age in which we live ; and it is an impediment rather than a help to us to possess what he possessed in such an overflowing measure, an ardent public spirit, an ambition to serve the State, such as Burke thought it the highest praise to declare that his dead son possessed.

" . . . When we meet around the grave of our dead brother to-day, we can say of him, and be proud to say it, that he was not only a great lawyer, but was, what is better, a ripe and gracious scholar, and, what is better still, a patriotic citizen, who served not only the law, but also the State, who was brave as becomes a gentleman in every circumstance of his life, and who left in the hearts of those who were privileged to know him best such sorrow as will not soon pass away."

Honorable Henry M. Teller, of the Arthur Cabinet, said,—

" . . . I did not come here to speak of the legal attainments and the high reputation of Benjamin Harris Brewster. His fame is not that of Philadelphia, or of Pennsylvania, or the nation, but of the English-speaking world. I could add nothing to what has been said. His name has been inscribed among the great lawyers of the country—and that is enough.

" It was my fortune to serve with him in another capacity—a capacity that required abilities of high order, an extended acquaintance with politics in its highest sense. For three years I sat by his side from two to three times a week in the Cabinet counsels of Mr. Arthur, the President of the United States, and I want simply to bear testimony here that this great lawyer was not only a great lawyer, but a great statesman ; that upon all questions presented to the Cabinet he was as ready upon international law, upon political economy, upon the science that should govern a great people, as he was in the forum he had chosen for his life-work.

" I repeat that it was for him to demonstrate that he was not only a great lawyer, but a great statesman. Brought in close communion with him every day in connection with one of the Departments of this government, I found it of great advantage to consult him upon the many intricate and difficult questions that were presented to me for my determination, and I always found him, as has been testified here, kind, courteous, capable, ready, willing, with intelligence of the highest order ; and if success crowned my efforts, I feel like recognizing the fact that much of it was due to his advice, and I can say to the members of his profession that I availed myself most freely of his great learning and his sound judgment, I only want to add this meed of praise that it may be known by his friends that, if he was great in the department of which they speak, he was equally great in the other."

Rev. Dr. E. A. Foggo, rector of Christ Church, conducted a brief service at Mr. Brewster's home, No. 205 S. Twelfth Street. Then the remains were conveyed to Christ Church, on Second Street above Market. The office for the burial of the dead was read by Dr. Foggo. The choir sang, "I heard a voice from Heaven."

The interment was made at Woodlands Cemetery, by the side of

Maria Hampton Brewster, his mother. Only the immediate friends and family servants went to the cemetery.

Mr. Brewster's Will.

"In the name of God, Amen. I, Benjamin Harris Brewster, of the county of Philadelphia, in the State of Pennsylvania, attorney-at-law, being of sound mind and understanding, but considering the uncertainty of this transitory life, do make and publish this my last will and testament, hereby revoking all other wills by me at any time heretofore made.

"First, it is my will and I do order that all my just debts and funeral expenses be duly paid as soon as conveniently can be after my decease, and I direct that my funeral shall be conducted in an inexpensive, simple way without parade or ostentation, and that my body shall be buried in the Woodlands Cemetery by the side of my mother.

"Item: I give, devise, and bequeath all of my estate of which I may die seized and possessed, real, personal, and mixed, to Frank R. Savidge, in trust for my son, Benjamin Harris Brewster, Jr., to hold the same in trust for him, and during his minority to apply as much of the income thereof as may be necessary for his support, education, and maintenance. And also in trust to pay over to the said Benjamin Harris Brewster, Jr., until he is thirty years of age, all of the income and profits of the said estate after he reaches his majority. And when he becomes thirty years of age, to pay over to the said Benjamin Harris Brewster, Jr., the entire property and corpus of said trust for his sole exclusive use and benefit, to be owned and enjoyed by him, the said Benjamin Harris Brewster, Jr., absolutely; *Provided*, however, that if the said Benjamin Harris Brewster, Jr., should die under the age of thirty without issue, or after attaining the age of thirty years he should die without issue and intestate, then I give, devise, and bequeath the whole of the said estate so devised to my son to the Sisters of Saint Francis of Philadelphia, absolutely in fee simple, to be used by them for the care of the sick in their hospitals.

"And lastly, I nominate, constitute, and appoint my said friend, Frank R. Savidge, to be the executor of this my will, and I also constitute and appoint him, the said Frank R. Savidge, to be the guardian of the person of my son, Benjamin Harris Brewster, Jr., during his minority, and I enjoin and entreat him to be kind to the dear boy, and to guide him to acquire habits of independence and gentlemanly thrift. And I request my said executor not to file in any public office any inventory of my private property or estate, but an inventory thereof should be made in some book, under the direction of my executor, and preserved among the books and papers of the estate, so that any and all persons having any interest under my will may have access thereto at proper times."

Witnesses to this will were Messrs. James S. Nickerson, H. Gilbert Cassidy, James P. Donoghue, Henry S. McCaffrey.

EULOGIES, DISCOURSES, AND ADDRESSES

OF

BENJAMIN HARRIS BREWSTER.

263

DISCOURSES AND ADDRESSES.

ALEXANDER HAMILTON. *

IT is a difficult thing to do that which I have been deputed to do.
The career of this wonderful man whose statue you are now about to
see unveiled is full of marked historical events. It is impossible to
relate his life, or even to sketch an outline of his remarkable thoughts
and deeds, without repeating the history of our country. He took
part in the first utterances of remonstrance and proposed resistance
to the arbitrary acts of the Mother Country, and, from that moment
down to the fatal end of his great and useful life, he was personally
associated with many of the prominent and triumphant results of that
Revolution, and when our independence was secured he was the
father and the author of the main principles of our national Constitution.

The government was established chiefly by his efforts. As the
financial minister of President Washington, he organized the action
and guided the executive and other functionaries in the inauguration
and administration of the first constitutional democratic republic that
had ever existed. How, then, in the presence of all these startling
and wonderful events associated with the actings and doings of the
great and good who were the actors, can I be able to compress the
object of this discourse within convenient limits? It is hardly
possible, and yet I must attempt it. Those I address must help
me, and with their memories supply all I am obliged to omit, and
thus complete in their own minds that which will be only an imperfect and shadowy sketch. The whole subject thus considered is
majestic and colossal. The magnitude and grandeur of it overawe
me. Alexander Hamilton is the glory of this nation. Jurists, states-

---

* An Address delivered in the Central Park of the city of New York, on
November 22, 1880, on the erection and presentation to the city of New York, by
J. C. Hamilton, Esq., of the statue of his father, ALEXANDER HAMILTON. The
statue was accepted on behalf of the city by Mayor Cooper.

men, and philosophers of all nations will honor and reverence his name. He will be ranked with the greatest and wisest of law-givers and philosophers. Solon and Lycurgus and Aristotle could have sat down with him and found in him a kindred spirit.

We are almost too near to him to take in fully the vast dimensions of his almost superhuman wisdom and genius. Time, like distance, can alone display to men the magnitude and height of his works and thoughts. " In general he has been little weighed and appraised, and in spots only,—never as a whole. His true valuation will be found in the diamond scales of posterity." In this, one of the greatest of cities, he has ever been reverenced.

John C. Hamilton, a surviving son, to-day, with filial piety and gratitude for your veneration of his father, bestows upon you this just resemblance of him whose gentle care he lost at the threshold of his boyhood. This work is to give to you and to posterity some memorial of his presence and bearing, so that men hereafter may see what manner of man he was, to whom such honor is due, and from whom we have received so much. Let me tell you who he was.

He was of an historic and noble race of men. His father was a Scot, his mother French,—a happy mixture of blood conferring qualities that were conspicuous in his whole career. He was born on the 11th of January, 1757, in Nevis, one of the smallest of the Leeward Islands,—a possession of the British crown. Early in life he was left an orphan. His means were slender. Obeying the impulse of his nature, which is in the spirit of his people, in his boy-hood he sought and obtained employment. It was not in his temper to eat the bread of idle dependence ; occupation and usefulness were essential to his very existence. Dignity and independence were the laws of his being, and imparted force and power to all he did.

When he was twelve years old he entered the counting-house of a merchant, and soon commanded the confidence of his employer, who when absent committed his affairs to his control. In this, as in every pursuit he adopted, he displayed aptitude and industry. Incessant, continuous, conscientious labor was the rule of his life. It was soon plain to those around him that he possessed a superior mind that needed and demanded an opportunity for instruction and learning.

To complete his education, in 1772 he was sent to New York, and there he entered King's College, now Columbia College, and while there he was the most diligent of students. In 1774, when he was but seventeen years old, a great meeting was held to protest against the policy and action of the British government. After others had spoken, urged by his convictions and zeal for the cause of the country, he arose to speak, and by the magic of his words and the justice of his thoughts excited the wonder and applause of all. This was followed by a series of articles written by him in defence of the country, which, their authorship being unknown, were imputed to men of established reputation and ability. Those who will read them now will be amazed, as people were then, when they learned they were the production of a college boy. As I read them, they startled me by their concise clearness of expression and precocious wisdom. I am almost tempted to cite here the passages I had marked. I can only ask you to read them, that you may be filled with the same sense of wonder that all have felt who have read them.

When remonstrance repelled ended in resistance, he at once sought and obtained a company of artillery; in command of this he served with skill and conspicuous courage. He was then but nineteen. He is thus described as he marched through Princeton : " This company was a model of discipline. At their head was a boy, and I wondered at his youth ; but what was my surprise when, struck with his slight figure, he was pointed out to me as that Hamilton of whom we had heard so much. He was a youth,—a mere strippling,—small, slender, almost delicate in frame, marching beside a piece of artillery, with a cocked hat pulled down over his eyes, apparently lost in thought, with his hand resting on a cannon and every now and then patting it as if it were a favorite horse or pet plaything."

At the head of this company he continued until March, 1777, when, by special request of Washington, he accepted a place on his staff as aide, with the rank of lieutenant-colonel. Transferred thus from the line of active service in the field, he took his stand close by the side of the general-in-chief, and forthwith obtained and retained his entire confidence. I shall not detail the multitude of important and critical affairs that were committed to him in the dark and dismal days of his military life : affairs that related to regulation and disposition of the army and its commanders ; to intercourse with foreign courts ; to intercourse with Congress and other public authorities, and to and with individuals interested in and connected with the cause of the country. That cannot be done here. The correspondence of Washington with all of these important persons and on all of these serious subjects was committed to him and executed by him, and as they are read they excite admiration and astonishment at his prodigious knowledge and forecast. They would be pronounced the work of a great mind had they been written by a mature man ; but, when it is remembered that he began this service at the age of nineteen and ended it when he was but twenty-two, we are filled with amazement. I cannot recount them, or even do more than mention them in a cursory way as I have done.

While thus in his youth two things were suggested by him which have since been accepted and applied, not only in this but in other countries, the public advantage of which all have experienced, and they were these : When commanding his artillery company and but nineteen, by a letter to Congress he suggested the promotion from the lowest grade of service as the reward of merit and as an incentive to brave deeds excited by high and honorable hopes. His suggestion was adopted. Again, when he was about twenty-two, in a letter to Colonel Laurens, of South Carolina, he proposed to raise battalions of negroes, pointing out how their very habits of servile obedience fitted them for subordination and prepared them for the duties of soldiers. He ended his suggestion by saying, " An essential part of the plan is to give them their freedom with their swords. This will secure their fidelity, animate their courage, and, I believe, will have a good influence upon those who remain by opening the door to their emancipation. This circumstance, I confess, has no small weight in inducing me to wish the success of the project, for the dictates of humanity and true policy equally interest me in favor of this unfortunate class of men."

In 1781 he resigned from the staff and accepted a commission as lieutenant-colonel, and in the same year joined the army and obtained the command of a battalion of New York troops, which became a part of the advanced corps, and, when the British forces entered Virginia, he followed the army to Yorktown with his command, and there signalized himself by acts of daring personal courage and took part at the memorable surrender of the Earl of Cornwallis. This closed his military life. The war was soon ended, and he returned to his civil duties and pursuits.

In this city he prosecuted the study of the law, was admitted to the bar, and at one step assumed the leadership in that profession. Independence had been secured, but with it came a host of dreadful evils.

The whole social, commercial, and political order and economy of society were in confusion, approaching anarchy. The currency was worthless, and all standard measures of value had been destroyed. Debtors were penniless, and creditors without remedy. The very foundations of society were shaken. The States asserted the shadow of public authority for local purposes, and the Congress of the Confederation was without means or credit and too feeble to enforce its enactments. The army was in a state of mutiny and destitution. Those were indeed dark days. For a season despair possessed almost all men. The liberties we had secured we were powerless to maintain and too prostrate to enjoy.

Hamilton never despaired. The causes of this distress he had considered, and the necessary relief he had brought forward. When he was but twenty-two years old, he wrote to Robert Morris, then a delegate in Congress, a letter expounding fully his views on the subject of the finances of the country, and suggested that a foreign loan was the only means of relief. In the next year, on the 3d of September, 1780, when he was but twenty-three years old, he laid before Mr. James Duane, a member of Congress from this city, his plan for organizing the government of this people on a firm and stable foundation. He had at that early age fathomed the whole subject, and with a force of reason that was his great gift he set forth in clear and well-defined words the public wants of the confederated colonies. It was a profound and searching exposition of the actual state of things, and it gives the ruling features of that plan of union which was afterwards adopted and under which we now live. It was the first draft of a great Title Deed conveying supreme popular power to a government created by the people for the public good. I do not use an exaggerated expression when I say that it was an astonishing work of knowledge, wisdom, and genius. It is an unexampled document. There is not another like it in the records of this world's history,—and by a youth of twenty-three years! The plan of the constitution which he afterwards propounded in the Convention, and of which I shall presently speak, was but an elaboration and more detailed proposal of the same thoughts and ideas.

Impressed as by a supernatural call with a sense of the duty that was set before him,—his appointed task, his mission,—he began the work of construction. With this disintegrated, chaotic condition of bewildered colonies walking with tottering steps in the pathways of public authority, with this confused and anxious body of unhappy and enfeebled communities, he proposed to deal. They were to be subjects of his intellectual and moral care.

He knew what had been before attempted from time to time with the same material in the early days of their colonial life. But then they were crawling in their infancy,—then they were the subjects of the Crown,—then they were free from the sorrows of that tribulation which they had passed through, and were now bending under. Now we were independent and must take our place among nations. The necessities of the colonies had in former times united them. In 1643 they had a compact that continued for forty years, and it was for deliberating on all matters of peace and common concern and to provide against impending wars,—a league offensive and defensive. After this, in 1754, at the instance of the mother country, a congress was convened to provide for the necessities of the French War, and this congress proposed a plan of union that was not accepted by the colonies and was rejected by the Crown. In 1765 Massachusetts invited a congress of the colonies to digest a Bill of Rights and deny the power of taxation to the British Crown, and this was followed by the Congress of 1774, and that by the Confederation of 1778, under which we were living when the ratification of peace was obtained in 1783.

With his voice and his pen he labored incessantly to impress upon the people the necessity of establishing a permanent and supreme government, as the only means of restoring order and maintaining the independence we had fought for and won. Here in this State he organized the action of its public authorities to aid in effecting his purpose. He was sent to the Congress of the Confederation, and there, with earnest, persistent zeal, he labored. Finally, as the fruits of his efforts, the States authorized delegates to convene, and they met in Philadelphia on the 14th of May, 1787.

This convention deliberated and sat until the 17th of September of the same year. Of this body he was a member. The Virginia plan, and the plan of Mr. Charles Pinckney, of South Carolina, and what was called the Jersey plan, presented by Mr. Patterson, were all submitted and discussed.

The Virginia plan gave supreme authority in all national matters, with a negative on the State laws and with express authority to use the public force against a delinquent State. The Jersey plan made one single legislature, and, among other peculiar and impractical features, acknowledged the sovereignty of the States. On the adoption of one of these plans the Convention was much divided. They were both dangerous. The Virginia plan, as Hamilton said, was " to enact civil war." The other led to anarchy. The dissolution of the Convention was feared.

Hamilton stood alone, and at this critical moment he presented his own plan. Mr. Madison has said of it, that it was "so prepared that it might have gone into immediate effect if it had been adopted." Read it now, and read it side by side with the Constitution, and we can at once see how near the one is the counterpart of the other. It was changed and modified to meet conflicting opinions and to avoid objections, but as an entire paper the resemblance remains. It is a marvellous production of intellect and of wisdom; no such thing was ever done before; no such plan of nationality was ever projected by the reason or wit of man. That it could have thus been done passes human understanding. It is the best-adjusted scheme for composing all differences in dispute and reconciling all points of contention that could have been suggested.

The danger that attended the execution of the national powers and the existence of State authority he foresaw and dealt with. The fierce trial through which we have just gone he predicted and provided for. State sovereignty he regarded as the seed of anarchy—

> " Tractas et incedis per ignes
> Suppositos cineri doloso."

Had public men in authority heeded his warning and repressed this dangerous element, the war that well-nigh destroyed us would never have happened; but the value of his wisdom was seen and felt in the power that was retained to assert the national authority and maintain the national life.

How finely he expresses the spirit of our government, which is the spirit of our people, when he said, " We are now forming a republican government. Real liberty is neither found in despotism nor in the extremes of democracy, but in moderate government. Those who mean to form a solid republican government ought to proceed to the confines of another government. As long as offices are open to all men and no constitutional rank is established, it is pure republicanism. But if we incline too much to democracy, we shall soon shoot into monarchy." This was but the echo of what he had written and published when he was but seventeen years old. " But a REP-RESENTATIVE DEMOCRACY, where the right of election is well secured and regulated, and the exercise of the legislative, executive, and judicial authorities is vested in select persons chosen really and not nominally by the people, will, in my opinion, be most likely to be happy, regular, and durable."

And as to pure democracies he said, "No position in politics is more false than this. The ancient democracies did not possess one feature of good government; their very character was tyranny, their figure, deformity. The true principle of a republic is that the people should choose whom they please to govern them. Representation is imperfect in proportion as the current of popular favor is checked. This great power of free government, popular election, should be practically pure, and the most unbounded liberty allowed."

These expressions of his thoughts and convictions, uttered by him in the debates and discussions in the Convention and elsewhere, I give that it may be seen how clear and well-defined then were his ideas of the use and beauty of popular liberty and popular suffrage to express popular will, maintain public order, secure private right, and enforce public and private duties. They are all plain enough to us now, but then men were startled with them. No such thoughts of organized popular power to produce such stable results for national ends had ever before then been enforced and uttered. To all but to him they were ideal and theoretical. Now they are real, institutional, practical, common.

Then there were but three millions of people for whom the government was provided; but he pointed out that it was prepared for an empire of millions. He said, "We have three millions of people, in twenty-five years we shall have six, in forty years nine millions." And now we have over forty millions, and, at the same ratio of increase, at the close of this century it will be one hundred millions; and by the year 1930 it will be swollen to the enormous number of two hundred and forty-six millions, nearly equal to the present population of Europe! When we contemplate this in its almost superhuman and unexampled growth, we can but feel a sense of gratitude and awe for the genius of that one man who thus foresaw the needs of such a people, and provided, from the chaotic fragments of its early being, the form and order of government that made it a nation and prepared the way for its growth and the preservation of its rights and liberties. This intellectual vision could see the promised land he was not to enter. Thus he prophesied as if inspired with supernatural power.

The Constitution was adopted, and to that great paper are appended the names of George Washington, Benjamin Franklin, and Alexander Hamilton,—a conjunction of human greatness, human wisdom, and human genius never before so united.

Then began his real labor. With his pen, with his speech, and with his personal influence in the New York Convention and elsewhere, he was tireless. In the *Federalist,* written mainly by him, aided in part by Mr. Madison and Mr. Jay, he expounded those doctrines that were to secure the adoption of the Constitution. For all time those papers will remain as the just and true exposition of its purpose and fitness for its end. Other papers he prepared and issued, and all to effect the same result. From his pen flowed limpid streams of pure thought and demonstration on those high themes of public right and private duty that have never been surpassed, and which he submitted to the reason and the moral sense of the nation. When Congress first assembled it enacted and proposed for the ratification of the States the first ten amendments to the Constitution. All but one of them were contained in the declaration and amendments before offered by Hamilton in the Convention of New York.

President Washington was inaugurated, and Mr. Hamilton was chosen by him to occupy the post of danger and difficulty,—the Treasury. All other positions then, as compared with it, were mere formalities of state. The first important act was the organization of his department, and to this day the order and discipline he established stand untouched, and are admitted to be perfect and complete for all the purposes of its vast and intricate necessities. The adjustment of the finances of the nation was the great task that he was to execute.

The war had left the country deluged with valueless paper and weighed down with debt, and the States were alike crippled with what were then debts of vast amount. To the cry of the dishonest he would not listen. He proclaimed that the public debt was the price of our liberty and it must be accounted for. Public honor and private morals alike demanded its payment. Furthermore, he advocated the assumption by the nation of the State debts incurred in the prosecution of the war, and after angry and fierce resistance he sustained himself and prevailed, and his measures were all adopted. He always prevailed, for he appealed to the conscience and the moral sense of the people to scorn dishonor and uphold justice. His plans were prosperous, and soon the credit of the whole country rose ; confidence was established; tranquillity existed in every avenue of public and private affairs. His Reports to Congress were numerous and frequent. They were submitted to stern and searching legislation and popular criticism. They are now, and they will be to the end of our natural life and far beyond it, memorials of the marvellous knowledge, wisdom, and thought of this wonderful man. What they maintained and propounded became the fundamental law of the land, and through them we secured (and as long as they are observed will retain) the vigorous national life we now enjoy. All concerns of the public administration were treated of by him.

The mint, the currency, public debt, public credit, public loans, and the foundation of national banks, foreign and internal commerce, the laws of navigation, foreign and internal taxes and duties, public highways, internal improvements, the American system of protection for domestic industry, the public lands, the organization of the army and navy, the foundation of a military school at West Point, the extinction of foreign title to and authority over dominions within our national territorial limits, the disposition of the Indian tribes, the rights of belligerents and neutrals, the rights and duties of States and their citizens, the establishment of the national judicial authority and the reorganization of it as the sole arbiter in disputed questions of Constitutional construction, which he pronounced to be what it has been and is,—the citadel of public justice and public purity ; the liberation of the slaves, the naturalization of foreigners,—all of these were the subject of his thoughtful consideration. Sovereignty he believed and taught was of necessity vested in the United States as the supreme authority of the nation. To the States he conceded rights that were to be held inviolate and inviolable. Local authority must be maintained to establish and preserve local order, local protection, and local relief. That was needed for the peace of society and to secure the possession and enjoyment of private property and personal, individual rights ; and in a vast territory like ours, as it then was, with a scattered population and imperfect means of intercourse, it was also essential as a political element to excite and keep alive a public feeling, and to interest men in the support of all government, general and local, and to check the undue exercise and action of national authority through unreasonable and irrepressible agents.

State sovereignty he saw and said would lead to anarchy, and that he resisted. The object of government was unity of power in one supreme head, for the sake of peace, for the sake of order, for the sake of law, for the general common good, and for the preservation of personal liberty.

I shall not even allude to the parties that were created or the men who led those parties. I shall not speak of those contentions. The motives and purposes and actions of other men towards him, or his opinion of or acts towards them, I shall hold beneath the dignity of this occasion. All of that I shall dismiss and pass by. I must speak of him and treat of him as he would have me do if I were now to speak in his great presence,—conflicting with the fame of no one, not arraigning the opinions, or acts, or motives of any man. We are in a purer, higher atmosphere of thought and reflection. I am here to recount the grand things that he did, and to remind you of the great debt we all owe to him. I shall not compare him with any one. The plane of his nature was distinct and apart from that of those around him, " for one star differeth from another star in glory." While he was at the head of the Treasury, intricate questions of foreign policy arose which were submitted to his consideration. The treaty with Great Britain was the occasion of much public excitement. It concerned our foreign commerce, our internal affairs, and the final adjustment of all outstanding questions of dispute between us and the mother country. In settling this, his advice guided the administration.

At the same time our relation with France was a subject of serious importance. The world was shocked and startled with its great Revolution. The public man who rose on the ruins of that ancient monarchy would have forced us into an offensive and defensive alliance with them. The popular sentiment here sympathized with the people of France, and our sense of gratitude for the aid that Frenchmen had given us prompted a public wish to be united with them. But against this heat and frenzy Hamilton opposed his judgment, and so shaped the course of the administration that we were not entangled with those contentions which soon made a continent one great camp, and all Christian Europe a battle-field. " Storms and darkness, under cover of which innocent blood was shed like water, fields were fought, frenzies of hatred gathered among nations, such as cried to Heaven for help and for retribution."

This he foretold, and this, too, he avoided. But I am admonished by the multitude of events that he ruled and which I must relate if I continue thus, and so I must pause. He had frequently resolved to retire. The growth of his family and his diminished means worried him. The object he had in accepting the Treasury was attained. The methods he had proposed had been accepted and were prospering. The relief he had promised had been secured and his end was answered; beside all, the contentions of public life were odious to him. By the persuasion of Washington he had remained, but in 1795 he surrendered his seat in the Cabinet and retired to follow his profession and to enjoy the tranquillity and happiness of his home. Now let me read to you what Washington at this time wrote to him.

"PHILADELPHIA, February 2, 1795.

"DEAR SIR,—After so long an experience of your public services, I am naturally led, at this moment of your departure from office (which it has always been my wish to prevent), to review them.

"In every relation which you have borne to me I have found that my confidence in your talents, exertions, and integrity has been well placed.

"I the more freely render this testimony of my approbation because I speak from opportunities of information which cannot deceive me and which furnish satisfactory proof of your title to public regard.

"My most earnest wishes for your happiness will attend you in your retirement, and you may assure yourself of the sincere esteem, regard, and friendship of, dear sir,

"Your affectionate,
"GEORGE WASHINGTON."

He returned to the practice of his profession, and in it he prospered. The necessities of his position and his personal associations, combined with his anxiety to see the administration of the government properly conducted, still obliged him to take part in the selection of candidates for public office. Of this interest he could not divest himself. It was a part of his nature.

He was born to lead and think and feel for the public. In those days party feeling was strong even to personal violence. We do not now know of such bitterness. Then it degenerated into rancor and malice. The institutions he bestowed on us have civilized and humanized men.

His opposition to some aspiring men, and his open censure of their ways and purposes and actions as being hurtful to the general public good, and the fact that his opposition was destructive of their hopes, excited a hatred for him that was deep and fierce. It was resolved that he should be removed. A man of note, but of desperate fortunes and wicked ways of life, sought a quarrel with him, and called him to account on an indefinite charge of having spoken of him words of condemnation.

It resulted in a challenge. I do not propose to enlarge on this sorrowful, wretched subject; but I will say that at this day few men would hold themselves responsible thus on such a complaint and so presented.

The purpose was to have his life. Then men answered to such calls under an impulse of military honor. We had just emerged from a long war, with the habits and principles of the camp infused into our social, personal, and public life. He met this adversary, a man prepared by practice and determination of purpose, who, with cold, merciless deliberation, murdered him.

> " That hand shall burn in never-quenching fire
> That staggered thus his person."

The man who did this act turned aside from the scene of his guilt to meet a punishment that few have suffered. He lingered through a prolonged life of bad deeds and meanness, an object of detestation in this community, who looked upon him to the end of his evil days with mingled feelings of contemptuous abhorrence and scorn.

Thus passed away this soldier, this patriot, this orator, this statesman, subtle in his knowledge of mankind, this philosopher and perfect citizen. There was nothing vile or mean in his nature; all was heroic and noble. His intellect was clear and high; his understanding sound; his heart pure; his will imperial and commanding. " *Justum et tenacem propositi.*"

I must not omit to make mention of one other conspicuous feature of his character. He was not inflamed with that sense of self-sufficient conceit which scoffs at faith and glories in unbelief. With all his triumphant genius and splendor and force of intellect, he believed with humility and bowed with submissive awe. He had read and learned that " Blessed is the man that walketh not in the counsel of the ungodly, nor standeth in the way of sinners, nor sitteth in the seat of the scornful; but his delight is in the law of the Lord, and in his law doth he meditate day and night." He did not " sit in the seat of the scornful." There, then, behold this presentment of him. Reverence him; obey his precepts and glory in the result of his grand labors, and be equal to the duties of that great citizenship of this mighty nation which he of all men was the first to secure for you. His fame cannot pass away. It will last forever. It will be as plain and enduring to all mankind hereafter as if it were written in the face of Heaven and every letter were a star.

THE RELIGIOUS FOUNDATION OF COLLEGIATE LEARNING.*

PROMPT acceptance of such a duty as I am now about to perform is a tribute that all educated men owe to society and to the State at large. Nothing but other and pressing obligations should ever hinder us from gladly responding to the partial kindness of those who invite us to contribute to these annual academic holidays.

I said all educated men owe it to the State to come out on these great days, when boys put aside the things that are childish and, clothed with the academic "toga virilis," are soon to be enrolled in the ranks of that quiet army of cultivated men, whose solemn duty it is to maintain public order and to enforce by blameless lives the precepts of sound morality.

In a monarchy the man owes all to his sovereign. In a republic of freemen each man owes all to the State, and his first and greatest duty is to strengthen the moral tone of his own life, so that his action may prompt others, and thus public morality may flow in a pure, broad, deep current, and the examples of public life be examples of heroic virtue and individual usefulness. Educated men should live as if they devoted themselves to public duties, and if necessary sacrifice themselves; and those who do may best claim the title of heroes.

This faculty of sacrifice and devotion has been well called divine. Superior talents favored by opportunity and education may exalt some; but they can never compete with those who possess this divine heroic quality.

I have been moved to these reflections by the recollections of my own life. Young gentlemen, as I sat down to prepare this discourse, I paused and cast back my mind to the time when I stood where you now stand. It is forty-five years ago, and yet it looks as if it were but last year.

All who were with me then are with me now, and time and space and all the incidents of being are passed away, and I am in the presence of those who honored me with my commission of early manhood.

---

* An address delivered before the Literary Societies of Dickinson College, Carlisle, Pa., June 24, 1879,—ninety-sixth Commencement.

Then, again, I remember the time when I was recalled from the active pursuits of a stirring life, and commanded to give an account of my own experiences, and speak for and to the fellows of my Alma Mater, as I now speak for and to you. These recollections reminded me of the necessity for the service I now undertake, and the object of these eventful celebrations.

It is not an occasion for idle display; you did not come to hear verbal flights of vapid rhetoric and high-sounding phrases. It is for a more serious purpose. This is one of the recurring necessities of civilized, cultured, social life. I am to speak a layman's homily, not a declamation filled with patriotic platitudes or fantastic sentimentalities. Let us then reason together as we can and should; for we all of us are academics, old and young, and have much in common.

The light-hearted lads who surround me, and the serious and sedate seniors now present, all stand on a common platform, all stand on the same level of scholastic and philosophic training,—students all. In retreats like these we all acquire habits of life, and of thought, and of feeling that can be obtained nowhere else. The peculiar characteristics and qualities of a collegiate student are known with no other order of men, and they have prevailed and will prevail all over the world wherever such institutions exist, modified only by surrounding associations; but still in all their elements and consequences the same. It is a guild of men,—a brotherhood,—a service that has its traits, and obligations, and duties that are conspicuous and point out and mark them wherever they may go.

The disciples who followed the footsteps of Socrates, or hung on the golden words of Plato, or listened with trembling intensity of thought to the subtilties of Aristotle, were inspired with the same zeal for knowledge and culture that must have prompted most of you, and had the elements of the same remarkable ways of life that have unconsciously been adopted by you. As I before said, students all—all alike.

The men who thronged the halls of public teaching in Athens and Rome and Alexandria, ofttimes in large numbers, listening to and learning from the Philosophers, the Sophists, and the Rhetoricians, were in their day men such as you are and will be.

After the wild and ferocious tribes had swept away Roman, Grecian, and Egyptian civilization, and blasted all things with the consuming fire of their savage desolation, the first centres of thought, of learning and culture, were the great monastic homes of the Benedictines. From the sixth to the thirteenth century the education of Europe was Benedictine. In their mountain cells they were preparing for the European intellectual growth. They were planting the seed of its future intellectual harvest. But all this was passing away. Soon the world was stirred by the crusades, the spiritual, martial, commercial, and intellectual enterprise of those days. Then from the gloom of cloistered life, where they were almost hidden, learning, knowledge, and culture went out and deserted the quiet of those homes of stability and meditation (where men thought much and talked but little), and mingled in the concourse of the world and in the tumults of great cities.

Monte Casino, Fulda and Bec, St. Gall and Citeaux and Cluny were avoided; and Paris and Naples and Bologna and Cologne were swarming with students and scholastics and clerks, all active, and often boisterous, and even rebellious and riotous, in their pursuit of intellectual excitement, and too often wild and sensual pleasures.

In the twelfth century these multitudes were drawn to Paris as a common focal point, there to listen to the eloquence of Anselm, of William of Champeaux, and of the marvellous Abelard. At the same time Bologna and Modena and Orleans and Padua and Salerno and Salamanca and Toledo and Oxford were crowded with scholars. But of all these Paris was pre-eminent in the dazzling attainments and parts of her illustrious teachers, and in the vast population of its students. Scholars from all quarters of Europe flocked there. They were divided into nationalities, and not by schools. Popes patronized and protected, censured and blessed them. Kings were present at their pageants, where oftentimes five thousand graduates would receive their degrees. Once the University sent twenty-five thousand students to take part and represent it in a great funeral.

At other universities great teachers were surrounded by vast followings. Why, Olfred lectured to ten thousand pupils and listeners at Padua.

All this was in the twelfth and thirteenth centuries. These Parisian students were a fierce body of intellectual demagogues— a flaming commune of brawling scholars.

Mixed with those who came for study were those who came for excitement and love of riotous disorder. Some were poor and destitute, and others were rich and prodigal; some were modest and laborious, others were conceited and ostentatious, noisy and vain-glorious. There were those who were starving and friendless; some-times one garment served for three who wore it by turns. Two went to bed, while the third put it on and went to the school. Paris was then the centre of dialectical disputations, and of intellectual gym-nastics.

From its gates went seven popes, and there were cardinals, arch-bishops, and bishops without number. Lully, the Spaniard, Albertus Magnus, St. Thomas Aquinas, the angelical doctor and Christian rival of Aristotle, with Dante and Petrarch, three great Italians, and scores of other men, illustrious in their day and known even in ours, sat in its school and gloried in having disputed in the presence of Duns Scotus. At Padua, in the sixteenth century, there were forty thou-sand students.

Before Luther's day there were sixty-six universities, sixteen of which were German. In 1231 Oxford had thirty thousand students. From these nurseries of reason and the understanding descended the modern schools of learning and science. But the grandeur and glory of this kind of life have passed away. The great followings and attendance of the German universities of our own day and of the past generation cannot compare with the legions of students that darkened the halls of these learned colleges of the middle ages.

They were like great camps of armed men, gathered together for conquest and glory. These hosts exist no more in such vast congre-gations, but the students yet exist, scattered everywhere. They are not weakened in their thirst for knowledge. The universities and colleges and schools have multiplied, and the army is divided, stationed at the different posts of learning. It is not disbanded, intellectual culture is scattered, and floods of its light beam on the whole earth, and a few men are no longer supereminently conspicu-ous. Mankind is elevated to a higher table-land of knowledge gradually diffused, and comfort, refinement, and gentleness follow in its train. Like the sword of the Cid and the cimeter of Saladin this spirit of culture gains glory and honor wherever it goes.

Thus far my thoughts have rested with those houses and asylums of learning and dialectical acuteness. They were the intellectual granaries of the old world and of redeemed Europe. Their influence is stamped deep into the substance of European thought and European life, and is felt at this hour in this far-off American seminary of learning, thought, and religion,—felt, too, in the numberless schools and colleges and universities that fill our land to enlighten and exalt our people.

We must remember that the great colleges and universities were the first fruit of the monastic life of early Christian Europe. They were the product of religious minds, and were maintained and established to propagate religious knowledge and theological learning. They were presided over by men of religious vocation, and their chief lecturers and teachers were all attached to the Church by some official relation, or as members of some of the great order of monks. The great divinity scholars of the times were the most conspicuous in their faculties. From those days to ours, in England and in this country, such has been the origin of nearly all of the schools of learning. On the Continent the rule has been otherwise. The great universities I have spoken of are no more. They have been supplanted and supplied by new schools in new places. In France and Germany, and even in Italy, the successors of those learned and subtle scholastics and clerics have been and are generally laymen, disengaged from the Church, pursuing science and letters professionally.

The important chairs of modern European schools are filled by scholars and scientists appointed by the State or its officials, to whom it delegates the power of appointment and visitation, and not by priests or clergymen selected by the Church or its representative bodies. The great English universities, and nearly all of the prominent and prosperous colleges and universities of our country, are in the custody of the religious denominations that founded and established them. In 1636, sixteen years after the settlement of Plymouth colony, Harvard University was established at Cambridge. It was then the centre of all puritanic practice and dogma, and was founded to maintain, by means of education, the faith that then pervaded the whole of that rigid and stern race of religionists. William and Mary, of Virginia, was founded in 1693, and so in 1700 Yale, and in 1748 Princeton, in 1753 the University of Pennsylvania, Columbia College in New York City in 1754, and Dartmouth in 1770, while this, your own dear nursing-mother, Dickinson, soon followed, in 1783. Now, of all these, but one in the outset was disconnected with denominational control, and that was the University of Pennsylvania; and even it was from the first moment of its life influenced and supervised by clergymen. The additional charter of 1775 selected the Rev. William Smith as Provost, and the Rev. Francis Allison as Vice-

Provost, while the act of 1779, among other things, especially provides that the senior minister in standing of the Episcopal, Presbyterian, Baptist, Lutheran, German Calvinistic, and Roman churches, in the city of Philadelphia, or within two miles of the old Court-House, on High Street, together with other eminent laymen, shall be trustees of the University of Pennsylvania.

From these five nurseries have grown up a throng of academic senates that yearly scatter their graduates through this nation. For we have now more than four hundred colleges and universities, schools of divinity and medicine, and of these there are not fifty that are not directly under the protection and control of some religious society—some branch of the Church of Christ, so that the pious influence that first moved the secluded monasteries in those far-off patristic days to educate men and to train them for usefulness here and for the joys of a better life hereafter, still breathes its holy and harmonizing spirit over these our retreats of learning, philosophy, and religion. Thirty-five years after Princeton had been founded by the fathers of the Presbyterian Church on this continent was this, another of their schools, planted here in this fertile valley.

The State endowed it, and the great Church of our revolution possessed it. Then that denomination exercised a powerful influence. Its form of government was that of a representative democracy, and the doctrines of its confession were cast in all of the stern severity of Calvinistic logic. The intellectual training of its clergy, and the educational fruit of their preaching upon their people, had excited a spirit of independence of men and heroic faith in God. Can it not be said that it is to their united fidelity in the cause of their country, and unflinching assertion of human rights, we mainly owe the liberties we now possess? It was the patriotic Church of the country. Its members organized the revolution that ended in independence. The very form of their church government furnished to us the draft of that which when modified and adapted to public and political purposes became the Constitution of this nation. Their churches were schools where men were taught their religious duties, and where their minds as well as their hearts were cultivated. They were and are a great race of men, thinkers and workers equal to all fortunes and superior to adversities. We owe them much, for they infused into our early public life a manly spirit of Christian faith that never has forsaken us, and which has been the greatest element of our national dignity, virtue, and prosperity. The name of a colonial governor of the State was given to this college, and it proudly retains it yet. Its first president, like Witherspoon and McCosh of Princeton, came from Scotland. Dr. Charles Nesbit, a man of eminence as a scholar and a divine, at the age of fifty was tempted by a desire to do good, and he came here, and his coming was felt to be a great gain. Under such auspices did the life of this college begin. The credit and renown of his learning linger around your halls to this hour. Dr. Benjamin Rush was one of the first and most zealous patrons of this college. As an intellectual and scientific thinker and as an active and earnest man he was one of the greatest of those times. His name will long be remembered by Americans as that of a philanthropist, patriot, and philosopher. Thomas Cooper, a most conspicuously learned and accomplished Englishman, also in those early days taught here, as he did in the University of Pennsylvania, and afterwards in the University of South Carolina, where he died.

I do not propose to enlarge on the history of this college: I only advert to those noted and able men whose names are linked with the first fifty years of its fitful and feverish life. During those times it enjoyed some years of prosperity and of fame. Nearly five hundred graduates received their degrees, and many of them were men of mark and usefulness in their after life, men that our country is proud of; such men as James Buchanan and Roger B. Taney and Robert C. Grier would adorn the annals of any college, for they were able and upright public men and illustrious citizens.

Princeton was first founded by and first attracted the love of the Presbyterian Church. It was the Geneva of America. The public men who came up from the South to Congress, at Philadelphia, then the commercial and social metropolis of the country and the political capital, brought with them their sons, and sent them to Princeton because it was convenient to them, and because their teachers and pastors at home commended that great school to their pupils; and thus it was that Nassau Hall enjoyed their patronage, and from that source a great number of students were diverted from Carlisle, and gave to the college of New Jersey the long roll of public men whose names are historical and whose political honors reflect such lustre on their Alma Mater. It is thus I can explain how it was that Presbyterians did not much add to the practical prosperity of this college. For a while adversity and poverty seemed to follow its career, until finally its doors were closed and it slept, but to awaken to a new day of usefulness, happily under the control of another sect of evangelizing Christians, whose great works are felt as a stimulating and fermenting element of action throughout all Christendom, and whose vitalizing influence has since been felt and will be felt through all time. In 1833 the buildings, grounds, and apparatus of the college passed into the custody of the Methodist Episcopal Church, and at its head was placed Dr. John P. Durbin. It was my good fortune to know that gentleman, and I can readily understand how well he guided and ruled over its interests.

He was a man of remarkable simplicity, and ease, and grace of manner, and tenacity of purpose; he had unusual business abilities and aptitude for the affairs of men, while he was quiet and modest in his bearing. He had a large store of learning, and was gifted by nature and grace with a pure, pious intellect, that imparted a sense of serenity and tranquillity wherever he went, and to all this he added a nobility of soul that made his whole life a grand career of public usefulness and private worth. About him he gathered a working faculty of earnest and well-prepared men. Among them was John McClintock, whose sad and early loss the Church and the scholars of the country yet mourn. I am tempted by my knowledge and recollection of this superior man to pause and dwell upon his works and merits. We were boys together, and fifty years ago studied at the same school, kept by that grand old Hebrew and Greek scholar, Samuel B. Wylie. Then in his boyhood he was conspicuous for his aptitude and industry in acquiring knowledge. He was a rapid and ready scholar, and a bright, clear, accurate thinker. In him, truly, " the child was father to the man." His career was easily foreseen. He did not mislead the hopes of any one : all that he promised to be he was to the fullest measure of expectation. Alas for all of us! he was swept away. "*Pallida mors æquo pulsat pede pauperum tabernas, regumque turres.*" I could and would gladly say much more in honor of his worth, goodness, wonderful attainments, and bright points ; but the necessity of brevity admonishes me, and I will pass on and resume the current of my discourse. I said that happily this college was now under the control of the Methodist Episcopal Church. It is well for the college and its prosperity, but it is better for the public at large, and especially for the Methodists, that it is so.

From the hour that they assumed the care and control of it, the career of its usefulness has been widened, and the community of learned and unlearned have had a conviction that its power must become established and permanent. The very educational wants of that vast religious authority will secure it a favor and following that can maintain it. That Church needed just such a post of learning, to which, in the heart of its great sphere of action, it could bring its growing young men and prepare them for the ministry, or under the influence of its own trained doctors—men of piety and learning and science—fit them for the other walks of life, while they kept alive within them the sacred flame of holy religion. There was a time when, strange to say, the educated and better class of people in this country and in England believed all Methodist clergymen to be illiterate, ranting zealots,—blind leaders of the blind. Those days have passed away, and those people now know their error. Why, the Methodist Church was, and is, a branch of the Established Church of Great Britain. John Wesley, founder of this immense organization, was the son of a clergyman of the Established Church. Both father and son were graduates of Oxford, and so was his brother Charles Wesley, the right arm of his mission. They were both men of thorough classical, biblical, and intellectual training, and so were others of that Church, companions and the associates and co-operators of theirs, at that time. There was the inspired evangelical orator George Whitefield, an Oxford man also, and the famous biblical scholar Adam Clarke, and with them were Fletcher, Benson, and Doctor Coke, and Pilmoor, and Burridge, and Romaine, learned in Hebrew, and Doctor Walker, a senior fellow of Trinity College, Dublin, and others, whose names I cannot pause to repeat. Aside from the sacred and inspired acts of his marvellous career, no educated man will deny to John Wesley wonderful attainments and gifts as a mere man. Lord Macaulay has well said of him, that he would have ranked with Richelieu, or any others of the great organizing and executing spirits, that have established empires and directed their destinies. His labors, trials, and sufferings were incessant, and lasted for sixty-four years; he died when he was eighty-eight years old. During his great mission he preached forty-two thousand four hundred sermons alone. What a life of real glory was that !

But before I pass from this, let me recall the grandeur of the career of George Whitefield, his companion and friend. Of him men of the greatest learning and parts, and such, too, as Hume, Bolingbroke, and Chesterfield, have spoken in terms of unrestrained applause. Doctor Franklin, a man of calm, dispassionate, exact, and cautious nature, records his evidence, testifying to the almost superhuman influence of this chosen messenger of God. His voice, his delivery, his action, his methods, and his flowing thoughts and sublime bursts, swept over multitudes as with the flash of Pentecostal flames of consuming and converting power. His work was not confined within the limits of Methodism. Providentially for the cause of evangelizing Christianity, he differed with Wesley in doctrines, and rejecting Arminius, he stood upon the faith and taught the dogmas of Calvin. Thus he transferred the spirit he had acquired with Wesley to other churches, and the benefit of his work was felt by the Scotch Presbyterian, the English, and other churches in Europe and this country. He was an apostle, if ever a man was. He crossed the Atlantic thirteen times, and preached eighteen thousand sermons during the thirty-four years of his career, and spoke to more people than any other man that ever lived. He left a name that never will be forgotten.

With him, too, was Adam Clarke, of whom I have before spoken. He was another of those wonderful men. He gave forty years to his "Commentaries." The learning and ability as a biblical scholar displayed in it made it a standard authority. As a preacher he labored with astounding zeal and industry. On the Norwich Circuit in 1781 he preached, in eleven months, four hundred and fifty sermons, travelling on foot a circuit of two hundred and sixty miles in extent, carrying his saddle-bags on his back. The Church grew under the ministry of such men. Within twenty years after the death of John Wesley, it had in England upwards of one hundred thousand members, and in 1876 there were in the United Kingdoms twenty-four thousand eight hundred and six itinerant preachers, and three million nine hundred and twenty-eight thousand five hundred and twelve members; while now it is believed that throughout the world there are over twelve millions of this body of Christian men.

It is to be remembered that in the history of the whole world no other religion or form of belief was ever pronounced and propagated as the Christian religion has been. We are told in an uncertain way that it was thus that the religion of Buddha was taught and spread; but the teaching of that belief was confined to the race who now possess it. To them it was preached, for them it was intended by its human founder. Its mission was not to all mankind. Its teachers were not directed to go and teach all nations; but the apostles of our own faith were so commanded, and they did go. No other religion ever sent out its missionaries to convert mankind by preaching the word of its faith, and no such miraculous results have ever been produced as have been brought about by the simple preaching and practice of Christian evangelists, to the civilized and the savage. Pagan beliefs grew and spread with the growth of the tribes and people by whom they were adopted in the infancy of their being, and the ancient heathen and the Mohammedan established their forms of worship at the spear's point. In that way, and in that way only, were they diffused among men. The Grecians and Romans alike, but more especially the Romans, adopted the deities of the barbarians they traded with, or fought with and overcame. But Christ alone founded his Church on the divine command of " Go you into all the world and preach the gospel." And from that day to this, thus it has been taught and accepted. I cannot detain you with a detail of the marvellous history of its early career and adoption ; its peculiar and new influence upon whole nations, and upon the most conspicuous men of those ancient days. From the time that the apostles went forth the world has been beatified with the results of their super-human deeds of love and mercy. Those who took up their work where they left it carried it on with the same holy zeal. The deserts of Egypt were populous with the anchorites who followed in the lead and life of Saint Anthony. Saint Augustine went to England, and Saint Patrick to Ireland, and Saint Boniface laid down his life in the wilds of Germany, and multitudes of other pious men like them went forth in a like way. When was such as this done in the world before ? when and where were men thus rescued from religious and moral degradation and physical destitution, and nations and king-doms established where only tribes and petty states existed ? The vicissitudes of human affairs and evil spirits of evil men would for a while overcome the labors of these evangelists, and social order and all religious faith would seemingly be threatened with extinction; but new men would be raised up to the work, and the lost ground regained, and new energy imparted to the faith and the faithful.

In the thirteenth century, because of the pestilences and famines, and the wars and oppressions of kings and princes and nobles and ecclesiastics, the European people were reduced to a pitiable con-dition of suffering and want. At the same time many of the learned, who were all clerics or churchmen, were poisoned with a spirit of unbelief, and were fascinated by and daringly adopted and taught the principles and precepts of Oriental philosophy and practical atheism. Those were dreadful days, and yet in the darkest hour there came Saint Dominic, a Spanish noble, who with the power of his preaching and his preachers persuaded the men of his own rank, and the proud prelates who were abasing their high offices and holy calling, into a purity of life and a submission to their religious duties. And then, too, came Saint Francis of Assisi, with his visions and raptures and his heroic poverty, and gathered into his huge organization of preaching friars a body of workers that befriended the poor and sick, rebuked the haughty and high-born, and revolutionized and chastened the political, social, and ecclesiastical life of Italy, and, passing into France, with the aid of the Dominicans did battle with the malcontents, the rationalists and sceptics of Paris, and beat them on their own chosen ground, routing their sophisticating infidelity, and reasserting and re-establishing the divine mission of evangelical Christianity. And so has the sacred flame from age to age been handed down.

It is often said that Methodism was designed for the New World. When we remember the prodigious results of its labors on our people and on our national existence, we are also tempted to accept this saying as just and true; but some reflection will show it to be a narrow view of its purpose and object. It is, and has been, catholic in its works and utterance. Remember the triumphant results of its missions all over the world, in the wildest places and with the most savage races, as with the oldest religions and most accomplished and intellectual of heathens. Turn then to the history of England at and about the time of its establishment, and we will immediately see how potential it was for the political, social, and temporal security of that kingdom. When John Wesley felt the divine impulse within him, when, chosen and sanctified by God's grace, he went forth to save men, there was a season of lassitude and indifference. The very devil of sensual impiety and heartless irreligion pervaded all walks of life. Christianity was not believed in. It was treated as if it were untrue, but permitted because it was necessary for society to have some form of religious belief. Its teachings were cold and colorless, and many of its priests apathetic or unbelieving and sceptical. The chief ministers of the Church, often stained with sin and puffed up with pride, delivered over to underlings the people they were deputed to guide and save. The rich were growing richer, the poor poorer. The vulgar vices of those in authority were readily taken up and imitated by the untaught and unprotected population. Infidelity was active, aggressive, and generally diffused; rebellious discontent was fermenting in the souls of men, who saw no happiness in this life and who believed they were doomed to a fate of perpetual labor, living on the edge of starvation. Society was sick, sick to its heart of hearts, and a fearful storm was gathering. That sentiment of nihilism which Peter Lombard, the Master of the Sentences, is reported to have taught in the twelfth century, and Abelard is accused of having been the author of, and which now infests the Russian Empire, and was the ruling principle of communistic action, was crawling over the public mind of the common people of Great Britain.

At intervals in the world's history, in all organized nationalties such despairing opinions are hatched out like vipers and vermin by the fermenting heat of rotting social order. The plebeian revolts, the servile wars of antiquity, the Jacquerie and the peasant wars of the middle ages, and Anabaptist revolt at Munster, under John of Leyden, and the dreadful uprisings of the Swabian starving field laborers, in Luther's time, under Munser, and the great French Revolution of 1792, and like events are familiar instances. They are all of them startling evidences that such things must and shall be whenever public life has lost its virtue, and whenever a people are driven to the wall by the dead pressure of abused social and political authority, and whenever, too, a people have no hope of help here, no trust in God, and do not know of or have rejected Revelation.

The bloodshed and blasphemy of the French Revolution would have been repeated in England, had it not been for the interposition of this religious zeal excited and organized by John Wesley. The middle and lower classes were captivated with its influence, and thus diverted from righting their grievances with the sword or the flames of revolution. The very men who suffered most, and would have been the first to have revolted against the evils that enveloped them, were the first to repel all attempts to excite them to acts of resistance and popular tumult.

They were the emotional, sympathetic, and suffering who would have been swept away into the whirlwind of insurrection had they not surrendered their whole souls to the peaceful influence of practical piety.

The men who shouted with Wesley and Whitefield at their chapels and in their field preaching would have been raving with anarchy and burning with hatred for all religion.

Justified by faith, sanctified and made perfect, they put behind them all sense of earthly sorrow, and were more than reconciled to their present sufferings. They had drawn from the wells of salvation. They had seen and known the joy of the drawing of waters. "He who had not known that joy, knew no joy!" Life was no longer a state of trial alone. To them it was one exulting march. They were lifted up with the delights of the soul and the transports and glories of an everlasting hereafter. Thus was it that their heads were bowed down with submission to the authority of princes and nobles, and thus was it that England was saved from the ruin and rancor of a revolt of suffering men led by blaspheming infidels. Had that revolution taken place, the terror of it would have been as the abomination of desolation.

It would not have been like the great rebellion against Charles. That was the organized action of the religious, educated as well as uneducated, to maintain and obtain civil and religious liberty. The men in that day were not scattering the flames of social ruin and impiety. They were wielding the sword of Justice, which, as Milton grandly puts it, "is the sword of God, superior to all mortal things, in whose hands soever by apparent signs his testified will is to place it."

This is what the Methodists did for England. That which they did for this country I can only advert to. It was preceded in the colonies by the labor of Jonathan Edwards, who has recorded the history of his apostolic work in the "great awakening" of 1729. Strange to say, at that time, in the very heart of Puritan New England, religious zeal languished. There was a visible decay of faith, and a growth of doubting, hypercritical unbelief. The impulse of the reviving work of Edwards had all reacted, and the religious condition of the colonies had sunk to a low point. Frelinghuysen, Blair, and the two Tennents were preaching, with the earnestness of apostles, in New Jersey and Pennsylvania. The old Tennent school- and meeting-house still stands in Monmouth County, New Jersey, a dear memorial of the labors of those devoted men in the cause of education and religion.

While this dark cloud was thus oppressing the public mind, in August, 1760, Philip Embury, the leader of a little colony of emigrants from Ireland, landed in New York. In a little room in his small house on Barrack Street, now Park Place, began the work of Methodism in this country. There were but few members then, and now it numbers three million two hundred and twenty-three thousand five hundred and thirty members! Its growth was steady, and in some places rapid. Soon such men as Coke and Rankin were sent across the sea by Wesley.

In 1784, Cokesbury College was established at Abingdon, twenty-five miles from Baltimore, and now there belong to this denomina tion more than one hundred academies and preparatory schools, and over fifty colleges and universities, while there are also at least ten divinity schools, with full faculties imparting theological training and instruction to those who propose to take Holy Orders.

There are many subjects connected with the rise and growth of this great religious organization in America, that would be instructive to consider and reflect on; but I must pass them by. I have enlarged upon its early history and the causes of its birth; for they were all incidental to the subject of my discourse, and suitable to the exercises of this commencement, under control of its members and chosen officials. What I have asserted and maintained, in a brief way, is that the foundation of all academic and collegiate learning was with the religious. Through them we have received the blessings of such training and education as we now possess, all of which is the sole cause of our form of civilization. These schools have been in the keeping of religious men, and they should continue so, and I firmly believe they will continue so. For, let men say what they will about the narrowing influence of such teachers, their illiberality, bigotry, and want of general scientific enlightenment,—let them say all this; still they dare not say they are not the best men to guard and guide the young, and restrain their wild, irregular impulses, and give a moral tone to their thoughts and actions. And that, I affirm, is more precious to a people than all of the fantastic teachings of philosophical speculators; but I do not assent to the assertion that the clergy are illiberal, or bigoted, or unenlightened. Their liberality is conservative liberality, which guards the three foci of life, "family, country and humanity," and not the liberality of destructives. They organized the elements of order that prevail in modern civil life, and they will maintain it to the end.

They are not bigoted; they stand by their convictions and rightfully maintain the truth of the faith that is in them, and they should do so. The days of religious persecution are over. That and other forms of persecution have passed away. The persecutors of this world have not been all of them religionists, or the ministers of religion, neither have all of the causes of ostracism and persecution been in the name of religion. It is the cant of intellectual quacks and political adventurers to say so, but it is not the truth. Neither are they unenlightened in the ways and teachings and doctrines of physical philosophy. They do not run after and adopt each new theory or fancy of visionary investigators and teachers. They receive, study, and inwardly digest before they accept and advocate.

Disregarding the spiritual sanction and influence of Christianity on the lives of men, and the fact that it gives a firm assurance of an eternity of joy or of sorrow, according to the deeds done in the body, —disregarding all that, let me ask what has philosophy done for the human race, compared with that which we have received from revealed religion? The great thinkers of antiquity were familiar with much of the elements of physical truth, and certainly theorized and conjectured over all of the known phases of metaphysical speculation.

From Orpheus, Pythagoras, Plato, Aristotle, Zeno, down to Porphyrius, Plotinus, and Proclus, all came as near to the truths of our spiritual and moral being as man can come by reason alone, unaided by revelation. How has all of their wisdom availed mankind? Where did it leave them? In ruins; yes, ruins. Did all this philosophy save Egypt, or Greece, or Rome from their fate? Empires were dissolved, cities destroyed, whole nations and their people were extinguished, and nature itself blasted, and prosperous and fertile countries became howling wildernesses. The savages came and spread like the sea, and washed out the men and their possessions. The civilization of these times, the civilization of these philosophers passed away forever. Could this have been so had they been enlightened and influenced by revelation? Do these wise unbelievers think that we, too, are to pass away in like manner? Did it happen to the Hebrews? With all of their spirit of disobedience and sinful resistance of God, with all of their punishment,—punished but saved as was promised,—they still exist, a monument of divine wrath, a monument of divine protection; the covenant that God made with Abraham one thousand years before Homer sang of ruined Troy has been kept to this hour, and will be kept until time shall be no more. How is it with the Chaldeans, the Assyrians, the Persians, the Chinese, the Hindoos, the Arabians,—that vast swarm of Orientals? Were they not possessed of some of the most subtle secrets of the exact sciences, and of nature too? Was not their mental philosophy and theology as spiritual and refined as ever the brain of man conceived? And what did it do or has it done for them? Where has it left them?

Some of them are extinct and swallowed up in endless night, and those who remain are lost in outer darkness yet, and their social, political, moral, and intellectual condition is barren and fruitless of good to themselves or of advantage to mankind. Those old philosophers of the East and West were, as Abelard said of Anselm, " Like the barren fig-tree cursed by Christ, covered with leaves but without a single fruit." When these men passed away and their clouds of thought were dissolved by the tempest of barbarians that swept over the face of nature and over the works of man, there was the silence of death, till men were called to a mental and moral consciousness by the voice of revealed religion, proclaimed by its apostles, chosen messengers of divine mercy.

When social consciousness had returned, and intellectual activity began, and schools of learning were established, then came with it the evil that ever follows in the train of all human action. Blasted with intellectual conceit, the teachers propagated opinions at war with revelation, and at war with the being of God himself. One reads with a shudder the blasphemy of Simon of Tournai, a famous teacher in the University of Paris. He had lectured on the proofs of the truth of Christianity, and was applauded by his class for his happy demonstration, when, filled with vainglory, he burst out, "Oh, little Jesus, little Jesus, how I have exalted thy law! If I chose, I could more easily cast it in the dust!" At the same time Abelard, the most polished and subtle mind of those days, was whirled away by the delusions of his own conceits, and became a disciple of the devil, corrupting the minds of his hearers with his intellectual poisons. Checked and rebuked by Saint Bernard, the sense of his error and the evil of his ways came to him, and he retracted all, and ended his days a penitent and true believer.

Europe was cursed then as she is now with the vile pretensions of human philosophy. The hostile opinions of those unbelievers then were not new, and they are the same that we confront now, reproductions of pagan belief, or rather unbelief. They are as old as sin itself. I should say they began with the first sin,—

> " Man's first disobedience, and the fruit
> Of that forbidden tree whose mortal taste
> Brought death into the world and all our woe."

Atheism, materialism, pantheism, deism, and rationalism were all then preached and propagated as they are now preached and propagated. Averroes, that learned Moorish infidel, saturated the scientific jugglers of those days with his specious speculations,—a mixture of Mohammedan theosophy and the philosophy of Aristotle with Oriental mysticism. He said that philosophy was nearer to truth than religion : learned men begin with religion, do not stop at it; with the aid of philosophy they pass through belief to the results and proofs of science; religion is for the people, they cannot comprehend science; all religions are alike, all are true. Thus he taught, and this the sciolists of those days believed. The Emperor Frederick the Second, the most accomplished monarch of those times, embraced these opinions and devoted his talents and genius to the teaching of all these deluding sophistications, that were brought from the East and infused into the minds of Christian men, corrupting their faith and degrading their moral nature. He was an abandoned, licentious man. He had Saracen guards, a Saracen university, and Arab concubines. The Sultan of Egypt was his nearest friend.

The infamous book, " De Tribus Imposteribus, Moses, Christ, and Mohammed," was imputed to him. It was supposed by many that Frederick might be antichrist. I do not propose to recount or dwell on the history of these phantasies and conceits of self-sufficient evil men. Neither do I propose to assume the office of a theologian, and contend with the propounders of these opinions; I only desire here, as the necessary incident of my discourse, to point out how old those vices of human reason are that come to you tricked out with the appearance of originality, and professing to be new revelations of scientific inspiration.

In those days they were confronted and refuted on their own ground of reason by many, but by no one with greater force and effect than by Saint Thomas Aquinas, the Angelical Doctor, who combined the logic of Aristotle with the sympathetic revelations of Plato. The study of his profound analysis and demonstrations of the fundamental principles of theological thought, and the true philosophy of our intellectual and moral being, is now reviving to re-enlighten, and to sweep away the ostentatious parades of scientific pretenders. Men begin again to learn from them, and reverence and accept them.

An acute thinker of our own day, and one not addicted to pietism, has said, " observation distinguishes, logic identifies; suffer the latter to have her way, she will resolve men into God, God into nature; she will still the universe into an indivisible unity, absorbing liberty, morality, and all the action of life." Meditate on this just statement, and see to what a fatal abyss of nihilism reason reduces us ! Who would exchange revelation and its peaceful, moral influence, its spirit of enlightened intellectual repose, its hope of future happiness, for such dark and bewildering speculations, ending in the everlasting destruction of all things of nature, of sense, of being, and of God?

> "O star-eyed science! hast thou wandered there
> To waft us home the message of despair?"

Fifty years ago there resided in this town a man noted in his day, and known and honored in ours. He was a Judge of the Supreme Court of this State. He was a good and wise man, and a lawyer of great fame. Thomas Duncan was his name, and it became his duty to deliver the opinion of the Supreme Court, in the great case of Updegraph against the Commonwealth, reported in 11th Sergeant and Rawle. Had he never performed any other act of professional or judicial duty, he would, by this judgment alone, have earned a name that men will not willingly forget.

The opinion was the product of learning, wisdom, culture, and faith. Read it, and it will delight you with its felicity of expression and its purity and depth of thought. That case decided Christianity to be a part of the common law of Pennsylvania, and to vilify it maliciously an indictable offence.

A man had proclaimed these blasphemous words, and was indicted for it: "The Holy Scriptures are a mere fable; they are a contradiction; although they contain a number of good things, yet they contain a great many lies." When we hear this read, we could well fancy that we heard the annunciation of some of our scientific sophists, for this is the result and conclusion of all they strive to teach, frequently by skilful indirection, and often by words as bold and impious. Listen, now, to what Judge Thomas Duncan then said on the subject of these poisonous words of unbelief:

"Christianity, general Christianity, is, and always has been, a part of the common law of Pennsylvania; Christianity without the spiritual artillery of European countries, for this Christianity was one of the considerations of the royal charter, and the very basis of its great founder, William Penn: not Christianity founded on any particular religious tenets, not Christianity with an established church and tithes and spiritual courts, but Christianity with liberty of conscience to all men."

Lord Mansfield, in a case which made much noise at the time, said,—

" Conscience is not controllable by human laws and answerable to human tribunals; prosecutions or attempts to enforce conscience will never produce conviction, and were only calculated to make hypocrites or martyrs."

There never was a single instance, from the Saxon times down to our own, in which a man was punished for erroneous opinions. For atheism, blasphemy, and reviling the Christian religion, there have been instances of prosecution " at common law; but bare non-conformity is no sin by the common law. The true principles of natural religion are a part of the common law, so that a person vilifying, ridiculing, or subverting may be prosecuted at common law. But temporal punishment ought not to be inflicted for mere opinions." I would gladly continue to quote from this convincing and clear judgment; but I cannot. I must soon end my discourse. Read it for yourselves, and you will be charmed with its directness and fulness, and instructed by its reasoning and learning. I have cited it to show what is the law of the community in which we live, and to show that it is in harmony with sound morality and reason, and to show you how wise and good men, founders of this commonwealth, thought, believed, and acted in the support of that Christian religion, to maintain which this college was founded, " So that men might know thee, the only true God, and Jesus Christ, whom thou has sent."

Young gentlemen, I have attempted, from the first words I have spoken, to direct your minds and hearts in the way of sound conservative thought and convictions. If you have not a sense of practical religious duty upon you, let me admonish you to, at least, reverence it.

Stand firmly and squarely on the principles of your early teachings. Never be tempted by a feeling of self-conceit or levity of disposition to slight it or scoff at it. " Sit not in the seat of the scorner." If you cannot worship with a sense of piety, or acknowledge by open acts of obedience the duties of your faith, you can, at least, respect and maintain morality; for that is the shadow, as well as the revelation in the heart of man, of the weak and unsafe thing we profess to respect and acknowledge as natural religion. Deference and submission to morality will in part fulfil your duty to your country and society, and probably, with God's help, may lead the way to that faith which purifies, and sanctifies, and maketh all things perfect.

CHESTER A. ARTHUR.

*Eulogy pronounced before the Legislature of the State of New York,
April 20, 1887.*

GENTLEMEN,—

We have been called by high authority to pay our united honors
to the memory of our departed great. Having accepted the distinction bestowed upon me, I will attempt to fulfil the duty I have
assumed. Concerning the history and early career of General
Arthur before he became the President I will not speak. Of that
the gentleman * who succeeds me will fully treat. Neither do I propose to relate the many public acts and events that were done and
sanctioned by him when President. A detailed historical narrative
will not answer the purpose of these solemnities. A few simple
words of allusion to those acts is all that could be called for. I wish
to bring together in one view his high qualities,—his magnanimity,
his gentleness, and all of the other traits of his nature which have
commanded our love and honor.

The manly grief of a whole nation and a great people that was
raised like a wild wail of terrified sorrow on the frightful murder of
Garfield was followed by a bewildered sense of public distrust and
doubt. The hot partisan hostilities prevailing before that calamity
were then inflamed by fierce and harsh misjudgments of General
Arthur and all who were associated with him in close personal and
political relations. With the knowledge of these hatreds before him
and keenly conscious of the intense and painful sense of public
anxiety and expectation, he calmly and firmly accepted the murdered
President's place. He took the oath of office, and at once issued that
inaugural to the people of the nation which I will here recite. By
its solemn tones of wisdom, speaking by lawful authority, it dispelled
all dread of commotion and subdued all anger.

" For the fourth time in the history of the republic its chief magistrate has been removed by death. All hearts are filled with grief
and horror at the hideous crime which has darkened our land; and
the memory of the murdered President, his protracted sufferings, his
unyielding fortitude, the example and achievements of his life, and
the pathos of his death, will forever illumine the pages of our history.

---

* Chauncey M. Depew.

For the fourth time the officer elected by the people and ordained by the Constitution to fill a vacancy so created is called to assume the executive chair. The wisdom of our fathers, foreseeing even the most dire possibilities, made sure that the government should never be imperilled because of the uncertainty of human life. Men may die, but the fabrics of our free institutions remain unshaken. No higher or more assuring proof could exist of the strength and permanence of popular government than the fact that, though the chosen of the people be struck down, his constitutional successor is peacefully installed, without shock or strain except the sorrow which mourns the bereavement. All the noble aspirations of my lamented predecessor which found expression in his life, the measures devised and suggested during his brief administration to correct abuses, to enforce economy, to advance prosperity, and promote the general welfare, to insure domestic security, and maintain friendly and honorable relations with the nations of the earth, will be garnered in the hearts of the people, and it will be my earnest endeavor to profit and to see that the nation shall profit by his example and experience.

" Prosperity blesses our country, our fiscal policy is fixed by law, is well grounded and generally approved. No threatening issue mars our foreign intercourse, and the wisdom, integrity, and thrift of our people may be trusted to continue undisturbed the present assured career of peace, tranquillity, and welfare. The gloom and anxiety which have enshrouded the country must make repose especially welcome now. No demand for speedy legislation has been heard; no adequate occasion is apparent for an unusual session of Congress. The Constitution defines the functions and powers of the Executive as clearly as those of either of the other two departments of government, and he must answer for the just exercise of the discretion it permits and the performance of the duties it imposes. Summoned to these high duties and responsibilities, and profoundly conscious of their magnitude and gravity, I assume the trust imposed by the Constitution, relying for aid on Divine guidance and the virtue, patriotism, and intelligence of the American people."

Your admiration must here be excited by the display of the qualities of his mind in this his first great act when clothed with power.

" Mighty is the storm, but mightier the calm that binds the storm."

Our existence, like a stream, flows smoothly on, and then suddenly dashes itself in a dark abyss where all worldly honor and power are gone forever, swallowed up as rivers are by the ocean. It was thus that Garfield, in the first months of his advancement, was swept into that eternal gulf; but not to be forgotten. His horrid murder is yet remembered, and will be remembered with a sense of humility and sorrow. Penetrated with these emotions partaken by a whole nation, General Arthur took up the reins of public authority. From the hour that he felt the obligations of the high duties thus forced upon him he seemed by a sudden and natural aptitude to be filled with power to execute them. From that moment he made it evident to all that he knew what to do, what he wanted to do, and how to do it. He was every inch a President. With deliberation he selected his Cabinet,—a body of gentlemen whose acts have been approved, whose official lives with him and with each other were one of cordial unity. There was no discord, no contention in the history of that administration. The firm, just, and peaceful qualities of its chief gave tone to the acts and utterances of his advisers.

From the first between him and the representatives of the nation there was established a sense of high respect. They saw at once that his purpose was the public good, not the perpetuation of party rule or personal power. He made it plain to them that his only law of official and personal life was to think the truth, act the truth, speak the truth. By his words and deeds he convinced them and the whole people of this nation that he believed in and lived by the ever-to-be-remembered preamble of our Constitution, which proclaims and declares that the true purpose of our government was and is " to establish justice, to insure domestic tranquillity, to provide for the common defence, to promote the general welfare, and to secure the benefit of liberty to us and to our posterity forever."

When his convictions would not permit him to assent to acts presented to him for his approval, he exercised his power of forbidding and dissenting in mild terms of wisdom and admonition that were received by Congress in the calm and friendly spirit with which they were given. He roused no sense of personal or political hostility or public discord. Words of objection uttered as an act of duty were accepted with deference if not with acquiescence. He was trusted, honored, and applauded by them and by all men from the time he first met Congress to the time when he laid down his high public honors to pass into that private domestic life where he was so much loved and wherein his own worth exalted him more than all the glories of his wise public career.

For the social and personal duties of this great office he was pre-eminently fit. I must speak of his presence as Tacitus in his affectionate panegyric describes his father-in-law, the great Agricola: "His figure was tall and comely; in his countenance there was nothing to inspire awe, but its character was generous and engaging. You would have readily believed him a good man and willingly a great one." There was never a man whose gracious elegance of manners better conformed to the refined usages of society. The public and the public man soon saw his fitness in the attractive hospitalities of the executive mansion—abundant, elegant, refined. The people were proud of the chief magistrate who could receive all with cordial dignity, and entertain with grace and liberality without waste or glittering pomp.

Thus passed his great public life. A time never to be forgotten, an era of public repose and of public and private prosperity, to which we all now look back with a sense of approval, I must say of praise, applauding him for securing it out of discord and maintaining it by his sense of justice and calm forbearance.

Because of his modest and unpretending career he was unknown by the people. At first they hesitated to accept him as fit, and then they were surprised when they found how suited he was for every exigency of his position. His mind was very prompt. He was resolute upon all principles of general public policy; but where his act would prejudice persons to their injury, such was the benevolence and gentleness of his nature that he would hesitate and act with reluctance. But when he did act he acted firmly always. He was stern with himself but liberal and forbearing with others. He had every attribute that one would wish to see in a chief executive. He never spoke of party politics, and always stood by what was right and practically proper. He was not visionary. He understood the world and men thoroughly. Their littleness did not sour his nature, for he was full of generosity. He had not a mean, unmanly element in his character. He was heroic but not ostentatious. He had an extended experience in public affairs and a large knowledge in public history. He had various reading in every direction, and what he had read he remembered with elegant taste and great accuracy.

Beginning life in a frugal way, by steady industry he advanced his means, but his wishes as to that were moderate. He had no sordid

thought in his mind. Money to him was but a means of personal
independence—no more. He knew how a man may " gain the
whole world and lose his own soul." And he lived up to that conviction. Thus far the public men of this country have all been of
moderate means—most of them what would be called poor men.
That is the glory and honor of the country. The plain, moderate
people who organized our social and public life so ordained it. Our
great offices were intended to be great honors, not sinecures. The
compensation attached to the best of them will not equal that which
any man can earn who is fit to have them, and it should be so.

Until of late there have been very few men holding high public
honors who were rich or even more than comfortable. The people
distrust all those who, being poor, follow a public career, take office
and become rich. Such rancid statesmen are objects of public hatred,
and ever will be. This country is ruled by two classes of workmen,
—the mechanics and men who work with their hands for their daily
bread, and the men who work with their intellects and in the great
professions. No such men can ever hope to be rich and possess es-
tates, and they will forbid the advancement of the sordid—those who
hold office to use it for gain. When they enter upon their career
they, in effect, take a vow of poverty. They know they can never
hope to acquire great wealth. At the best they can only obtain a
moderate competency suitable to their condition in life. These men
never will tolerate for official life as a class those who love money.
They look upon all such as public enemies. As I have said, they
hate them.

Can we not congratulate ourselves that we have come of such a
lineage of simple, honest men, who loved God and not lucre; who
loved God as He is the Father of natural and rational liberty,—the
liberty of obedience to law and subordination to natural and social
duty? May we not exultingly say that a hundred years and more
of such national life, under such national principles, has brought us
to this point of glory, the peaceful glory of a prosperous, plain people; of sixty millions who sprang from the few who sought refuge
here, inspired with a belief in revelation and living strictly by a
sense of moral duty, who erected a temple of human rights, into
which all men who love law and obey order can enter and find happiness and peace?

Before I close these remarks I must remind you that all these fine
qualities of his character were not unconsecrated by religious con-

victions. If this were wanting we could have found no consolation in our sorrow. His excellence of nature would have been but a shadow. He was trained in a home of religious teaching, by a father who taught him and others the truths of revealed religion. He was not tainted with any philosophical pretensions. He had no affinity with the hostile opinions of unbelievers. He was blasted with no such intellectual conceit. He believed that Christianity was the product of Divine revelation, not the result of human reason; that philosophy did not make it and could not destroy it; that it dwelt in realms of thought and understanding, far above the region of the philosophy of schools. He thought that " to reduce Christianity to philosophy would be to strip it of the future and to strike it dead;" that there is one science which is religious and another which is not, and that is impious science. By these convictions he lived and died.

Having thus recounted all that my disturbed and unhappy mind will permit me to express, overcome as I am, standing in the presence of those memories which endeared him to me, I feel I can say no more. My hand trembles as I write, and my mind refuses to express the thoughts and feelings with which it is now crowded. My heart is full of sorrow. My eyes are filled with tears. No sooner had he finished his great work than he was hurried to the grave. How this teaches us our nothingness and insignificance! Here he was exalted and honored above all men. And there he lies subdued by the mysterious forces of nature and doomed by the very law of our existence to fall, as it were, a victim for our warning. If we needed such terrors to wean us from our devotion to the world and its glories, this calamity which we now consider should be sufficiently appalling.

FIRST CENTENNIAL ADDRESS.*

FELLOW CITIZENS,—

Coming from many urgent occupations, I have been suddenly called on and deputed to speak to you to-night. The occasion is so important, and the call so unexpected, that I am at loss to know what

----

* At midnight, January 1, 1876, before Independence Hall, at the request of Select and Common Councils of Philadelphia.

to say. A few words of serious but cheerful thought will better answer than a long discourse.

At this instant we stand upon the verge of a new year. The old one that is to pass away is one of a hundred like it, that have been freighted with the joys and sorrows of a young nation, and the new one that is to enter in will begin another century of national life, matured by serious trials, and strengthened by a career of marvellous prosperity. It is a solemn moment. Throughout this land, imperial in the majesty of its career as it is imperial in the vastness of its domain, the unmeasured value of its wealth, the dignity of its people, there reigns a conscious sense of the importance of this approaching hour. We all know how much has been given to us, and how much we now enjoy, and how much will be expected of us; and we all know the peril of such great trusts.

Behind us lie the early years of oppression, trial, sorrow; the after-years of success and public triumph; and before us lie the crowning years of duty—duty to be performed with religious fidelity for the sake of ourselves and our children, and for the sake of the future of the human race.

Let us pause and look at the past; meditate upon its wholesome lessons. Let us pause and gaze on the future approaching us with measured tread. We have now come to years of national manhood, and with its honors will come its cares and calamities. May we be able to use them all, and accept them as our fathers accepted their mission with its glories and its adversities! God has prospered us as a people. As men were never before blessed have we been blessed. How this should admonish us to remember Him in this the day of our youth and strength! When we forget Him, the virtue will have gone from us, and we will pass away in a whirlwind of anarchy and bloodshed. We are to preserve our own liberties that we may secure liberty for the human race. Here, on this spot, our fathers declared their own freedom from foreign dominion, and piously claimed for mankind that freedom which they heroically resolved to secure for themselves. It was a noble and majestic act of national power, and from that moment have we lived up to the full measure of its greatness and goodness. From that hour a message went forth to all the corners of the world proclaiming man to be free, and from that moment has the human race seemed roused to a just sense of popular power based on personal and individual freedom. We have taken our place " among the powers of the earth," and we have begun to evangelize men in the cause of human rights for the sake of human liberty. Our example has subverted the tyranny that once cursed men, and roused them to a sense of more perfect manhood. This is our mission, and thus far have we well performed it. Let us silence the noise of all discord at home. Let us unite in future as our fathers were united in their days of trial. Let us acknowledge and maintain, as they did, our nationality for the sake of our common liberty, and then we will be an example for others to imitate and honor.

In those days there were men of great public usefulness, but among them were three of surpassing merit,—three to whom we owe all that we have of public life or public power,—Franklin, Washington, and Jefferson: Franklin, who first united public opinion here, and then secured for us by his wisdom and skill the aid and protection of foreign powers; Washington, who fought in the field as he ruled in the council, with a conservative wisdom that avoided rash action, while it led to prosperous results; Jefferson, who knew the real genius of our people, and recognized that their duty was to stand by human freedom while they fought for their own. These men were the leaders of the great events we meet to commemorate, and that which we now have came from their joint labors. This city—this spot —was the scene of those labors, and it is because we rejoice over their deeds that we now come together here at this dark hour of midnight to greet the coming year.

Soon will those new days be with us, and from all nations of the earth will come wanderers across the seas to join with us in our great jubilee. When they come we must receive them with cordial hospitality, and be ourselves in fraternal unity. No such event has ever adorned the annals of history. Men have flocked to see religious rites, to aid in public games and exhibitions; but mankind never before came together to recognize and celebrate the hundredth birthday of a nation. It never happened before, as no such nation ever lived. No people ever before thus proudly asserted its liberty and took "its place among the powers of the earth."

The result of this event will send back those who visit us, filled with new thoughts and new resolutions that may change the order of human affairs and create new destinies for old nationalities. We will profit by their coming; we will take help from their more polished tone of civilization, and subdue our sense of self-importance; but they will learn lessons of public policy and private right practically enforced, that will strengthen their manhood and reform their national and individual beings.

But I must end this. The hour as it approaches admonishes me to be done. Here we are happy in our prosperity, happy in our past history, happy in our hopes for the future, and happy in a common confidence in Divine protection. May another hundred years see freemen of our united nation like ourselves thus gathered together for a like purpose, and in a like spirit, to tell all men that their mission as ours is " on earth, peace, good-will toward men."

FREDERICK THE GREAT.*

SOME time before the year 1170, when Henry the Second, the son of Maud the Empress and Geoffrey Plantagenet, Count of Anjou, had reigned in England for near sixteen years, and during which year St. Thomas à Becket was cruelly murdered at the high altar of Canterbury, Conrad, a younger son of a Swabian baron, set out to seek his fortune, from his father's old castle of Hohenzollern, perched high up in the Alp country. From the home of their house in the Black Forest his race took their name, Hohen- (high) Zollern (tollery), which means, that clear up in those remote regions stood a castle, or hold, whose owner commanded the way and exacted toll from all travellers. For centuries, no doubt, there they had resided, wielding absolute authority, and earning their revenues from the merchants and traders that passed out by the Swiss valleys or from Italy on their way to Germany.

In those days the castles of these knights and nobles were but robbers' nests. They pillaged the churchman and merchant; they captured their rivals and enemies and the wealthy travellers, to secure ransom; and their young men, under color of military occupation, spent their days and nights in the saddle, prosecuting their petty feuds or gaining their living by what were then called the earnings of the stirrup. The Crusades came as a practical blessing, not only to open

---

* A lecture delivered on the evening of December 10, 1872, at the Academy of Music, Philadelphia, in aid of Saint Mary's Hospital.

the way to a higher civilization by intercourse with the East, but by affording a new field of action for these restless and penniless sons of these wild and savage nobles. They were a hardy, resolute, and not over-scrupulous race of men.

This youth thus starting out into the world was the founder of the present race of Prussian kings. From him in a direct line came the subject of my present discourse, Frederick the Second, the third king of Prussia, known by all the world as Frederick the Great; and from him also descended the present emperor of Germany.

This young Conrad Hohenzollern entered the service of the kaiser of the Holy Roman Empire, Frederick the First, the second of the Hohenstaufen race of the Swabian line of emperors, and the nephew of Conrad the Third.

The Emperor Frederick, surnamed by the Italians Barbarossa for his beautiful light-golden beard, was a man of singular merit and renown. He was a politician of subtle skill, a soldier of great achievements, and a monarch of right royal and imperial nature.

The fame of his deeds and the history of his career read like the narratives of romance, rather than the sober realities of an age of hard and almost savage necessities. To this day the Swabian peasants believe that their great kaiser is not dead, but that he has withdrawn from our upper and earthly life, by some supernatural power to be again restored as a national deliverer when the hour shall come.

In a deep cleft in the Kyffhäuserberg, on the golden meadow of Thuringia, still sleeps the mighty emperor, his head resting on his arm; he sits by a granite block, through which his red beard has grown in the lapse of time; but, when the ravens no longer fly around the mountain, he will awake and restore the golden age to the expectant world.

By another legend he still sits in sleep in the Untersberg, near Salzburg, and when the dead pear-tree blossoms in the Walserfeld, which has been thrice cut down, but ever grows anew, then he will come forth, hang his shield on the tree, and commence a battle, in which the whole world shall join, and the good shall overcome the bad.

By this great prince Conrad was advanced. He was a young fellow of merit, and in the service of such a monarch promotion and opportunity were sure to follow. After a while he contracted a marriage with the heiress of the Vohburg family, who had been before that the hereditary Burggrafs of Nuremberg, which place in time he acquired for himself and his posterity.

The next step in the history of this race of men is the purchase of the electorate of Brandenburg. In 1415 the Emperor Sigismund, the last of the Bavarian line of emperors, sold this electorate to one of the Hohenzollern Burggrafs for four hundred thousand gulden, equal in our money at this time to about one million dollars. On the 14th of April, 1417, in the market-place of Constance, was the investiture of this honor publicly and with great ceremony bestowed, one hundred thousand people looking on. This great dignity, thus acquired by money, was the fruit of that thrift and skill which have from the first signalized the career of the descendants of those old mountain robbers and toll-gatherers. Fully to understand and appreciate the value and importance of this promotion we must remember that there was acquired the territory, the sovereign power, and the electoral dignity. The cadet of a robber lordship had become one of the seven sovereigns in whose hands were lodged the power and duty of selecting the master of the Holy Roman Empire.

At that time Germany was divided into seven of these sovereignties, styled kurfürsts, or electors. There were three ecclesiastical states and four secular principalities. Mentz, Cologne, and Treves were the ecclesiastical; the Palatinate, Saxony, Bohemia, and Brandenburg were the secular. In years afterwards Bavaria and Hanover were added. Whenever a vacancy occurred on the imperial throne, these princes of the church and state elected a successor, and their vote conferred on the fortunate candidate the purple of Charlemagne and the Cæsars.

From the investiture of Frederick, the First Elector (on the 14th of April, 1417), to the 6th of February, 1620 (the date of the accession of Frederick Wilhelm, styled the Great Elector), there were in all eleven electoral princes, during a period of about two hundred years; and he was succeeded by his son Frederick the Third, the twelfth and last elector, for this sovereign was created and acknowledged (by the kaiser) as king of Prussia on the 18th of January, 1701.

During these years, in addition to the dominion of Brandenburg, by inheritance and marriage this house acquired the territory of Prussia proper, a region of country originally conquered from the pagans by the Teutonic knights, with the aid of Ottocar, king of

Bohemia and duke of Austria, about the year 1228. It was from this province thus acquired that the new kingdom took its name.

Before I proceed further with this narrative I will here rest for a moment, to draw your attention to the conspicuous merits of Frederick Wilhelm, the eleventh elector, the great-grandfather of the great Frederick. This prince well deserved the fame of noble deeds. Of all his ancestors the great Frederick admired him the most. It is related of him that, when in the year 1750 a new cathedral had been finished at Berlin, and the remains of the electoral race were moved from the vaults of the old to the vaults of the new, he witnessed the operation, and, when the great kurfürst's coffin came, he had it opened. In silence he gazed on his features, which were perfect and untouched even in death. He laid his hand on the cold and long-dead hand and said to his attendants, "Gentlemen, this one did great work." To this day he is honored in Prussia. A large, majestic man, his statue in bronze adorns the long bridge at Berlin. I have seen it, and can recall it as I now write of it, and I can also recall the admiration with which they yet speak of him.

The flames of the Thirty Years' War had swept over his territories, and the cinders and ashes of its fury were scattered far and wide in his dominions. Brandenburg had sunk very low under its tenth elector, it had been well-nigh annihilated; but this wise, valiant, and thrifty prince restored it. For over thirty years it had been the scene of a multitude of battles, and it had been scoured from end to end by hostile armies. Tilly and Wallenstein had both carried their hordes there. The Evangelical Union troops and the English under Sir Horace Vere had swept over its plains ; Pomerania was seized first by the kaiser and then by the Swedes under Gustavus Adolphus. As has been said of these fearful years when all the furies of the most dismal contest were at their height, "all horrors of war and of being a seat of war that have been since heard are poor to those then practised, the detail of which is still horrible to read. Famine about Langemünde had risen so high that men ate human flesh,—nay, human creatures ate their own children."

In this wretched condition did the Great Elector come to his inheritance in 1640, and when he died, in 1688, all trace of these horrors had passed away. The Swede was driven from his foothold, the homage from Prussia to Poland was given up. His army was organized and made efficient; he drained bogs, established colonies in the wild waste places, constructed canals, encouraged trade, and stimulated industry; and when he had ended his energetic, earnest, honest, God-fearing life, he left his people prosperous and happy, to his successor a large treasury of accumulations, the product of his skill, industry, and German thrift, and to the world the example of a high life, spent in the strict performance of his public and private duties. Truly was he a great elector!

His son was a man of a different stamp. In his infancy he received a hurt that slightly deformed him and affected the history of his life. He was fond of pomp and gayeties and ceremonies. He bought his elevation to a kingship with the treasure left him by his thrifty and prosperous father. He surrounded himself with all the glitter and ceremonial of a royal court, and spent his days in the pursuit of such vanities. He was an expensive, costly man. He left no mark of his name behind, but the fact of his promotion and his foolish ostentation. He was a harmless, well-intentioned man, and would have passed away to be forgotten forever, with the mob of kings that fill this world's history, had it not been that he was the first Hohenzollern who was a king. The descendant of that Conrad whom we have seen, before 1170, coming down from his father's robber home in the far-off German Alps, resolved to seek a higher fortune, and to go out among men and earn a name, and secure advancement by honorable deeds of arms and state-craft in the service of the great Barbarossa.

From 1170 to 1702 (when they became kings) will be near to six hundred of as momentous years as we can trace on the map of our civilized history. I will not even glance at the political and social, moral and physical, events that happened during this period; but I will remind you how, while in this time kingdoms were extinguished, and empires broken into fragments, and dynasties of emperors and kings were blotted out forever, that these Hohenzollerns remained untouched, growing year by year to the fitness of that grand destiny that was waiting for them.

King Frederick the First died, but it was a sad ending to a life spent in such gilded felicities. For a third wife he had a princess of Mecklenburg. After a time she went mad, and was confined in the charge of keepers. The king, with a feeble body, worn out, weary with life, sat one morning in his apartment, when suddenly the glass door was broken to atoms, and then rushed before him what at first seemed to be the apparition of the traditional "White Lady" of his house, who is supposed to be ever present to announce the death of any of the race. There she stood, robed in white, her hair floating around her, her eyes blazing with fury, and her body dripping with great gouts of blood! The king shrieked and fainted. It was not an apparition : it was his mad wife, who had eluded her keepers and, finding her way to his room, flung herself thus wildly into his presence. The king was carried to his bed; he never recovered from the shock. This happened on the 13th of February, 1713, and twelve days after (on the 25th of February) he died.

At this time the great Frederick was just about fourteen months old. Frederick Wilhelm the First (but the second king of Prussia) succeeded. He was a man of most unaccountable and singular qualities. No sooner was his father dead than he forthwith dismissed the whole entourage of court followers and officers,—stewards and chamberlains and pages and lords in waiting and lackeys and other court riffraff and idlers. That which delighted the heart of his father and was the glory of his life was an abomination to him. The large and wasteful expenditure caused by such a crew of worthless hangers-on was at once arrested, and ended forever. And so in other ways he increased his revenues by diminishing his expenses and prosecuting plans of domestic and public policy that multiplied the productive power of his people and stimulated and directed their industries.

He had but one passion, and that was training and disciplining his army, although he never had but one campaign.

Charles the Twelfth of Sweden, on his sudden return from his mysterious residence of five years in Turkey, reappeared in Stralsund, on the shores of the Baltic. This was a part of Pomerania, still held by the Swedes, and from it the Prussian king resolved to drive them. Promptly he collected an army, and with the aid of some few Russians and Saxons, and about sixteen thousand Danes, headed by their king, besieged the once mighty lion of the North. The town was invested, it was but slightly garrisoned, and in a few months it was taken, Charles escaping in a Swedish vessel of war, to return again to his long-abandoned home, soon to end his wild career of almost supernatural victories and defeats by the ball of an assassin. This was his only war.

By the help of Leopold, prince of Anhalt-Dessau, an old soldier who had served under Prince Eugene and Marlborough, he trained and organized his army. This officer was a man of worth and valor, and without him and his experience and his system the troops of the great Frederick would never have achieved the results they did. He it was who first invented and used the iron ramrod. He invented the equal step and all the modern military tactics. The words of command and the whole system of drill long used in all European forces were invented and introduced by this remarkable military man.

By the most persistent industry and vigilant devotion to his army, a body of soldiery was created that was not surpassed in discipline by any in the world. This army numbered at least sixty thousand, and all of this he maintained in his little kingdom, and with its small population, without burthening his people or impoverishing his treasury. His economy and frugality were strict, his discipline stern and severe. He had one eccentric freak of the mind, that made him an object of derision to some, and to others suspected of madness, when it was associated with the harsh and violent acts of his peculiar and unusual life. His passion was the possession of a regiment of giants. He searched the whole world to find recruits for his Titanic cohort. In one instance he even snatched from the altar an Italian priest, whose large form and grand proportions made him an object to be coveted, and, with his emissaries infesting every city of the world, he abducted and spirited away to his service all whose height exceeded the common stature of common men. Some of them were as tall as nine feet, and none were less than seven. Of this body of prodigious monsters the king himself was colonel; before he was fifteen Frederick was created a captain, and soon after a major. Had he not been mounted, his diminutive figure would have made him an object of ridicule as a pigmy by the side of giants.

This king is worthy of some remark here. Indeed, I cannot well give you a fair insight into the character or deeds of the son without pausing for a time over the life of the father. Much that followed in the history of that son was the inevitable result of what had been done by the father and with the father,—as, in fact, it so runs through all such human affairs.

Men in their station are oftentimes believed to be acting of themselves and from their own unimpelled impulses, when in truth they are only obeying necessities that have been put upon them as trusts or bequests which they are obliged to fulfil or use. This monarch was of a frank, honest nature, fearfully rough and arbitrary, inflexible as iron in his will, abrupt, violent, fiery, but bluntly just and downright in his determinations and intentions. Sometimes men have thought him insane, so strange, so fierce, so wilful and exaggerated were his ways. He certainly was more than eccentric, if, indeed, he was not at times almost mad. But with all his fierce and boisterous ways, his fantastical hardness and cruelty, he had a fixed and settled rule of life,—I should rather say, an exact rule of life for himself and those about him. He was intensely practical, and had a resolute detestation for all that was hollow, false, trashy, or vain. He looked on life as a real, positive thing, in which certain duties were inevitable, and at all risks to be prepared for and done, not shirked or sneaked out of. He believed that his station was a trust, and that he would have to answer to God for his wilful neglect or abuse of that trust. His office was to rule for the well-being of his people, and not for the enjoyment of his own appetites or passions. He was to be an example to them in his public and private life, and, further, it was his place to oblige them to follow the same path that he walked, to be diligent in their daily doings, and to live with frugality and without foolishness or ostentation. Indeed, his habit of economy has been called parsimony and avarice. Perhaps it was, in one sense; but to judge of him we must see things as he saw them, and know them as he knew them.

His kingdom was given over to him on his father's death much demoralized by that father's prodigality and vanities. His kingdom was an object of derision to some whose crowns were older and whose dominions were larger, and of disgust and envy to others who hankered after the same advancement. It was composed of various patches of territory, partly purchased and partly acquired by negotiation and marriage, and of people of divers races. It was a long, narrow strip of land, with an extended and seemingly defenceless frontier. Indeed, it was all frontier, surrounded with enemies, and within itself having no strongholds, no points of military power, where resistance could be offered, protected by natural advantages. So during the Thirty Years' War it had been easily overrun, and was an attractive field for open fights.

His royalty was brand new. It commanded no respect from past deeds, national or individual. Princes and public men had no sense of awe of it: before the assembled congress of kingships military men sneered at its resources and its power, as courtiers and flunkeys laughed scornfully at his father's pompous retinue of regalities and his theatrical pageants of state ceremonials. He resolved to be a king in fact as he was in name, and to have his people, what he was himself, respectful and submissive to the forms of the faith he was bred in and believed in, obedient to the ordained laws of the land, industrious and frugal and temperate in their daily lives, and, above all, dutifully silent and yielding to his will for their own good. Consider this man's purpose witnessed by his acts and his whole scheme of life, and strip from it the angry, arbitrary manner with which he conformed to it himself and enforced it on all others, and you will feel that he lived not without a great public use,—a public use felt to this hour abroad as well as at home. From the moment he took up the threads of order and unravelled them from their sad confusion and meshes of tangle, and restored the fabric to what it had been when the Great Elector laid them down,—from that moment to this the designs of their workmanship have been plain to all men, and the result has been useful to a whole great people and useful to the world.

At this minute Prussia (the territory he ruled over) contains a people who, by their wise economy, industry, and practical good sense, find their pleasures at home, in the performance of domestic duties and in the cultivation of the domestic virtues, and who obtain prosperity by reasonable and practical industry, and happiness in life without pretentious competition for social importance and the mimicry of fashionable vanities. His diligence became their rule of life, his thrift and penurious exactness their habit, his prudence and forecast their nature.

Think how small a place his kingdom then was,—not five millions of people. Think, too, of the sad and dismal condition of things everywhere—in other lands and with other kings. Look at France, with the infamies of the regency; contrast its court with that of Prussia; and England, too! with a German prince like himself, no less than himself in dignity and rank and importance, lording it over that heroic race, with his fat and lean German trulls be-titled and bowed down to by a super-serviceable crew of courtiers! Look over the face of Germany, and see the minor sovereigns who crowded round him and his people. Look at the court of that Sybarite and animal, Augustus the Strong, of Saxony. Look at them all, and see how they were whirling around in a wild dance of accursed vanities and sins, how they lived only in wickedness and selfishness and sinful foolishness. They were disciples of the devil! In France they were dancing and yelling on the very confines of hell itself; Tartarus, with all its filthy vapors foaming up from its dark abyss and flashing out in lurid flames, was yawning before them. Eyes had they, and yet did they not see; ears had they, and yet did they not hear. Kings by the Grace of God, Defenders of the Faith, were living in lust and sumptuousness, and were grinding their people into the mire of moral degradation and physical want. They were debasing their souls and starving and murdering their bodies. The German potentates were swelling with silliness and vaporing conceits, imitating like stage-players the pomps and vanities of Versailles; and Versailles was leading the way to destruction. These are strong words; but they are not as strong as the deeds I speak of were infamous.

All this the Prussian king saw, and in his soul he loathed it, and he resolved, in his savage, fierce way, to live by a higher and purer rule of life, for a loftier and holier destiny. Remember the nature of the man, and remember the detestable, beastly things he saw and knew to be done by the whole world of Christian European rulers. It was enough to make him wild when he saw what a work he had before him. He had no warlike propensities, or, if he had, he wisely restrained them; but he well knew and felt that to avoid them, and give his people time to grow and strengthen, and to be ready for the crisis whenever it should come, as come it would, he or his heir must be armed to the teeth, and his soldiers must be in all the qualities of soldierhood as far beyond his adversaries as they excelled him and his dominions in extent of territory and number of people. He not only prepared his army, but he increased his treasury, and, above all, he trained his people with a habit of life and thought and disposition that fitted them to front the evil day with a stern power of self-reliance and self-control and heroic fortitude.

He not only knew that this general reign of wild disorder would end in strife, but he remembered and kept constantly in view the position of his kingdom towards the empire and the other powers about him. He remembered the adjourned dispute about Silesia, wrongfully wrested from his race by the grasping kaiser, and the suspended and unacknowledged right he had to the duchies of Cleves and Jülich, all of which must some day ripen into cause of open rupture. For be it observed that in all these hundreds of years these Hohenzollerns never forgot a claim or surrendered a right they had ever a color of. The traditional policy of this race is persistent, indefatigable, inflexible possession or pursuit of their own, whether they hold it themselves or it has been seized and claimed by others. They are unyielding, and, when the right time comes as inevitably as the law of gravitation, they march on steadily to take their own against all the world in arms if need be. The very severities of the father made the heroic temper of the son, and prepared him for the hard necessities he was to inherit with his crown. He too must obey the law of his race, he must mount to the very pinnacle of kingly power and dominion, he must overcome ruin and gain imperishable glory; but it must be by confronting terrors such as few kings ever faced and such as none ever faced with so little hope and with such undaunted fortitude.

Much that we know of the inner life of this king is taken from a sad, undutiful book written by his daughter Wilhelmina, afterwards the margravine of Baireuth. She was the favorite sister of Frederick, but she and he were destined for a time to fall under their father's displeasure. All the domestic troubles and griefs that should have been concealed and forgotten are unveiled and exposed to the gaze of the unthinking and wicked, who delight to learn of such in-door scandals and calamities. Much that she writes is no doubt true, but possibly exaggerated, and even then, when she tells the truth, she does not tell the whole truth. Enough, however, is revealed to show how this positive and angry man was irritated by petty cabals, and domestic treacheries and diplomacies, the end of which was not only to derange his well-ordered and well-designed discipline, but also to cross the very pathway of his public ends and purposes. His wife and daughter encouraged his son in his idle, silly, disobedient, and almost godless ways, and his wife was ever scheming against his will to form alliances for her daughters and her son, when those connections were a part of the state policy, and things to be dealt with only by him to whom such things were alone committed. The very welfare of his kingdom, of his race, and of his people were concerned in the proper disposition of his children by judicious and suitable marriages; and yet, while he was striving to effect results that should accord with that policy and that purpose, known only to himself, his wife and daughters were following their own wilful inclinations by clandestine means, and to the injury of all his plans. I do not intend by this to glorify this man or to hold him up to you as one without blemish or fault. He was often savage and despotic. His family lived with him sometimes as if they were living with a madman in a mad-house. His whole domestic career was one unbroken current of tyranny. He loved his wife, but he knew her weak, vain ways, no doubt the transmitted qualities of her weak and almost criminal mother, repudiated by her husband for her sad doings with Count Koenigsmark, the brother of that Aurora who was one of the Pompadours of Augustus the Strong and the mother by him of the celebrated Marshal Saxe. He knew how they were encouraging his heir in habits of thought and ways of life that might lead to ruin and unfit him for the crown he was to wear and the stern duties that were awaiting him. He was a harsh, wild man; in his rugged bosom he had a kind, loving heart, but that heart never ruled his conscience or ensnared his reason.

He was brutal and avaricious; but he was brutal when he felt that fraud and contrivance and sloth were to be driven out with blows, and he was avaricious when he knew that economy could alone prepare him with the means of self-protection and save his people from destitution, and when he saw unthrift and prodigality and wilful, wicked waste. As he feared God, and was a virtuous, wife-loving king, and a firm, affectionate father, in a generation of infidels and scoffers and adulterers; as he ruled his people justly and peaceably, and for their good, when other monarchs who were soft and courteous and mild sent theirs forth to die by myriads, from lust of conquest or malignant piques, or robbed them of their gains till they reduced them to starving,—as he was all this, we must respect if not venerate his name and not scoff at his infirmities.

The last mention I made of the great Frederick was that at about the age of fifteen he had been promoted to the rank of major in his father's own regiment of grenadier guards. By the time he was eighteen he was its lieutenant-colonel.

Here it will be proper to give some account of his early education. His father's notions were as peculiar in this as they were in other matters, and yet they were rational and highly practical. The success of that prince in after-life can be traced to the influence of this discipline and to a correct knowledge of the very subjects as to which his father exacted from his teachers a rigid training. The prince did not relish the duties of his station or sympathize with the tastes of his father. Nothing but the sharpest of teachers could have given to his nature the turn it took in life. Adversity and necessity forced him to acquire that which was the foundation of all his glory.

The father was a soldier. His monarchy was a military monarchy. His civil rule was like the rule of the camp. His amusements were those of drilling, hunting, drinking, smoking. The prince was a fine gentleman. He had been infected with a fondness for fine things,—for music, for belles-letters, for sceptical philosophy, fantastic speculations, and equally fantastic fine clothing. The father was all German to the core; the son was French. The father was resolute and believed in serious employments; the son was frivolous and licentious. These tendencies were strengthened by his association with French teachers and intimates who were refugees and thronged Berlin at that time. All this his father detested, and, with a resolution which was the law of his nature, he determined to force the prince to learn those arts and take up those habits which would fit him for the terrible task that he knew he must some day work out. Oftentimes the severities of the father were almost brutal; but we must remember how his purpose was the good of the young man, and that the means were necessary and were only taken after milder treatment had failed.

Frederick bore himself in a haughty, resistant way, and finally resolved to fly the country. He planned his escape. He had two associates, Lieutenant Katt and Lieutenant Keith. These young men were his intimates. Katt, it is said, was addicted to vices of a flagrant nature, and abused his great cleverness and culture and precocity by the sin of scoffing infidelity. They were both men of noble birth and high connections. For a long time they had encouraged and even instigated the prince to the vain pursuits so odious to his father and so derogating to his own manhood and princely dignity.

The immediate cause of his proposed flight was personal chastisement, inflicted on him by his father when on a visit to the king of Poland and elector of Saxony, Augustus the Strong, at Dresden. While there he had been guilty of some acts of depravity as well as of personal disrespect to the king, and when admonished and checked answered with a haughty and rebellious air. We must not think of him as a prince, but we must remember that he was a lad of fifteen, and that his father was a stern, high-tempered, God-fearing man, who looked with sorrow on these evil deeds, and who believed, as I do, in whipping such devils out of boys, so that they may be spared soul and body for future good and not become a curse to society and to themselves. The purpose of the prince became known, and he was watched.

Some time after this visit to Dresden the king resolved on a journey through the Imperial dominions. The prince was taken with him, and the officers who were his companions were men of high rank and sterling worth. They were especially cautioned to watch the young man. They did; and when, on their way home, he stole out in the gray of the morning, at the village of Steinfurth, leaving, as he thought, all asleep, and, with one foot in the stirrup and bridle in hand, he was ready to mount and ride forth into the world and desert his home and his duties in his wicked wish to find liberty to sin, he was suddenly stopped. Lieutenant-Colonel Rochou, one of his suite, had been called by his valet, who was on the watch, walked quietly out to him, and ended that attempt.

When the king heard this, his rage was without restraint, and the prince by his attitude of defiance provoked him further and further till his father again severely chastised him. Keith fled to Holland and thence to England. Katt was arrested, tried, convicted, and sentenced; and Frederick was arrested, imprisoned, and tried also. They were all conspirators, and had proposed an offence of most serious and dangerous character. They were deserters from their military duty, and as such were condemned to death. The king threatened to execute his son, but the sovereigns of Europe united and protested against this act of cruelty. I have never believed that the king intended to carry out his threat. The parental instinct, his real rough goodness of heart, the religious rule of his life, all disfavor the thought. His object was to shock the young man into a sense of the peril of his own position, and teach him the value of those two potent words *duty* and *obedience,* and put an end to the schemes and cabals that infested his household with their treasonable petty diplomacy and mean shifts.

The prince's life was spared. Katt was executed in his presence, and died repentant, and begging the prince to reform his life and yield to the rule of his father. Frederick was then exiled to Cüstrin, a small town about seventy miles east of Berlin, and placed under strict watch. He was restricted in all his ways and enjoyments, and obliged to set about at once acquiring a perfect knowledge of the management and direction of the internal economy of the government. The very details of such affairs he was required to take part in, and with his own hand to report to his father the result of his labor, and this he did with diligent earnestness. He surrendered and put behind him all the stubborn airs and idle conceits and wicked practices that had well-nigh worked his ruin and broken the heart of his earnest, honest, rough, and passionate father. A year passed by. During that time the father knew all about him, and, knowing how happy the influence of this confinement and discipline had been, relented, and resolved to visit him and see for himself,—and go he did. The interview was a painful—was a distressing one. We have the record of it, and can learn how touching it was. Hearken to the father as he speaks: "Nothing touches me so much as that you had not any trust in me. All this that I was doing for the aggrandizement of the house, the army, and the finances could only be for you if you made yourself worthy of it. I here declare I have done all things to gain your friendship, and all has been in vain!" They were reconciled, and embraced, with tears and sobs, that one may almost see if not hear to this day.

For fifteen months he remained at Cüstrin. After this visit of his father the regulations were relaxed; but he was still kept there, that he might, away from temptation, be taught the tasks that were set before him, and prepare himself for life and its hard, stern realities, and that he might in solitude learn to walk cautiously and in good earnest study to become a new creature and be ruled by his own good sense.

His sister Wilhelmina was married to the margrave of Baireuth, and during the festivities at an immense ball she was dancing with great delight. As she tells it, "I liked dancing and was taking advantage of my chances. Grumkow came up in the middle of a minuet. 'O madame! you seem to have got bit by the tarantula. Don't you see those strangers who have just come in?' I stopped short, and, looking all around, I noticed at last a young man dressed in gray whom I did not know. 'Go, then, embrace the prince royal; there he is before you!' said Grumkow. All the blood in my body went topsy-turvy for joy. I sprang upon him with open arms; I was in such a state I could speak nothing but broken exclamations. I wept, I laughed, I was like one gone delirious. I never felt such joy. I took him by the hand, and entreated the king to restore him his friendship; this was so touching that all wept." This tells the story: he had returned to his place, he was restored, and he was changed; he was a man, and as she says, "He wore a proud air and seemed to look down on everybody." Soon after this he was appointed to the Goltz regiment as its colonel commandant, and went to Rupin, about thirty miles northwest from Berlin, where it was stationed, and took charge of it.

This ends the boyhood and youth of this wonderful man: conspicuous in it (at a time when others are obscure), as he was in all of the events of his calamitous, intrepid, and triumphant career. Wilhelmina was now married. She too was restored to her father's love by her dutiful submission to his will. She married a man who was a good husband to her, and she was happy and made him a good wife, and so she testifies in her strange, improper book, in which she records the secrets of her father's house, and I believe much exaggerates, as, indeed, such a babbler would, and of necessity must. It is from her that we have learned all of the accounts of her father's dreadful outbursts and his passionate assaults on the prince, and they are to be taken with all due caution. Had she had her way and the way of her mother, she would have been the wife of Frederick, Prince of Wales, the father of George III. She would have been the unhappy, miserable consort of a dissolute, depraved, and drunken husband. Her father, no doubt, knew this, and he hindered it for her good. Her brother learned to understand her, and in after-life treated her with gentleness and love, but with a proper sense of her real merits and qualities.

The next step in the life of the prince was his marriage. After some serious negotiations, a wife was chosen for him. It was a princess of Brunswick-Bevern.

He was married on the 12th of June, 1733. She is described as a young person of eighteen, and of a clear, beautiful complexion ; rather simple, if not awkward, in her ways, but of upright, honest heart; rather silent, but still of good sound sense. His father purchased him a fine residence at Rheinsberg, about ten miles away from Ruppin. This place the prince adorned with considerable taste and skill, and then established himself with his wife and his little court, and lived a tranquil, happy life for near seven years, till the death of the king.

Before he went, after his marriage at Rheinsberg, he spent a winter as a volunteer at the siege of Philipsburg in the war between the emperor and Louis XV., growing out of the election of the king of Poland, wherein the emperor had hindered the elevation and restoration of Stanislaus Leszinski to that crown, for which his father-in-law, Louis XV., felt himself aggrieved, and with the Spaniards took up arms, and during two or three years despoiled the emperor of his possessions in Italy, took from him and his family the kingdom of Naples and the two Sicilies, and established there in his stead the Spanish Bourbons, who were but the other day and in our time expelled from these ill-gotten regalities.

v

This siege of Philipsburg was remarkable for two things only. The Duke of Berwick, the natural son of James II. by Arabella Churchill, the sister of the great John Churchill, the Duke of Marlborough, was commander of the French forces, and was a man of remarkable gifts, and had signalized his career by many acts of military greatness. While he was inspecting the enemy's lines, incautiously he stepped on an elevation so dangerous that soldiers were forbidden to go there. He was hardly on it, with his glass to his eye, when a cannon-ball dashed his brains out and thus ended his brilliant life in an instant.

The Austrians were commanded by the greatest Continental officer of that age, Prince Eugene of Savoy, the victor of the Turks at the battle of Zenta, and the conquerer in eighteen pitched battles. He was now an old man, hard on to eighty. His presence there drew around him nearly all of the princely persons in Germany. The fact that such a leader was again in arms after a lifetime of glories has given a character to the siege of this otherwise insignificant place.

At Rheinsberg the prince spent his time in the performance of his public and military duties and close and serious study. He cultivated music and surrounded himself with all of the musical celebrities within his reach. His own skill as master of the flute is well attested. To him his music was ever a consolation, and it has been said of him, that in the solitude of his soul, when in grief at Cüstrin, or in after-life, when overwhelmed with disasters, he found his relief in the wild and piteous wailings of his own adagios that expressed his sorrow. The marriage of Frederick was one of state convenience urged by his father, in his anxiety to settle and establish the boy, accepted by him as a convenient means of independence. His wife and he at Rheinsberg lived contentedly, and in after-years she adverted to those days as the happiest of her life—her joyless life. He was not a good husband to her. Indeed, how could he love any woman? for early he had learned in his dissolute doings to measure woman by the standard of the low creatures who were the companions of his sinful levities. His soul was stained with impurities; its wings were soiled and bedraggled with mire. Much of his own misfortune in after-life he owed to his harsh and malicious sayings of women, some of whom merited censure, and others as to whom his jeers were calumnies. It was because of this scorn of women and derogation of their just dues that, soon after he ascended the throne, he quietly deserted his simple true wife, and left her, as I have before said, with her honest heart to lead a joyless, cheerless life. For two or three years at intervals he sought her society; they grew rare, and then he dropped her altogether.

She never unveiled to the public the griefs that afflicted her; but, with a patience as heroic and a courage as intrepid as his own, bore her calamities with silent dignity, and suffered with a calm serenity of soul that made her life beautiful.

He never failed in all external evidences of ceremonious respect towards her. He exacted from others implicit deference for her, and once each year, on her birthday, in high punctilious state, he called on her, and extended the most formal and gracious courtesies to her, and that was all. After that he left her—he to go on his stormy ways of ferocious struggle for fame, and sometimes for land and life itself, or to the hard duties of his civil employments, or the gay enjoyments of his literary and philosophic followers; and she to her solitude and her life of goodness.

To his mother he was ever gracious and attentive. When she first said "Your Majesty," he interposed, "Call me son! that is the title of all others most agreeable to me." When in Berlin—no matter how busy—he never failed to visit her each day, and never spoke to her but with his hat in his hand.

While at Rheinsberg he wrote and composed much. Of course all that he wrote was in French—in truth he knew but little of German, and it is said that his knowledge of his native German was very imperfect. It is related of him that once he tried to understand a German translation of Racine's Iphigénie. He held the French original in his hands as the German was read to him, and he was obliged to say that he could not understand it. All that he knew of German was some colloquial talk—"enough to scold his servants or give the word of command to his soldiers," says a great historical scholar and critic; and the same author says his "French was, after all, the French of a foreigner." By some, and they great names, his productions, especially his poetic flights, or rather studies, are lightly spoken of, and even sneered at.

The easy voluptuous life thus led by the prince persuaded many that when his reign began it would be one of refinement and elegance, an era of letters and science and art and luxury, if not of pomp and magnificence.

But in this they erred, as we shall presently see. His father was rigid and exacting, and even penurious, and so was the son. The purpose and necessities of both made thrift and parsimony the rules of their lives.

In 1740 the king died, and at twenty-eight years of age Frederick II. inherited his crown. Men were startled at the conduct of their new sovereign. His first acts were peremptory and imperious, and free from all trace of folly and expense. From the hour he became king he held the reins of authority with a stern, unyielding sense of power. The light-headed vanities of his bad boyhood had passed away, and would have been remembered only by contrast with his subsequent industry, love of order, love of business austerity, and despotic will as a ruler, had he not then, along with his fooleries and wickedness, learned to scoff and sneer at things most holy. And men recalled all when, in after-life, they saw the libertine and sceptic become the tyrant and infidel. That spirit of impious mockery followed him to his dark and hopeless grave. Frederick was not a good man ; his principles were bad. He venerated nothing on earth or in heaven. His mind was quick, vivacious ; his wit was sharp and brilliant ; his knowledge of men was keen, and searching, and subtle ; he was crafty and unscrupulous, and selfish to the bone— cruelly selfish. With all his fortitude and almost superhuman intrepidity and undaunted industry—with all of these majestic traits of a heroic nature, he was not a good man, and left to the world a record of successes that will astound men when they read of his adversities and calamities ; but that is all he left. He led a life of superhuman trial and of miraculous triumphs, the product of an almost supernatural force of will and genius for his occupation ; but he was heartless and callous. His sense of justice towards his subjects was only a conviction of his reason as a principle of policy, and his occasional traits of feeling were mere ebullitions of romantic sentiment. He was a hard mocking infidel ; he had no fear of God or real love for man.

He was his father in all of his rigor but without his rugged sense of truth and straightforwardness. He was the same soldier and martinet, but he never hankered for military monstrosities or trifles. The day after his father's burial the whole of the four thousand giants were disbanded with a dash of his pen. He had a will, and he knew from the instant he put his foot on the first step of his throne what he wanted to do and how to do it. He was every inch a king!

Charles the Sixth, Emperor of Germany, died a few months after the accession of Frederick. This emperor was the last of the male line of his house. His son was dead and he had two daughters; one of them, the eldest, was Maria Theresa, who was married to Francis, Duke of Lorraine. As the law of succession then stood the female line was excluded. Many crowns were in the possession of these Hapsburgs. The hope of the emperor was to transmit them, together with the imperial dignity itself, to his daughter and her issue. To effect this he announced a new law of regal and imperial succession, and by what was called the Pragmatic Sanction he decreed that to his daughter and her husband should descend those vast dominions and dignities. The whole of the latter part of his life was given to diplomatic negotiations to secure the assent of all the European powers to this innovation. He not only diverted the course of descent as to his own inherited kingdoms, but he assumed to seize for his daughter by his will the imperial dominions and the imperial title, when it was not in his gift, but was to be had only by the voice of the electoral princes of the Holy Roman Empire. This was an arbitrary and revolutionary act, and those who assented to it had no power to assent. That which they gave was not theirs to give. The constitution of the empire, gray with ages, was not to be thus overturned by the usurping will of an incumbent who held not by inheritance, but by election, and to whom it was only a trust, and in whom there was no personal right of ownership or property.

There were princes of the empire who would not give even a color of confirmation to this usurpation.

Dissatisfaction from the first was felt, and this ripened into a hostile and angry feeling when Maria Theresa undertook to assume the dignities thus settled on her and seized for her aggrandizement.

She was a woman of commanding and attractive qualities of person and disposition, almost heroic in her tone. Her life was pure, but her nature was haughty and dominating.

As I have stated, the Austrian crown had a century before seized the province of Silesia. By solemn and recognized compact between the duke who owned it and the elector of Brandenburg, the possessions of each were to descend from the one who died without heirs to the one who survived.

The duke died heirless, and the province, by the deed, devolved on Brandenburg. Such contracts were common among these princes, and were sometimes encouraged by the empire as useful and conducive to peaceful results.

Various attempts and shifts had been adopted by the Austrians to obtain a surrender of their right from the Brandenburg electors; but these offers were all rejected, and the electors persisted in a continual claim of ownership from the hour that the province was taken to the hour of Frederick's accession to the crown.

This province Frederick resolved to take. To this he was moved by many motives, and among them was not only his " desire to make people talk about him," as he said himself, but it was the knowledge that this was his opportunity, the blazing opportunity for which his race had been watching through long nights of years and years, and for which they had day by day been mustering and drilling and organizing those forces which had been the wonder of Europe, as they were soon to be the wonder of the world. And he had personal reasons that were close to his heart, for these Hohenzollerns bequeath their wrongs from father to son, and through the long dreary years of their pilgrimage up, from the days of Conrad their adventurous cadet up to the days of Frederick, each had in due time collected the score due to his predecessor. It was the law of their race, and it is to this day.

We, too, have seen them at Sedan and in Paris wiping out an old score of this kind, that touched a nice point of honor, but till then not wholly adjusted between them and the French.

He had his father's wrongs, he had personal wrongs to avenge,—wrongs inflicted on him by the direct machinations of the Austrian crown. For years Seckendorf, the imperial envoy, had enjoyed the closest relation with the dead king. In fact (with Grumkow, his prime minister), he had ruled him and directed the public and private policy of the crown. Grumkow was his paid instrument, and he the paid emissary sent to delude and cheat the rough but honest monarch.

The king had affinities for his imperial chief, and that feeling swayed him, for he was conservative and loyal by nature, and he was made to believe that his suspended claims for Silesia and Julich and Cleves and Berg should be finally and justly settled.

The alliances of his own prince and his daughters were influenced by this heartless, obtrusive, artful spy and envoy.

Some of the conflicts between Frederick and the king were instigated by this meddler and prince of scoundrels, as a part of the policy of his master, the emperor. Frederick knew this, and had waited for his hour.

And, further, after the king had betrothed Frederick to his wife—and all done in strict accord with the wishes of the emperor and his envoy—that officer, in the name of his sovereign, urged him to break his faith and open anew negotiations with England for a daughter of its king. So honest and faithful to his word was that violent old man that he resented the request as a personal indignity. It provoked his sense of honor and pierced to the heart his chivalric spirit of loyalty to his imperial chief. As he said, " It was as if you had turned a dagger in my heart," and for years after the event he now and then, in violent cries of resentment, raged over it; and once, as he approached the grave, and as he began to observe the hard, unrelenting, and fierce qualities of his son, and to discover the soldier and the king in his boy concealed under his silken surface, he exclaimed, " There is one that will avenge me !" Yes, one ! And there is one now who will avenge you, and avenge himself, though he set Europe in a flame, and bring himself, his land, his title, his people, and his family to the very jaws of desolation and ruin !

On the 20th of October, 1740, the kaiser died. On the 12th of December, 1740, a grand ball was given by the king and he was present; privately he quitted it, and on the 13th of December he was on the way to Frankfort to join his troops, suddenly and promptly assembled, all in fighting trim for this the first great step of his life.

This act was planned and executed in the true spirit of his nature. With despatch and secrecy he prepared himself, and, swift as a bolt from the ethereal blue, he launched himself on his object; onward he swept, and, though it was the depth of winter, by the end of January he owned the province, and his victorious muskets garrisoned every town of importance and held undisputed occupation of the open country.

He returned to Berlin, and in the spring he joined his forces. The Austrians were in the field. At Mollwitz a battle was fought, the first battle of his life. Field-Marshal Schwerin was at his side, and by him the fight was fought and won, and the Austrians lost eight thousand men. Frederick became bewildered by the rout of the cavalry commanded by himself; he fled the field, and almost lost his honor, believing he had lost the day.

After this the French and Bavarians united with him in his assault on Austria. The electors advanced the Bavarian to the imperial crown. Maria Theresa was now in peril, and her enemies were hunting her in her patrimonial dominions. The Pragmatic Sanction was in tatters, and the work of a lifetime and years of scheming diplomacy vanished before the flash of the first musket fired by Frederick.

Onward in his impetuous way he pushed his fortunes and drove his enemy before him,—aggressive from the first, aggressive to the last.

At Chotusitz the king met Prince Charles of Lorraine,—the brother-in-law of the Queen of Hungary,—who gave battle to the Prussians and lost it. Though skilful and valiant, he was not a prosperous officer. This victory the king owned that he owed to the discipline and valor of his men and not to his own skill.

After this he made peace with Austria, deserting his allies without compunction, and obtaining from the Empress Queen the cession of Silesia and for himself and for his troops repose and opportunity.

In 1742 he withdrew himself and his forces from the field, and so continued until 1744. In the mean time, the Austrians, relieved from him and joined by the Saxons and English, soon retrieved their shattered fortunes, and drove the French and Bavarians and their other enemies with dreadful slaughter from their borders, and even reclaimed by military occupation a part of the German territory seized on and kept by the victorious armies of Louis the Fourteenth.

In 1745, Charles the Seventh, the Bavarian emperor, lay down and died. In May, 1744, the king of France, the Emperor Charles the Seventh, the king of Prussia, the Elector Palatine, and the king of Sweden as landgrave of Hesse, formed an alliance at Frankfort. To this step he was led from the knowledge that it was the resolution of the Austrians and English (with whom afterwards were the Saxons and Sardinians and the Dutch) to force France into a treaty of peace without stipulating for any guarantee for Silesia.

He had been advised that in the negotiations between the queen of Hungary and George the Second, Maria Theresa had complained that she had been forced to surrender Silesia, to which the king replied, " Madame, that which it is good to take, it is good to retake."

This scheme of spoilation he wished to resist. While resting, he had increased his army by eighteen thousand men; it was refreshed and prepared, and in the autumn of 1744 he took the field with his usual energy, and his very presence sent terror to the courts that had been plotting him mischief.

At first his operations were unsuccessful, but after a time he regained all he had lost, and by the battles of Hohenfriedberg and Sorr he signally routed the Austrians and Saxons, and convinced all men that he was the master of his art and the first general in the world.

After this a peace was negotiated and concluded at Dresden in January, 1746, and on his return to Berlin his people exultingly bestowed on him the title of Frederick the Great. Nothing escaped him. His mind was ever on the alert; had he not been the ever-present and all-doing man he was, he never could have reached the goal he started for. It was essential to his fortunes that his kingdom should be conducted by him alone. His necessities and wants no man must know, or it would have been his ruin. His hopes and resolutions no man must ever be able to conjecture, or he would fail. Convinced of this, there was not a thing done, from the recruiting and drilling of his men to the collection of his taxes, the conduct of his household, the government of his family, the police regulations of his towns, the details of their extension and improvement, the administration of public justice, the diplomatic intercourse with other states,—no, not a thing, of which he was not in person the superintendent and director.

During the period I have spoken of, early in his reign, he watched the course and purpose of other crowns and had his paid agents in each court and by the side of each foreign functionary.

He knew all that others said, wrote, or designed that related to him or his fortunes, and thus it was he was ever in advance of them and their schemes for his harm. We have seen how in 1744 he anticipated the plans of the Empress Queen and George II. to despoil him of Silesia. He suddenly joined the king of France and took up arms to check the Austrians, now too high in their flight, and grown too strong with victory. At the same time, with the forecast of an older man, he provided for his future and most dreaded danger from Russia, by securing an influence at that court which in his darkest hour, when all seemed gone and his enemies were grinding him to dust, helped if not saved him.

At his instance the heir to that empire was married to the only daughter of a poor prince of Anhalt-Zerbst, then a field-marshal in his service. By him Catherine the Second, the Semiramis of the North, when a little girl of fifteen, was taken from a garrison town of his, Stettin, and sent to be the bride of that heir, herself to become renowned for more than manlike vigor, atrocities, and depravities.

28*

Then, also, he obtained a foothold in the Swedish court, marrying his sister Ulrica to the crown prince of that kingdom.

In the campaign of 1745 he was well-nigh ruined, and so all men thought. His disasters were many, and his expenses had exhausted the whole of his treasure. His people he would not retax. He provided in various ways for his wants by his never-ending thrift, by quietly melting up all of the plate of the crown, the grand silver chandeliers of his palace, and the superb silver music balcony in his great ball-room. They were all secretly taken away in the night-time and converted into coin. With these helps and with his sword and his subtle craft he beat aside his enemies and conquered fortune.

For ten years he enjoyed perfect peace, and these were the years of real glory. For like a subordinate and dependent, and not like a monarch, he gave each hour of each day to the duties of his station and to bettering the condition of his people. He was diligent in mind and body. In summer he rose at three, and in winter at four o'clock, and worked incessantly.

His army was his first object of care. With a population of five millions, he had as many men in arms as had Louis XV., with twenty-five millions of subjects. A seventh of his men were his soldiers. His discipline was severity itself. The men who were to fear nothing on earth on the day of battle were trained to stand in terror of the corporal's cane. The precision and velocity with which they per-formed the most difficult manœuvres, even in the face of an enemy, astounded all soldiers. There were no forces in being then that were not as raw militia when compared with them. His kingdom was new,—he was almost an upstart among kings,—its rank was hardly that of second-rate, and yet he raised it to be the first of the first. He glittered not as one of a constellation of sovereignties; he blazed as a planet flaming with rays of glory. He encouraged both letters and science. His court was the refuge of all persecuted and unrecog-nized merit. He created an academy of science and letters, and himself often presided, and to it read papers of his own composition. He adorned his capital with grand buildings. He improved his highways; he systematized his revenue. He reformed his juris-prudence and supervised its workings. The poorest man was heard in person by him and his wrongs righted. He built places of amuse-ment and directed their spectacles and plays. He abolished the tor-ture, and rarely punished with death. He was tolerant on the subject of religion, and when, from motives of state policy, the Order of

Jesus was driven from all the courts and kingdoms of Europe, he gave them a welcome asylum. He encouraged and promoted education, and in his own life furnished an example to others of frugality and moderation. He surrounded himself with some men of letters and science whose names will not readily be lost to mankind, and others who got fame only by their association with him,—Maupertuis, Euler, D'Arget, Algarotti, La Mettrie, Rothenburg, and the two Keiths, James and George. And then, too, he had Voltaire with him. To this Frenchman all cultivated minds then, as now, accorded a pre-eminence in the domain of letters.

He was a man of various attainments, of exalted genius, of refined and acute perceptions, and of brilliant wit. He was monarch in the realms of human thought and in the power of human expression. Whatever he said or wrote or did, the world heard and read and saw, and the world applauded " to the echo that doth applaud again."

Early in life Frederick was attracted and dazzled with this man's fame, and emulated his achievements. For a long time, while he was the prince, they corresponded. After he became king, Voltaire visited him casually three or four times. Once or twice, under color of paying his court to the Prussian king, his friend, he was the secret agent of Louis XV., and, while seemingly devoted to letters and the courtesies of royal hospitality, he was striving by finesse and craft to persuade Frederick to the purposes of the French court. Frederick, with his swift intuition and insight, perceived all this, and, without disclosing his knowledge of Voltaire's purpose, he softly turned away from it and enjoyed his visitor and his elegant fascinations of conversation and stores of information.

Frederick longed for the society of this man ; he desired the advantage of his help in his studies and the charm of his never-failing fountain of thought, of sentiment, and feeling. After some entreaty and solicitation he consented to come. When he came he was adorned with titles and dignities and offices. He had a life pension given him, and a residence by the side of the king in the palace itself. All that could gratify his vanity or pride, or contribute to his comfort or happiness, was bestowed on him by his royal friend ; so they lived together in harmony and delight for a while.

These two men were not made for each other ; their stations in life were too remote to admit of the close intercourse each sought to establish ; they were both exacting and both unprincipled, and both vain and ambitious. The one followed the business of a hero, the other was after all but a kind of glorious sycophant. The one was a right royal king of men, the other was but a king of critics. They both scoffed at religion and almost defied God. How then could they respect or trust each other ? Voltaire was guilty of acts of petty meanness and malevolence, and complicated and annoyed the king with his spiteful quarrels with others, and finally excited the disgust of Frederick, who parted with him in anger.

Voltaire went his way screeching with rage at his royal patron, and Frederick followed him on the road with acts of petty and tyrannical malice, and so ended their personal intercourse. Afterwards they had a kind of hollow truce, an outward show of reconciliation, and corresponded, but Voltaire never forgot his punishment, and Frederick at heart looked on him as a cross between a monkey and a cat inflamed with an inspired gift for letters.

While thus occupied the king never for a moment forgot his enemies. He well knew that Austria would not surrender all hope of regaining her lost province, and he further knew that other crowns were eager to see him punished and repressed. He had given some cause for this hostile feeling. His sharp, caustic speeches and reflections on other princes had been repeated and circulated through Europe, and they rankled with malicious resentment towards him. He had unwisely attracted the hatred of two powerful and wicked women, Elizabeth of Russia, and Madame Pompadour. His sneers and flings at their infamies had roused their keenest sense of hatred. Both of them he had repelled, and both of them were solicited by Maria Theresa, who forgot the dignity of her race and station and the purity of her fame and womanhood, to court favor and alliance with two such conspicuous criminals, outcasts from decency, daughters of depravity itself.

Prince Kaunitz, the Austrian chancellor, was a subtle and adroit man. His heart was with the cause of his mistress, the Empress Queen. He devised an alliance the purpose of which was the ruin of Frederick. For centuries France and Austria had been traditional hereditary enemies, and the face of Europe ran with streams of human blood poured out in their vindictive and unrelenting conflicts. By his designs and dexterous management, all this animosity was to be forever abandoned, and these two rival powers were to become friends, and unite to punish their common foe and rival, this upstart king, this rebellious subject, this ferocious foe, this treacherous ally.

The product of all this diplomacy was a secret treaty between them. France, Austria, Russia, Saxony, and Sweden, and the Germanic princes, were all united to trample him and his kingdom out of life. They were to divide his territory and almost obliterate him. Austria was to take Silesia, Russia East Prussia, Saxony Magdeburg, and Sweden Pomerania. To the French Austria was willing to cede a part of the Netherlands as compensation.

These were fearful odds. No one man and no one state ever before encountered such and survived. Look at it, think of it. He had about five millions of people, his enemies reigned over full a hundred millions. He was able to bring into the field about two hundred thousand fighting men, but they commanded over six hundred thousand; his territory was open and easy of occupation, and one-fourth of his dominions, Silesia, was new and disaffected in religion and in allegiance. All of this would have cowed any other spirit than that of Frederick.

He had been advised of it, and knew each step that had been taken in the plot, and was secretly preparing himself and his army for the strife. He knew his advantages and what feats his men could achieve against all odds.

He was the sole commander, while his enemies were divided in their councils and in their leaders. He knew himself and he knew them, and he felt he had skill and valor enough for all of them, and so he had.

Quietly he lay by watching, and when all was ripe for action and when they had nearly consummated their designs and begun their preparations, he proclaimed to the empress his knowledge of her purpose, and demanded to know what the massing of her military forces meant and against whom they were to be sent. He had an evasive, haughty reply. This was enough for him, and swift as thought itself his army of two hundred thousand men, led by himself and his brother, and Schwerin and Keith, and Bevern and Ferdinand of Brunswick, and Winterfeldt and Seidlitz and the prince of Wirtemberg, marched forth in August, 1756.

Before it was known that he had started, he was in Saxony and soon possessed of Dresden. Then he seized the archives, and notwithstanding the personal resistance of the queen, her husband having fled to the camp at Pirna, he opened them and took from them written evidence of this guilty combination to destroy him. It was for that he was so prompt in his march on Saxony. By his spies he was advised that such documents were there, and he knew their publication would justify him and expose the conspirators against him and the peace of Europe.

He met Marshal Browne with the Austrians at Lowositz and drove them before him. Saxony capitulated, and its king fled to Poland. From that hour and during the war he treated it as a conquered province, and in it levied troops and money as he never did from his own Brandenburg.

Now, behold! one of his conspiring enemies is at his feet, and only a few months had gone by since that evening when at a dinner-party he whispered to Mitchell, the British envoy, to come to him at three o'clock the following morning, and when he arrived, he took him to his camp, near Berlin, and said, " There are one hundred thousand men setting out at this instant,—not one of them knows where. Write to the king, your master, and say that I go to defend his majesty's dominions and my own," and now—hardly two months—his foot is on the Saxon! The winter suspended all operations in the field. He lived in Dresden during that winter, organizing and preparing for the spring, sequestering the revenues of that state, levying contributions, enrolling their forces with his own, and treating them as a conquered and subjugated people. Once only he went to Berlin, and that for nine days, in January, 1757,—the last time he was to see his capital for six long years.

Let those who wish to know how well he understood the peril of his position, read his letter of secret instructions to Graf Von Finck-ensten, written while on this visit. He calmly contemplates the worst and provides for all disasters. It is direct, simple, and exact; each line of it shows the depth of his determination to conquer his enemies or perish in his resistance. Then he bade good-by forever to his mother,—they never met again. She died while he was in the wilderness of his calamities. Then it was, too, that he provided himself with poison,—a few small pills in a little glass tube with a bit of ribbon to it; these he always carried on his person. How sad a tale do they reveal! They were found in his drawer after his death.

Early in 1757 the king with his forces passed into Bohemia, and in May of that year had the dreadful fight before the walls of Prague. The slaughter was horrible on both sides. The Austrians were beaten and driven into the city, and Marshal Browne, its commander, was killed.

It was there that Frederick lost Marshal Schwerin, who, charging at the head of his regiment with his colors in his hand, fell, at seventy-two years of age, one of the last of Marlborough's veterans and the best of Frederick's captains. In June he rashly attacked Marshal Daun at Kolin, and was beaten with great carnage. Indeed, it seemed for a while as if he were down never to rise. He was stupefied with horror at the blow, his very brothers reproached him with the impending ruin of their race. It was in this midnight of disasters he lost his mother. He gathered up his forces and withdrew from Bohemia.

At this time Winterfeldt was killed in action. "Against my multitude of enemies I may contrive resources, but I shall find no Winterfeldt again," said the king, with tears.

The Russians were in possession of his eastern provinces and Silesia was regained by the Austrians, and the French, under command of Marshal Soubise with the imperial troops, were advancing from the West. United they were seventy thousand in number.

His enemies shouted with exultation. Now they had him in their toils. He gathered up his loins and girded himself for the fight, and history shows but few records of such a victory as she then recorded. It was audacity itself that fired his soul. Beaten down and almost hunted out of his dominions, he faced a force of seventy thousand fresh and exultant troops with his squadrons of but twenty thousand men. At Rossbach he met them. Let me speak of it as Voltaire, a Frenchman, tells of it. "The defeats of Agincourt, Cressy, and Poictiers were not so humiliating." This battle was on the 5th of November, 1757, and it scattered the French and German troops into rags and tatters. They never again lay in his way.

From this scene he galloped off into Silesia to repair the losses there. At a council of his officers he addressed them; after saying a few but impressive things, he concluded, "But if there should be one or another who dreads to share all these dangers with me he can have his discharge this evening, and shall not suffer the least reproach from me," and the answer was no! And then he added, "The cavalry regiment that does not, on the instant an order is given, dash full plunge into the enemy, I will directly after the battle unhorse and make it a garrison regiment. The infantry battalion which, meet with what it may, shows the least signs of hesitating, loses its colors and its sabres, and I cut the trimmings from its uniform. Now, good-night, gentlemen; shortly we have either beaten the enemy or we never see one another again !" And he kept his word; he did meet the enemy at Leuthen, and on the 5th of December, 1757, with thirty thousand men he drove eighty thousand Austrians before him and cleared Silesia of their presence. This battle was one of the finest masterpieces of military skill, and was so pronouned by the great Napoleon. Thus by his grand feats he raised his fame and retrieved his fortunes. After this he received aid from England; an annual subsidy of seven hundred thousand pounds was paid him; and with it he increased his forces.

In 1758 he beat the Russians at Zorndorf with great slaughter. In less than a year he had vanquished vast armies of those great nations, France, Austria, and Russia. Then followed a series of calamities, and ruin again seemed impending. At Hochkirchen he was surprised at the dead of night and suffered terrible loses, but the greatest of all was the death of his friend the Field-Marshal James Keith, for whom he had a sense of fraternal affection. And thus from victory to defeat, and from defeat to victory, swayed to and fro the tide of this merciless and bloody conflict. At Kunersdorf the Austrians and Russians united nearly exterminated him. His own firmness gave way, and in his despair he meditated suicide. His enemies failed to follow up their advantage. They disputed among themselves and threw away their chance, their only chance. To him but a few days were all that was wanted. He re-collected his scattered squadrons and gathered in arms and materials for resistance. Five years had now gone by, and another man and another people must have been trampled out of life; but no, not he; his capital was taken and taken again, and every inch of his territory had been occupied by hostile forces, and yet he made fight to the last moment; wherever he faced them he attacked them, no matter about their force and no matter what were the odds.

He knew he could out-general them, and he knew the valor and the unquestioning faith of his people in him and his fortunes. 1761 came and his fate seemed sealed, but yet there he stood sword in hand defying the world. The English (from a change in politics) withdrew their help, and it looked as if the end had come, when Elizabeth of Russia died. The Emperor Peter III. succeeded. On the instant he withdrew his troops and concluded peace with Frederick, for whom he had a profound veneration. Indeed, he did more; he furnished troops and money to help him, and thus enabled him before the year to drive the Austrians before him and regain Silesia.

Peter was assassinated, Catherine, his wife (the little Anhalt-Zerbst girl of whom I spoke), became the empress, and while she did not help, she would not harm him. France and England concluded a peace, and finally, on the 15th of February, 1763, Austria sullenly and reluctantly assented to a peace, and at Hubertsburg, near Dresden, the treaty was signed that ended this prolonged contest of seven years of carnage and ruin.

He, of all who had engaged in that conflict, came out triumphant. Not one inch of ground had he lost, and he acquired a fame that men will not willingly let die.

But his people had suffered; whole provinces were devastated; one-sixth of the male population had been swept off as if the noon-day devil had walked forth. Famine had carried off its thousands and penury afflicted all that survived.

But one thing must not be forgotten,—he went into this war without debt, and he ended it without debt! His dexterity and thrift were as marvellous as his courage and skill. He straightway set about the restoration of his country.

From the year 1763 to 1786, when occurred his death, he was un-wearied in his efforts to replace all that had been destroyed, and to rouse the energies of his people and encourage their productive industries. I cannot here relate or detail the history of these years of practical usefulness.

These latter days were days of real glory and exhibit him in colors most attractive to the thoughful and judicious. " Peace hath her victories no less renowned than war," and those victories, those un-stained and unselfish victories, were his also. Steadily and firmly he restored all things. He did more; he increased the wealth and ad-vanced the standard of civilization and culture in his kingdom and with his people, and founded their greatness as on a rock, against which the winds and waves might dash and beat themselves in vain.

The real glory of these warlike struggles and peaceful victories is as much due to the temper and disposition of his people as to the policy and wisdom and prowess of their sovereign; and mankind acknowledge it, for without a grave and earnest and faithful people, he and all would have been whirled from the face of the earth.

Before I close, I must and will allude to two other important events in which he took part. One has been designated the crime of the age. i mean the partition of Poland. If any one of those sovereigns who took part in that offence had color of excuse, it was Frederick, for the portion assigned to him in the partition was only restored to Germany,—the Germans from whom it had been taken by the Poles in 1411, at the battle of Tannenburg, where the Teutonic knights were almost exterminated.

Those Christian warriors had reclaimed that wild region from the pagans and made it a part of Germany, when they were deprived of it in battle by the Poles and Tatars.

Men generally have blamed Austria and Russia for that robbery, and have been silent as to Frederick. He certainly did not plot it, and he took what was given to him when the result was inevitable, and in taking it, he took a people who owed their civilization to Germans, and whose affinities were with Germany, and who but three hundred years before had been under German rule.

The other event was the war of the Bavarian succession in 1777. The Elector of Bavaria died childless, and the Austrian crown, disregarding the claims of the Duke de Deux-Ponts to the succession, proceeded to seize upon the better part of Bavaria as an escheat to the emperor. Frederick had been watching the preparations of his old foe, and was resolved, for the sake of the integrity of the empire, to arrest this act of rapacity. He was appealed to to intervene, and he did, and in July, 1778, at the age of sixty-six, he marched forth at the head of one hundred thousand men, and at the same time sent his brother, Prince Henri, with another one hundred thousand. The king poured his forces into Bohemia, and his brother started from Dresden to assail them on the west. Maria Theresa was filled with terror. She dreaded a war for the sake of her people, and she dreaded this contest because her sons, Joseph and Leopold, were in the field, and Joseph the kaiser was ambitious of a soldier's fame, and would win laurels against so great a captain.

However, no results followed of a serious character. After an almost bloodless campaign Russia and France mediated, and their arbitration was accepted, and the cloud passed away and peace came. Frederick was glad enough to be done with it. His object was a good one; he gained his point and checked the grasping arrogance of Austria.

He was now within eight years of his death; those eight years were given to toil such as few young men would willingly endure. " The strictest husbandman was not busier with his farm than he with his kingdom."

Nothing but such habitual labor was left for him. He had no other refuge. Age had deadened his sense of enjoyment in those pursuits that were once the delight of his leisure.

A new era in the world was dawning on men. Just as he was tottering towards the twilight of life, "amid rifle-volleys and death-groanings at Bunker Hill, American Liberty had been born, and whirlwind-like was to envelop the whole world."

One by one his old generals had gone before him, and he was all alone. Indeed, his whole life had been one apart from others, and he was stern and lonesome, for he had no intimates and few friends in all of the retinue of associates and followers that he had gathered about him. He was a sad, silent, scornful old man. What had all of his toils and terrors, his conquests and glories, brought him to in these dark December days of his closing years? Oh, how painful and wretched must those doleful hours have been to him, when on his solitary summit he gazed back on a life of such labor and slaughter, and saw how little of real golden harvest it yielded, the golden harvest of good deeds, which with his great gifts he might have gathered! —when he remembered how he had walked among men with a soft and stealthy tread, wrapped in his "polite cloak of darkness," and all to gain the whole world and lose his own soul! What had it availed him, this mighty, this lonesome man? Verily, had he not sought to gather grapes of thorns and figs of thistles?

Down in the great plain of the Rhine country not far from Cologne, in the little village of Kempen, now a part of Prussia, in 1380, nearly five centuries ago, there was born a simple-hearted, pious peasant boy, Thomas, his real surname now hardly known, but called by men à Kempis, from the place of his birth, all else of him unknown, so humble and hidden was his secluded conventual life; lonely contemplation and secret prayer filled up his days; but his thoughts are known and will be known for ages and ages and ages to the end of time.

The consolation and joy that he has given to many a soul "weary and heavy laden;" the succor and comfort that he will give to millions yet to come, will glorify him with the beauty of a seraph. By the side of his pious meditations, "The Imitation of Christ," shining like a star leading to angelic ways, how dark and dismal look the doings of this king of men and lord of battles!

The history through which we have toiled (of over six hundred years) is filled to the brim with memorials of human sorrow and human cruelty; but, of all I ever read, the saddest is the one I am now about to tell you.

It chanced in the first days of Frederick's kingship, when his people believed they had a young, magnanimous, humane prince. On one of his first visits to Potsdam, a thousand children beset him in his way, all with the red string around their necks, that tells they are to be taken as soldiers,—a thousand little children! and cry out with one wild wail, " Oh, deliver us from slavery ! Must we be taken for soldiers ?" The cry of these little ones pierces us to this day. How could he have heard it and not quailed before it? The Emperor Joseph said the cry of people for bread, in a famine, had sent a chill of terror to his heart ; but this wail of little children palsies the soul. Alas! alas! he felt it not. He moved right on, brooding over those plans of conquest that would before long carry these children to the field and scatter the ashes of their households. And here he is passing away, passing away, poor, hard-worked, exhausted, stern old man, and on Thursday, the 17th of August, 1786, he is dead, and at eight o'clock in the evening, on Friday, the 18th, he was borne to the garrison church of Potsdam and laid beside his father in the vault behind the pulpit there, where the two coffins are still to be seen. *Sic transit gloria mundi.*

BREWSTERIANA.

A PHILADELPHIA lawyer, in an address to the jury, referred to Mr. Brewster's personal disfigurement. Mr. Brewster replied:

"When I was a baby I was a beautiful blue-eyed child. I know this, because my dear dead mother told me so; but a careless nurse let me fall into the fire, and when I was picked up from the burning coals my face was as black as the heart of the scoundrel who has referred to my disfigurement here."

PROFESSIONAL FEES.

An entry, made after a dispute of a bill for professional services, reads:

"Here our connection closes. I have charged them about one-half the amount I should, and in return receive an insolent letter. Hereafter I charge all persons a full price, and make no abatement whatever."

During the Star Route trials, Mr. Brewster wrote: "It is a rule of my life to have no trouble in professional matters with anybody about money."

FROM AN ADDRESS IN 1853 (COLLEGE OF NEW JERSEY).

A few short years ago where you are I was, and where I am some of you will hereafter stand, as I now do, and see rise up around you a host of recollections you had long forgotten. But for those who were with you here you will search in vain. Indeed, it is a sad and doleful thing thus to pause in the mid-current of life's impetuous stream, and look back for those who, with exulting shouts of light-hearted boyhood, plunged with you into the angry flood. Where are they? We may call plaintively, and piteously, and eloquently, as once did a great old lawyer, mourning for an extinguished and illustrious race of nobles: "Where is Bohun? Where is Mowbray? Where is Mortimer? Nay, which is more and most of all, where is Plantagenet? They are entombed in the urns and sepulchres of mortality. . . ."

The highest works of human skill and human thought outlive through ages the creatures that produced them. Southey thus relates:

When Wilkie was in the Escurial, looking at Titian's famous picture of the Last Supper, an old Jeronymite said to him: "I have sat daily in sight of that picture for now nearly threescore years. During that time my companions have dropped off, one after another, all who were my seniors, all who were my contemporaries, and many or most of those who were younger than myself; more than one generation has passed away, and there the figures in the picture have remained unchanged. I look at these until I sometimes think they are the realities and we are the shadows."

If you are poor in knowledge do not pine over the past, but forthwith rouse yourself and set about repairing your neglect. Your training has at least taught you where and how you can get the bright armor with which you are to march out and face the world in strife. Go after it forthwith. Be not daunted by the past or the painful consequences of your own feebleness and poverty. Take courage from the history of many men who, like you, have loitered through college, and like you have felt the necessity of exertion when standing on the very verge of manhood. Remember that " every man who rises above the common level has received two educations,—the first from his teachers, and the second, more permanent and important, from himself."

GENIUS.

Genius—that which men call genius—the dazzling results of irregular and bewildered intellects—the sensuous thoughts of voluptuous men—can intoxicate and degrade—can enchant and enervate; but it cannot purify and exalt—it cannot give content to life or confidence in death.

Human nature is prone to ennoble those who are inspired with the dangerous gift of genius; few men who are endowed with it are fit to use it. It would seem almost as if they were blemished with defects and stained with vices lest mankind should worship them.

CALUMNY.

So vile is it that, as Simonides has said, " those ought to be deemed calumniators who lightly give credit to calumny." The devil himself

is the father of lies—the calumniator—the accuser; he who is called
devil because he blows against you the polluted breath of defamation.
Of it a great pontiff has said, "It is more dangerous because it is
difficult to be discovered. The very wisest of men find it so bar-
barous and intolerable that they cannot hinder their constancy from
being shaken, be their minds ever so strong." Truly it is well called
Scandal, which in Greek signifies a stumbling-block.

PENN AND FRANKLIN.

Penn and Franklin are names that will never be forgotten; they
will pass down through time linked with Solon and Lycurgus, Pythagoras and Archimedes, and Socrates, and Plato, and Aristotle,—the
crowned monarchs of human thought. Benjamin Franklin is still
the greatest man this country ever produced.

FAIRMOUNT PARK ART ASSOCIATION ADDRESS, 1872.

. . . And so from year to year we garnish this chosen spot of
innocent delights with creations of genius exalting in their influences,
and embellishing and ennobling our dear, dear Philadelphia.

It is in such public objects of decoration and use that we are
wanting. The luxuries, the pomps and vanities of the Old World
attract the idle and sumptuous from the New—the sudden rich, eager
for notoriety and hungry for indulgence; but the thoughtful and
trained men of our country journey and tarry there to see their people
and the influences of ages of kingcraft upon them, and to behold
with solemn joy the marvellous and majestic beauties of their archi-
tectural and artistic wonders. . . . In those countries, such grand
things are seen and felt and enjoyed by the rich and cultivated
only. The poor and laboring and needy have no heart for
them.

Gladly and eagerly they turn from these marvels of beauty and
taste, and sometimes landmarks of history. They cross the waters
of the stormy sea to find protection, and comfort, and prosperity here
. . . Our poor and their poor come together, and our moderate and
sober, whose souls are not dead, but who live for a purer and a higher
life, by a purer and higher law of being, remain here and enjoy that
which has been given us. . . .

Should we not learn from this that such things can neither make
nor save a people? Greece, Rome, Gothic and Arabic Europe, in all

their sublimity and splendor of architecture and artistic decorations, are deserted by men suffering with want, and out of whom the necessities of life eat all consciousness of their influence. . . .

The possession of creations of art will not alone make us good and happy. The public moral sense that precedes their production and demands their creation is the only true test of their usefulness and fitness; and even then, if we degenerate and become sensuous, and voluptuary, and ostentatious, and full of folly, then their presence will only gratify a half-animal, half-intellectual passion, but it will not excite that joy which, like "the joy of the drawing of waters," exceeds all other joys,—the joy of a serene moral nature, tranquil and content, because its aim is above self, and its object is the good of all, and its means natural and truthful.

May such things as these cover our land, and they will, like the great aqueducts and canals and public works of antiquity, remain to testify our civilization when other and more fanciful productions of art shall have crumbled into dust. . . .

We must cultivate the useful, the natural, and we will thus keep alive a sense of simplicity and truth, which is the life of the beautiful; and we must be thankful, as that is the life of righteousness, for in a thankful heart dwells righteousness. "Righteousness alone can exalt a nation or promote a man."

PHILADELPHIA.*

I have seen and lived in almost all the capitals of Europe, and I have read of all the great cities of the world, but I have never seen or read of such a city as this. There is no town in the world of its dimensions or population, and there never has been one, that possesses such accommodations for its people. . . .

Of all the cities in this nation Philadelphia is pre-eminently American. The vast body of its population is the product of its own people, who were here almost from the beginning. The descendants of the men who were here at its foundation, and were here at the outbreak of the Revolution, are the men who now compose the body of its citizens. We are not governed by strangers, and never have been willing to submit to such rule. We have a manly local pride of citizenship; other sea-board cities are provincial, or filled

---

* From an address at the laying of the corner-stone of the Philadelphia Public Buildings, July 4, 1874.

with strangers from other parts of the nation and from other countries; and the western cities are like New York, the homes of new men from old places.

If a foreigner were to ask me, where will I find a real American, untouched in his character and nationality by the ever-drifting tide of emigration, domestic and foreign, and with no taint of provincial narrowness, I would say, go to Philadelphia. . . .

Such is my love for and faith in this city that I feel possessed with the conviction, which might even be called a superstition, that it will again be, as it once was, the real metropolis of the nation. The capitol and the public offices of the Union will never return; the foreign trade may cluster at New York as it does at Liverpool; but Philadelphia will be again, as she first was, the real centre of finance, of commerce, of wealth. . . .

She is at the head of the mechanic arts and of manufacturing, and she has ever led in refinement, in science, and in jurisprudence. We have done and are doing a great work, and it will inspire our posterity to live up to our standard, as we are inspired by the standard of our ancestors. . . We can say, as Franklin said when writing of his home,—dear, dear Philadelphia. Do we not say it in enduring words with this day's work, and when we leave behind us this noble building to say it for us?

FROM THE SECOND CENTENNIAL ADDRESS.*

. . . When I have recalled the incidents of our history from the earliest days of colonial existence to the blessed hour when it was solemnly declared that we were, " and of right ought to be, free and independent States," I have observed that, in all of the great events where public order, private right, or public duty was the subject of popular action, they proceeded with deliberation, and with a rigid regard to the strict forms of legislative order and of public legal enactment. No element of the conspirator, outlaw, or communist was part of their natures. They were serious, God-fearing, God-loving men, and from the beginning had solemn work to do, and they knew it, and within the strictest forms of legal order they asserted their natural and legal rights. They had known the harsh usage of ad-

---

* In Independence Square, July 1, 1876, the Centennial Commemoration of the passage of the Resolution declaring Independence. At the request of the Historical Society of Pennsylvania.

versity; they had felt its discipline. Many of them possessed that knowledge which is the fruit of study, learning, and experience, and they all bowed with submission before the obligations of religion, and acknowledged the supremacy of public will.

. . . I have no recollection of such public records in the history of any other people. It is peculiar to us. It is part of the glory of our career that the pen has ever been mightier than the sword. While we have perpetuated in our annals the formal declarations of our principles and our acts, so have we likewise in the same way embalmed in our history the living words recorded at the time, which were to protect us, and teach mankind through us the doctrines we had maintained and the liberties we have secured.

With us the sword was only drawn to justify the written word that uttered the convictions of the very souls of our great ancestors.

This thought I shall not further follow by reciting each incident of public action, for the time will not permit me so to do. The events illustrating the fact are too numerous to repeat. When in the fulness of time our grievances had ripened into wrongs, and the attempts to enforce the royal will had degenerated into acts of oppression, then, too, step by step, as we approached the great crisis of our separation, did the people at various times and in different places publish and declare, in formal and apt words, as were thereafter published and declared here by the Continental Congress, that we were free, and of right ought to be free and independent States.

. . . Let me congratulate you that we came of such a lineage of heroic men,—the statesmen of the human race,—who loved God, as He is the father of natural liberty—the liberty of obedience to law and subordination to natural and social duty. Let me congratulate you that a hundred years of such national life have brought us to this point of national glory, the peaceful glory of a prosperous people of forty millions who sprang from the few who sought refuge here, and here erected a temple of human rights into which all men who love law and obey order can enter and find happiness and peace.

APPENDIX.

THE STAR ROUTE TRIALS.

INCLUDING AN ACCOUNT OF THE DURATION, COST, THE NUMBER OF WITNESSES EXAMINED, AND AN ABSTRACT OF TESTIMONY, SHOWING HOW THE RING OPERATED, AND DETAILS OF THE JURY CORRUPTION.

THE first Star Route trial began June 1, 1882, and continued until September 15th, when the court discharged the jury, who were unable to agree. The *First Star Route trial.* following constituted the jury: W. K. Brown, G. W. Cox, Wm. Dickson, E. D. Doniphan, Wm. Holmead, M. G. McCarthy, E. J. McLain, M. McNulty, Thomas Martin, H. T. Murray, H. A. Olcott, Z. Tobriner.

Jury deliberations began Friday, September 8th, and were continued over Sunday. There were seven ballottings. Brown, Dickson, Holmead, Martin, voted for acquittal.

There were one hundred and seventeen witnesses examined, twenty-three hundred pages of testimony, three thousand two hundred and eighty-six pages of record, and twenty-three indictments.

The second trial began December 4, 1882, and ended June 4, 1883. It was a repetition of the first in point *Second trial.* of tactics. There were one hundred and fifty witnesses examined, two thousand seven hundred and sixty-one pages offered in evidence, four thousand four hundred and eighty-one pages of testimony, five thousand eight hundred and seventy-six pages of record, and twenty-six indictments.

It was proved that not only were the jurors purchased in this case, but signals were arranged by which the defendants knew how matters were going in the jury-room. The signal which told that the jury had agreed for acquittal was "bringing hands together near the centre of the window, and pulling them away from each other out towards the extremities of the window. This was the understanding between us all who were working for the defence." (Confession of Nelson.)   A verdict was rendered to acquit.

A Washington lawyer subsequently arose in Judge Wylie's court and solemnly moved that George Bliss, of New York, and Wm. W. Ker, of Philadelphia, be debarred for having publicly and privately stated that it was impossible to secure an impartial jury in the district, thereby placing a stigma on the entire body of the citizens of the District of Columbia, without cause or provocation.

The judge declined to entertain the motion, or allow the paper in which it was set forth to be placed on file.

The cost has been estimated at $1,000,000.   Special counsel, B. H. Brewster, $5000; George Bliss, $50,813.55; R. L. Merrick, $32,500; W. W. Ker, $28,970; W. A. Cook, $5250; A. M. Gibson, $5000; H. H. Wells, $2622.45; P. H. Woodward, $7076; in addition, witness fees, expenses, detective service, printing, etc.

Expenses of the trials.

AFFIDAVIT OF RERDELL.

When the investigation began under the Garfield administration, I saw from the public prints that the authorities were getting down to substantial facts.   After reflection, I decided for myself to tell the truth and take the consequences, though well aware that my course would lead to the severance of long-continued business and social relations.   With this end in view, I sought the interview with Postmaster James, and the statements made by me at the Arlington Hotel, to Messrs. James, Clayton, and Woodward, were true.   The statements subsequently made by me to Attorney-General MacVeagh were also true.

Rerdell decides to turn State's evidence.

After thus committing myself, I determined, acting under the countenance of the Attorney-General, to save ex-Senator Dorsey, if possible, as well as to furnish written proof to sustain all I had told.   I accordingly . . . first went to the office of Dorsey (New York) and secured the journal which contained the original entries both in my writing and that of Donnelly.   I then called on Dorsey at the Albemarle Hotel.   He received me angrily, nay, furiously, having learned of my disclosures, as he alleged, from Mr. S. B. Elkins, as I believe, from A. M. Gibson.   He remarked that no steps were taken but

Determines to save Dorsey.

what he was fully advised of. Finding him in no frame of mind to discuss matters reasonably, I soon rose to leave. He was still in his night-clothes, and, as I was about to close the door, remarked that he wanted to see me again as soon as he was dressed. On reaching the street, I grew more and more indignant at his treat-ment. Without returning to the Albemarle, I started for Washington. I telegraphed Dorsey from Jersey City :

Dorsey threatens.

"The affidavit story is a lie; but confidence between us is gone. I resign my position, and will turn everything over to any one you designate."

At Philadelphia two despatches were handed to me, both from Dorsey. The first one ran substantially :

"Why did you leave without seeing me again? Return by first train to New York." The second one : "Will you ruin my wife and children? Return to New York, and all will be made right. I will not accept your resignation." I answered from Baltimore : "I can do no good returning. Will do nothing to injure you, but send some one to take my place."

In the morning, I received by mail a long, pathetic, and fervent appeal from Dorsey, imploring me to do nothing to disgrace him and his family. The same morning United States Senator ——— sent me a message to come at once

Dorsey appeals.

to the National Hotel. I complied. He proceeded to say that he had left Dorsey the night before nearly crazy; that he had already been terribly punished by the scandal; that since March 4th he had fallen from a dizzy height, and that I had nothing but ruin to gain by making disclosures. By way of warning, he pointed to the fate of witnesses in the whiskey cases. The interview lasted a couple of hours, and left me unshaken in my purpose. . . .

On Sunday, Dorsey arrived in Washington, and sent for me to come to his house. He met me at the door,—an unusual proceeding,—shook hands cordially, and led me to the office. He made the most eloquent and affective appeals to me, dwelling particularly upon his wife and children. I replied that I would do anything in the world for him except perjure myself. He replied, "What in hell does an oath amount to when the fate of a friend is at stake? Under such circumstances I would not hesitate."

Meanwhile, Mr. J. W. Bosler came in and entered into the con-versation. The talk continued from 10 A.M. until 3 P.M. Bosler and I then left, walking down to Willard's Hotel together. On reaching his hotel, after dinner we resumed the conversation. I then repeated the admission I had made to Mr. Mac-Veagh. He argued that this did no essential harm, as in an Indian investigation he was once confronted by a witness to whom he had made compromising admissions, when he escaped by acknowledging the admissions, and by claiming that he was not under oath at the time, and that they were made for the express purpose of entrapping his accuser. He added that I was now in the same fix, and that if I would make affidavit on that line, Messrs. James and MacVeagh would be driven out of the Cabinet inside of ten days.

Arranging to recant.

The next day I began preparation of the affidavit, Dorsey and Bosler being present and offering frequent suggestions. The last two or three pages were written by Dorsey and copied by me. I was exhausted and hungry when the paper was completed; notwithstanding, Bosler insisted that it should be sworn to before I dined. We drove to Middleton's bank, where the notary affixed his jurat. A copy was then made by Miss Nettie White, when the original was sent to President Garfield, or rather was taken by Messrs. Ingersoll and Dorsey in person to the White House. I accompanied them, remaining in the anteroom, expecting to be called in. While seated there I saw Messrs. James, Cook, and Woodward enter the house. About ten o'clock Dorsey and I left together, Ingersoll remaining. This occurred the week the President was shot.

The hungry, exhausted clerk.

The famous White House meeting.

EXTRACT FROM TESTIMONY OF JOHN A. WALSH.

The investigation commenced and I was very early subpœnaed. I appeared before the sub-committee, of which Mr. Blackburn was the chairman. . . . I stated the case clearly and plainly. . . . Well, after this investigation, I was approached by Charles Andrews, who said, " Mr. Walsh, here is a list." Well, I was glad to see any list, and I said I was favored. " You see," said he, " you are down here for $8000." I said, " Favored again." He said, " Yes, you are favored again." I said, " What is that for, Andrews?" " Oh, well," said he, " Congressional business. You don't suppose we got that appropriation through for fun?" I said, " I do not know. I was examined very largely and exhaustively up there, and I didn't notice that anybody asked me for any money. My route was particularly the subject of investigation, but I saw no indication of any one wanting money." "Oh, well," said he, "if you don't understand it, let it drop. The old man will want to see you." "The old man" was Mr. Brady. A few weeks after, Brady sent for me. . . . Said he, " What are you going to do about that, Walsh?" " About what?" said I. Said he, " What Andrews spoke to you about." I tried to turn it off jocularly, though it was quite a serious thing to me, and I said, laughingly, " Really, Andrews was not in earnest, was he?" " You do not think so?" said Brady. Said I, " How could he be? Eight thousand dollars! Egad, I haven't anything to pay $8000 for." " Well," said Brady, " that's all right." It was not long after that that an order was issued on my route cutting off one trip, and reducing the pay about $20,000 a year.

The corruption fund.

Brady disciplining a contractor.

In the mean time, I had discounted some of Brady's notes, some of them he had paid. . . . About the end of December, I thought it would be well to have a settlement. I made an appointment to meet him. . . . He came and took the notes and said it was a settlement, that that was the end of the business, and that I could never have assumed for a moment that he was doing these things, increasing service and so on, for any particular amusement. I said, " Well, general, I did not know you were doing it for amusement, but I thought you were doing it in accordance with the law. I presented petitions for the increase you gave me." Said he, " Walsh, it is silly to talk about petitions. You have seen enough to know that petitions do not operate unless the fates are propitious. You have sent in a good many petitions to get your service put back to seven times a week. Have you succeeded?" I said, " No, I have not." " Well," said he, " there is an illustration for you that petitions are sometimes ineffective." " Now," said he, " for you to assume that I owe you any money is absurd. You never at heart could have believed anything of the kind. You have seen enough to know better than that." I said, " Wherein have I had opportunity to know better, general?" " Well," said he, " you collected Price's drafts, amounting to $20,000, and you credited me with $10,000 of it. What do you think it meant?" Said I, " I never stopped to inquire. It is not part of my business to inquire into other people's business." Said he, " There was the Price draft, $25,000, on the Indianola and Corpus Christi route. Then, too,

Petitions and propitious fates.

you affected not to believe that your share of that Congressional assessment was $8000. Mr. Price did not assume that. Mr. Price paid it." "Well," said I, "general, just favor me with an account. Let us see how we stand. Perhaps I owe you some money." He said that if he were to figure it down closely, he did not doubt that I did.

He said, "You found this contract at $74,500 a year."

Brady figuring his share. "No," said I, "I found the contract at $18,000 a year." Said he, "Oh, no; McDonough and that crowd had the pay increased to $74,000 per annum. Now, that was paid for." "Yes," said I, "I am painfully aware that that was paid for. It was my money that paid for it. Now, I understand that my money went to Brown." "Yes," said Brady, "it went to Brown." . . . "Now," said Brady, "the difference between $74,000 and $135,000 is, in round numbers, $60,000." "Undoubtedly," said I. Said he, "$60,000 per annum for three years at 20 per cent. per annum is $36,000, Mr. Walsh, ain't it?" "Undoubtedly," said I. "Your share of the Congressional fund, $8000, which you seem to forget you owe, added to the $36,000 will make $44,000, won't it?" I said, "Yes, sir." "Now," said he, "I remitted those fines in your case, amounting to about $6000." Said I, "Those fines were unjustly imposed." "That's all right about the unjust part," said he; "I remitted them, didn't I?" I said, "Yes." "Well," said he, "fifty per cent. of them amounts to $3000." Said I, "General, that is a very comprehensive statement, and it is quite evident that I owe you some money, but do you really think you are going to settle in that way?" Said he, "What other way will you settle it?" "Well," said I, "up here I will settle it in court, but if we lived in the South perhaps I might adopt some other remedy." "Well," said he, "you can go to court if you want to, but it won't do you any good." "Perhaps it won't; but I will tell you that it will really cost you a good deal of money before you get through." "Oh," said he, "that's all right; Walsh, do your best." . . .

Hinds went to work very assiduously for Brady's scalp. . . . He went to the District Attorney here, Mr. Corkhill; he went to the Postmaster-General; he went to the Attorney-General, at that time

Brady boasting of a "corner on the grand jury." Mr. Devens. He offered to produce proof of the grossest fraud . . . but he got no satisfaction. He employed counsel, Mr. Charles F. McLean, of New York. . . . In the mean time, I thought I would try to make Brady feel badly, and I said to him, "It is my opinion that you will be indicted." "That's all right," said Brady. "*Don't concern your-self about me, Walsh. I have a corner on that grand jury.* I assure you there is no danger."

TESTIMONY OF P. H. WOODWARD.

In May, 1881, Mr. Gibson ardently urged the employment of William A. Cook in these cases, and invoked my aid. So far as I remember, his recommendations were oral, and I orally, but mildly, reinforced them.

Shortly after the engagement of Mr. Cook was publicly announced, I received a summons from President Garfield to be at the White House at a designated hour. Without much preface he said he had sent for me to ask if I could explain how the appointment came to be made; that the day before a judge of the Supreme Court had in-formed him that Cook was one of the most disreputable members of the Washington bar, and that the selection was a disgrace to the administration. *[President Garfield displeased at Cook's employment.]*

I attempted to justify the action of the Attorney-General on the ground that, as the investigation widened, it would be desirable to have in the cases a local lawyer who possessed an intimate and extensive knowledge, not only of the criminal class, but also of the darker elements that go to make up the life of the district. I added that the experience of post-office special agents was of little aid in fitting them to work successfully in the social strata referred to, as they traced crime to its source, not by communication with the guilty, but by purely intellectual processes. The President seemed partially satisfied.

A few days later . . . the President took me one side and asked if I did not regard as confidential the conversation above referred to. I replied that I did. "Why, then," he continued, with some severity, "did you report it to Mr. Cook?" I answered him that I had never mentioned the subject to any one. He then said that Mr. Cook had written him a letter, making special reference to the imputations of a Supreme Court judge, and defending his own character. I assured Mr. Garfield that the fact had been disclosed through some other channel. . . .

Mr. Cook testified that he had several private interviews with General Garfield, by whom he was instructed to communicate directly

x   30*

with himself on Star Route matters, thus, in a degree, ignoring the Attorney-General.

From events in which I bore a share I know with the assurance of certainty that these representations are false. Mr. Cook was introduced to General Garfield by Postmaster-General James in my presence on the Wednesday evening preceding the assassination. The event was pre-arranged. Mr. Cook called at the Arlington in a carriage at twilight. Thence we three drove to the White House. We were ushered into one of the lower rooms. Shortly after the President entered. Mr. Cook was presented to him by Mr. James. They met each other as persons hitherto unacquainted. I cannot believe that the Executive of this nation arranged a job with a man whom a Supreme Court judge had only a few weeks before denounced to him as disreputable, for the purpose of deceiving an honored member of his own official family.

Cook's alleged secret dealings with the President.

Mr. Cook insisted that immunity should be granted to Stephen W. Dorsey, on account of his great services to the Republican party. In answer, I modestly suggested that penal laws and penitentiaries were not devised for the exclusive benefit of Democrats.

When comfortably seated in his new chair Mr. Cook proceeded to employ a number of local detectives, to report to him personally. The discoveries resulting from their joint labors were not added to the common stock of information, and, so far as I am aware, not a ray of light emanating from either that luminary or his satellites ever disclosed a scrap of evidence for the benefit of the prosecution.

Cook's personal detectives.

About the same time Frederick B. Lilley was brought before United States Commissioner Charles S. Bundy for a preliminary hearing. William A. Cook appeared for the government. After putting in the formal parts of the proof and identifying the handwriting of the defendant, Mr. Cook placed me upon the stand to establish the essential points of the case by hearsay testimony. As this was promptly and properly ruled out, the prosecution broke down ignominiously, the commissioner refusing to grant even a continuance. We left the room with our papers amid the derisive laughter of the crowd which had gathered there.

Cook's weak efforts.

Mr. Cook read before this committee an extract from the *Evening Star* to prove that he is the leading criminal lawyer of the city. He is not a chicken in years or experience. Why, then, did he thus engineer this lamentable fiasco ?

William Lilley, the father of Frederick B., told me often that William A. Cook, for $1000, guaranteed immunity to his son, and that on the very day when we appeared before Commissioner Bundy, $250 of the fee, through the underground channels employed for the conduct of the business, had already found its way into the pocket of Cook.

Cook guaranteeing immunity for $1000.

From the quarters of Commissioner Bundy I accompanied Mr. Cook to his office, where, against my indignant protests, he proceeded to subpœna Mrs. Brott to appear before the grand jury as a witness against her husband. This was the last official interview I ever had with the man.

Cook "killing" a government witness.

In August or September, 1881, the attitude of Mr. A. M. Gibson towards certain combinations, notably the Salisburys, underwent a sudden and remarkable change. Previously he had been the zealous advocate of sweeping reductions of service. All at once he discovered that the department was going too fast and too far. He expostulated with Mr. Lyman against the continuance of a policy which hitherto he had earnestly approved. As the new condition of things developed, both General Elmer and Mr. Lyman began to suspect him of treachery. An incident illustrates the feeling. One day Colonel Ingersoll brought some matter of business in behalf of his client, Mr. Salisbury, to the attention of General Elmer, who jocosely replied, " Yes; your associate counsel, Mr. Gibson, took the same view." By those faithful officers I was gently warned, but my eyes were not yet opened. . . .

Gibson's work for the ring while in Government employ.

In December, 1881, William Lilley informed me that he had learned some time before that A. M. Gibson had become the paid agent of the contractors on route No. 40,116, from Phœnix to Prescott, Arizona. I at once examined the papers on that route and found the following extraordinary document over the signature of A. M. Gibson :

40,116.

There is no proof of fraud in this case. There are *suspicious* circumstances, such as the advertisement of the route as one hundred and forty miles long when in reality it is only one hundred and eight miles, and the bid of six hundred and eighty dollars, and the subsequent raising to thirty-two thousand six hundred and forty dollars ; but, in the first instance, the advertisement of the distance as greater than it really is, the contractor cannot be held responsible for the laches of the Post-Office Department; and, in the second place, while the enormous increase of price is suspicious, still the department cannot base its action upon mere suspicion. There must be *absolute* proof of fraud either in obtaining the increase or in performing the service after the increase has been obtained. In this case there is, as remarked above, no proof whatever of fraud. The service is, according to all the evidence, capitally performed, the contractor employing first-class stock and equipments, and making faster time by several hours than the terms of his contract call for. The necessity of the present schedule time is admitted by all who speak or testify in regard to this route. There have been large reductions already made in the service leading to and from Prescott, and I do not believe the department would be justified either by the evidence or public policy in making any change in this route. Inspector Sharpe does not recommend that the old schedule be restored, but, on the contrary, says it would be unwise to do so. The schedule cannot legally be changed unless proof of fraud is clear and positive. There can be no half-way work—it must be either left where it is or put back to the original schedule. The latter, in my judgment, as before stated, would be illegal, and of course unwise public policy.

A. M. Gibson,
Special Counsel.

EXTRACT FROM AFFIDAVIT OF F. C. SHAW.[*]

While serving as juror . . . I received a letter, . . . worded as follows :

"If you are down this way to-morrow, please let me see you. . . .

"HOWARD FRENCH."

. . . I called at the census office . . . and asked for Mr. French, with whom I had no previous acquaintance. He . . . asked, "Is this Mr. Shaw?" and said, "I don't recognize you as the party I want to see." He then said, "It is too bad for you to come so far for nothing; suppose we walk up to Willard's." We . . . went to Willard's, . . . where Mr. French was approached by one Colonel William P. Rice, whom he introduced to me. French handed Rice five dollars, thanking him for the loan of it, when Rice remarked, "It has been so long I had forgotten it; let's go in and break it up." We went into the saloon . . . took drinks . . . came out . . . talked a while in the lobby, when Rice suggested we go to the restaurant. . . When we came out, Rice

Approached through a third party.

The pilot-fish and the whale.

---

[*] Shaw was a member of the panel, and was challenged by the government because of actual knowledge that he had already pledged himself to the accused.

and French engaged in a private conversation, after which Rice excused himself . . . French again excused himself for bringing me on a wild-goose chase; he said he understood I was a mighty good clerk, and that Rice was a man for me to cultivate. . . "He's a damn good man to know."

"A good man to know."

April 29, 1882, the following note was brought to my house by a colored boy, whom I afterwards recognized in the employment of Rice: " MR. SHAW,—Meet me at Willard's Hotel at 4 P.M.—FRENCH. . . ." I was at the hotel, and while waiting to see French, Rice came up . . . after talking a few moments he suggested that we go to the Ebbett House saloon, as French was more likely to be there. We went in and sat down . . . Rice commenced a running conversation . . . asking me how long I had been in the city, the extent of my acquaintance, who I knew among public men, and my circumstances and present employment. After answering his questions in a general way he ordered two more beers, and then said he would like me to come to his office; that he liked me and might be useful to me. When we got to his office he pulled out a roll of money, and, laying two twenty-dollar notes on the table, said, " I want you to get some information that is of importance to me: I do this on French's recommendation." I had previously told Rice I was doing nothing except serving as juror. Rice then took from his pocket a list of the jurors . . . and asked me to look over the list and tell him all I could about each member, his politics, habits, financial standing, and the names of his nearest friends and acquaintances. I told him . . . I did not want to say anything in reference to the jury. He said . . . there was nothing improper in his request; he simply wanted to compare my views with information he had already obtained. I looked over the list and gave him my knowledge . . . which he noted on the margin of the same slip. Notes had previously been made opposite several names. I left him, with a promise to meet him at his office the following Monday. . . I kept this appointment . . . and gave him additional points I had gathered. As I was about to leave he gave me ten dollars, and said, " Use this around among the boys, and I will give you money in a few days to fix up your own matters." . . I continued to meet him from time to time in reference to these matters.

The tempter.

Money for "the boys."

May 3, Rice came to my house and was introduced to my wife and children. . . . He said to my wife that an important business

matter was developing . . . which would be to our mutual advantage.
. . . He put $40 into my hand, which I handed to my
wife . . . she remarking that I would get into trouble.
. . . Rice told me that " Holmead had been seen," and
. . . I could talk with him, and learn something to my advantage.

May 4 I remarked to Holmead that I had an intimation that he
had been " seen." He said he had been approached
by a warm personal friend, who said, " You are an old
contractor, and know how contractors have to turn
corners to get out, and that is all there is of the Star
Route business, and you ought to make some money out of it; that
the defendants would like to have me foreman of the jury, and that
in that case I would get double any one else did." He
further stated that he had agreed that if I would join
him he should accept the proposition, remarking that
the money must be paid in advance. I told him to go ahead and I
would be with him.

The following week Holmead . . . said, " Well, I am satisfied
now. I would not have gone ahead on uncertainties." I asked him if
money had been put up, and he said he had the word of a *man* that
it was all right, and that was as good as money to him.

I saw Rice every day. . . . May 30 he gave me $70. This was
my last interview with Rice until after the trial commenced.

June 1 I saw Rice. . . . He asked me what I thought about
Murray and Tobriner. . . . He said, " If those two men are all
right, it (meaning the jury) will stand twelve to nothing. I have
told Dorsey that your services will probably be valuable,
and you can consider yourself under pay, and report to
me every morning about ten o'clock, when I will give
you such points as we want you to look up, and you can report such
information as you have obtained." Under this arrangement I was
employed in the interest of Stephen W. Dorsey during the trial,
reporting regularly to Rice, and frequently holding conversations with
Dorsey himself. At our first interview under this arrangement, Rice told me that Stephen W. Dorsey had
placed $12,000 in his hands to fix the jury. This was
when he referred to Tobriner and Murray. And then
he said, as he had nothing to do with Tobriner and
Murray, it left him a balance of $2000 in his hands, and he proposed
to lay back a little and see what Brady and the other defendants

would do for Tobriner and Murray, and that would leave him a stake to work for without calling on Dorsey for more funds. Rice told me he had been boat-riding with (juryman) Doniphan's daughter "Flossie," and that "he had got on to him," and believed him all right. *[Juror Doniphan and "Flossie."]*

. . . We (Holmead and Shaw) had a conversation. Holmead said if he had known I would have been challenged he would not have served as juror; but having made the arrangement he would go through with it. I told him he would not be alone, and need not feel nervous about it. . . . Holmead said, "We must be mighty careful about this thing; no one will mistrust me, as I have a good deal of property in my own name." . . . On the second or third Sunday in July, we (Holmead and Shaw) arranged signals to be given by him from the jury-room. . . . *[Arranging signals for jury-room.]*

Rice came to my office August 26. He seemed a good deal excited, and said that Dorsey had given him $1000 for Doniphan, and he (Dorsey) supposed he (Rice) had placed it; but he (Rice) had been led to believe that Doniphan was all right, and had held the money. . . . I should bring Rice and Doniphan together, as Rice wanted to give Doniphan some money. . . . Doniphan missed seeing Rice. *[Excitement. A juryman neglected.]*

Friday, September 1, I saw Doniphan. . . . From what he said about the standing of the jury I felt satisfied that Dorsey had been "played." . . . During recess, Dorsey asked me what was the matter. I said, "Do you know when Rice will be in town?" He replied, "What do you want with him? I gave him your money before he went away; and if he has not fixed it, I will." I said, "That is all right. I can wait until he comes; it is your matters that bother me. I don't like the looks of things, and think Rice ought to be here." Dorsey then asked, "What is the matter?" I said, "Well, Doniphan, I am satisfied, hasn't got a cent." Dorsey replied, "Why, I gave Rice $1000 for him." I then repeated the conversation between Rice and myself. *[Dorsey "played" by his agents.]* *[Doniphan's $1000 appropriated.]* Dorsey then told me to see Doniphan and find out what I could. . . . September 3, I went to Dorsey's house. . . . He said, "Now, tell me about this Rice business." I then went over the whole matter, and told him that from what I learned there were not more than two men on the jury he could depend on. Dorsey telegraphed for Rice, . . .

and said this is the first intimation of any hitch; whom can we depend on ? I told him there was no question about Holmead.

September 6 I met Doniphan. He said if Dorsey proposed to do anything, now was the time. . . . He said he could control Martin. He then went on to say that he was hard pressed, or hard up, not having drawn any money for some time. I told him that the party I had spoken to him about, and wanted to introduce him to, . . . was still out of town; but that I could possibly arrange to get hold of a little money for him, and arrange things satisfactorily, and told him all he had to do was to say the word. He said, " Well, wait and see what turns up, and I will see you this evening." . . . The same day Dorsey . . . called me to him. He asked me if I had seen Doniphan. I told him I had, and gave him the conversation in substance. Dorsey made some remark about Rice not being here, and asked me if I could fix this. I replied, " If you have got a friend who will act for you, I will bring him and Doniphan together to-night." He replied, impatiently, " God damn it, no; there are enough in this already; you must do it, Shaw; all may depend on him. I will stand by you as long as you live." I said, " I will see him to-night." . . . I met Dorsey at Chamberlain's. . . . Dorsey handed me $250. . . . Dorsey remarked, " Don't make any mistake; I will take care of you."

At our previous interview, Dorsey told me I could give Doniphan a small amount for immediate use, and that he (Dorsey) would stand by any further arrangement that I made with Doniphan. Dorsey further stated that he had plenty of influence, and could get all the places in the departments he wanted, and that I could guarantee Doniphan a good position in addition to any money he might receive.

September 7 I met Doniphan. . . . I asked why he did not keep his appointment, and he replied that things looked bad; that Dickson had been offered $25,000, and had reported it to the court, and there was likely to be hell when the court met. . . . September 8 I passed him, neither of us stopping. I remarked, " Do the best you can : I will guarantee everything to be all right." He answered, " I will see how they stand" (meaning the jury). . . . A. B. Williams wanted to see me . . .; he (Williams) told me that Doniphan had " squealed." . . . Williams asked me several questions about the matter, and I told him I had nothing to say to any one except Senator Dorsey. . . . In a few minutes Dorsey came in. Williams walked to the rear, and Dorsey says, " Now, Shaw, what are you going to do ?" I told him I was going to stand; that I wasn't the "squealing" kind. Dorsey said, " Well, what are you going to say ?" I said my idea was to make light of it, . . . that I was merely sounding Doniphan, and had no money, and no idea of bribing him. He then remarked, " Then you didn't succeed in getting the money into his hands?" I replied, " No;" and Dorsey replied, " That is good; now I want you to go out and tell Colonel In-gersoll." I went to the carriage standing at the curb and said to Ingersoll, " This whole thing is a put-up job, and there is nothing in it so far as Dorsey is concerned." Ingersoll replied, " Of course not; I know that, my boy." . . . Dor-sey told me to keep away from Rice, adding, " You keep the money you have got on account of anything Rice may owe you; keep away from him; I will settle with him." He then called Williams and told him that he (Williams) was to act as my attor-ney. . . . Since then Williams has been my coun-sel. . . . Dorsey further stated I could have Colonel Ingersoll, William A. Cook, Davidge, or all of them, if necessary. This was the last interview I had with Dorsey until meeting him at the Court House during the progress of the second trial.

F. C. SHAW.

Sworn and subscribed before me the 28th day of February, A.D. 1884.

WARREN C. STONE, *Notary Public.*

AFFIDAVIT OF JAMES A. NELSON.

. . . About the first Monday in December, 1882, I was employed by the defence in the Star Route cases. I was engaged by Mr. A. B. Williams to look out and watch government counsel, government spotters, and members of the Star Route jury. My instructions from Mr. Williams were to report to him daily whatever I could find out about the parties named, and such other useful information as might be of use to the defence, and particularly to watch the jury, morning, noon, and night. . . .

During the second trial, Crossman, who was agent or partner of John H. Crane, foreman of the jury, was daily around the Court House, and I saw him frequently in communication with John H.

Foreman of jury signalling to agents of accused.

Crane aforesaid and said A. B. Williams. Said Crossman was constantly around corner of the Court House, east and north of said City Hall, where the jury were locked up during the time when the jury were in their room, after they were charged by the judge, and I saw the said Crane send or give signals to said Crossman from east side of the jury-room. I saw Crane signal from said second window to said Crossman and to A. B. Williams, and saw both respond that they understood what Crane meant. . . .

JAMES A. NELSON.

Sworn and subscribed to before me this 7th day of March, 1884.

WARREN C. STONE, *Notary Public.*

AFFIDAVIT OF JAMES A. NELSON.

. . . Soon after the termination of the second Star Route trial, or about the time that Stephen W. Dorsey left the city for the West, . . . I had a conversation with one Clarence Shields, a juror on the second trial. . . . Shields stated that he

The disappointed juror.

had been treated badly by said Dorsey; that Dorsey had left the city without making any arrangements to carry out the agreement made with him (Shields), and that he (Shields) understood that the white men on the panel with him in said trial had been treated differently. Shields further said that he thought it more than likely that Dorsey had fixed matters, but that the parties who had charge of the matter for Dorsey had failed to

Dorsey's agents appropriating the corruption fund.

carry out his instructions, and that he (Shields) intended to see Dorsey personally when he (Dorsey) returned to Washington, and have a full understanding about it. . . . Subsequently, Shields told me something had been done for him, but that the agreement had not been fully carried out, and that it would have to be done when Dorsey came to the city. When Dorsey came to the city. . . .

Partial payment.

I had a talk with Shields, and he told me that at that time he was on his way to . . . see Dorsey, and that he (Dorsey) had to do something for him or get a position for his friends. I am also informed by a reliable party, whose affidavit can be obtained, that he saw Charles Jones, in company with a brother of Jackson Howard (another juror on said second trial), go to house of said Jackson Howard on the night after said Howard was accepted as juror in the Star Route case, and that said Charles Jones was at that time in the employment of Star Route defendants, *A juror visited early by agent of defence.* and received immediate instructions from A. B. Williams, one of Dorsey's lawyers.

JAMES A. NELSON.

Sworn to and subscribed before me this 18th day of March, A.D. 1884.

WARREN C. STONE.

INDEX.

THE END.

"WALLINGFORD:"

A Story of American Life.

BY

EUGENE COLEMAN SAVIDGE.

"The author is a student of the world and its inhabitants. He looks into nature and the human heart, drawing truly from both. He is an uncommon observer and thinker."—*Washington National Republican.*

"Characters skilfully drawn, especially the young medical student, and the book is well conceived and executed."—*Boston Globe.*

"Well written . . . not wanting in descriptive power."—*New York Times.*

"A pretty love-story. The proneness of people not to understand and appreciate those who possess genius is made very plain."—*Savannah Morning News.*

"Descriptions are very fine and always truthful. Written with pathos and ability."—*Norristown Herald.*

"Interest does not flag for an instant."—*Baltimore Evening News.*

"Original in plot and character-drawing."—*San Francisco Chronicle.*

"Will be read with keen enjoyment."—*Pittsburgh Chronicle-Telegraph.*

"Charmingly told—a story of our own home life and ways, full of pointed thought and interesting descriptions."—*Davenport, Iowa, Democrat.*

"Observing the mental gymnastics of the author we are tempted to say the book is 'most excellent, full of comic.' In this book is promise of power."—*New York Epoch.*

"Attention held with intensest interest. . . . Enough of sadness, of life's true experience, to bring added charm."—*Easton Press.*

12mo, 308 Pages, Extra Cloth, $1.25.

For sale by all booksellers, or sent by mail, post-paid, on receipt of the price, by

J. B. LIPPINCOTT COMPANY,

715 and 717 Market Street, Philadelphia.